Once Upon
a Dream

Also by Nora Roberts, Jill Gregory, Ruth Ryan Langan, and Marianne Willman in Large Print:

Once Upon a Castle

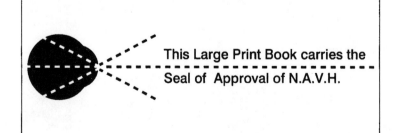

This Large Print Book carries the
Seal of Approval of N.A.V.H.

Once Upon a Dream

Nora Roberts, Jill Gregory, Ruth Ryan Langan, and Marianne Willman

Thorndike Press • Thorndike, Maine

Published in 2001 by arrangement with The Berkley
Publishing Group, a member of Penguin Putnam Inc.

Thorndike Press Large Print Romance Series.

The tree indicium is a trademark of Thorndike Press.

The text of this Large Print edition is unabridged.
Other aspects of the book may vary from the original edition.

Set in 16 pt. Plantin by Christina S. Huff.

Printed in the United States on permanent paper.

Library of Congress Cataloging-in-Publication Data

Once upon a dream / Nora Roberts . . . [et al.].
   p. cm.
In dreams / Nora Roberts — The sorcerer's daughter /
Jill Gregory — The enchantment / Ruth Ryan Langan —
The Bride of Sighs / Marianne Willman.
   ISBN 0-7862-3338-9 (lg. print : hc : alk. paper)
1. Love stories, American. 2. Dreams — Fiction.
I. Roberts, Nora.
PS648.L6 O53 2001
813'.08508—dc21   2001027307

LARGE
PRINT
FICTION
Once

Contents

IN DREAMS
Nora Roberts   7

THE SORCERER'S DAUGHTER
Jill Gregory   143

THE ENCHANTMENT
Ruth Ryan Langan   277

THE BRIDGE OF SIGHS
Marianne Willman   431

In Dreams

Nora Roberts

For those who believe in magic

Prologue

All he had were the dreams. Without them he was alone, always and ever alone. For the first hundred years of his solitude, he lived on arrogance and temper. He had plenty of both to spare.

For the second, he lived on bitterness. Like one of his own secret brews, it bubbled and churned inside him. But rather than healing, it served as a kind of fuel that pushed him from day to night, from decade to decade.

In the third century, he fell into despair and self-pity. It made him miserable company, even for himself.

His stubbornness was such that it took four hundred years before he began to make a home for himself, to struggle to find some pleasure, some beauty, some satisfaction in his work and his art. Four hundred years before his pride made room for the admission that he may have been, perhaps, just slightly and only partially responsible for what had become of him.

Still, had his actions, his attitude, deserved such a harsh judgment from the Keepers? Did his mistake, if indeed it had been a mistake, merit centuries of imprisonment, with only a single week of each hundred-year mark in which to really live?

When half a millennium had passed, he surrendered to the dreams. No, it was more than surrender. He embraced them, survived on them. Escaped into them when his soul cried out for the simple touch of another being.

For she came to him in dreams, the dark-haired maid with eyes like blue diamonds. In dreams she would run through his forest, sit by his fire, lie willing in his bed. He knew the sound of her voice, the warmth of it. He knew the shape of her, long and slender as a boy. He knew the way the dimple would wink to life at the corner of her mouth when she laughed. And the exact placement of the crescent moon birthmark on her thigh.

He knew all of this, though he had never touched her, never spoken to her, never seen her but through the silky curtain of dreams.

Though it had been a woman who had betrayed him, a woman who was at the root of his endless solitude, he yearned for this dark-haired maid. Yearned for her, as the years passed, as much as he yearned for what had been.

He was drowning in a great, dark sea of alone.

1

It was supposed to be a vacation. It was supposed to be fun, relaxing, enlightening.

It was not supposed to be terrifying.

No, no, terrifying was an exaggeration. Slightly.

A wicked summer storm, a strange road snaking through a dark forest where the trees were like giants cloaked in the armor of mists. Kayleen Brennan of the Boston Brennans wasn't terrified by such things. She was made of sterner stuff. She made a point of reminding herself of that, every ten seconds or so as she fought to keep the rental car on the muddy ditch that had started out as a road.

She was a practical woman, had made the decision to be one quite deliberately and quite clearly when she was twelve. No flights of fancy for Kayleen, no romantic dreams or foolish choices. She had watched — was still watching — such occupations lead her charming, adorable, and baffled mother into trouble.

Financial trouble. Legal trouble. Man trouble.

So Kayleen had become an adult at twelve, and had stayed one.

An adult was not spooked by a bunch of trees and a few streaks of lightning, or by mists that thickened and thinned as if they breathed. A grown woman didn't panic because she'd made a wrong turn. When the road was too narrow, as this one was, to allow her to safely turn around, she simply kept going until she found her way again.

And a sensible person did not start imagining she heard things in the storm.

Like voices.

Should have stayed in Dublin, she told herself grimly as she bumped over a rut. In Dublin with its busy streets and crowded pubs, Ireland had seemed so civilized, so modern, so urbane. But no, she'd just had to see some of the countryside, hadn't she? Just had to rent a car, buy a map, and head out to explore.

But honestly, it had been a perfectly reasonable thing to do. She'd intended to see the country while she was here and perhaps find a few treasures for her family's antique shop back in Boston. She'd intended to wander the roads, to drive to the sea, to visit the pretty little villages, and the great, grand ruins.

Hadn't she booked her stay in a licensed bed-and-breakfast for each night that she'd be traveling? Confirmed reservations ensured there would be no inconvenience and no surprises at the end of each day's journey.

Hadn't she precisely mapped out her route and each point of interest, how long she intended to stay studying each?

She hadn't anticipated getting lost. No one did. The weather report had indicated some rain, but this was Ireland, after all. It had *not* indicated a wild, windy, wicked thunderstorm that shook her little car like a pair of dice in a cup and turned the long, lovely summer twilight into raging dark.

Still, it was all right. It was perfectly all right. She was just a bit behind schedule, and it was partly her own fault. She'd lingered a bit longer than she intended at Powers-court Demesne on her way south. And a bit longer again at the churchyard she'd come across when she headed west.

She was certainly still in County Wicklow, certainly somewhere in Avondale Forest, and the guidebook had stated that the population through the forested land was thin, the villages few and far between.

She had expected to find it charming and atmospheric, a delightful drive on her way to her night's stay in Enniscorthy, a destination she'd been scheduled to reach by seven-thirty. She tipped up her arm, risked a quick glance at her watch, and winced when she saw she was already a full hour late.

Doesn't matter. Surely they wouldn't lock the doors on her. The Irish were known for their hospitality. She intended to put that to the test as soon as she came across a town, a village, or even a single cottage. Once she did, she'd get her bearings again.

But for now . . .

She stopped dead in the road, realizing she hadn't even seen another car for over an hour. Her purse, as ruthlessly organized as her life, sat on the seat beside her. She took out the cell phone she'd rented, turned it on.

And swore softly when the readout told her, as it had since she'd driven into the forest far enough to realize she was lost, that she had no signal.

"Why don't I have a signal?" She nearly rapped the phone against the steering wheel in frustration. But that would have been foolish. "What is the point of renting mobile phones to tourists if they're not going to be able to use them?"

She put the phone away, took a deep breath. To calm herself, she closed her eyes, tilted her head back, and allowed herself two minutes of rest.

The rain lashed the windows like whips, the wind continued its feral howl. At jolting intervals the thick darkness was split by yet another lance of blue-edged lightning. But Kayleen sat quietly, her dark hair still tidy in its band, her hands folded in her lap.

Her mouth, full and shapely, gradually relaxed its tight line. When she opened her eyes, blue as the lightning that ripped the sky, they were calm again.

She rolled her shoulders, took one last cleansing breath, then eased the car forward.

As she did, she heard someone — something — whisper her name.

Kayleen.

Instinctively, she glanced to the side, out the rain-spattered window, into the gloom. And there, for an instant, she saw a shadow take shape, the shape of a man. Eyes, green as glass, glittered.

She hit the brakes, jerking forward as the car slid in the mud. Her heart raced, her fingers shook.

Have you dreamed of me? Will you?

Fighting fear, she quickly lowered the

window, leaned out into the driving rain. "Please. Can you help me? I seem to be lost."

But there was no one there. No one who would — could — have said, so low and sad, *So am I.*

Of course there was no one. With one icy finger she jabbed the button to send the window back up. Just her imagination, just fatigue playing tricks. There was no man standing in the forest in a storm. No man who knew her name.

It was just the sort of foolishness her mother would have dreamed up. The woman lost in the enchanted forest, in a dramatic storm, and the handsome man, most likely a prince under a spell, who rescued her.

Well, Kayleen Brennan could rescue herself, thank you very much. And there were no spellbound princes, only shadows in the rain.

But her heart rapped like a fist against her ribs. With her breath coming fast, she hit the gas again. She would get off of this damned road, and she would get to where she intended to be.

When she got there, she would drink an entire pot of tea while sitting neck-deep in a hot bath. And all of this. . . . inconvenience would be behind her.

She tried to laugh it off, tried to distract herself by mentally composing a letter home to her mother, who would have enjoyed every moment of the experience.

An adventure, she would say. Kayleen! You finally had an adventure!

"Well, I don't want a damn adventure. I want a hot bath. I want a roof over my head and a civilized meal." She was getting worked up again, and this time she couldn't seem to stop. "Won't somebody *please* help me get where I'm supposed to be!"

In answer, lightning shot down, a three-pronged pitchfork hurled out of the heavens. The blast of it exploded the dark into blinding light.

As she threw up an arm to shield her eyes, she saw, standing like a king in the center of the road, a huge buck. Its hide was violently white in the slash of her headlights, its rack gleaming silver. And its eyes, cool and gold, met her terrified ones through the rain.

She swerved, stomped on the brakes. The little car fishtailed, seemed to spin in dizzying circles propelled by the swirling fog. She heard a scream — it had to be her own — before the car ran hard into a tree.

And so she dreamed.

Of running through the forest while the rain slapped down like angry fingers. Eyes, it seemed a thousand of them, watched her through the gloom. She fled, stumbling in the muck stirred up by the storm, her bones jolting as she fell.

Her head was full of sound. The roar of the wind, the booming warning of thunder. And under it a thousand voices chanting.

She wept, and didn't know why. It wasn't the fear, but something else, something that wanted to be wrenched out of her heart as a splinter is wrenched from an aching finger. She remembered nothing, neither name nor place — only that she had to find her way. Had to find it before it was too late.

There was the light, the single ball of it glowing in the dark. She ran toward it, her breath tearing out of her lungs, rain streaming from her hair, down her face.

The ground sucked at her shoes. Another fall tore her sweater. She felt the quick burn on her flesh and, favoring her left arm, scrambled up again. Winded, aching, lost, she continued at a limping run.

The light was her focus. If only she could make it to the light, everything would be all right again. Somehow.

A spear of lightning struck close, so close she felt it sear the air, felt it drench the night with the hot sting of ozone. And in its afterglow she saw that the light was a single beam, from a single window in the tower of a castle.

Of course there would be a castle. It seemed not odd at all that there should be a castle with its tower light glowing in the middle of the woods during a raging storm.

Her weeping became laughter, wild as the night, as she stumbled toward it, tramping through rivers of flowers.

She fell against the massive door and with what strength she had left, slapped a fist against it.

The sound was swallowed by the storm.

"Please," she murmured. "Oh, please, let me in."

By the fire, he'd fallen into the twilight-sleep he was allowed, had dreamed in the flames he'd set to blaze — of his dark-haired maid, coming to him. But her eyes had been frightened, and her cheeks pale as ice.

He'd slept through the storm, through the memories that often haunted him even in that drifting place. But when she had come into those dreams, when she had turned those eyes on him, he stirred. And spoke her name.

And jolted awake, that name sliding out of his mind again. The fire had burned down nearly to embers now. He could have set it roaring again with a thought, but didn't bother.

In any case, it was nearly time. He saw by the pretty crystal clock on the ancient stone mantel — he was amused by such anachronisms — that it was only seconds shy of midnight.

His week would begin at that stroke. For seven days, and seven nights, he would *be*. Not just a shadow in a world of dreams, but flesh, blood, and bone.

He lifted his arms, threw back his head, and waited to become.

The world trembled, and the clock struck midnight.

There was pain. He welcomed it like a lover. Oh, God, to *feel*. Cold burned his skin. Heat scorched it. His throat opened, and there was the blessed bliss of thirst.

He opened his eyes. Colors sprang out at him, clear and true, without that damning mist that separated him for all the other time.

Lowering his hands, he laid one on the back of his chair, felt the soft brush of velvet. He smelled the smoke from the fire, the rain that pounded outside and snuck in through his partially open window.

His senses were battered, so overwhelmed with the rush of sensations that he nearly swooned. And even that was a towering pleasure.

He laughed, a huge burst of sound that he felt rumble up from his belly. And fisting his hands, he raised them yet again.

"I am."

Even as he claimed himself, as the walls echoed with his voice, he heard the pounding at the door. Jolted, he lowered his arms, turned toward a sound he'd not heard in five hundred years. Then it was joined by another.

"Please." And it was his dream who shouted. "Oh, please, let me in."

A trick, he thought. Why would he be tortured with tricks now? He wouldn't tolerate it. Not now. Not during his week to be.

He threw out a hand, sent lights blazing. Furious, he strode out of the room, down the corridor, down the circling pie-shaped stairs. They would not be allowed to infringe on his week. It was a breach of the sentence. He would not lose a single hour of the little time he had.

Impatient with the distance, he muttered the magic under his breath. And appeared again in the great hall.

He wrenched open the door. Met the fury of the storm with fury of his own.

And saw her.

He stared, transfixed. He lost his breath, his mind. His heart.

She had come.

She looked at him, a smile trembling on her lips and sending the dimple at the corner of her mouth to winking.

"There you are," she said.

And fainted at his feet.

2

Shadows and shapes and murmuring voices. They swirled in her head, swelling, fading in a cycle of confusion.

Even when she opened her eyes, they were there. Revolving. What? was her only thought. What is it?

She was cold and wet, and every part of her was a separate ache. An accident. Of course, an accident. But . . .

What is it?

She focused and saw overhead, high overhead, a curved ceiling where plaster faeries danced among ribbons of flowers. Odd, she thought. How odd and lovely. Dazed, she lifted a hand to her brow, felt the damp. Thinking it blood, she let out a gasp, tried to sit up.

Her head spun like a carousel.

"Uh-oh." Trembling now, she looked at her fingers and saw only clear rainwater.

And, turning her head, saw him.

First came the hard jolt of shock, like a vicious strike to the heart. She could feel panic gathering in her throat and fought to swallow it.

He was staring at her. Rudely, she would think later when fear had made room for annoyance. And there was anger in his eyes. Eyes as green as the rain-washed hills of Ireland. He was all in black. Perhaps that was why he looked so dangerous.

His face was violently handsome — "violent" was the word that kept ringing in her ears. Slashing cheekbones, lancing black brows, a fierce frown on a mouth that struck her as brutal. His hair was as dark as his clothing and fell in wild waves nearly to his shoulders.

Her heart pounded, a primal warning. Even as she shrank back, she gathered the courage to speak. "Excuse me. What is it?"

He said nothing. Had been unable to speak since he'd lifted her off the floor. A trick, a new torment? Was she, after all, only a dream within a dream?

But he'd felt her. The cold damp of her flesh, the weight and the shape of her. Her voice came clear to him now, as did the terror in her eyes.

Why should she be afraid? Why should she fear when she had unmanned him? Five hundred years of solitude hadn't done so, but this woman had accomplished it with one quick stroke.

He stepped closer, his eyes never leaving her face. "You are come. Why?"

"I . . . I don't understand. I'm sorry. Do you speak English?"

One of those arching brows rose. He'd spoken in Gaelic, for he most often thought in the language of his life. But five hundred years of alone had given him plenty of time for linguistics. He could certainly speak English, and half a dozen other languages besides.

"I asked why you have come."

"I don't know." She wanted to sit up but was afraid to try it again. "I think there must have been an accident. I can't quite remember."

However much it might hurt to move, she couldn't stay flat on her back looking up at him. It made her feel foolish and helpless. She set her teeth, pushed herself up slowly. Her stomach pitched, her head rang, but she managed to sit.

And sitting, glanced around the room.

An enormous room, she noted, and filled with the oddest conglomeration of furnishings. There was an old and beautiful refectory table that held dozens of candlesticks.

Silver, wrought iron, pottery, crystal. Pikes were crossed on the wall, and near them was a dramatic painting of the Cliffs of Mohr.

There were display cabinets from various eras. Charles II, James I. Neoclassic bumped up against Venetian, Chippendale against Louis XV. An enormous big-screen television stood near a priceless Victorian davenport.

Placed at random were Waterford bowls, T'ang horses, Dresden vases, and . . . several Pez dispensers.

Despite discomfort, the eccentricity tickled her humor. "What an interesting room." She glanced up at him again. He'd yet to stop staring. "Can you tell me how I got here?"

"You came."

"Yes, apparently, but how? And . . . I seem to be very wet."

"It's raining."

"Oh." She blew out a breath. The fear had ebbed considerably. After all, the man collected Pez dispensers and Georgian silver. "I'm sorry, Mister . . ."

"I'm Flynn."

"Mister Flynn."

"Flynn," he repeated.

"All right. I'm sorry, Flynn, I can't seem

to think very clearly." She was shivering, violently now, and wrapped her arms around her chest. "I was going somewhere, but . . . I don't know where I am."

"Who does?" he murmured. "You're cold." And he'd done nothing to tend to her. He would see to her comfort, he decided, and then . . . He would simply see.

He scooped her off the couch, faintly irritated when she pushed a hand against his shoulder defensively.

"I'm sure I can walk."

"I'm more sure I can. You need dry clothes," he began as he carried her out of the room. "A warm brew and a hot fire."

Oh, yes, she thought. It all sounded wonderful. Nearly as wonderful as being carried up a wide, sweeping staircase as if she weighed nothing.

But that was a romantic notion of the kind her mother lived on, the kind that had no place here. She kept that cautious hand pressed to a shoulder that felt like a sculpted curve of rock.

"Thank you for . . ." She trailed off. She'd turned her head just a fraction, and now her face was close to his, her eyes only inches from his eyes, her mouth a breath from his mouth. A sharp, unexpected thrill stabbed clean through her heart. The strike was followed by a hard jolt that was something like recognition.

"Do I know you?"

"Wouldn't you have the answer to that?" He leaned in, just a little, breathed. "Your hair smells of rain." Even as her eyes went wide, he skimmed his mouth from her jawline to her temple. "And your skin tastes of it."

He'd learned to savor over the years. To sip even when he wished to gulp. Now he considered her mouth, imagined what flavors her lips would carry. He watched them tremble open.

Ah, yes.

He shifted her, drawing her ever so slightly closer. And she whimpered in pain.

He jerked back, looked down and saw the raw scrape just below her shoulder, and the tear in her sweater. "You're injured. Why the bloody hell didn't you say so before?"

Out of patience — not his strong suit in any case — he strode into the closest bedchamber, set her down on the side of the bed. In one brisk move he tugged the sweater over her head.

Shocked, she crossed her arms over her breasts. "Don't you touch me!"

"How can I tend your wounds if I don't touch you?" His brows had lowered, drawn together. She was wearing a bra. He knew they were called that, as he'd seen them worn on the television and in the thin books that were called magazines.

But it was the first time he had witnessed an actual female form so attired.

He liked it very much.

But such delights would have to wait until he saw what condition the woman was in. He leaned over, unhooked her trousers.

"Stop it!" She shoved, tried to scramble back and was hauled not so gently into place.

"Don't be foolish. I've no patience for female flights. If I was after ravishing you, t'would already be done." Since she continued to struggle, he heaved a breath and looked up.

It was fear he saw — not foolishness but raw fear. A maiden, he thought. For God's sake, Flynn, have a care.

"Kayleen." He spoke quietly now, his voice as soothing as balm on a burn. "I won't harm you. I only want to see where you're hurt."

"Are you a doctor?"

"Certainly not."

He seemed so insulted, she nearly laughed.

"I know of healing. Now be still. I ought

to have gotten you out of your wet clothes before." His eyes stayed on hers, seemed to grow brighter. And brighter still, until she could see nothing else. And she sighed. "Lie back now, there's a lass."

Mesmerized, she lay on the heaps of silk pillows and, docile as a child, let him undress her.

"Sweet Mary, you've legs that go to forever." His distraction with them caused the simple spell to waver, and she stirred. "A man's entitled to the view," he muttered, then shook his head. "Look what you've done to yourself. Bruised and scraped one end to the other. Do you like pain, then?"

"No." Her tongue felt thick. "Of course not."

"Some do," he murmured. He leaned over her again. "Look at me," he demanded. "Look here. Stay."

Her eyes drooped, half closed as she floated where he wanted, just above the aches. He wrapped her in the quilt, flicked his mind toward the hearth and set the fire roaring.

Then he left her to go to his workshop and gather his potions.

He kept her in the light trance as he tended her. He wanted no maidenly fidgets when he touched her. God, it had been so long since he'd touched a woman, flesh against flesh.

In dreams he'd had her under him, her body eager. He'd laid his lips on her, and his mind had felt her give and arch, her rise, her fall. And so his body had hungered for her.

Now she was here, her lovely skin bruised and chilled.

Now she was here, and didn't know why. Didn't know him.

Despair and desire tangled him in knots.

"Lady, who are you?"

"Kayleen Brennan."

"Where do you come from?"

"Boston."

"That's America?"

"Yes." She smiled. "It is."

"Why are you here?"

"I don't know. Where is here?"

"Nowhere. Nowhere at all."

She reached out, touched his cheek. "Why are you sad?"

"Kayleen." Overcome, he gripped her hand, pressed his lips to her palm. "Do they send you to me so I might know joy again, only to lose it?"

"Who are 'they'?"

He lifted his head, felt the fury burn. So

he stepped away and turned to stare into the fire.

He could send her deeper, into the dreaming place. There she would remember what there was, would know what she knew. And would tell him. But if there was nothing in her, he wouldn't survive it. Not sane.

He drew a breath. "I will have my week," he vowed. "I will have her before it's done. This I will not cast off. This I will not abjure. You cannot break me with this. Not even with her can you break Flynn."

He turned back, steady and resolved again. "The seven days and seven nights are mine, and so is she. What remains here at the last stroke of the last night remains. That is the law. She's mine now."

Thunder blasted like cannon shot. Ignoring it, he walked to the bed. "Wake," he said, and her eyes opened and cleared. As she pushed herself up, he strode to a massive carved armoire, threw the doors open, and selected a long robe of royal blue velvet.

"This will suit you. Dress, then come downstairs." He tossed the robe on the foot of the bed. "You'll want food."

"Thank you, but —"

"We'll talk when you've supped."

"Yes, but I want —" She hissed in frustration as he walked out of the room and shut the door behind him with a nasty little slam.

Manners, she thought, weren't high on the list around here. She dragged a hand through her hair, stunned to find it dry again. Impossible. It had been dripping wet when he'd brought her up here only moments before.

She combed her fingers through it again, frowning. Obviously she was mistaken. It must have been all but dry. The accident had shaken her up, confused her. That was why she wasn't remembering things clearly.

She probably needed to go to a hospital, have X rays taken. Though a hospital seemed silly, really, when she felt fine. In fact, she felt wonderful.

She lifted her arms experimentally. No aches, no twinges. She poked gingerly at the scrape. Hadn't it been longer and deeper along her elbow? It was barely tender now.

Well, she'd been lucky. And now, since she was starving, she'd take the eccentric Flynn up on a meal. After that, her mind was bound to be steadier, and she'd figure out what to do next.

Satisfied, she tossed the covers back. And let out a muffled squeal. She was stark naked.

My God, where were her clothes? She remembered, yes, she remembered the way he'd yanked her sweater off, and then he'd . . . Damn it. She pressed a trembling hand to her temple. *Why* couldn't she remember? She'd been frightened, she'd shoved at him, and then . . . then she'd been wrapped in a blanket, in a room warmed by a blazing fire and he'd told her to get dressed and come down to dinner.

Well, if she was having blackouts, the hospital was definitely first on the agenda.

She snatched up the robe. Then simply rubbed the rich fabric over her cheek and moaned. It felt like something a princess would wear. Or a goddess. But certainly nothing that Kayleen Brennan of Boston would slip casually into for dinner.

This will suit you, he'd said. The idea of that made her laugh, but she slid her arms into it and let herself enjoy the lustrous warmth against her skin.

She turned, caught her own reflection in a cheval glass. Her hair was a tumble around the shoulders of the deep blue robe that swept down her body and ended in a shimmer of gold lace at the ankles.

I don't look like me, she thought. I look like something out of a fairy tale. Because that made her feel foolish, she turned away.

The bed she'd lain in was covered with velvet as well and lushly canopied with more. On the bureau, and certainly that was a Charles II in perfect condition, sat a lady's brush set of silver with inlays of lapis, antique perfume bottles of opal and of jade. Roses, fresh as morning and white as snow, stood regally in a cobalt vase.

A fairy tale of a room as well, she mused. One fashioned for candlelight and simmering fires. There was a Queen Anne desk in the corner, and tall windows draped in lace and velvet, pretty watercolors of hills and meadows on the walls, lovely faded rugs over the thick planked floors.

If she'd conjured the perfect room, this would have been it.

His manners might be lacking, but his taste was impeccable. Or his wife's, she corrected. For obviously this was a woman's room.

Because the idea should have relieved her, she ignored the little sinking sensation in her belly and satisfied her curiosity by opening the opal bottle.

Wasn't that strange? she thought after a sniff. The bottle held her favorite perfume.

3

Flynn had a stiff whiskey before he dealt with the food. It hit him like a hot fist.

Thank God there were still some things a man could count on.

He would feed his woman — for she was unquestionably his — and he would take some care with her. He would see to her comfort, as a man was meant to do, then he would let her know the way things were to be.

But first he would see that she was steadier on her feet.

The dining hall fireplace was lit. He had the table set with bone china, heavy silver, a pool of fragrant roses, the delicacy of slim white candles and the jewel sparkle of crystal.

Then closing his eyes, lifting his hands palms out, he began to lay the table with the foods that would please her most.

She was so lovely, his Kayleen. He wanted

to put the bloom back in her cheeks. He wanted to hear her laugh.

He wanted her.

And so, that was the way things would be.

He stepped back, studied his work with cool satisfaction. Pleased with himself, Flynn went out again to wait at the base of the stairs.

And as she came down toward him, his heart staggered in his chest. *"Speirbhean."*

Kayleen hesitated. "I'm sorry?"

"You're beautiful. You should learn the Gaelic," he said, taking her hand and leading her out of the hall. "I'll teach you."

"Well, thank you, but I really don't think that'll be necessary. I really want to thank you, too, for taking me in like this, and I wonder if I might use your phone." A little detail, Kayleen thought, that had suddenly come to her.

"I have no telephone. Does the gown please you?"

"No phone? Well, perhaps one of your neighbors might have one I can use."

"I have no neighbors."

"In the closest village," she said, as panic began to tickle her throat again.

"There is no village. Why are you fretting, Kayleen? You're warm and dry and safe."

"That may be, but . . . how do you know my name?"

"You told me."

"I don't remember telling you. I don't remember how I —"

"You've no cause to worry. You'll feel better when you've eaten."

She was beginning to think she had plenty of cause to worry. The well-being she'd felt upstairs in that lovely room was eroding quickly. But when she stepped into the dining room, she felt nothing but shock.

The table was large enough to seat fifty, and spread over it was enough food to feed every one of them.

Bowls and platters and tureens and plates were jammed end to end down the long oak surface. Fruit, fish, meat, soups, a garden of vegetables, an ocean of pastas.

"Where —" Her voice rose, snapped, and had to be fought back under control. "Where did this come from?"

He sighed. He'd expected delight and instead was given shock. Another thing a man could count on, he thought. Women were forever a puzzle.

"Sit, please. Eat."

Though she felt little flickers of panic, her voice was calm and firm. "I want to know where all this food came from. I want to know who else is here. Where's your wife?"

"I have no wife."

"Don't give me that." She spun to face him, steady enough now. And angry enough to stand and demand. "If you don't have a wife, you certainly have a woman."

"Aye. I have you."

"Just . . . stay back." She grabbed a knife from the table, aimed it at him. "Don't come near me. I don't know what's going on here, and I'm not going to care. I'm going to walk out of this place and keep walking."

"No." He stepped forward and neatly plucked what was now a rose from her hand. "You're going to sit down and eat."

"I'm in a coma." She stared at the white rose in his hand, at her own empty one. "I had an accident. I've hit my head. I'm hallucinating all of this."

"All of this is real. No one knows better than I the line between what's real and what isn't. Sit down." He gestured to a chair, swore when she didn't move. "Have I said I wouldn't harm you? Among my sins has never been a lie or the harm of a woman. Here." He held out his hand, and now it held the knife. "Take this, and feel free to use it should I break my word to you."

"You're . . ." The knife was solid in her hand. A trick of the eye, she told herself. Just a trick of the eye. "You're a magician."

"I am." His grin was like lightning, fast and bright. Whereas he had been handsome, now he was devastating. His pleasure shone. "That is what I am, exactly. Sit down, Kayleen, and break fast with me. For I've hungered a long time."

She took one cautious step in retreat. "It's too much."

Thinking she meant the food, he frowned at the table. Considered. "Perhaps you're right. I got a bit carried away with it all." He scanned the selections, nodded, then sketched an arch with his hand.

Half the food vanished.

The knife dropped out of her numb fingers. Her eyes rolled straight back.

"Oh, Christ." It was impatience as much as concern. At least this time he had the wit to catch her before she hit the floor. He sat her in a chair, gave her a little shake, then watched her eyes focus again.

"You didn't understand after all."

"Understand? Understand?"

"It'll need to be explained, then." He picked up a plate and began to fill it for her. "You need to eat or you'll be ill. Your injuries will heal faster if you're strong."

He set the plate in front of her, began to fill one for himself. "What do you know of magic, Kayleen Brennan of Boston?"

"It's fun to watch."

"It can be."

She would eat, she thought, because she did feel ill. "And it's an illusion."

"It can be." He took the first bite — rare roast beef — and moaned in ecstasy at the taste. The first time he'd come to his week, he'd gorged himself so that he was sick a full day. And had counted it worth it. But now he'd learned to take his time, and appreciate.

"Do you remember now how you came here?"

"It was raining."

"Yes, and is still."

"I was going . . ."

"How were you going?"

"How?" She picked up her fork, sampled the fish without thinking. "I was driving . . . I was driving," she repeated, on a rising note of excitement. "Of course. I was driving, and I was lost. The storm. I was coming from —" She stopped, struggling through the mists. "Dublin. I'd been in Dublin. I'm on vacation. Oh, that's right, I'm on vacation and I was going to drive around the countryside. I got lost. Somehow. I was on one of the little roads through the forest, and it was storming. I could barely see. Then I . . ."

The relief in her eyes faded as they met his. "I saw you," she whispered. "I saw you out in the storm."

"Did you now?"

"You were out in the rain. You said my name. How could you have said my name before we met?"

She'd eaten little, but he thought a glass of wine might help her swallow what was to come. He poured it, handed it to her. "I've dreamed of you, Kayleen. Dreamed of you for longer than your lifetime. And dreaming of you I was when you were lost in my forest. And when I awoke, you'd come. Do you never dream of me, Kayleen?"

"I don't know what you're talking about. There was a storm. I was lost. Lightning hit very near, and there was a deer. A white deer in the road. I swerved to avoid it, and I crashed. I think I hit a tree. I probably have a concussion, and I'm imagining things."

"A white hind." The humor had gone from his face again. "You hit a tree with your car? They didn't have to hurt you," he muttered. "They had no *right* to hurt you."

"Who are you talking about?"

"My jailers." He shoved his plate aside. "The bloody Keepers."

"I need to check on my car." She spoke slowly, calmly. Not just eccentric, she decided. The man was unbalanced. "Thank you so much for helping me."

"If you want to check on your car, then we will. In the morning. There's hardly a point in going out in a storm in the middle of the night." He laid his hand firmly on hers before she could rise. "You're thinking, 'This Flynn, he's lost his mind somewhere along the way.' Well, I haven't, though it was a near thing a time or two. Look at me, *leannana*. Do I mean nothing to you?"

"I don't know." And that was what kept her from bolting. He could look at her, as he was now, and she felt tied to him. Not bound by force, but tied. By her own will. "I don't understand what you mean, or what's happening to me."

"Then we'll sit by the fire, and I'll tell you what it all means." He rose, held out his hand. Irritation washed over his face when she refused to take it. "Do you want the knife?"

She glanced down at it, back up at him. "Yes."

"Then bring it along with you."

He plucked up the wine, and the glasses, and led the way.

He sat by the fire, propped his boots on the hearth, savored his wine and the scent of the woman who sat so warily beside him. "I was born in magic," he began. "Some are. Others apprentice and can learn well enough. But to be born in it is more a matter of controlling the art than of learning it."

"So your father was a magician."

"No, he was a tailor. Magic doesn't have to come down through the blood. It simply has to *be* in the blood." He paused because he didn't want to blunder again. He should know more of her, he decided, before he did. "What is it you are, back in your Boston?"

"I'm an antique dealer. That came through the blood. My uncles, my grandfather, and so on. Brennan's of Boston has been doing business for nearly a century."

"Nearly a century, is it?" he chuckled. "So very long."

"I suppose it doesn't seem so by European standards. But America's a young country. You have some magnificent pieces in your home."

"I collect what appeals to me."

"Apparently a wide range appeals to you. I've never seen such a mix of styles and eras in one place before."

He glanced around the room, considering. It wasn't something he'd thought of, but he'd had only himself to please up until now. "You don't like it?"

Because it seemed to matter to him, she worked up a smile. "No, I like it very much. In my business I see a lot of beautiful and interesting pieces, and I've always felt it was a shame more people don't just toss them together and make their own style rather than sticking so rigidly to a pattern. No one can accuse you of sticking to a pattern."

"No. That's a certainty."

She started to curl up her legs, caught herself. What in the world was wrong with her? She was relaxing into an easy conversation with what was very likely a madman. She cut her gaze toward the knife beside her, then back to him. And found him studying her contemplatively.

"I wonder if you could use it. There are two kinds of people in the world, don't you think? Those who fight and those who flee. Which are you, Kayleen?"

"I've never been in the position where I had to do either."

"That's either fortunate or tedious. I'm not entirely sure which. I like a good fight myself," he added with that quick grin. "Just one of my many flaws. Fact is, I miss going fist to fist with a man. I miss a great many things."

"Why? Why do you have to miss anything?"

"That's the point, isn't it, of this fireside conversation. The why. Are you wondering, *mavourneen,* if I'm off in my head?"

"Yes," she said, then immediately froze.

"I'm not, though perhaps it would've been easier if I'd gone a bit crazy along the way. They knew I had a strong mind — part of the problem, in their thinking, and part of the reason for the sentence weighed on me."

"They?" Her fingers inched toward the handle of the knife. She could use it, she promised herself. She *would* use it if she had to, no matter how horribly sad and lonely he looked.

"The Keepers. The ancient and the revered who guard and who nurture magic. And have done so since the Waiting Time, when life was no more than the heavens taking their first breath."

"Gods?" she said cautiously.

"In some ways of thinking." He was brooding again, frowning into the flames. "I was born of magic, and when I was old enough I left my family to do the work. To heal and to help. Even to entertain. Some of us have more of a knack, you could say, for the fun of it."

"Like, um, sawing a lady in half."

He looked at her with a mixture of amusement and exasperation. "This is illusion, Kayleen."

"Yes."

"I speak of magic, not pretense. Some prophesy, some travel and study, for the sake of it. Others devote their art to healing body or soul. Some choose to make a living performing. Some might serve a worthy master, as Merlin did Arthur. There are as many choices as there are people. And while none may choose to harm or profit for the sake of it, all are real."

He slipped a long chain from under his shirt, held the pendant with its milky stone out for her to see. "A moonstone," he told her. "And the words around are my name, and my title. *Draiodoir*. Magician."

"It's beautiful." Unable to resist, she curved her hand around the pendant. And felt a bolt of heat, like the rush of a comet, spurt from her fingertips to her toes. "God!"

Before she could snatch her hand away, Flynn closed his own over hers. "Power," he murmured. "You feel it. Can all but taste it. A seductive thing. And inside, you can make yourself think there's nothing impossible. Look at me, Kayleen."

She already was, could do nothing else. Wanted nothing else. There you are, she thought again. There you are, at last.

"I could have you now. You would willingly lie with me now, as you have in dreams. Without fear. Without questions."

"Yes."

And his need was a desperate thing, leaping, snapping at the tether of control. "I want more." His fingers tightened on hers. "What is it in you that makes me crave more, when I don't know what more is? Well, we've time to find the answer. For now, I'll tell you a story. A young magician left his family. He traveled and he studied. He helped and he healed. He had pride in his work, in himself. Some said too much pride."

He paused now, thinking, for there had been times in this last dreaming that he'd wondered if that could be so.

"His skill, this magician's, was great, and he was known in his world. Still, he was a man, with the needs of a man, the desires of a man, the faults of a man. Would you want a man perfect, Kayleen?"

"I want you."

"*Leannana.*" He leaned over, pressed his lips to her knuckles. "This man, this magician, he saw the world. He read its books, listened to its music. He came and went as he pleased, did as he pleased. Perhaps he was careless on occasion, and though he did

49

no harm, neither did he heed the rules and the warnings he was given. The power was so strong in him, what need had he for rules?"

"Everyone needs rules. They keep us civilized."

"Do you think?" It amused him how prim her voice had become. Even held by the spell, she had a strong mind, and a strong will. "We'll discuss that sometime. But for now, to continue the tale. He came to know a woman. Her beauty was blinding, her manner sweet. He believed her to be innocent. Such was his romantic nature."

"Did you love her?"

"Yes, I loved her. I loved the angel-faced, innocent maid I saw when I looked at her. I asked for her hand, for it wasn't just a tumble I wanted from her but a lifetime. And when I asked, she wept, ah, pretty tears down a smooth cheek. She couldn't be mine, she told me, as much as her heart already was. For there was a man, a wealthy man, a cruel man, who had contracted for her. Her father had sold her, and her fate was sealed."

"You couldn't let that happen."

"Ah, you see that, too." It pleased him that she saw it, stood with him on that vital point. "No, how could I let her go loveless to another? To be sold like a horse in the marketplace? I would take her away, I said, and she wept the more. I would give her father twice what had been given, and she sobbed upon my shoulder. It could not be done, for then surely the man would kill her poor father, or see him in prison, or some horrible fate. So long as the man had his wealth and position, her family would suffer. She couldn't bear to be the cause of it, even though her heart was breaking."

Kayleen shook her head, frowned. "I'm sorry, but that doesn't make sense. If the money was paid back and her father was wealthy now, he could certainly protect himself, and he would have the law to —"

"The heart doesn't follow such reason," he interrupted, impatiently because if he'd had the wit in his head at the time, instead of fire in his blood, he'd have come to those same conclusions. "It was saving her that was my first thought — and my last. Protecting her, and yes, perhaps, by doing so having her love me the more. I would take this cruel man's wealth and his position from him. I vowed this, and oh, how her eyes shone, diamonds of tears. I would take what he had and lay it at her feet. She would live like a queen, and I would care for her all my life."

"But stealing —"

"Will you just listen?" Exasperation hissed through his voice.

"Of course." Her chin lifted, a little tilt of resentment. "I beg your pardon."

"So this I did, whistling the wind, drawing down the moon, kindling the cold fire. This I did, and did freely for her. And the man woke freezing in a crofter's cot instead of his fine manor house. He woke in rags instead of his warm nightclothes. I took his life from him, without spilling a drop of blood. And when it was done, I stood in the smoldering dark of that last dawn, triumphant."

He fell into silence a moment, and when he continued, his voice was raw. "The Keepers encased me in a shield of crystal, holding me there as I cursed them, as I shouted my protests, as I used the heart and innocence of my young maid as my defense for my crime. And they showed me how she laughed as she gathered the wealth I'd sent to her, as she leapt into a carriage laden with it and fell into the arms of the lover with whom she'd plotted the ruin of the man she hated. And my ruin as well."

"But you loved her."

"I did, but the Keepers don't count love as an excuse, as a reason. I was given a choice. They would strip me of my power, take away what was in my blood and make me merely human. Or I would keep it, and live alone, in a half world, without companionship, without human contact, without the pleasures of the world that I, in their estimation, had betrayed."

"That's cruel. Heartless."

"So I claimed, but it didn't sway them. I took the second choice, for they would not empty me. I would not abjure my birthright. Here I have existed, since that night of betrayal, a hundred years times five, with only one week each century to feel as a man does again.

"I am a man, Kayleen." With his hand still gripping hers, he got to his feet. Drew her up. "I am," he murmured, sliding his free hand into her hair, fisting it there.

He lowered his head, his lips nearly meeting hers, then hesitated. The sound of her breath catching, releasing, shivered through him. She trembled under his hand, and he felt, inside himself, the stumble of her heart.

"Quietly this time," he murmured. "Quietly." And brushed his lips, a whisper, once . . . twice over hers. The flavor bloomed inside him like a first sip of fine wine.

He drank slowly. Even when her lips parted, invited, he drank slowly. Savoring the texture of her mouth, the easy slide of tongues, the faint, faint scrape of teeth.

Her body fit against his, so lovely, so perfect. The heat from the moonstone held between their hands spread like sunlight and began to pulse.

So even drinking slowly he was drunk on her.

When he drew back, her sigh all but shattered him.

"*A ghra.*" Weak, wanting, he lowered his brow to hers. With a sigh of his own he tugged the pendant free. Her eyes, soft, loving, clouded, began to clear. Before the change was complete, he pressed his mouth to hers one last time.

"Dream," he said.

4

She woke to watery sunlight and the heady scent of roses. There was a low fire simmering in the grate and a silk pillow under her head.

Kayleen stirred and rolled over to snuggle in.

Then shot up in bed like an arrow from a plucked bow.

My God, it had really happened. All of it.

And for lord's sake, for *lord's* sake, she was naked again.

Had he given her drugs, hypnotized her, gotten her drunk? What other reason could there be for her to have slept like a baby — and naked as one — in a bed in the house of a crazy man?

Instinctively, she snatched at the sheets to cover herself, and then she saw the single white rose.

An incredibly sweet, charmingly romantic crazy man, she thought and picked up the rose before she could resist.

That story he'd told her — magic and betrayal and five hundred years of punishment. He'd actually believed it. Slowly she let out a breath. So had she. She'd sat there, listening and believing every word — then. Hadn't seen a single thing odd about it, but had felt sorrow and anger on his behalf. Then . . .

He'd kissed her, she remembered. She pressed her fingertips to her lips, stunned at her own behavior. The man had kissed her, had made her feel like rich cream being gently lapped out of a bowl. More, she'd *wanted* him to kiss her. Had wanted a great deal more than that.

And perhaps, she thought, dragging the sheets higher, there had been a great deal more than that.

She started to leap out of bed, then changed her mind and crept out instead. She had to get away, quickly and quietly. And to do so, she needed clothes.

She tiptoed to the wardrobe, wincing at the creak as she eased the door open. It was one more shock to look inside and see silks and velvets, satins and lace, all in rich, bold colors. Such beautiful things. The kind of clothes she would covet but never buy. So impractical, so frivolous, really.

So gorgeous.

Shaking her head at her foolishness, she snatched out her own practical trousers, her torn sweater . . . but it wasn't torn. Baffled, she turned it over, inside out, searching for the jagged rip in the arm. It wasn't there.

She hadn't imagined that tear. She couldn't have imagined it. Because she was beginning to shake, she dragged it over her head, yanked the trousers on. Trousers that were pristine, though they had been stained and muddy.

She dove into the wardrobe, pushing through evening slippers, kid boots, and found her simple black flats. Flats that should have been well worn, caked with dirt, scarred just a little on the inside left where she had knocked against a chest the month before in her shop.

But the shoes were unmarked and perfect, as if they'd just come out of the box.

She would think about it later. She'd think about it all later. Now she had to get away from here, away from him. Away from whatever was happening to her.

Her knees knocked together as she crept to the door, eased it open, and peeked out into the hallway. She saw beautiful rugs on a beautiful floor, paintings and tapestries on the walls, more doors, all closed. And no sign of Flynn.

She slipped out, hurrying as quickly as she dared. Wild with relief, she bolted down the stairs, raced to the door, yanked it open with both hands.

And barreling through, ran straight into Flynn.

"Good morning." He grasped her shoulders, steadying her even as he thought what a lovely thing it would be if she'd been running toward him instead of away from him. "It seems we've done with the rain for now."

"I was — I just —" Oh, God. "I want to go check on my car."

"Of course. You may want to wait till the mists burn off. Would you like your breakfast?"

"No, no." She made her lips curve. "I'd really like to see how badly I damaged the car. So, I'll just go see and . . . let you know."

"Then I'll take you to it."

"No, really."

But he turned away, whistled. He took her hand, ignoring her frantic tugs for release, and led her down the steps.

Out of the mists came a white horse at the gallop, the charger of folklore with his mane flying, his silver bridle ringing. Kayleen managed one short shriek as he arrowed toward them, powerful legs shredding the mists, magnificent head tossing.

He stopped inches from Flynn's feet, blew softly, then nuzzled Flynn's chest.

With a laugh, Flynn threw his arms around the horse's neck. With the same joy, she thought, that a boy might embrace a beloved dog. He spoke to the horse in low tones, crooning ones, in what she now recognized as Gaelic.

Still grinning, Flynn eased back. He lifted a hand, flicked the wrist, and the palm that had been empty now held a glossy red apple. "No, I would never forget. There's for my beauty," he said, and the horse dipped his head and nipped the apple neatly out of Flynn's palm.

"His name is Dilis. It means faithful, and he is." With economical and athletic grace, Flynn vaulted into the saddle, held down a hand for Kayleen.

"Thank you all the same, and he's very beautiful, but I don't know how to ride. I'll just —" The words slid back down her throat as Flynn leaned down, gripped her arm, and pulled her up in front of him as though she weighed less than a baby.

"I know how to ride," he assured her and tapped Dilis lightly with his heels.

The horse reared, and Kayleen's scream mixed with Flynn's laughter as the fabulous beast pawed the air. Then they were leaping forward and flying into the forest.

There was nothing to do but hold on. She banded her arms around Flynn, buried her face in his chest. It was insane, absolutely insane. She was an ordinary woman who led an ordinary life. How could she be galloping through some Irish forest on a great white horse, plastered against a man who claimed to be a fifteenth-century magician?

It had to stop, and it had to stop now.

She lifted her head, intending to tell him firmly to rein his horse in, to let her off and let her go. And all she did was stare. The sun was slipping in fingers through the arching branches of the trees. The air glowed like polished pearls.

Beneath her the horse ran fast and smooth at a breathless, surely a reckless, pace. And the man who rode him was the most magnificent man she'd ever seen.

His dark hair flew, his eyes glittered. And that sadness he carried, which was somehow its own strange appeal, had lifted. What she saw on his face was joy, excitement, delight, challenge. A dozen things, and all of them strong.

And seeing them, her heart beat as fast as the horse's hooves. "Oh, my God!"

It wasn't possible to fall in love with a stranger. It didn't happen in the real world.

Weakly, she let her head fall back to his chest. But maybe it was time to admit, or at least consider, that she'd left the real world the evening before when she'd taken that wrong turn into the forest.

Dilis slowed to a canter, stopped. Once again, Kayleen lifted her head. This time her eyes met Flynn's. This time he read what was in them. As the pleasure of it rose in him, he leaned toward her.

"No. Don't." She lifted her hand, pressed it to his lips. "Please."

His nod was curt. "As you wish." He leapt off the horse, plucked her down. "It appears your mode of transportation is less reliable than mine," he said, and turned her around.

The car had smashed nearly headlong into an oak. The oak, quite naturally, had won the bout. The hood was buckled back like an accordion, the safety glass a surrealistic pattern of cracks. The air bag had deployed, undoubtedly saving her from serious injury. She'd been driving too fast for the conditions, she remembered. Entirely too fast.

But how had she been driving at all?

That was the question that struck her now. There was no road. The car sat broken on what was no more than a footpath through the forest. Trees crowded in everywhere, along with brambles and wild vines

61

that bloomed with unearthly flowers. And when she slowly turned in a circle, she saw no route she could have maneuvered through them in the rain, in the dark.

She saw no tracks from her tires in the damp ground. There was no trace of her journey; there was only the end of it.

Cold, she hugged her arms. Her sweater, she thought, wasn't ripped. Cautiously, she pushed up the sleeve, and there, where she'd been badly scraped and bruised, her skin was smooth and unmarred.

She looked back at Flynn. He stood silently as his horse idly cropped at the ground. Temper was in his eyes, and she could all but see the sparks of impatience shooting off him.

Well, she had a temper of her own if she was pushed far enough. And her own patience was at an end. "What is this place?" she demanded, striding up to him. "Who the hell are you, and what have you done? How have you done it? How the devil can I be here when I can't possibly be here? That car —" She flung her hand out. "I couldn't have driven it here. I couldn't have." Her arm dropped limply to her side. "How could I?"

"You know what I told you last night was the truth."

She did know. With her anger burned away, she did know it. "I need to sit down."

"The ground's damp." He caught her arm before she could just sink to the floor of the forest. "Here, then." And he lowered her gently into a high-backed chair with a plump cushion of velvet.

"Thank you." She began to laugh, and burying her face in her hands, shook with it. "Thank you very much. I've lost my mind. Completely lost my mind."

"You haven't. But it would help us both considerably if you'd open it a bit."

She lowered her hands. She was not a hysterical woman, and would not become one. She no longer feared him. However savagely handsome his looks, he'd done her no harm. The fact was, he'd tended to her.

But facts were the problem, weren't they? The fact that she couldn't be here, but was. That he couldn't exist, yet did. The fact that she felt what she felt, without reason.

Once upon a time, she thought, then drew a long breath.

"I don't believe in fairy tales."

"Now, then, that's very sad. Why wouldn't you? Do you think any world can exist without magic? Where does the color come from, and the beauty? Where are the miracles?"

"I don't know. I don't have any answers. Either I'm having a very complex dream or I'm sitting in the woods in a" — she got to her feet to turn and examine the chair — "a marquetry side chair, Dutch, I believe, early eighteenth century. Very nice. Yes, well." She sat again. "I'm sitting here in this beautiful chair in a forest wrapped in mists, having ridden here on that magnificent horse, after having spent the night in a castle —"

" 'Tisn't a castle, really. More a manor."

"Whatever, with a man who claims to be more than five hundred years old."

"Five hundred and twenty-eight, if we're counting."

"Really? You wear it quite well. A five-hundred-and-twenty-eight-year-old magician who collects Pez dispensers."

"Canny little things."

"And I don't know how any of it can be true, but I believe it. I believe all of it. Because continuing to deny what I see with my own eyes makes less sense than believing it."

"There." He beamed at her. "I knew you were a sensible woman."

"Oh, yes, I'm very sensible, very steady. So I have to believe what I see, even if it's irrational."

"If that which is rational exists, that which is irrational must as well. There is ever a balance to things, Kayleen."

"Well." She sat calmly, glancing around. "I believe in balance." The air sparkled. She could feel it on her face. She could smell the deep, dark richness of the woods. She could hear the trill of birdsong. She was where she was, and so was he.

"So, I'm sitting in this lovely chair in an enchanted forest having a conversation with a five-hundred-and-twenty-eight-year-old magician. And, if all that isn't crazy enough, there's one more thing that tops it all off. I'm in love with him."

The easy smile on his face faded. What ran through him was so hot and tangled, so full of layers and routes he couldn't breathe through it all. "I've waited for you, through time, through dreams, through those small windows of life that are as much torture as treasure. Will you come to me now, Kayleen? Freely?"

She got to her feet, walked across the soft cushion of forest floor to him. "I don't know how I can feel like this. I only know I do."

He pulled her into his arms, and this time the kiss was hungry. Possessive. When she pressed her body to his, wound her arms around his neck, he deepened the kiss, took more. Filled himself with her.

Her head spun, and she reveled in the giddiness. No one had ever wanted her — not like this. Had ever touched her like this. Needed her. Desire was a hot spurt that fired the blood and made logic, reason, sanity laughable things.

She had magic. What did she need of reason?

"Mine." He murmured it against her mouth. Said it again and again as his lips raced over her face, her throat. Then, throwing his head back, he shouted it.

"She's mine now and ever. I claim her, as is my right."

When he lifted her off her feet, lightning slashed across the sky. The world trembled.

They rode through the forest. He showed her a stream where golden fish swam over silver rocks. Where a waterfall tumbled down into a pool clear as blue glass.

He stopped to pick her wildflowers and thread them through her hair. And when he kissed her, it was soft and sweet.

His moods, she thought, were as magical as the rest of him, and just as inexplicable. He courted her, making her laugh as he plucked baubles out of thin air and painted rainbows in the sky.

She could feel the breeze on her cheeks, smell the flowers and the damp. What was in her heart was like music. Fairy tales *were* real, she thought. All the years she'd turned her back on them, dismissed the happily-ever-after that her mother sighed over, her own magic had been waiting for her.

Nothing would ever, could ever, be the same again.

Had she known it somehow? Deep inside, had she known it had only been waiting, that he had only been waiting for her to awake?

They walked or rode while birds chorused around them and mists faded away into brilliant afternoon.

There beside the pool he laid a picnic, pouring wine out of his open hand to amuse her. Touching her hair, her cheek, her shoulders dozens of times, as if the contact was as much reassurance as flirtation.

She'd never had a romance. Never taken the time for one. Now it seemed a lifetime of love and anticipation could be fit into one perfect day.

He knew something about everything. History, culture, art, literature, science. It was a new thrill to realize that the man who held her heart, who attracted her so completely, appealed to her mind as well. He could make her laugh, make her wonder, make her yearn. And he brought her a contentment she hadn't known she'd lived without.

If this was a dream, she thought, as twilight fell and they mounted the horse once more, she hoped never to wake.

5

A perfect day deserved a perfect night. She had thought, hoped, that when they returned from their outing, he would take her inside. Take her to bed.

But he had only kissed her in that stirring way that made her weak and jittery and asked if she might like to change for the evening.

So she had gone up to her room to worry and wonder how a woman prepared, after the most magical of days, for the most momentous night of her life. Of one thing she was certain. It wouldn't do to think. If she let her thoughts take shape, the doubts would creep in. Doubts about everything that had happened — and about what would happen yet.

For once, she would simply act. She would simply be.

The bath that adjoined her room was a testament to modern luxury. Stepping from the bedchamber with its antiques and plush velvets into this sea of tile and glass was like stepping from one world into another.

Which was, she supposed, something she'd done already. She filled the huge tub with water and scent and oil, let the low hum of the motor and quiet jets relax her as she sank in up to her chin.

Silver-topped pots sat on the long white counter. From them she scooped out cream to smooth over her skin. And watched herself in the steam-hazed window. This was the way women had prepared for a lover for centuries. Scenting and softening themselves for a man's hands. For a man's mouth.

A woman's magic.

She wouldn't be afraid, she wouldn't let anxiety crowd out the pleasure.

In the wardrobe she found a long gown of silk in the color of ripe plums. It slid over her body like sin and scooped low over her breasts. She slipped her feet into silver slippers, started to turn to the glass.

No, she thought, she didn't want to see herself reflected in a mirror. She wanted to see herself reflected in Flynn's eyes.

He felt like a green youth, all eager nerves and awkward moves. In his day, he'd had quite a way with the ladies. Though five hundred years could certainly make a man rusty in certain areas, he'd had dreams.

But even in dreams, he hadn't wanted so much.

How could he? he thought as Kayleen started down the staircase toward him. Dreams paled next to the power of her.

He reached out, almost afraid that his hand would pass through her and leave him nothing but this yearning. "You're the most beautiful woman I've ever known."

"Tonight" — she linked her fingers with his — "everything's beautiful." She stepped toward him and was confused when he stepped back.

"I thought . . . Will you dance with me, Kayleen?"

As he spoke, the air filled with music. Candles, hundreds of them, spurted into flame. The light was pale gold now, and flowers blossomed down the walls, turning the hall into a garden.

"I'd love to," she said, and moved into his arms.

They waltzed in the Great Hall, through the swaying candlelight and the perfume of roses that bloomed everywhere. Doors and windows sprang open, welcoming the glow of moon and stars and the fragrance of the night.

Thrilled, Kayleen threw back her head and let him sweep her in stirring circles. "It's wonderful! Everything's wonderful. How can you know how to waltz like this when there was no waltz in your time?"

"Watching through dreams. I see the world go by in them, and I take what pleases me most. I've danced with you in dreams, Kayleen. You don't remember?"

"No," she whispered. "I don't dream. And if I do, I never remember. But I'll remember this." She smiled at him. "Forever."

"You're happy."

"I've never in my life been so happy." Her hand slid from his shoulder, along his neck, to rest on his cheek. The blue of her eyes deepened. Went dreamy. "Flynn."

"Wine," he said, when fresh nerves kicked in his belly. "You'll want wine."

"No." The music continued to swell as they stood. "I don't want wine."

"Supper, then."

"No." Her hand trailed over, cupped the back of his neck. "Not supper either," she murmured and drew his mouth to hers. "You." She breathed it. "Only you."

"Kayleen." He'd intended to romance her, charm her. Seduce her. Now she had done all of that to him. "I don't want to rush you."

"I've waited so long, without even knowing. There's never been anyone else. Now I think there couldn't have been, because there was you. Show me what it's like to belong."

"There's no woman I've touched who mattered. They're shadows beside you, Kayleen. This," he said and lifted her into his arms, "is real."

He carried her through the music and candlelight, up the grand stairs. And though she felt his arms, the beat of his heart, it was like floating.

"Here is where I dreamed of you in the night." He took her into his bedchamber, where the bed was covered with red silk and the petals of white roses, where candles stood flaming and the fire shimmered. "And here is where I'll love you, this first time. Flesh to flesh."

He set her on her feet. "I won't hurt you, that I can promise. I'll give you only pleasure."

"I'm not afraid."

"Then be with me." He cupped her face in his hands, laid his lips on hers.

In dreams there had been longing, and echoes of sensations. Here and now, with those mists parted, there was so much more.

Gently, so gently, his mouth took from

hers. Warmth and wanting. With tenderness and patience, his hands moved over her. Soft and seductive. When she trembled, he soothed, murmuring her name, and promises. He slid the gown off her shoulders, trailed kisses over that curve of flesh. And thrilled to the flavor and the fragrance.

"Let me see you now, lovely Kayleen." He skimmed his lips along her throat as he eased the gown down her body. When it pooled at her feet, he stepped back and looked his fill.

There was no shyness in her. The heat that rose up to bloom on her skin was anticipation. The tremble that danced through her was delight when his gaze finished its journey and his eyes locked on hers.

He reached out, caressed the curve of her breast, let them both absorb the sensation. When his fingertips trailed down, he felt her quiver under his touch.

She reached for him, her hands not quite steady as she unbuttoned his shirt. And when she touched him, it was like freedom.

"*A ghra.*" He pulled her against him, crushed her mouth with his, lost himself in the needs that stormed through him. His hands raced over her, took, sought more, until she gasped out his name.

Too fast, too much. God help him. He

fought back through the pounding in his blood, gentled his movements, chained the raw need. When he lifted her again, laid her on the bed, his kiss was long and slow and gentle.

This, she thought, was what the poets wrote of. This was why a man or a woman would reject reason for even the chance of love.

This warmth, this pleasure of another's body against your own. This gift of heart, and all the sighs and secrets it offered.

He gave her pleasure, as he had promised, drowning floods of it that washed through her in slow waves. She could have lain steeped in it forever.

She gave to him a taste, a touch, so that sensation pillowed the aches. He savored, and lingered, and held fast to the beauty she offered.

When flames licked at the edges of warmth, she welcomed them. The pretty clouds that had cushioned her began to thin. Falling through them, she cried out. A sound of triumph as her heart burst inside her.

And heard him moan, heard the quick whispers, a kind of incantation as he rose over her. Through the candlelight and the shimmer of her own vision she saw his face, his eyes. So green now they were like dark jewels. Swamped with love, she laid a hand on his cheek, murmured his name.

"Look at me. Aye, at me." His breath wanted to tear out of his lungs. His body begged to plunge. "Only pleasure."

He took her innocence, filled her, and gave her the joy. She opened for him, rose with him, her eyes swimming with shocked delight. And with the love he craved like breath.

And this time, when she fell, he gathered himself and plunged after her.

Her body shimmered. She was certain that if she looked in the mirror she would see it was golden. And his, she thought, trailing a hand lazily up and down his back. His was so beautiful. Strong and hard and smooth.

His heart was thundering against hers still. What a fantastic sensation that was, to be under the weight of the man you loved and feel his heart race for you.

Perhaps that was why her mother kept searching, kept risking. For this one moment of bliss. Love, Kayleen thought, changes everything.

And she loved.

Was loved. She repeated that over and over in her head. She was loved. It didn't matter that he hadn't said it, in those precise words. He couldn't look at her as he did, couldn't touch her as he did and not love her.

A woman didn't change her life, believe in spells and fairy tales after years of denial, and not be given the happy ending.

Flynn loved her. That was all she needed to know.

"Why do you worry?"

She blinked herself back. "What?"

"I feel it. Inside you." He lifted his head and studied her face. "The worry."

"No. It's only that everything's different now. So much is happening to me in so little time." She brushed her fingers through his hair and smiled. "But it's not worry."

"I want your happiness, Kayleen."

"I know." And wasn't that love, after all? "I know." And laughing, she threw her arms around him. "And you have it. You make me ridiculously happy."

"There's often not enough ridiculous in a life." He pulled her up with him so they were sitting tangled together on silk roses. "So let's have a bit."

The stone in his pendant glowed brighter as he grinned. He fisted his hands, shot them open.

In a wink the bed around them was covered with platters of food and bottles of wine. It made her jolt. She wondered if such things always would. Angling her head, she lifted a glass.

"I'd rather champagne, if you please."

"Well, then."

She watched the glass fill, bottom to top, with the frothy wine. And laughing, she toasted him and drank it down.

6

All of her life Kayleen had done the sensible thing. As a child, she'd tidied her room without being reminded, studied hard in school and turned in all assignments in a timely fashion. She had grown into a woman who was never late for an appointment, spent her money wisely, and ran the family business with a cool, clear head.

Looking back through the veil of what had been, Kayleen decided she had certainly been one of the most tedious people on the face of the planet.

How could she have known there was such freedom in doing the ridiculous or the impulsive or the foolish?

She said as much to Flynn as she lay sprawled over him on the bed of velvety flowers.

"You couldn't be tedious."

"Oh, but I could." She lifted her head from his chest. She wore nothing but her smile, with its dimple, and flowers in her hair. "I was the queen of tedium. I set my alarm for six o'clock every morning, even when I didn't have to get up for work. I even set alarms when I was on vacation."

"Because you didn't want to miss anything."

"No. Because one must maintain discipline. I walked to work every day, rain or shine, along the exact same route. This was after making my bed and eating a balanced breakfast, of course."

She slithered down so that she could punctuate her words with little kisses over his shoulders and chest. "I arrived at the shop precisely thirty minutes before opening, in order to see to the morning paperwork and check any displays that might require updating. Thirty minutes for a proper lunch, fifteen minutes, exactly, at four for a cup of tea, then close shop and walk home by that same route."

She worked her way up his throat. "Mmmm. Watched the news during dinner — must keep up with current affairs. Read a chapter of a good book before bed. Except for Wednesdays. Wednesdays I went wild and took in an interesting film. And on my half day, I would go over to my mother's to lecture her."

Though her pretty mouth was quite a distraction, he paid attention to her words, and the tone of them. "You lectured your mother?"

"Oh, yes." She nibbled at his ear. "My beautiful, frivolous, delightful mother. How I must have irritated her. She's been married three times, engaged double that, at least. It never works out, and she's heartbroken about it for, oh, about an hour and a half."

With a laugh, Kayleen lifted her head again. "That's not fair, of course, but she manages to shake it all off and never lose her optimism about love. She forgets to pay her bills, misses appointments, never knows the correct time, and has never been known to be able to find her keys. She's wonderful."

"You love her very much."

"Yes, very much." Sighing now, Kayleen pillowed her head on Flynn's shoulder. "I decided when I was very young that it was my job to take care of her. That was after her husband number two."

He combed his fingers through her flower-bedecked hair. "Did you lose your father?"

"No, but you could say he lost us. He left us when I was six. I suppose you could call him frivolous, too, which was yet another motivation for me to be anything but. He never settled into the family business well. Or into marriage, or into fatherhood. I hardly remember him."

He stroked her hair, said nothing. But he was beginning to worry. "Were you happy, in that life?"

"I wasn't unhappy. Brennan's was important to me, maybe all the more so because it wasn't important to my father. He shrugged off the tradition of it, the responsibility of it, as carelessly as he shrugged off his wife and his daughter."

"And hurt you."

"At first. Then I stopped letting it hurt me."

Did you? Flynn wondered. Or is that just one more pretense?

"I thought everything had to be done a certain way to be done right. If you do things right, people don't leave," she said softly. "And you'll know exactly what's going to happen next. My uncle and grandfather gradually let me take over the business because I had a knack for it, and they were proud of that. My mother let me handle things at home because, well, she's just too good-natured not to."

She sighed again, snuggled into him. "She's going to get married again next month, and she's thrilled. One of the reasons I took this trip now is because I wanted to get away from it, from those endless plans for yet another of her happy endings. I suppose I hurt her feelings, leaving the way I did. But I'd have hurt them more if I'd stayed and spoke my mind."

"You don't like the man she'll marry?"

"No, he's perfectly nice. My mother's fiancés are always perfectly nice. Funny, since I've been here I haven't worried about her at all. And I imagine, somehow, she's managing just fine without me picking at her. The shop's undoubtedly running like clockwork, and the world continues to spin. Odd to realize I wasn't indispensable after all."

"To me you are." He wrapped his arms around her, rolled over so he could look down at her. "You're vital to me."

"That's the most wonderful thing anyone's ever said to me." It was better, wasn't it? she asked herself. Even better than "I love you." "I don't know what time it is, or even what day. I don't need to know. I've never eaten supper in bed unless I was ill. Never danced in a forest in the moonlight, never made love in a bed of flowers. I've never known what it was like to be so free."

"Happy, Kayleen." He took her mouth, a

little desperately. "You're happy."

"I love you, Flynn. How could I be happier?"

He wanted to keep her loving him. Keep her happy. He wanted to keep her beautifully naked and steeped in pleasures.

More than anything, he wanted to keep her.

The hours were whizzing by so quickly, tumbling into days so that he was losing track of time himself. What did time matter now, to either of them?

He could give her anything she wanted here. Anything and everything. What would she miss of the life she had outside? It was ordinary and tedious. Hadn't she said so herself? He would see that she never missed what had been. Before long she wouldn't even think of it. The life before would be the dream.

He taught her to ride, and she was fearless. When he thought of how she'd clung to him in terror when he'd pulled her up onto Dilis the first time, he rationalized the change by saying she was simply quick to learn. He hadn't changed her basic nature, or forced her will.

That was beyond his powers and the most essential rule of magic.

When she galloped off into the forest, her laughter streaming behind her, he told himself he let his mind follow her only to keep her from harm.

Yet he knew, deep inside himself, that if she traveled near the edge of his world, he would pull her back.

He had that right, Flynn thought, as his hands fisted at his sides. He had claimed her. What he claimed during his imprisonment was his to keep.

"That is the law." He threw his head back, scowling up at the heavens. "It is *your* law. She came to me. By rights of magic, by the law of this place, she is mine. No power can take her from me."

When the sky darkened, when lightning darted at the black edges of clouds, Flynn stood in the whistling wind, feet planted in challenge. His hair blew wild around his face, his eyes went emerald-bright. And the power that was his, that could not be taken from him, shimmered around him like silver.

In his mind he saw Kayleen astride the white horse. She glanced uneasily at the gathering storm, shivered in the fresh chill of the wind. And turned her mount to ride back to him.

She was laughing again as she raced out of

the trees. "That was wonderful!" She threw her arms recklessly in the air so that Flynn gripped the halter to keep Dilis steady. "I want to ride every day. I can't believe the *feeling*."

Feeling, he thought with a vicious tug of guilt, was the one thing he wouldn't be able to offer her much longer.

"Come, darling." He lifted his arms up to her. "We'll put Dilis down for the night. A storm's coming."

She welcomed it too. The wind, the rain, the thunder. It stirred something in her, some whippy thrill that made her feel reckless and bold. When Flynn set the fire to blaze with a twist of his hand, her eyes danced.

"I don't suppose you could teach me to do that?"

He glanced back at her, the faintest of smiles, the slightest lift of brow. "I can't, no. But you've your own magic, Kayleen."

"Have I?"

"It binds me to you, as I've been bound to no other. I will give you a boon. Any that you ask that is in my power to give."

"Any?" A smile played around her mouth now as she looked up at him from under her lashes. The blatantly flirtatious move came to her much more naturally than she'd anticipated. "Well, that's quite an offer. I'll have to consider very carefully before making any decision."

She wandered the room, trailing a fingertip over the back of the sofa, over the polished gleam of a table. "Would that offer include, say, the sun and the moon?"

Look at her, he thought. She grows more beautiful by the hour. "Such as these?" He held out his hands. From them dripped a string of luminous white pearls with a clasp of diamonds.

She laughed, even as her breath caught. "Those aren't bad, as an example. They're magnificent, Flynn. But I didn't ask for diamonds or pearls."

"Then I give them freely." He crossed to her, laid the necklace over her head. "For the pleasure of seeing you wear them."

"I've never worn pearls." Surprised by the delight they brought her, she lifted them, let them run like moonbeams through her fingers. "They make me feel regal."

Holding them out, she turned a circle while the diamond clasp exploded with light. "Where do they come from? Do you just picture them in your mind and . . . poof?"

"Poof?" He decided she hadn't meant

that as an insult. "More or less, I suppose. They exist, and I move them from one place to another. From there, to here. Whatever is, that has no will, I can bring here, and keep. Nothing with heart or soul can be taken. But the rest . . . It's sapphires, I'm thinking, that suit you best."

As Kayleen blinked, a string of rich black pearls clasped with brilliant sapphires appeared around her neck. "Oh! I'll never get used to . . . Move them?" She looked back at him. "You mean take them?"

"Mmm." He turned to pour glasses of wine.

"But . . ." Catching her bottom lip between her teeth, she looked around the room. The gorgeous antiques, the modern electronics — which she'd noticed ran without electricity, the glamour of Ming vases, the foolishness of pop art.

Almost nothing in the room would have existed when he'd been banished here.

"Flynn, where do all these things come from? Your television set, your piano, the furniture and rugs and art. The food and wine?"

"All manner of places."

"How does it work?" She took the wine from him. "I mean, is it like replicating? Do you copy a thing?"

"Perhaps, if I've a mind to. It takes a bit more time and trouble for that process. You have to know the innards, so to speak, and the composition and all matter of scientific business to make it come right. Easier by far just to transport it."

"But if you just transport it, if you just take it from one place and bring it here, that's stealing."

"I'm not a thief." The idea! "I'm a magician. The laws aren't the same for us."

Patience was one of her most fundamental virtues. "Weren't you punished initially because you took something from someone?"

"That was entirely different. I changed a life for another's gain. And I was perhaps a bit . . . rash. Not that it deserved such a harsh sentence."

"How do you know what lives you've changed by bringing these here?" She held up the pearls. "Or any of the other things? If you take someone's property, it causes change, doesn't it? And at the core of it, it's just stealing." Not without regret, she lifted the jewels over her head. "Now, you have to put these back where you got them."

"I won't." Fully insulted now, he slammed his glass down. "You would reject a gift from me?"

"Yes. If it belongs to someone else. Flynn, I'm a merchant myself. How would I feel to open my shop one morning and find my property gone? It would be devastating. A violation. And beyond that, which is difficult enough, the inconvenience. I'd have to file a police report, an insurance claim. There'd be an investigation, and —"

"Those are problems that don't exist here," he interrupted. "You can't apply your ordinary logic to magic. Magic is."

"Right is, Flynn, and even magic can't negate what's right. These may be heirlooms. They may mean a great deal to someone even beyond their monetary value. I can't accept them."

She laid the pearls, the glow and the sparkle, on the table.

"You have no knowledge of what governs me." The air began to tremble with his anger. "No right to question what's inside me. Your world hides from mine, century by century, building its pale layers of reason and denial. You come here, and in days you stand in judgment of what you can't begin to comprehend?"

"I don't judge you, Flynn, but your actions." The wind had come into the room. It blew over her face, through her hair. And it was cold. Though her belly quaked, she lifted her chin. "Power shouldn't take away human responsibility. It should add to it. I'm surprised you haven't learned that in all the time you've had to think."

His eyes blazed. He threw out his arms, and the room exploded with sound and light. She stumbled back, but managed to regain her balance, managed to swallow a cry. When the air cleared again, the room was empty but for the two of them.

"This is what I might have if I lived by your rules. Nothing. No comfort, no humanity. Only empty rooms, where even the echoes are lifeless. Five hundred years of alone, and I should worry that another whose life comes and goes in a blink might do without a lamp or a painting?"

"Yes."

Temper snapped off him, little flames of gold. Then he vanished before her eyes.

What had she done? Panicked, she nearly called out for him, then realized he would hear only what he chose to hear.

She'd driven him away, she thought, sinking down in misery to sit on the bare floor. Driven him away with her rigid stance on right and wrong, her own unbending rules of conduct, just as she had kept so many others at a distance most of her life.

She'd preached at him, she admitted with

a sigh. This incredible man with such a magnificent gift. She had wagged her finger at him, just the way she wagged it at her mother. Taken on, as she habitually did, the role of adult to the child.

It seemed that not even magic could burn that irritating trait out of her. Not even love could overcome it.

Now she was alone in an empty room. Alone, as she had been for so long. Flynn thought he had a lock on loneliness, she thought with a half laugh. She'd made a career out of alone.

She drew up her knees, rested her forehead on them. The worst of it, she realized, was that even now — sad, angry, aching — she believed she was right.

It wasn't a hell of a lot of comfort.

7

It took him hours to work off his temper. He walked, he paced, he raged, he brooded. When temper had burned off, he sulked, though if anyone had put this term on his condition, he'd have swung hard back into temper again.

She'd hurt him. When anger cleared away enough for that realization to surface, it came as a shock. The woman had cut him to the bone. She'd rejected his gift, questioned his morality, and criticized his powers. All in one lump.

In his day such a swipe from a mere woman would have . . .

He cursed and paced some more. It wasn't his day, and if there was one thing he'd learned to adjust to, it was the changes in attitudes and sensibilities. Women stood toe-to-toe with men in this age, and in his readings and viewings over the years, he'd come to believe they had the right of it.

He was hardly steeped in the old ways. Hadn't he embraced technology with each new development? Hadn't he amused himself with the quirks of society and fashion and mores as they shifted and changed and became? And he'd taken from each of those shifts what appealed most, what sat best with him.

He was a well-read man, had been well read and well traveled even in his own time. And since that time, he'd studied. Science, history, electronics, engineering, art, music, literature, politics. He had hardly stopped using his mind over the last five hundred years.

The fact was, he rarely had the chance to use anything else.

So, he used it now and went over the argument in his head.

She didn't understand, he decided. Magic wasn't bound by the rules of her world, but by itself. It was, and that was all. No conscientious magician brought harm to another deliberately, that was certain. All he'd done was take a few examples of technology, of art and comfort, from various points in time. He could hardly be expected to live in a bloody cave, could he?

Stealing? Why, the very idea of it!

He sat on a chair in his workshop and indulged in more brooding.

It wasn't meant to be stealing, he thought now. Magicians had moved matter from place to place since the beginning of things. And what were jewels but pretty bits of matter?

Then he sighed. He supposed they were considerably more, from her point of view. And he'd wanted her to see them as more. He'd wanted her to be dazzled and delighted, and dote on him for the gift of them.

Much as he had, he admitted, wanted to dazzle and delight the woman who'd betrayed him. Or, to be honest, the woman who'd tempted him to betray himself and his art. That woman had greedily gathered what he'd given, what he'd taken, and left him to hang.

What had Kayleen done? Had she been overpowered by the glitter and the richness? Seduced by them?

Not in the least. She'd tossed them back in his face.

Stood up for what she believed was right and just. Stood up to him. His lips began to curve with the image of that. He hadn't expected her to, he could admit that. She'd looked him in the eye, said her piece, and stuck to it.

God, what a woman! His Kayleen was strong and true. Not a bauble to ride on a man's arm but a partner to stand tall with him. That was a grand thing. For while a man might indulge himself in a pretty piece of fluff for a time, it was a woman he wanted for a lifetime.

He got to his feet, studied his workroom. Well, a woman was what he had. He'd best figure out how to make peace with her.

Kayleen considered having a good cry, but it just wasn't like her. She settled instead for hunting up the kitchen which was no easy task. On the search she discovered Flynn had chosen to make his point with only that one empty room. The rest of the house was filled to brimming, and in his fascinatingly eclectic style.

She softened by the time she brewed tea in a kitchen equipped with a restaurant-style refrigerator, a microwave oven, and a stone fireplace in lieu of stove. It took her considerable time to get the fire going and to heat water in the copper pot. But it made her smile.

How could she blame him, really, for wanting things around him? Pretty things, interesting things. He was a man who needed to use his mind, amuse himself, challenge himself. Wasn't that the man she'd fallen in love with?

She carried the tea into the library with its thousands of books, its scrolls, its manuscripts. And its deep-cushioned leather chairs and snappy personal computer.

She would light the fire, and enough candles to read by, then enjoy her tea and the quiet.

Kneeling at the hearth, she tried to light the kindling and managed to scorch the wood. She rearranged the logs, lodged a splinter painfully in her thumb, and tried again.

She created a hesitant little flame, and a great deal of smoke, which the wind cheerfully blew back in her face. She hissed at it, sucked on her throbbing thumb, then sat on her heels to think it through.

And the flames burst into light and heat.

She set her teeth, fought the urge to turn around. "I can do it myself, thank you."

"As you wish, lady."

The fire vanished but for the smoke. She coughed, waved it away from her face, then got to her feet. "It's warm enough without one."

"I'd say it's unnaturally chilly at the moment." He walked up behind her, took her hand in his. "You've hurt yourself."

"It's only a splinter. Don't," she said when he lifted it to his lips.

"Being strong-minded and being contrary are two different matters." He touched his lips to her thumb, and the throbbing eased. "But not contrary enough, I notice, to ignore the comforts of a cup of tea, a book, and a pleasant chair."

"I wasn't going to stand in an empty room wringing my hands while you worked out your tantrum."

He lifted his eyebrows. "Disconcerting, isn't it? Emptiness."

She tugged her hand free of his. "All right, yes. And I have no true conception of what you've dealt with, nor any right to criticize how you compensate. But —"

"Right is right," he finished. "This place and what I possessed was all I had when first I came here. I could fill it with things, the things that appealed to me. That's what I did. I won't apologize for it."

"I don't want an apology."

"No, you want something else entirely." He opened his hands, and the rich loops of pearls gleamed in them.

"Flynn, don't ask me to take them."

"I am asking. I give you this gift, Kayleen. They're replicas, and belong to no one but me. Until they belong to you."

Her throat closed as he placed them around her neck. "You made them for me?"

"Perhaps I'd grown a bit lazy over the years. It took me a little longer to conjure them than it might have, but it made me remember the pleasure of making."

"They're more beautiful than the others. And much more precious."

"And here's a tear," he murmured, and caught it on his fingertip as it spilled onto her cheek. "If it falls from happiness, it will shine. If it's from sorrow, it will turn to ashes. See."

The drop glimmered on his finger, shimmered, then solidified into a diamond in the shape of a tear. "And this is your gift to me." He drew the pendant from beneath his shirt, passed his hand over it. The diamond drop sparkled now beneath the moonstone. "I'll wear it near my heart. Ever."

She leapt into his arms, clung to his neck. "I missed you!"

"I let temper steal hours from us."

"So did I." She leaned back. "We've had our first fight. I'm glad. Now we never have to have a first one again."

"But others?"

"We'll have to." She kissed his cheek. "There's so much we don't understand about each other. And even when we do, we won't always agree."

"Ah, my sensible Kayleen. No, don't frown," he said, tipping up her chin. "I like your mind. It stimulates my own."

"It annoyed you."

"At the first of it." He circled her around, lighting the fire, the candles as he did. "And I spent a bit of time pondering on how much more comfortable life would be if you'd just be biddable and agree with everything I said and did. 'Yes, Flynn, my darling,' you would say. 'No indeed, my handsome Flynn.' "

"Oh, really?"

"But then I'd miss that battle light in your eyes, wouldn't I, and the way your lovely mouth goes firm. Makes me want to. . . ." He nipped her bottom lip. "But that's another kind of stimulation altogether. I'm willing to fight with you, Kayleen, as long as you're willing to make up again with me."

"And I'm willing to have you stomp off in a temper —"

"I didn't stomp."

"Metaphorically speaking. As long as you come back." She laid her head on his shoulder, closed her eyes. "The storm's passed," she murmured. "Moonlight's shining through the windows."

"So it is." He scooped her up. "I have the perfect way to celebrate our first fight." He closed her hand over his pendant. "Would you like to fly, Kayleen?"

"Fly? But —"

And she was soaring through the air, through the night. Air swirled around her, then seemed to go fluid so it was like cutting clean through a dark sea. The stone pulsed against her palm. She cried out in surprise, and then in delight, reaching out as if she could snatch one of the stars that shone around her.

Fearless, Flynn thought, even now. Or perhaps it was more a thirst for all the times she'd denied herself a drink. When she turned her face to his, her eyes brighter than the jewels, brighter than the stars, he spun her in dizzying circles.

They landed in a laughing tumble to roll over the soft cushion of grass by the side of his blue waterfall.

"Oh! That was amazing. Can we do it again?"

"Soon enough. Here." He lifted a hand, and a plump peach balanced on the tips of his fingers. "You haven't eaten your supper."

"I wasn't hungry before." Charmed, she took the peach, bit into the sweetness. "So

101

many stars," she murmured, lying back again to watch them. "Were we really flying up there?"

"It's a kind of manipulation of time and space and matter. It's magic. That's enough, isn't it?"

"It's everything. The world's magic now."

"But you're cold," he said when she shivered.

"Mmm. Only a little." Even as she spoke, the air warmed, almost seemed to bloom.

"I confess it." He leaned over to kiss her. "I stole a bit of warmth from here and there. But I don't think anyone will miss it. I don't want you chilled."

"Can it always be like this?"

There was a hitch in his chest. "It can be what we make it. Do you miss what was before?"

"No." But she lowered her lashes, so he was unable to read her eyes. "Do you? I mean, the people you knew? Your family?"

"They've been gone a long time."

"Was it hard?" She sat up, handed him the peach. "Knowing you'd never be able to see them again, or talk to them, or even tell them where you were?"

"I don't remember." But he did. This was the first lie he'd told her. He remembered that the pain of it had been like death.

"I'm sorry." She touched his shoulder. "It hurts you."

"It fades." He pushed away, got to his feet. "All of that is beyond, and it fades. It's the illusion, and this is all that's real. All that matters. All that matters is here."

"Flynn." She rose, hoping to comfort, but when he spun back, his eyes were hot, bright. And the desire in them robbed her of breath.

"I want you. A hundred lifetimes from now I'll want you. It's enough for me. Is it enough for you?"

"I'm here." She held out her hands. "And I love you. It's more than I ever dreamed of having."

"I can give you more. You still have a boon."

"Then I'll keep it. Until I need more." Because he'd yet to take her offered hands, she cupped his face in them. "I've never touched a man like this. With love and desire. Do you think, Flynn, that because I've never felt them before I don't understand the wonder of knowing them now? Of feeling them now for one man? I've watched my mother search all of her life, be willing to risk heartbreak for the chance — just the chance — of feeling what I do right at this moment. She's the most important person to me outside this world you've made. And I know she'd be thrilled to know what I've found with you."

"Then when you ask me for your heart's desire, I'll move heaven and earth to give it to you. That's my vow."

"I have my heart's desire." She smiled, stepped back. "Tell me yours."

"Not tonight. Tonight I have plans for you that don't involve conversation."

"Oh? And what might they be?"

"Well, to begin . . ."

He lifted a hand and traced one finger down through the air between them. Her clothes vanished.

8

"Oh!" This time she instinctively covered herself. "You might have warned me."

"I'll have you bathed in moonlight, and dressed in starshine."

She felt a tug, gentle but insistent, on her hands. Her arms lowered, spread out as if drawn by silken rope. "Flynn."

"Let me touch you." He kept his eyes on hers as he stepped forward, as he traced his fingertips down her throat, over the swell of her breasts. "Excite you." He took her mouth in quick, little bites. "Possess you."

Something slid through her mind, her body, at the same time. A coiled snake of heat that bound both together. The rise of it, so fast, so sharp, slashed through her. She hadn't the breath to cry out, she could only moan.

He had barely touched her.

"How can you . . . how could I —"

"I want to show you more this time." Now

his hands were on her, rough and insistent. Her skin was so soft, so fragrant. In the moonlight it gleamed so that wherever he touched, the warmth bloomed on it. Roses on silk. "I want to take more this time."

For a second time he took her flying. Though her feet never left the ground, she spun through the air. A fast, reckless journey. His mouth was on her, devouring flesh. She had no choice but to let him feed. And his greed erased her past reason so that her one desire was to be consumed.

Abandoning herself to it, she let her head fall back, murmuring his name like a chant as he ravished her.

He mated his mind with hers, thrilling to every soft cry, every throaty whimper. She stood open to him in the moonlight, soaked with pleasure and shuddering from its heat.

And such was his passion for her that his fingers left trails of gold over her damp flesh, trails that pulsed, binding her in tangled ribbons of pleasure.

When his mouth found hers again, the flavor exploded, sharp and sweet. Drunk on her, he lifted them both off the ground.

Now freed, her arms came tight around him, her nails scraping as she sought to hold, sought to find. She was hot against him, wet against him, her hips arching in rising demand.

He drove himself into her, one desperate thrust, then another. Another. With her answering beat for urgent beat, he let the animal inside him spring free.

His mind emptied but for her and that primal hunger they shared. The forest echoed with a call of triumph as that hunger swallowed them both.

She lay limp, useless. Used. A thousand wild horses could have stampeded toward her, and she wouldn't have moved a muscle.

The way Flynn had collapsed on her, and now lay like the dead, she imagined he felt the same.

"I'm so sorry," she said on a long, long sigh.

"Sorry?" He slid his hand through the grass until it covered hers.

"Umm. So sorry for the women who don't have you for a lover."

He made a sound that might have been a chuckle. "Generous of you, *mavourneen*. I prefer being smug that I'm the only man who's had the delights of you."

"I saw stars. And not the ones up there."

"So did I. You're the only one who's given me the stars." He stirred, pressing his lips to the side of her breast before lifting his head. "And you give me an appetite as well — for all manner of succulent things."

"I suppose that means you want *your* supper and we have to go back."

"We have to do nothing but what pleases us. What would you like?"

"At the moment? I'd settle for some water. I've never been so thirsty."

"Water, is it?" He angled his head, grinned. "That I can give you, and plenty." He gathered her up and rolled. She managed a scream, and he a wild laugh, as they tumbled off the bank and hit the water of the pool with a splash.

It seemed miraculous to Kayleen how much she and Flynn had in common. Considering the circumstance and all that differed between them, it was an amazing thing that they found any topic to discuss or explore.

But then, Flynn hadn't sat idle for five hundred years. His love of something well made, even if its purpose was only for beauty, struck home with her. All of her life she'd been exposed to craftsmanship and aesthetics — the history of a table, the societal purpose of an enameled snuffbox, or the heritage of a serving platter. The few pieces she'd allowed herself to collect were special to her, not only because of their beauty but also because of their continuity.

She and Flynn had enjoyed many of the same books and films, though he had read and viewed far more for the simple enjoyment of it than she.

He listened to her, posing questions about various phases of her life, until she was picking them apart for him and remembering events and things she'd seen or done or experienced that she'd long ago forgotten.

No one had ever been so interested in her before, in who she was and what she thought. What she felt. If he didn't agree, he would lure her into a debate or tease her into exploring a lighter side of herself rarely given expression.

It seemed she did the same for him, nudging him out of his brooding silences, or leaving him be until the mood had passed on its own.

But whenever she made a comment or asked a question about the future, those silences lasted long.

So she wouldn't ask, she told herself. She didn't need to know. What had planning and preciseness gotten her, really, but a life of sameness? Whatever happened when the week was up — God, why couldn't she remember what day it was — she would be content.

For now, every moment was precious.

He'd given her so much. Smiling, she wandered the house, running her fingers along the exquisite pearls, which she hadn't taken off since he'd put them around her neck. Not the gifts, she thought, though she treasured them, but romance, possibilities, and above all, a vision.

She had never seen so clearly before.

Love answered all questions.

What could she give him? Gifts? She had nothing. What little she still possessed was in the car she'd left abandoned in the wood. There was so little there, really, of the woman she'd become, and was still becoming.

She wanted to do something for him. Something that would make him smile.

Food. Delighted with the idea, she hurried back toward the kitchen. She'd never known anyone to appreciate a single bite of apple as much as Flynn.

Of course, since there wasn't any stove, she hadn't a clue what she could prepare, but . . . She swung into the kitchen, stopped short in astonishment.

There certainly was one beauty of a stove now. White and gleaming. All she'd done was mutter about having to boil water for tea over a fire and — poof! — he'd made a stove.

Well, she thought, and pushed up her sleeves, she would see just what she could do with it.

In his workroom, Flynn gazed through one of his windows on the world. He'd intended to focus on Kayleen's home so that he could replicate some of her things for her. He knew what it was to be without what you had, what had mattered to you.

For a time he lost himself there, moving his mind through the rooms where she had once lived, studying the way she'd placed her furniture, what books were on her shelves, what colors she'd favored.

How tidy it all was, he thought with a great surge in his heart. Everything so neatly in place, and so tastefully done. Did it upset her sense of order to be in the midst of his hodgepodge?

He would ask her. They could make some adjustments. But why the hell hadn't the woman had more color around her? And look at the clothes in the closet. All of them more suited to a spinster — no, that wasn't the word used well these days. Plain attire without the richness of fabric and the brilliance of color that so suited his Kayleen.

She would damn well leave them behind if he had any say in it.

But she would want her photographs, and that lovely pier glass there, and that lamp. He began to set them in his mind, the shape and dimensions, the tone and texture. So deep was his concentration that he didn't realize the image had changed until the woman crossed his vision.

She walked through the rooms, her hands clasped tightly together. A lovely woman, he noted. Smaller than Kayleen, fuller at the breasts and hips, but with the same coloring. She wore her dark hair short, and it swung at her cheeks as she moved.

Compelled, he opened the window wider and heard her speak.

"Oh, baby, where are you? Why haven't you called? It's almost a week. Why can't we find you? Oh, Kayleen." She picked up a photograph from a table, pressed it to her. "Please be all right. Please be okay."

With the picture hugged to her heart, she dropped into a chair and began to weep.

Flynn slammed the window shut and turned away.

He would not be moved. He would not.

Time was almost up. In little more than twenty-four hours, the choice would be behind him. Behind them all.

He closed his mind to a mother's grief. But he wasn't fully able to close his heart.

His mood was edgy when he left the workroom. He meant to go outside, to walk it off. Perhaps to whistle up Dilis and ride it off. But he heard her singing.

He'd never heard her sing before. A pretty voice, he thought, but it was the happiness in it that drew him back to the kitchen.

She was stirring something on the stove, something in the big copper kettle that smelled beyond belief.

It had been a very long time since he'd come into a kitchen where cooking was being done. But he was nearly certain that was what had just happened. Since it was almost too marvelous to believe, he decided to make sure of it.

"Kayleen, what are you about there?"

"Oh!" Her spoon clattered, fell out of her hand and plopped into the pot. "Damn it, Flynn! You startled me. Now look at that, I've drowned the spoon in the sauce."

"Sauce?"

"I thought I'd make spaghetti. You have a very unusual collection of ingredients in your kitchen. Peanut butter, pickled herring, enough chocolate to make an entire elementary school hyper for a month.

However, I managed to find plenty of herbs, and some lovely ripe tomatoes, so this seemed the safest bet. Plus you have ten pounds of spaghetti pasta."

"Kayleen, are you cooking for me?"

"I know it must seem silly, as you can snap up a five-star meal for yourself without breaking a sweat. But there's something to be said for home cooking. I'm a very good cook. I took lessons. Though I've never attempted to make sauce in quite such a pot, it should be fine."

"The pot's wrong?"

"Oh, well, I'd do better with my own cookware, but I think I've made do. You had plenty of fresh vegetables in your garden, so I —"

"Just give me a few moments, won't you? I'll need a bit of time."

And before she could answer, he was gone.

"Well." She shook her head and went back to trying to save the spoon.

She had everything under control again, had adjusted the heat to keep the sauce at low simmer, when a clatter behind her made her jolt. The spoon plopped back into the sauce.

"Oh, for heaven's sake!" She turned around, then stumbled back. There was a pile of pots and pans on the counter beside her.

"I replicated them," Flynn said with a grin. "Which took me a little longer, but I didn't want to argue with you about it. Then you might not feed me."

"My pots!" She fell on them with the enthusiasm of a mother for lost children.

More enthusiasm, Flynn realized as she chattered and held up each pan and lid to examine, than she'd shown for the jewels he'd given her.

Because they were hers. Something that belonged to her. Something from her world.

And his heart grew heavy.

"This is going to be good." She stacked the cookware neatly, selected the proper pot. "I know it must seem a waste of time and effort to you," she said as she transferred the sauce. "But cooking's a kind of art. It's certainly an occupation. I'm used to being busy. A few days of leisure is wonderful, but I'd go crazy after a while with nothing to do. Now I can cook."

While the sauce simmered in the twenty-first-century pot, she carried the ancient kettle to the sink to wash it. "And dazzle you with my brilliance," she added with a quick, laughing glance over her shoulder.

"You already dazzle me."

"Well, just wait. I was thinking, as I was putting all this together, that I could spend weeks, months, really, organizing around here. Not having a pattern is one thing, but having no order at all is another. You could use a catalogue system for your books. And some of the rooms are just piled with things. I don't imagine you even know what there is. You could use a listing of your art, and the antiques, your music. You have the most extensive collection of antique toys I've ever seen. When we have children . . ."

She trailed off, her hands fumbling in the soapy water. Children. Could they have children? What were the rules? Might she even now be pregnant? They'd done nothing to prevent conception. Or she hadn't, she thought, pressing her lips together.

How could she know what he might have done?

"Listen to me." She shook her hair back, briskly rinsed the pot. "Old habits. Lists and plans and procedures. The only plan we need right now is what sort of dressing I should make for the salad."

"Kayleen."

"No, no, this is my performance here. You'll just have to find something to do until curtain time." She heard the sorrow in his voice, the regret. And had her answers. "Everything should be ready in an hour. So, out."

She turned, smiling, shooing at him. But her voice was too thick.

"I'll go and tend to Dilis, then."

"Good, that's fine."

He left the room, waited. When the tear fell from her eye he brought it from her cheek into his palm. And watched it turn to ashes.

9

He brought her flowers for the table, and they ate her meal with the candles glowing.

He touched her often, just a brush of fingers on the back of her hand. A dozen sensory memories stored for a endless time of longing.

He made her laugh, to hear the sound of it and store that as well. He asked her questions only to hear her voice, the rise and fall of it.

When the meal was done, he walked with her, to see how the moonlight shone in her hair.

Late into the night, he made love with her, as tenderly as he knew how. And knew it was for the last time.

When she slept, when he sent her deep into easy dreams, he was resolved, and he was content with what needed to be done.

She dreamed, but the dreams weren't easy

ones. She was lost in the forest, swallowed by the mists that veiled the trees and smothered the path. Light shimmered through it, so drops of moisture glittered like jewels. Jewels that melted away at the touch of her hand, and left her nothing.

She could hear sounds — footsteps, voices, even music — but they seemed to come from underwater. Drowning sounds that never took substance. No matter how hard she tried to find the source, she could come no closer.

The shapes of trees were blurred, the color of the flowers deadened. When she tried to call out, her voice seemed to carry no farther than her own ears.

She began to run, afraid of being lost and being alone. She only had to find the way out. There was always a way out. And her way back to him. As panic gushed inside her, she tried to tear the mists away, ripping at them with her fingers, beating at them with her fists.

But her hands only passed through, and the curtain stayed whole.

Finally, through it, she saw the faint shadow of the house. The spear of its turrets, the sweep of its battlements were softened like wax in the thick air. She ran toward it, sobbing with relief. Then with joy as she saw him standing by the massive doors.

She ran to him now, her arms flung out to embrace, her lips curved for that welcoming kiss.

When her arms passed through him, she understood he was the mist.

And so was she.

She woke weeping and reaching out for him, but the bed beside her was cold and empty. She shivered, though the fire danced cheerfully to warm the room. A dream, just a dream. That was all. But she was cold, and she got out of bed to wrap herself in the thick blue robe.

Where was Flynn? she wondered. They always woke together, almost as if they were tied to each other's rhythms. She glanced out the windows as she walked toward the fire to warm her chilled hands. The sun was beaming and bright, which explained why Flynn hadn't been wrapped around her when she woke.

She'd slept away the morning.

Imagine that, she thought with a laugh. Slept away the morning, dreamed away the night. It was so unlike her.

So unlike her, she thought again as her hands stilled. Dreaming. She never remembered her dreams, not even in jumbled pieces. Yet this one she remembered exactly, in every detail, almost as though she'd lived it.

Because she was relaxed, she assured herself. Because her mind was relaxed and open. People were always saying how real dreams could be, weren't they? She'd never believed that until now.

If hers were going to be that frightening, that heartbreaking, she'd just as soon skip them.

But it was over, and it was a beautiful day. There were no mists blanketing the trees. The flowers were basking in the sunlight, their colors vibrant and true. The clouds that so often stacked themselves in layers over the Irish sky had cleared, leaving a deep and brilliant blue.

She would pick flowers and braid them into Dilis's mane. Flynn would give her another riding lesson. Later, perhaps she'd begin on the library. It would be fun to prowl through all the books. To explore them and arrange them.

She would *not* be obsessive about it. She wouldn't fall into that trap again. The chore would be one of pleasure rather than responsibility.

Throwing open the windows, she leaned out, breathed in the sweet air. "I've changed so much already," she murmured. "I like the person I'm becoming. I can be friends with her."

She shut her eyes tight. "Mom, I wish I could tell you. I'm so much in love. He makes me so happy. I wish I could let you know, and tell you that I understand now. I wish I could share this with you."

With a sigh, she stepped back, leaving the windows open.

He kept himself busy. It was the only way he could get through the day. In his mind, in his heart, he'd said good-bye to her the night before. He'd already let her go.

There was no choice but to let her go.

He could have kept her with him, drawing her into the long days, the endless nights of the next dreaming. His solitude would be broken, the loneliness diminished. And at the end of it, she would be there for that brief week. To touch. To be.

The need for her, the desire to have her close, was the strongest force he'd ever known. But for one.

Love.

Not just with the silken beauty of the dreams he'd shared with her. But with the pains and joys that came from a beating heart.

He would not deny her life, steal from her what she had known, what she would be. How had he ever believed he could? Had he really thought that his own needs, the most selfish and self-serving of them, outweighed the most basic of hers?

To live. To feel heat and cold, hunger, thirst, pleasure and pain.

To watch herself change with the years. To shake the hand of a stranger, embrace a loved one. To make children and watch them grow.

For all his power, all his knowledge, he could give her none of those things. All he had left for her was the gift of freedom.

To comfort himself, he pressed his face to Dilis's neck, drew in the scents of horse and straw, of oat and leather. How was it he could forget, each time forget the wrenching misery of these last hours? The sheer physical pain of knowing it was all ending again.

He was ending again.

"You've always been free. You know I have no claim to keep you here, should you choose to go." He lifted his head, stroking the stallion's head as he looked into his eyes. "Carry her away safe for me. And if you go beyond, I'll not count it against you."

He stepped back, drew his breath. There

was work yet, and the morning was passing fast.

When it was done, the last spell, the thin blanket of forget spread at the edges of his prison, he saw Kayleen in his mind's eye.

She wandered through the gardens toward the verge of the forest. Looking for him, calling his name. The pain was like an arrow in the heart, almost driving him to his knees.

So, he was not prepared after all. He fisted his hands, struggled for composure. Resolved but not prepared. How would he ever live without her?

"She will live without me," he said aloud. "That I want more. We'll end it now, quick and clean."

He could not will her away, will her back into her world and into life. But he could drive her from him, so that the choice to go was her own.

Taking Dilis's reins, only for the comfort of contact, he walked for the last time as a man, for yet a century to come, through the woods toward home.

She heard the jingle of harness and the soft hoofbeats. Relieved, she turned toward the sound, walking quickly as Flynn came out of the trees.

"I wondered where you were." She threw her arms around his neck, and he let her. Her mouth pressed cheerfully to his, and he absorbed the taste of it.

"Oh, I had a bit of work." The words cut at his throat like shards of glass. "It's a fine day for it, and for your travels."

"For my travels."

"Indeed." He gave her a little pat, then moved away to adjust the stirrups of Dilis's saddle. "I've cleared the path, so you'll have no trouble. You'll find your way easily enough. You're a resourceful woman."

"My way? Where?"

He glanced back, gave her an absent smile. "Out, of course. It's time for you to go."

"Go?"

"There, that should do." He turned to her fully. Every ounce of power he owned went into the effort. "Dilis will take you as far as you need. I'd go with you myself, but I've so much to see to yet. I saw you have one of those little pocket phones in your car. Fascinating things. I have to remember to get one myself for the study of it. You should be able to use it once you're over the border."

"I don't understand what you're saying." How could she when her mind had gone numb, when her heart had stopped beating. "I'm not going."

"Kayleen, darling, of course you are." He patted her cheek. "Not that it hasn't been a delight having you here. I don't know when I've been so diverted."

"Di . . . *diverted?*"

"Mmm. God, you're a tasty bit," he murmured, then leaned down to nip at her bottom lip. "Perhaps we could take just enough time to . . ." His hands roamed down her, giving her breasts a teasing squeeze.

"Stop!" She stumbled back, came up hard against Dilis, who shifted, restless. "A diversion? That's all this was to you? A way to pass the time?"

"Passed it well, didn't we? Ah, sweetheart, I gave as much pleasure as I got. You can't deny it. But we've both got things to get back to, don't we?"

"I love you."

She was killing him. "God bless the female heart." And he said it with a chuckle. "It's so generous." Then he lifted his brows, rolled his eyes under them. "Ah, don't be making a scene and spoil this parting moment. We've enjoyed each other, and that's the end. Where did you think this was going? It's time out of time, Kayleen. Now don't be stubborn."

"You don't love me. You don't want me."

"I loved you well enough." He winked at

her. "And wanted you plenty." When the tears swam into her eyes, he threw up his hands as if exasperated. "For pity's sake, woman, I brought some magic and romance into a life you yourself said was tedious. I gave you some sparkle." He lifted her pearls with a fingertip.

"I never asked for jewels. I never wanted anything but you."

"Took them, though, didn't you? Just as another took the sparkles from me once. Do you think, after having a woman damn me to this place, I'd want another around for longer than it takes to amuse myself?"

"I'm not like her. You can't believe —"

"A woman's a woman," he said carelessly. "And I've given you a pretty holiday, with souvenirs besides. The least you can do is be grateful and go along when I bid you. I've no more time for you, and none of the patience to dry your tears and cuddle. Up you go."

He lifted her, all but tossed her into the saddle.

"You said you wouldn't hurt me." She dragged the pearls over her head, hurled them into the dirt at his feet. She stared at him, and in his face she saw the savageness again, the brutality, and none of the tenderness. "You lied."

"You hurt yourself, by believing what

wasn't there. Go back to your tame world. You've no place in mine."

He slapped a hand violently on Dilis's flank. The horse reared, then lunged forward.

When she was gone, swallowed up by the forest, Flynn dropped to his knees on the ground — and grieved.

10

She wanted to find anger. Bitterness. Anything that would overpower this hideous pain. It had dried up even her tears, had smothered any rage or sorrow before it could fully form.

It had all been a lie. Magic was nothing but deceit.

In the end, love hadn't been the answer. Love had done nothing but make her a fool.

Didn't it prove she'd been right all along? Her disdain of the happy ending her mother had regaled her with had been sense, not stubbornness. There were no fairy tales, no loves that conquered all, no grand sweep of romance to ride on forever.

Letting herself believe, even for a little while, had shattered her.

Yet how could she not have believed? Wasn't she even now riding on a white horse through the forest? That couldn't be denied. If she'd misplaced her heart, she couldn't deny all that she'd seen and done and experienced. How did she, logical Kayleen, resolve the unhappy one with the magnificent other?

How could he have given her so much, shown her so much, and thought of her as only a kind of temporary entertainment? No, no, something was wrong. Why couldn't she think?

Dilis walked patiently through the trees as she pondered. It had all happened so quickly. This change in him had come like a fingersnap, and left her reeling and helpless. Now, she willed her mind to clear, to analyze. But after only moments, her thoughts became scattered and jumbled once again.

Her car was unmarked, shining in the sunlight that dappled through the trees. It sat tidily on a narrow path that ran straight as a ruler through the forest.

He'd cleared the path, he'd said. Well, he certainly was a man of his word. She slid off the horse, slowly circled the car. Not a scratch, she noted. Considerate of him. She wouldn't have to face the hassle that a wrecked car would have caused with the rental company.

Yes, he'd cleared that path as well. But why had he bothered with such a mundane practicality?

Curious, she opened the car door and

sliding behind the wheel, turned the key. The engine sprang to life, purred.

Runs better than it did when I picked it up, she thought. And look at that, to top things off, we have a full tank.

"Did you want me out of your life so badly, Flynn, that you covered all contingencies? Why were you so cruel at the end? Why did you work so hard to make me hate you?"

He'd given her no reason to stay, and every rational reason to go.

With a sigh, she got out of the car to say good-bye to Dilis. She indulged herself, running her hands over his smooth hide, nuzzling at his throat. Then she patted his flank. "Go back to him now," she murmured, and turned away to spare her heart as the horse pranced off.

Because she wanted some tangible reminder of her time there, she picked a small nosegay of wildflowers, twined the stems together, and regardless of the foolishness of the gesture, tucked them into her hair.

She got into the car again and began to drive.

The sun slanted in thin beams through the trees, angled over the little lane. As she glanced in her mirror, she saw the path shimmer, then vanish behind her in a tumble of moss and stones and brambles. Soon there would be nothing but the silent wood, and no trace that she had ever walked there with a lover.

But she would remember, always, the way he'd looked at her, the way he would press his lips to the heart of her hand. The way he'd bring her flowers and scatter them over her hair.

The way his eyes would warm with laughter, or heat with passion when . . . His eyes. What color were his eyes? Slightly dizzy, she stopped the car, pressed her fingers to her temples.

She couldn't bring his face into her mind, not clearly. How could she not know the color of his eyes? Why couldn't she quite remember the sound of his voice?

She shoved out of the car, stumbled a few steps. What was happening to her? She'd been driving from Dublin on the way to her bed-and-breakfast. A wrong turn. A storm. But what . . .

Without thinking, she took another step back down the now overgrown path. And her mind snapped clear as crystal.

Her breath was coming short. She turned, stared at the car, the clear path in front of it, the impassable ground behind.

"Flynn's eyes are green," she said. His

face came clearly into her mind now. And when she took a cautious step forward, her memory of him went hazy.

This time she stepped back quickly, well back. "You wanted me to forget you. Why? Why if none of it mattered did you care if I remembered you or not? Why would it matter if I broke my heart over you?"

A little shaky, she sat down on the ground. And she began to do what she'd always done best. Be logical.

Flynn sat as he had on the night it had begun. In the chair in front of the fire in the tower. He'd watched in the flames until Kayleen had gotten into her car. After that, he hadn't been able to bear it, so he had hazed the vision with smoke.

He'd lost track of the time that he'd sat there now, chained by his own grief. He knew the day was passing. The slant of sunlight through the window had shortened and was dimming.

She would be beyond now, and would have forgotten him. That was for the best. There would be some confusion, of course. A loss of time never fully explained. But she would put that behind her as well.

In a year or two, or twenty, he might look into the fire again, and see how she was. But

133

he would never open his mind to her in dreams, for that would be more torment than he could ever possibly bear.

She would be changed a little by what had passed between them. More open to possibilities, to the magic of life. He lifted the strings of pearls, watched them glow in the light of the dying fire. At least that was a gift she hadn't been able to hurl at his feet.

With the pearls wrapped around his fingers, he lowered his face into his hands. He willed the time to come when pain could strike only his mind, when every sense wasn't tuned so sharply that he could smell her even now. That soft scent that whispered in the air.

"Bring on the bloody night," he muttered and threw his head back.

Then he was stumbling to his feet, staring. She stood not three feet away. Her hair was tangled, her clothes torn. Scratches scored her hands and face.

"What trick is this?"

"I want my boon. I want what you promised me."

"What have you done?" His knees unlocked and he lunged toward her, grabbing her hard by the arms. "How are you hurt? Look at you. Your hands are all torn and bleeding."

"You put briars in my way." She gave him a shove, and such was his shock that she knocked him back two full steps. "You bastard. It took hours to get through them."

"Get through." His head snapped back, as if she'd slapped him. "You have to go. Go! Now! What's the time?" He was pushing her out of the room, and when that wasn't quick enough he began to drag her.

"I'm not going. Not until you grant my boon."

"You damn well are." Terrified, he tossed her over his shoulder and began to run. As she struggled and cursed him, he began to fly.

The night was closing in. Time that had dripped began to flood. He went as deep into the forest as he dared. The edges of his prison seemed to hiss around him.

"There." Fear for her slicked his skin. "Your car's just up ahead. Get in it and go."

"Why? So I can drive a little farther and forget all this? Forget you? You'd have stolen that from me."

"I've no time to argue with you." He grabbed her shoulders and shook. "There is no time. If you stay past the last stroke of twelve, you're trapped here. A hundred years will pass before you can walk away again."

"Why do you care? It's a big house. A big

forest. I won't get in your way."

"You don't understand. Go. This place is mine, and I don't want you here."

"You're trembling, Flynn. What frightens you?"

"I'm not frightened, I'm angry. You've abused my hospitality. You're trespassing."

"Call the cops," she suggested. "Call your Keepers. Or . . . why don't you just flick me out, the way you flick things in? But you can't, can you?"

"If I could, you'd be gone already." He yanked her a few steps toward the car, then swore when the ground in front of his boots began to spark and smoke. That was the edge of his prison.

"Big, powerful magician, but you can't get rid of me that way. You couldn't bring me here, and you can't send me away. Not with magic, because I have heart and soul. I have will. So you tried to drive me away with careless words. Cruel, careless words. You didn't think I'd see through them, did you? Didn't think I'd figure it all out. You forgot who you were dealing with."

"Kayleen." He took her hands now, squeezing desperately. "Do this thing I ask now, won't you?"

"A diversion," she said. "That's a crock. You love me."

"Of course I love you." He shook her harder, shouted so his voice boomed through the forest. "That's the bloody point. And if you care for me, you'll do what I tell you, and do it now."

"You love me." Her breath came out on a sob as she flung herself against him. "I knew it. Oh, I'm so angry with you. I'm so in love with you."

His arms ached to grip, to hold. He made himself push her away, hold her at arm's length. "Listen to me, Kayleen. Clear the stars out of your eyes and be sensible. I've no right to love you. Be quiet!" he snapped when she started to speak. "You remember what I told you about this place, about me. Do you feel my hands on you, Kayleen?"

"Yes. They're trembling."

"After midnight, one breath after, you won't feel them, or anything else. No touch, no contact. You'll pick a flower, but you won't feel the stem or the petals. Its perfume will be lost to you. Can you feel your own heart beat? Beating inside you? You won't. It's worse than death to be and yet not be. Day by day into the decades with nothing of substance. Nothing but what's in your mind. And, *a ghra,* you haven't even the magic to amuse yourself into some sanity. You'll be lost, little more than a ghost."

"I know." Like the dream, she thought. A mist within the mist.

"There's more. There can be no children. During the dreaming nothing can grow in you. Nothing can change in or of you. You will have no family, no comfort. No choice. This is my banishment. It will not be yours."

Though her nerves began to dance, her gaze stayed steady. "I'll have my boon."

He swore, threw up his hands. "Woman, you try me to the bone. All right, then. What will you?"

"To stay."

"No."

"You took a vow."

"And so I break it. What more can be done to me?"

"I'll stay anyway. You can't stop me."

But he could. There was one way to save her in the time left him. One final way. "You defeat me." He drew her close, rocked her against him. "You've a head like a rock. I love you, Kayleen. I loved you in dreams, when dreams were all there was for me. I love you now. It killed me to hurt you."

"I want to be with you, no matter how short the time or how long. We'll dream together until we can live together again."

He took her mouth. A deep kiss, a drugging one that spun in her head, blurred her vision. Joy settled sweetly in her heart.

When she sighed, he stepped back from her. "Five hundred years," he said quietly. "And only once have I loved. Only you."

"Flynn." She started to move toward him, but the air between them had hardened into a shield. "What is this?" She lifted her fisted hands to it, pushed. "What have you done?"

"There's a choice, and it's mine to make. I will not damn you to my prison, Kayleen. No power can sway me."

"I won't go." She pounded a fist on the shield.

"I know it, and understand it as well. I should have before. I would never leave you, either. *Manim astheee hu.*" My soul, he said in the language of his birth, is within you. "You brought me a gift, Kayleen. Love freely given."

The wind began to kick. From somewhere a sound boomed, slow and dull, like a clock striking the hour.

"I give you a gift in return. Life to be lived. I have a choice, one offered me long ago. A hundred years times five."

"What are you . . . No!" She flung herself at the shield, beat against it. "No, you can't. You'll die. You're five hundred years old. You can't live without your powers."

"It's my right. My choice."

"Don't do this." How many strikes of the clock had there been? "I'll go. I swear it."

"There's no time now. My powers," he said, lifting his arms. "My blood, my life. For hers." Lightning spewed from the sky, struck like a comet between them. "For foolishness, for pride, for arrogance I abjure my gifts, my skills, my birthright. And for love I cast them away."

His eyes met Kayleen's through the wind and light as the clock struck. "For love, I offer them freely. Let her forget, for there is no need for her to suffer."

He fisted his hands, crossed his arms over his chest. Braced as the world went mad around him. "Now."

And the clock struck twelve.

The world went still. Overhead the skies broke clear so the stars poured free. The trees stood as if carved out of the dark. The only sound was of Kayleen's weeping.

"Do I dream?" Flynn whispered. Cautious, he held out a hand, opened and closed his fist. Felt the movement of his own fingers.

The air began to stir, a soft, sweet breeze. An owl called.

"I am." Flynn dropped to his knees beside Kayleen, with wonder in his eyes. "I am."

"Flynn!" She threw her arms around him,

dragging him close, breathing him in. "You're real. You're alive."

"I am restored." He dropped his head on her shoulder. "I am freed. The Keepers."

He was breathless, fighting to clear his mind. Drawing her back, he framed her face in his hands. Solid, warm. His.

"You're free." She pressed her hands against his. The tears that fell from her eyes shimmered into diamonds on the ground between them. "You're alive! You're here."

"The Keepers said I have atoned. I was given love, and I put the one I loved before myself. Love." He pressed his lips to her brow. "They told me it is the simplest, and most potent of magic. I took a very long time to learn it."

"So have I. We saved each other, didn't we?"

"We loved each other. *Manim astheee hu*," he said again. "These are the words I give you." He opened his hand and held out the pearls. "Will you take them, and this gift, as a symbol of betrothal? Will you take them, and me?"

"I will."

He drew her to her feet. "Soon, then, for I've a great respect for time, and the wasting of it. Now, look what you've done." He trailed his fingers gently over the scratch on her cheek. "There's a mess you've made of yourself."

"That's not very romantic."

"I'll fill you with romance, but first I'll tend those hurts." He scooped her off her feet.

"My mother's going to be crazy about you."

"I'm counting on it." Because he wanted to savor, he walked for a bit. "Will I like Boston, do you think?"

"Yes, I think you will." She twirled a lock of his hair around her fingers. "I could use someone who knows something about antiques in my family business."

"Is that so? Ha. A job. Imagine that. I might consider that, if there was thought of opening a branch here in Ireland, where a certain wildly-in-love married couple could split their time, so to speak."

"I wouldn't have it any other way."

She laughed as he spun her around, pressed her lips to his, and held on tight as they leaped into space and flew toward home.

And happily-ever-afters.

The Sorcerer's Daughter

Jill Gregory

This story is lovingly dedicated to Marianne, Nora, and Ruth — and all those who dream — and to my beloved father, who gave me so much, always believed in me, always was there for me — and whose joyous memory will always live in my heart

1

It's too dangerous, Willow. I won't allow it.

"You have no say in the matter, Father. I'm going, and that is that."

Willow of Brinhaven mounted her white mare, Moonbeam, and sat very straight in the saddle. As the sun set over the mountains behind the deserted keep where her father, Artemus, was imprisoned in a collapsing stone dungeon, its last fleeting rays turned her spiraling red-gold curls to molten fire.

But the Perilous Forest —

"It's no use arguing about it, Father. There's only one way to get you released from this place — and that is to pacify Lisha. Now, are you going to help me or not?"

She knew exactly what his answer would be.

Of course I'll help you. It was a grumble, not the least bit good-natured. *Since I can't stop you. I don't think the man has yet been*

145

born, Willow, who can stop you from doing something when you get a notion into your head. Except, perhaps, young Adrian —

Willow fought the pang that sliced through her heart whenever she thought of Sir Adrian. "Father," she murmured, "you know I'm the most agreeable creature alive. But in this case I must go against your wishes. If I don't find the Necklace of Nyssa and turn it over to Lisha, she'll stand by her word and keep you imprisoned here for a hundred years."

But the Perilous Forest, Willow. Please, for once be reasonable. All manner of outlaws and evil creatures inhabit that place — why, they say an army of knights would be hard put to return from its depths alive!

"Don't worry. I'll be careful." Despite her calm words, Willow knew the tales. Her stomach knotted a little as she reflected on the frightening stories she'd been told of the Perilous Forest ever since she was a child. But she had to free her father, and this was the only way. Lisha the Enchantress had cast a powerful spell that had lured him to the keep's dungeon, and then she'd collapsed the walls upon him, leaving him trapped. He had enough air to breathe to stay alive, and each day food and drink magically appeared. He had the length of the dungeon to roam, but he could not get out, and Willow, who'd tried for two days, could not get in.

Lisha's magic was too powerful, far more so than Artemus's own, and his powers were already dwindling. Trapping a sorcerer so that he cannot walk beneath the light of moon and stars is the surest way to drain him of his powers, and Willow knew that if she didn't hurry, even his Dream Powers, those for which he was best known, would fade to mere wisps, reaching no farther than the walls that hemmed him in.

"I'll take care, Father." Her violet eyes shone with purpose. Though she was fine-boned, her features dainty and lovely within her heart-shaped face, Willow of Brinhaven's eyes were as brilliant and determined as those of any soldier setting forth to battle. Large and luminous, they drew attention to her small, lightly freckled nose, her sculpted cheeks, and the beautiful shape of her chin and jaw. They were remarkably intelligent eyes, as bewitching as stars and tilted slightly up at the corners. They also tended to mirror her every emotion.

"I have my dagger and my pouch — and my wits," she said quietly. "So try not to worry. But should you get an inkling of precisely where within the Troll's Lair the necklace might be hidden, you will send it to me in a dream, won't you, Father?"

Of course. I was inside the lair myself once as a boy and actually glimpsed the necklace, but it was so long ago . . .

She heard his sigh as his gruff voice ran through her head, and she knew he was worried, frustrated, and bound and determined to be of help to her.

I'll surely remember something useful if I concentrate on it, and I'll send you anything that occurs to me. But, Willow, I wish you would reconsider. Or at least take along some male protector. I know of a most trustworthy knight — his name is Sir Dudley —

"Nearly every knight in three kingdoms is off trying to win the hand of Princess Maighdin by performing brave deeds," she retorted with a shake of her head. "Besides, a man would just slow me down and get in my way. He'd be constantly fussing over me and worrying about me, and I'd be exhausted from merely assuring him that I'm not frightened or cold, or hungry or —"

Willow. Listen to me. In her head, her father's voice sounded even more urgently pleading. *If anything were to happen to you, I could never forgive myself. Stop and think, my girl. This is a rash, foolish decision and —*

"Speaking of rash and foolish decisions,

Father, yours tops them all," she exclaimed. "I still don't see why you had to turn Lisha's lover into a toad." Her slender fingers tightened on the reins as the restive Moonbeam pranced in the fading light. "I've told you a thousand times that those transformations of yours only lead to trouble."

I didn't know that he was Lisha's lover when I did it — well, I mean, I wasn't completely sure if he was or not at the time. Artemus's thoughts rumbled through her head. He had no need to speak aloud to communicate with her, at least not at this range. But the spell Lisha had put on the keep would limit his powers, and once Willow ventured away from this place, only his Dream Powers would be strong enough to reach her.

But he was annoying me no end.

"And look where it led," Willow pointed out just as the sun slipped at last beneath the tip of the mountain and gray dusk shadowed the land.

It wasn't my fault that some stupid hawk swooped down and ate him before I could change him back, he protested irritably. *Lisha always was hotheaded. You know, it's possible that she'll settle down and change her mind and lift the spell in only twenty or thirty years.*

"But I will have the necklace for her in less than a fortnight." Willow's mouth was set with determination. "Farewell, Father. I'm headed north. Try not to worry — and don't forget to dream."

Be careful! His words thundered through her mind, and then she was off, Moonbeam's hooves flying like silver streaks across the earth as a gleaming full moon sailed in the sky.

Willow rode fast and low in the saddle, the hood of her midnight-blue cloak blowing behind her, her long, vibrant curls fluttering free. There was utter resolution and confidence in her eyes and in the way she handled the mare as they galloped across the high, rocky terrain. But though Willow had faith in her own abilities, she wasn't so foolish as to think they wouldn't be tested to their limits. True, she'd been trained by a master swordsman in the court of King Felix of Prute and was agile and quick-witted and able to move silently through woods or glen when she put her mind to it. She had the special pouch her father had prepared for her inside her cloak pocket, and she could throw a dagger and hit her target perfectly nine times out of ten. But evil creatures and outlaws did roam the Perilous Forest, and perhaps the most dangerous of all was the spirit of the dead Troll King, whose haunted lair she would have to enter to retrieve the fabled necklace that Lisha desired.

Her skin prickled just thinking of that.

But she had to get Artemus out of that dungeon. Though he didn't complain, she knew that any kind of confinement was torturous for him, and she wasn't about to let him suffer beneath a pile of stone rubble for a hundred years — or even twenty-five.

Not when she could use her own abilities to obtain his freedom.

She rode deep into the lonely hours of the night and at last made a solitary camp on the outskirts of a small town near the River Grith. Wearily she shook out her blankets in readiness for sleep. It was late autumn, and the night air was chill, but she didn't want to risk drawing attention by making a fire. She wished only to fall into a deep sleep so she could receive the dream.

She hoped Artemus's dreams could still reach her. If he could somehow conjure up an image of the Troll's Lair, and of precisely where the Necklace of Nyssa was hidden within it, her task would be far easier and quicker.

In no time at all, she was stretched out beneath the stars, huddled in her cloak and a blanket of fine green wool, letting the forest sounds lull her into sleep.

And waiting for the dream.

Artemus had been pacing and pacing the entire time Willow rode north toward the Perilous Forest. He knew he couldn't stop her, but he *could* help her. In the moments when the lustrous full moon had risen, the shimmering image of the necklace had suddenly come to him. And not only the necklace but the chamber in which it was housed as well. He saw it clearly — all of it. The staircase dominating the shadowy Great Hall, the raised dais in the marble-floored chamber with draperies of scarlet and gold, the heavy chest inlaid with gold and silver where the necklace was locked away. The chest's lid adorned by rubies in the shape of a troll. And more, Artemus saw the Troll's Lair itself, a spike-towered fortress built of blood-red stone, looming deep within the swampy depths of the forest.

All of these images he would send to Willow in a dream, and they would guide her to the necklace so that she could retrieve it speedily — and, he hoped with all his heart, safely.

But he was going to do more for her than that.

Artemus had devised the perfect plan to help his daughter, whether she liked it or not.

He was sending the dream not only to Willow but to another as well. A man who he knew would aid any lady in need that he came upon, as stalwart and dependable and chivalrous a knight as Artemus had ever encountered. Sir Dudley of Mulcavia was of middle years, middle height, and middle intelligence. But he was a solid soldier, and with his graying hair and beard, years of experience, and strict adherence to every knight's code of honor, he would be the perfect protector for the brave but impetuous Willow. Once Sir Dudley came upon her, a slender wand of a girl no more than nineteen years old bent upon a dangerous quest, Artemus knew he would stick by her side, loyal as a dog, and he would guard her with his life.

No worries here, Artemus reflected, his brows drawn together, of some young pup of a knight being smitten with Willow's beauty and grace and getting any ideas. No, there would be none of that.

Sir Dudley was too old, too reliable, and too above reproach in every way even to entertain such notions. Artemus had no doubt that he would conduct himself properly.

Well pleased with himself, the sorcerer settled his aching back against the cold stone wall, scrunched his silver cloak into a ball and stuck it behind his head for a pillow. He squeezed his eyes shut and set about conjuring up the dream.

It was more difficult than he'd expected. Lisha's damned spell was clouding his powers. He couldn't quite see Willow — or Sir Dudley, for that matter. Keeping his eyes closed tight, he took several deep breaths and was at last able to picture Willow's flowing red-gold curls. *That will be enough,* Artemus thought with relief. *Enough to send the dream to her.*

He then concentrated on calling to mind Sir Dudley's jowly face, but the knight's features remained blurred, and he had to settle for focusing upon the man's famed golden cloak instead. It was rumored that the High King himself had conferred the cloak upon him as a gift of appreciation, and Sir Dudley was so immensely proud of the cloak with its jeweled fastenings and fur lining that he wore it always, no matter the season.

Artemus smiled with satisfaction. Ah, yes, the cloak. There it was.

With a muttered spell and a slight wave of his fingers, he tilted his head back against the rough stone behind him, took one more deep, steadying breath, and turned all his energies to sending the dream.

From the cracked tower of the collapsing keep, two plumes resembling pale gray wisps of smoke drifted up and across the night sky. The plumes were fainter than smoke and shimmered as they floated away from the keep and sailed upon their way beneath the canopy of sky, moon, and stars.

Each plume contained a dream, and each followed its own separate path. One headed toward Willow, the sorcerer's daughter, as she lay curled fast asleep in the woods near the River Grith. The other moved across the sky to find the knight who wore the fur-lined golden cloak.

But unbeknownst to Artemus, at this point his plans went seriously awry. Miles away, in the Valley of Wye, events were transpiring at that very moment that altered Artemus's plans beyond his wildest contemplations.

The dream intended for Sir Dudley reached a man as different from him as night from day: a young, hawk-eyed, fearless man.

A man regarded warily by his enemies and respected by his friends. A mercenary soldier who despite his mere twenty-odd years was seasoned in battle and who hired out his services to the highest bidder. A man who owed allegiance to no one but himself.

A man whose heart had never been touched by a woman, but whose roguish instincts and rough good looks had drawn many smitten females of every imaginable rank to his bed.

A man called Blaine of Kendrick — known among his enemies and friends alike as the Wolf.

Blaine of Kendrick stood over Sir Dudley, smiling faintly at the snoring sounds the knight emitted as he lay huddled beneath his cloak.

"You won't mind, will you, my friend?" he muttered softly. In the darkness, Blaine's sharp black eyes glittered like coals. "I'll get this back to you before you ever know it's gone."

In one swift movement, he swept the rich golden cloak from the knight's chunky body and replaced it with his own plain black woolen one.

Sir Dudley twitched, his mouth opened, and another snore whistled out.

Blaine turned away, grinning as he donned the cloak.

At this very moment a certain acquaintance of his was drinking ale in the hamlet of Strachdale, less than ten miles away — an old comrade who had wagered him that he couldn't get his hands on Dudley's cloak. Blaine was about to win that wager and to impress a certain well-endowed tavern wench who had a fondness for riches.

Take what you want in life or else you've no one to blame for your troubles but yourself, Blaine thought. Then he pictured Chandra, who would be leading him to the small room at the top of the inn within the hour. He chuckled with pleasant anticipation, congratulating himself.

But things did not go as he had planned. For when he reached the inn and collected the gold coins from his friend for winning the bet, he found that Chandra was already busy with another man in the small room at the top of the stairs.

The only other wench serving that night was Ina, who'd been clinging a bit too much lately whenever he'd come by. The last time they'd gone to bed she'd even mentioned something about marriage. Blaine had choked on his ale and hadn't been able to speak for a full hour.

No, he would steer clear of Ina.

He waved warily as she caught his eye, and left with all due speed. She was working her way to the door to waylay him, but he moved faster. The cool night air felt good on his face as he headed back to camp.

The only woman he planned to marry was Princess Maighdin of the South Country. She was royal, highly sought after, rumored to be the most beautiful woman in five kingdoms.

And everyone wanted her.

For the Wolf of Kendrick, that was the real draw. The competition for her hand was intense. His old enemy, Sedgwick of Lothbar, was planning to slay a dragon and bring Maighdin its head. His old friend, Rolf of Cornhull, beside whom he'd fought often in battle, was off at this very moment pursuing a unicorn rumored to be hiding in the Elven Wood.

Sir Wallach of Graystone, who'd been his commanding officer when he offered his mercenary services to King Felix some years back, was on a quest to slay Angbar the Giant and bring back Angbar's Golden Throne.

I need a plan, Blaine decided as he settled alongside Sir Dudley in the soldiers' camp that night. He hadn't bothered to switch the cloaks back yet. He wanted to sample the feel of luxury, since once he beat out all the other men vying for Maighdin's hand in marriage, he would know nothing *but* luxury. So he would just keep Sir Dudley's cloak for tonight and let the old rooster have it back in the morning.

The cloak was thick and pleasantly warm. He felt himself drifting comfortably into sleep, still pondering what he could do to best everyone else in the field, how he could impress the princess, woo her, and capture her heart.

Losing to Sedgwick, or Rolf, or any other man simply would not do. He had never lost any competition and he wasn't about to lose now.

Think, man, he admonished himself as he yawned beneath the cold swirl of stars. *Think how to dazzle and delight a princess . . .*

The faint plume floated down, down, down . . . touched him, light as the wings of a moth.

He was standing before a fortress made of red stone, deep inside the murkiest forest imaginable. The fortress was high, grim, impenetrable. Then he was inside somehow, and he saw a great hall, a winding staircase, a torchlit chamber. There was a dais, and a chest inlaid with gold and silver, glittering brighter than a hundred suns. The lid of the chest opened slowly, slowly, and the inside of it was lined in white velvet. Resting upon this snowy bed was a necklace that shimmered . . . crystal . . . and rubies . . .

Entwined by gold.

He knew that necklace. Everyone knew

that necklace. It was the fabled necklace that had belonged to Nyssa, the greatest sorceress of all time. Some said it didn't exist. Others said a whole league of men had died trying to find it. It was purported to be magical — the stones in it contained a power that drew all things good, beautiful, powerful, and desirable to the wearer.

Gazing at it in that chest, within that chamber, deep inside that blood-red fortress, Blaine of Kendrick smiled in his sleep.

He awakened just as dawn broke and turned the horizon to pale amber. He knew precisely where to go and what to do in order to dispatch his rivals, every single one of them — and win.

Blaine of Kendrick, the Wolf, startled awake and stared grimly about him. His lean, handsome face was full of purpose.

The bastard son of a murdered duke, he'd been forced to make his own way in the world and survive in any manner he could for as long as he remembered. His mother had died giving birth to his stillborn twin only moments after he himself entered the world — and so he'd never known even a moment of her nurturing. Since his father's death when Blaine was barely nine, and his own subsequent exile, he'd had to work and scheme and fight and hide just to stay alive.

He'd proved tougher than any adversary he'd ever had to fight, and he'd come far from that ragged and starving boy who'd hidden in haylofts and trees, who'd nearly frozen to death one winter and nearly drowned in a stream the next spring while onlookers stood idly by, laughing as they watched.

He was a man now, who earned his own way, whose skills were in demand, whose future belonged only to himself.

And he had decided what that future would hold.

He knew now how to win the princess's hand, how to attain his goal. Fate had given him a dream and shown him what to do.

The magical Necklace of Nyssa was going to be his. A gift to his beautiful future wife.

Nothing and no one on this earth — not man, woman, or beast — had the power, strength, or means to stand in his way.

2

As a chill darkness swept down over the darkened countryside, Willow slipped into the bustling inn known as the White Hog in as inconspicuous manner as was possible. Weariness dragged at her after her second long day of solitary travel. She was in need of a decent meal, for tomorrow she would reach the edge of the Perilous Forest where the truly dangerous part of her journey would begin. *I'll sleep in the inn tonight, upon a real bed,* she thought, all too aware of her hunger and her aching muscles. *That will help me to gather my strength for what lies ahead.*

To her relief, no one in the White Hog paid much attention to her, not the stout, bearded innkeeper in his greasy tunic, nor the villagers, nor the fellow travelers scattered through the dim, smoky room that smelled of boiled ham and burnt lard and spilled ale. She'd disguised herself as a youth: her bright hair had been secured with a thong and tucked beneath a cap, her shapely form hidden beneath a coarse, bulky brown tunic and cloak. She had smeared dirt upon her cheeks, donned scuffed boots, and assumed a hunched posture. In the slight young man who seated himself at a small corner table and ordered ham, potatoes, and ale, no one saw a beautiful, slender woman whose eyes were the deep blue of violets, whose nose was dusted with a few pale, enchanting freckles, and whose soft lips and slender neck had drawn sighs of desire from countless young men.

A serving maid set her plate down with a clatter and departed without a second glance. Pleased with how smoothly things were going, Willow dug into the greasy food with abandon, paying scant attention to those around her — until the inn's door swung open with a sharp *thunk* and a very tall man with wide shoulders and cropped black hair appeared on the threshold and took a long, hard look around.

He looked to be a soldier, by his stance and bearing and dress. But it was not that which kept her attention riveted upon his rugged, handsome face. It was his eyes. He had the coolest, keenest, blackest eyes she'd ever seen — black as night they were, and just as impenetrable. They glittered with intelligence, within a swarthy masculine face that was too youthful to be so harsh. The man could not have been much older than she herself, perhaps less than four or five years her senior, but he looked anything but boyish. This was a warrior — a man accustomed to fighting and winning, she guessed, a man with a warrior's mind and heart. In that one swift moment, his glance seemed to weigh and appraise every occupant of the room, and when those eyes of his touched her, she felt a hot, honeyed flutter deep in the pit of her stomach.

For only a moment their gazes met, and she went breathless, certain that he saw through her disguise. Not knowing what he might do, she was already sliding her hand toward the sheathed dagger hidden beneath her tunic, but his glance moved past her and continued its swift, precise scan of the taproom.

He didn't notice anything. All is well. There's no reason for your heart to pound so, she scolded herself, but as luck would have it, the only empty table in the room was one alongside hers, very near the roaring log fire.

She forced her fork to her lips as the man strode right past her and seated himself at the trestle table less than five steps away. Yet

she didn't taste anything, for she found herself watching as every serving maid in the
room clamored to serve him.

"Bring the soup and a roast duckling and
brown bread," he ordered. His voice was
deep, curt, and decisive. "And I think I'll
have you, too, fair Rowena," he added with a
laugh. "Come here, my sweet."

The serving wench to whom he spoke
gave a squealing laugh and tossed her
stringy yellow hair behind her. "My name's
not Rowena, sir, it's Mattie," she gushed,
then gave a screech as the man pulled her
down upon his lap. But despite her cry, she
looked far from unwilling. She giggled and
opened her eyes very wide as her arms
snaked eagerly around his neck.

"Why, sir, whatever are you doing?" she
chortled.

"Getting to know you better. What a
pretty thing you are," he remarked with a
grin that could have melted snow. "You remind me of a Rowena I once knew. Succulent wench. I wonder if you taste as delicious
as she did, fair Mattie."

"Try me and see, sir," the girl challenged
with another giggle.

Willow gritted her teeth and forced her attention back to her plate of food. The poor
girl would no doubt fall prey to his silver-

tongued prattle and false compliments. With his handsome, hawklike features, lean and muscular physique, and the hardened air of command that he wore as easily as his cloak, it was easy to see how women would be drawn to him. Some women.

Not I, Willow thought gratefully, spearing a forkful of ham. *Such as he cannot compare to Adrian.*

At the thought of the beautiful, pale-haired young knight whom she'd loved all her life, a knot tightened in her chest. She and her father had lived for as long as she could remember in a comfortable stone cottage on the property of Adrian's father, Sir Edmund, who, courtesy of King Felix, was lord of the big manor house at Brinhaven and all the surrounding land, clear down to the river. She'd grown up watching Sir Edmund's man-at-arms training young Adrian in everything he needed to learn in order to become a knight like his father. And that he did, excelling even when brought to tutelage under King Felix's own man-at-arms. Adrian, with his keen mind and noble nature, had easily won the respect and admiration of all who knew him. A full ten years older than Willow, he was the kindest, gentlest young man she'd ever known, and handsome beyond compare with his tall, straight figure, his thick, fair hair that shone in the sun, and his crinkly eyes the color of warm honey. He had always treated her like a little sister, which both gratified and depressed her. For she'd loved him since she was nine years old, and even when she blossomed into womanhood she'd never had the courage to confess the truth to him. When he was twenty-six and she sixteen, he had ridden off to war, and she'd vowed to herself that she would tell him what was in her heart the day that he returned.

But Adrian had been killed in battle. His father had mourned, the entire village had wept, and Willow had been unable to stop sobbing for a week.

When at last she dried her eyes and rose from her bed, under the worried care of her father, she had known that she would never love another man, that none would ever touch her heart in the way that the noble and gentle Adrian had.

So now, in the White Hog Inn, she munched on bread and nibbled at ham, and thanked her lucky stars that *she* would never be in danger of falling prey to the lying, roguish charms of a man like the one seated near her — a man every bit as arrogant as he was handsome, a man who would bed any willing wench who crossed his path, who made a public spectacle of himself in a tavern with serving maids who ought to know better than to be drawn in by his charms and flattery.

But why was she so concerned with him? she wondered in irritation. Perhaps because he *was* so handsome. That was undeniable. There was something dark and sleek and dangerous in him, Willow sensed, beneath the ready charm. She'd glimpsed chain mail beneath his plain black cloak, and there was coiled power in the way he walked and in the swift, commanding way he had assessed all those in the room.

She brought herself out of her musings with a start and reminded herself sharply that she had a mission to accomplish — and she couldn't afford to be distracted by some hard-eyed stranger who mattered no more than a gnat.

Don't worry, Father. By dawn tomorrow I'll be setting off into the Perilous Forest. Before you know it, I'll hold the Necklace of Nyssa in my hands.

She sipped at the ale in her tankard and pondered again the dream Artemus had sent, the dream that told her where within the Troll's Lair she would find the prize. Even when the dark-haired stranger hailed a friend entering the tavern and the short, red-haired man broke into a huge grin and joined him at the trestle table, she refused to do more than glance over her shoulder.

For she had plans to make, preparations to consider, and so engrossed was she in her own thoughts that it was with a start that she suddenly heard a snatch of the conversation going on alongside her.

"You're not serious, man! You're not truly venturing into the Perilous Forest!"

"Quiet, Gurth." It was the stranger's deep voice, lowered, and rough with annoyance. "The whole village needn't know my business," he growled.

Willow tensed. *The Perilous Forest.* Now the two men had her full attention.

"What business could you possibly have in that place? Don't you know you'll never make it out of there alive?"

"Care to make a wager on that, my friend?" The stranger sounded amused. "Not only will I come out alive, but I'll come out with a tidy bit of treasure as well. You see, you're looking at the man who's going to win the hand of the Princess Maighdin."

Uproarious laughter from his companion greeted this statement, but Willow wasn't smiling. Her fingers clenched around her tankard.

"That's a good one, that it is." Gurth raised his tankard to his lips and drank greedily. "Every man old enough to walk and young enough to remember what to do with a maiden is scrambling to be the one she picks. I'd say it'd have to be some mighty fancy treasure to —" He broke off, then continued in a dazed tone. "Not the Necklace of Nyssa?"

"You're not as much of an idiot as I imagined, Gurth." The stranger gave a chuckle. He sounded well pleased with himself, cocky, and not at all afraid. "Stealing that necklace out of the Troll's Lair and getting out of the Perilous Forest alive will beat every other quest and prize brought before her all to hell."

"Well, that it might, Blaine, if you could do it."

Blaine. His name was Blaine. Curse him, this was all she needed. Some arrogant whelp trying to impress a stupid princess and getting in her way.

Willow's mind began to race. She had to slow him down somehow, leave him behind, so she could reach the forest and the Troll's Lair first.

She'd planned to start at first light tomorrow, but now she realized she would have to forgo her night's rest at the inn and get a head start by entering the forest tonight.

She would also have to make sure that he didn't follow any too quickly.

Fortunately she knew exactly how she could accomplish that.

As she tossed several coins on the table to pay for her meal, she reached for the plain woolen pouch stitched in silver threads that was tucked deep in her cloak pocket. From it she tugged a small blue vial no bigger than her thumb, which contained a gray powder resembling dust.

"I can do it all right," the stranger called Blaine assured his companion. "Trust me — it will be child's play."

The other man snorted. "Remember Duke Knut of Paragour? He went in after the necklace a year back — took a troop of ten or so of his best fighting men with him, vowed to return with the prize. None of 'em, not one, ever came back out."

"I will." Blaine sounded coolly, sublimely confident. "Never has there been a thing I set out to do that I *didn't* do. And I've set out to marry this princess."

"Why do you want to marry her so badly? Never thought you were the marrying type."

"I wasn't. I'm not."

Willow could hear the man drinking

heartily. Her eyes narrowed as she stared at the tiny vial clenched between her fingers.

"But a man has got to settle down sometime, and it strikes me that it might as well be with a princess. Hers is a rich kingdom. The palace floors are laid with gold and precious jewels. Not to mention that Maighdin is a beauty — the most beautiful girl in five kingdoms, or so they say. Seems to me I met her once, years ago, when she was a child. She was a sweet-looking little thing then. So now —"

"I know you, Blaine. You don't fool me. The only reason you want her is because you're itching to prove to everyone else that you can get her. You like to win, and this is the biggest contest ever to come your way."

"Could be." The black-haired man shrugged cheerfully. "I'm looking forward to seeing the expression on the face of every other man when I walk off with the precious prize. And then there's the fact that I wonder what it's like to bed a princess." He laughed, and Willow's gaze narrowed at the glint of amusement and lustful anticipation in his eyes.

The other man burst out laughing again, then stroked his beard. "Interesting notion, I've got to admit. A man like you, a duke's bastard, fighting and clawing your way up through the ranks — a warrior and a survivor if ever I saw one. But . . . sorry, Blaine, it's hard to imagine you married to some delicate little princess used to having her path strewn with rose petals. I mean, what's she going to do with the likes of you?"

"It's the thought of what I'm going to do with the likes of her that's going to get me through that forest alive," Blaine retorted with a grin.

Do whatever you want, you idiotic man, Willow thought, *but you'll just have to win your stupid princess without the Necklace of Nyssa.*

She pushed back her stool, made a show of glancing around for the serving maid. In the process, she inched her way a few feet sideways until she was standing alongside Blaine's table.

Suddenly the red-haired man stood up to leave, and she had her chance. As he bid farewell to his friend, Blaine's glance was fixed briefly on Gurth's ruddy face, and it was all the opening she needed. Quick as a blink she upended the vial and gave it a shake into Blaine's ale tankard.

An instant later, she felt a strong hand close over her wrist and jerk her forward.

"What'd you put in my drink, boy?"

Willow's heart lurched in her chest. She

tried to wrench her wrist away, only to find it manacled by Blaine's steely grip, which tightened with every attempt she made to tug free.

"You're mad, sir. Let go of me, or you'll be sorry," she growled, deepening her voice as much as she could and praying he couldn't see her fear.

But if the man called Blaine was the least bit frightened by this threat from the slight youth with the dirty face and thin arms, he gave not the faintest sign of it. His cold soldier's gaze was riveted on the vial in her fingers, and with his free hand he pried it from her.

"It's no use denying it. You tried to poison me." He spoke in a low, deadly tone. Still holding on to her, he rolled the vial slowly between his fingers. "And I'm going to know why."

Gurth had paused to watch, and now his shrewd glance skimmed over the youth in the ragged clothing. "Hired by one of your enemies, no doubt, my friend." His lips slashed upward in a grin. "Or else the boy's merely jealous of the attentions of that serving maid. Hey, boy, you wanted her for yourself, eh? Was that it?"

He stepped toward Willow and grabbed her by the front of her tunic. "Don't you know that no maid can resist the Wolf of Kendrick?"

He shook her, laughing uproariously.

"Shut up, Gurth." Blaine was staring hard into Willow's face. She fought back a rising terror. Never had she seen eyes so cold, so flat and frightening. Blaine knocked his friend's arm aside and came to his feet, towering over Willow. Still holding her wrist in a viselike grip, he swung her around so that she was pinned against the trestle table.

"Who hired you?" he demanded softly.

Willow spoke quickly. "No one, sir. It was an accident — I never meant harm to you. This is some medicine for my sister — a midwife in the village gave it to me. I didn't mean to spill it near your drink —"

"*In* my drink, you mean. And you're a filthy little liar." Suddenly Blaine began dragging her toward the door.

"What . . . what are you doing?" Desperately Willow tried to break free, but she may as well have struggled against iron chains.

No one paid much attention as he hauled her unceremoniously toward the inn's door, except Gurth, who called out, "Need any help?"

"With this whelp? I'll beat it out of him before you can take your next sip of ale," Blaine growled back over his shoulder.

Fear swept through Willow as she was dragged out the door and into the cold gray dusk. Her wrist ached where his fingers were clamped so tightly, and she wondered if she would be able to escape this man — this fiend — who was so strong and so clever as to have caught her trying to drug him. She must be slipping. Time was, she could have poured the entire contents of the vial into a bowl of soup and have no one the wiser. Either she was losing her touch or this man was far more keen-eyed than even she had given him credit for.

"You're making a mistake, sir," she cried, forcing her voice to remain low, but she couldn't control the quaver in it.

Blaine of Kendrick shoved her against the side of the barn, and she hit the wooden wall hard, then fell to her knees in a puddle of mud. Quickly, she scrambled to her feet, and her hand flashed out with her dagger.

"Keep back, or I'll kill you," she said breathlessly, yet her voice held confidence now. With the weapon she felt she might just be a match for him. He was huge and strong and ruthless, as she had already learned, but for all her slender build she knew she was quick and well trained.

King Felix's man-at-arms had seen to that.

But to her dismay, Blaine of Kendrick merely smiled. A wicked, unpleasant smile. The icy expression in his dark eyes was even more unpleasant, Willow thought as the shadows of the encroaching night fell and the cold air whistling down from the mountains sliced right through her garments to chill her skin.

Alone, she faced the formidable man whose chain mail glinted in the dusk.

"If you think that little knife is going to stop me, boy, you're mistaken," he told her grimly. "If you want to spare yourself a beating, you'll tell me right now what you were up to — because once I lay hands on you I'm not going to stop until you're dead or you've told me everything I want to know. And you won't like my methods."

Willow swallowed. Beneath her long, tattered tunic, her knees shook, but she managed to hold the dagger steady. "You won't like the feel of this in your heart," she said as calmly as she could. "That's where it'll go if you take one step toward me."

"We'll see about that." Blaine lunged toward her so suddenly that Willow barely had time to lash out with the dagger. But she did. And sidestepped quickly, just as she'd been taught. Yet the trick she'd worked so hard to master didn't work the way it was meant to. Blaine of Kendrick dove straight at her, and his hand somehow shot out and caught her wrist without feeling the bite of the knife. With one hard wrench that made her cry out in pain, he had the knife from her and tossed it into the dirt.

Then his fist shot out, and she went crashing back against the barn. The world swam, a dark place filled with gnarled trees and squawking chickens and cold night stars and the odor of dung.

A tall form loomed over her, stooped, yanked her upward, and she was futilely struggling once more against strong arms.

"If you think I'll spare you because you're so little and scrawny, you're wrong. You tried to murder me and —"

Suddenly he broke off. As Willow stared dizzily up at him, she saw the incredulity on his face. At the same moment she realized that in her struggles her cap had fallen off. The thong must have come loose from her tresses as well, because her hair tumbled down around her shoulders in a bright, wild tangle.

"What the devil?"

Blaine's skin flushed, and his cold black eyes flickered with an emotion she couldn't read as his gaze swept from her hair to her face. She glared defiantly back at him.

"A girl." He spoke slowly, beginning to sound amused. There was a light in his eyes she didn't care for, and his lips curled up in a mocking smile. "Well, well. Perhaps you're not so scrawny after all."

3

"Maybe I should get a better look at you." Blaine gripped the front of her cloak in his fist.

In that instant, Willow realized he intended to rip it away.

"No!" she whispered, her heart in her throat. "D-don't. Let me go, or I'll kill you!"

The amusement in his eyes deepened. "I fear I'm even less daunted by a woman than by a spindly boy," he said dryly. "Or are you even a woman? You look like a scrawny little imp. I'm tempted to find out. But," he continued as her eyes sparked with fury, "I'll let you be if you answer my question. This puzzle grows more interesting all the time."

"It was a mistake, I tell you. I never meant you any harm."

He saw the mark on her face then, where his fist had struck, and his mouth tightened. "I hurt you."

"Not a bit."

But Willow winced as his fingers brushed over the forming bruise, and her long-lashed eyes closed for a moment. She then opened them quickly to find him searching her face.

"You deserved it. And more," he added angrily. "It's time for answers, wench. Start with your name. You can tell me here and now or —" Suddenly his eyes gleamed in a way that made him look both boyish and menacing all at once, and her heart stopped.

"Wh-what are you thinking?" Still a bit dizzy, Willow could nevertheless read the dark devilment and equally dark determination in his face. "Whatever it is, I promise you you'll be sorry if you don't — Ohh, what are you doing?"

But this became immediately self-evident as the Wolf of Kendrick slung her over his shoulder like a sack of grain and stalked with her back toward the inn.

"Let me down! How dare you! You will pay dearly for this!"

She's well born, Blaine thought, striding through the inn. He spoke a few words to the innkeeper, grinned, and waved a salute to Gurth as he continued toward the narrow stairs. *Her voice is cultured. I should have seen she was a girl all along. Something about the way she moves. And speaks. Something in those eyes . . .*

With a sudden surge of curiosity, he found himself wondering what she looked like under that tunic and cloak and those dirty boots. Well, he would soon find out.

"So 'twas a girl trying to murder you!" Gurth shouted across the room and then let out a bark of laughter. "Aye, I should have known there'd be a woman involved. Hahahahaha!"

Blaine didn't bother to respond. He was thinking about the squirming bundle over his shoulder, anticipating the pleasure of uncovering all of her secrets.

"You should have told me the truth before, imp," he muttered as he reached the landing. He winced slightly, then grinned in admiration as she continued to rain pounding blows onto his broad back. "Lost your temper, have you, my girl? So you don't much fancy hanging upside down. Maybe, though, it will loosen your tongue."

Willow gave a shriek of pure fury. Wrath choked her as she bobbed helplessly over his shoulder. Never had she hated any man so much in her life. Even the vile, murdering outlaw Ervin of Gronze, whose hand she'd chopped off after he tried to attack a village girl, had not inspired such a torrent of violent emotions.

If she couldn't rout this lone soldier, how

could she hope to defeat the sinister outlaw bands roaming the Perilous Forest — not to mention the ghost of the Troll King.

The situation didn't appear promising.

Her dagger lay in the dirt by the barn, and her vial of sleeping powder was in her enemy's possession. She'd seen him drop it into his pocket just before he slung her over his shoulder.

Now she was hopelessly overpowered.

But she had to get away, get a head start into the forest. Somehow she had to leave this arrogant brute far behind, unable to catch up to her and beat her to the necklace.

By the time he had stomped into a room, kicked the door shut behind him, and swung her around, Willow was formulating a plan, but her head was spinning from both the blow and from being carried upside down, and her apprehension about the man who had captured her was growing by the moment. He was too quick, too strong, too intelligent. She'd underestimated him earlier. Though she usually enjoyed a worthy opponent, this matter was too important to have to waste time on a battle of wits and resources. This Wolf of Kendrick made a dangerous enemy. She would have to leave him behind — far, far behind.

Somehow or other, before the night was

over, she would make good her escape. If she couldn't defeat a shallow, self-important bully like him, she was not the woman she thought herself to be.

But in the meantime . . .

"Start from the beginning," Blaine ordered. He set her down on the floor with a thump that rattled her teeth. "What poison was it that you shook into my ale?"

He looked so daunting standing there before her, blocking the door, that Willow wanted to scurry to a far corner of the room. The single candle burning on the rough wood table near the window sent amber light flickering over his rugged features and thick black hair, illuminating his broad, muscled chest and powerful shoulders, and the clenched hardness of his lean jaw.

Never had she met so intimidating a man, and never had she found it necessary to summon up every drop of her courage merely to stand her ground.

But she did stand her ground, refusing to budge an inch, even as he stepped closer.

"Answer me, damn you. Or else, girl or no, you'll be sorry."

"Threats from a man who bullies youths and women." Willow's delicate chin lifted. "Pardon me if I don't quail before such as you."

"You'll quail, all right." Blaine grasped her arms in a brutal grip that she was beginning to know. "If you don't loose your tongue, perhaps I'll have to cut it out."

She stared into his eyes, gleaming like coals in the candlelight, and her breath caught in her throat. He just might mean it. He had the look of a man capable of anything. Anything at all.

"You're hurting me. Let me go, and I'll tell you the truth."

"Tell me, and then I'll let you go."

She winced as his grip seemed to tighten even more. But she reached a decision. Up until now, lies hadn't fooled him. Maybe the truth would serve better after all.

"It was a sleeping powder. Nothing worse. Now . . . please . . ."

She heard the quaver in her voice and hated it, but wasn't able to stop it anymore than she was able to stop the sudden tears brimming at her eyes. It was with mingled mortification and relief that she felt Blaine of Kendrick abruptly relax his grip on her arms. Those iron fingers did not release her, but they eased enough that she was able to draw a breath.

"Go on." It was a growl, edged with impatience.

Willow's violet eyes lifted earnestly to his

black ones. "I heard you speaking to your friend about venturing into the Perilous Forest."

"You were spying on me?"

"No . . . *no*. I just happened to overhear. I paid attention because . . . I am going there myself."

"You?" Incredulity and scorn showed in his face. Willow flushed with anger.

"You idiot girl, if you set one foot in that place, you'll be eaten alive. Don't you know of Eadric the Terrible? His roving band of outlaws live there when they're not raiding the countryside — killing and raping all they encounter. Then there's the wild boars, the poisonous snakes, and the evil spirit of the Troll King —"

"I know all about Eadric and the Troll King — and the necklace." In the candlelight, her eyes were brilliant as jewels. "And I know that you want it, badly. But you can't have it. That's what I have to say to you. I am going after the necklace. I need it for something far more important than the winning of a princess's hand in marriage," she told him with contempt. "And I'm going to get it."

For a moment he just stared at her. Those black eyes searched her face, keen and intent, and a muscle throbbed in his jaw. Suddenly he threw back his head and whooped with laughter.

"You? You think you're going to get the necklace — instead of me?" He gave her a shove that sent her spinning down onto the rough straw bed. "That's a good tale, my girl. Now tell me another — and make it the truth."

"That is the truth. Look into my eyes and if you have any sense at all, you'll see that I mean what I say."

Slowly she rose from the bed and faced him. Slowly he studied her face and saw the truth staring back at him.

Blaine shook his head. "Why would a little thing like you want to brave such danger? What makes the Necklace of Nyssa so important to you?"

"That is my concern, not yours." Willow's lovely mouth was firmly set. "But I assure you that my reasons are far more imperative than yours. To win the hand of a princess," she said with quiet scorn. "If that is your desire, you'll have to find another way to woo poor Maighdin."

He grinned at her. "I happen to like this way."

"That is unfortunate for you."

A ghost of a smile touched his lips. "You're very sure of yourself. I'll grant that you possess courage and mettle. You never wavered back there by the barn when I threatened to beat you to find out the truth. But even you, fair imp, would tremble if you were to set foot inside the forest." Suddenly he reached out and cupped her chin, tilting it up. "Tell me your name."

"Why?"

"Do you always answer a question with another question?"

"What concern is it of yours if I do?"

He laughed again. Some of the coldness left his eyes — indeed, she felt a certain heat in his gaze as it traveled over her, appraising her afresh.

"You are spirited."

"You are insufferable."

"Don't get in my way," he warned. "If you interfere with my quest for the necklace, all your beauty will not save you from my anger."

"Behold, I tremble," Willow retorted mockingly. Yet she was stunned. Beauty? He thought she possessed beauty? She had never felt less beautiful — her cheeks were dirty, her hair a tangled mass of curls, her garments — unflattering, to be sure.

The man was mad.

She started toward the door, only to have her path blocked again. He was too big, too strong. She knew she would not get past if he did not wish her to do so.

"Our business is finished, sir." She met his gaze squarely. Inwardly she was aware of a strange, fluttering excitement as those midnight eyes nailed hers, but she managed to keep her composure despite the intensity of his gaze. "Let me pass now — and as far as the necklace is concerned, may the better one of us win."

"There's something you should know, imp. I always win. Ever since I was a boy, I have won every contest, every game, every tournament, and every fight. I learned that was what I needed to do to survive."

"You wish to wed a princess so that you may survive?"

"To prove that I can."

"To yourself or to others?" Willow asked quietly.

He looked surprised. For a moment there was silence but for the din coming from the taproom far below. Then Blaine spoke, his tone matter-of-fact. "Both."

Willow smoothed her hair back from her eyes. In the light it glimmered like fire. "Poor Maighdin. Is that the *only* reason you wish to wed her?"

"What other reason could there be? Most men do not wish to tie themselves to a woman, one woman, unless it need be."

"Oh, so you do not seek fortune. Or power. Or ease and security. I see."

"Not really." His grin spread, and he shrugged, his hand falling lightly to her shoulder, sliding slowly down her arm. "I seek to win what others cannot achieve. It is my nature."

"And what of love?" Willow's voice was low.

"Love." He said the word as if it were a kind of worm not worthy of his notice. His arm slid around her waist before she could protest. She felt a shock of heat.

"What is love, little imp?" he asked mockingly.

For a moment she was mesmerized by the gleam in his eyes, then she wrenched free of his grasp. "I'm not your little imp!"

His face lit with amusement. And something else, something darker, deeper, that made her blood race. "You're very beautiful when your lip trembles just that way with anger," he said softly. "And your eyes spark like flames. Magnificent. I hope my princess will be as lovely."

Suddenly he stepped closer and seized her arms, not roughly, as he had before, but gently, as if she were some fragile thing that would break.

"You speak of love. That tells me you are young and foolish. And innocent. To believe in such things," he said with a curt laugh.

"Those who do not believe in love are the foolish ones."

One dark eyebrow slanted upward. Mockingly, he smiled. "Whom have you loved, imp?"

She felt hot color flooding her cheeks. "Let me go."

"When you answer my question."

An image of Adrian flashed into her mind. She saw him as he was the day that he had ridden off to battle, his fair hair tousled by the breeze, his smile easy and confident and kind. He had kissed her hand . . . oh, so gently. And bid her to take care — of herself and her father.

Willow's throat closed. She couldn't speak.

Seeing the emotions that passed across her fine-boned face, Blaine's jaw tightened. Who the devil was she thinking of? he wondered. He frowned, angry with himself. What did it matter? She was a pest, a hindrance, a foolish girl who believed in things he knew well did not exist. A girl who would try to get in his way if he didn't frighten her off.

Yet there was something about her that

made him hesitate. He'd seen many beautiful women in his travels, and most of them at one point or another had thrown themselves at him and invited him to taste of their lips — and much more. But there was something particularly appealing about this one, something that set her apart from the others. He couldn't see her curves beneath the bulky garments that covered her, but her face was heart-shaped, delicate, her eyes entrancing. And under the soot on her face, her small nose and her cheeks were lightly freckled. Charming.

But she's also troublesome, he reminded himself darkly.

"Never mind." Abruptly Blaine released her arms. "I don't care whom you've loved. I don't care anything about you — except that you keep out of my way."

"Nothing would please me more," Willow retorted, "so long as you keep out of mine."

Blaine scowled down at her. "You're a fool if you set one foot into that forest. You'd best not expect me to waste my valuable time helping you when you run into trouble."

"By the time you enter the Perilous Forest, I expect to be on my way out — with the necklace already in my possession!" she flashed.

He shook his head, unable to suppress a grin. His eyes traveled over her with increasing interest, trying to discern if she did in fact have any curves beneath that damned cloak and tunic. "You're either the stupidest or the most determined woman I've ever met. But I'd give ten pieces of gold to see what you really look like beneath all this soot and wool," he muttered.

I'd sooner eat a toad than show you, Willow thought, but aloud she said, "There is a clean gown in my traveling pack, tied to my pony. Shall I get it and change? We could have some wine, and you . . . you could tell me more about your desire to marry the princess."

He threw back his head and laughed. "Do you really think I'm such a fool? I don't intend to let you out of my sight 'til morning."

"That's absurd." Willow spoke sharply. "Surely you don't expect me to stay here all night?"

"Why not? It need not be unpleasant — for either of us. I'll send you packing at first light, when I'm ready to head for the forest."

"I'll simply follow you in."

"I'll lose you before the first fork in the trail."

"We'll see, won't we?"

But Willow knew she had to get out of

here this evening — she must get a head start on this infuriating man. Turning, she paced away from him, toward the window, and suddenly lifted a hand to her brow.

"I really . . . would like some . . . wine," she murmured weakly.

"Going to try to drug me again? It didn't work the first —" He broke off as she swayed on her feet. "What's the matter?" he demanded, reaching her in one quick stride and grasping her arm. "Is this a trick?"

Willow closed her eyes and shook her head. "No trick," she whispered. "Please . . . some air. The window. I feel . . . faint."

With a muttered oath, Blaine caught her as her knees buckled and she sagged into his arms. He lifted her and carried her to the bed, setting her down gently. Suspiciously he studied her drawn, still face. Damn, she was lovely. She looked so small and fragile on the coarse straw bed. And she appeared to be in a deep faint.

"Girl . . . girl?" He didn't even know her name. "Wake up."

He scowled, remembering how he'd thrown her against the barn, struck her with his fist. True, he'd held back on the blow, thinking it was aimed at naught but a scrawny boy, but still . . .

She looked more beautiful than ever,

lying there with her rose-gold hair swirled across the pillow, her long lashes sweeping across fair, exquisite cheeks.

He swore again and stalked to the window, opening it high, letting the chill fresh air blow in. Then he went back to find her stirring at last.

"Thirsty . . ." It was a whisper, faint and weak. She touched a hand to her throat.

Those incredible violet eyes opened, fixing upon him. The pleading he saw within their luminous depths stirred something inside him he hadn't thought he possessed.

"Some . . . wine . . ."

He went to the door, flung it open. The din from below surged through the hallway into the dank, narrow room.

"Innkeeper!" he shouted.

From the taproom came the sounds of laughter, singing, shouting, along with the odors of smoke and grease and ale.

"Innkeeper!" he roared.

No response. It was useless. No one could hear a blasted thing.

He threw one last glance toward the girl lying upon the bed. She hadn't moved a muscle; in fact, her eyes had drifted closed once again.

Blaine strode to the head of the stairs.

"Damn it — *innkeeper!*" he shouted again, and this time a fat red face appeared at the bottom of the landing.

"Bring me up wine. Plenty of it. And make it quick!"

He wheeled and returned to the room.

"It's all right, I'm getting you some —"

He broke off. The bed was empty but for the worn gray coverlet. And so was the room. He was alone with the poor furnishings and the open shutters flapping in the wind.

He charged to the window in time to glimpse a slim form riding a white mare through the gloom. Too late he saw the tree, whose thick branches were within jumping distance of the inn's window.

"Lying little sneak." Blaine gritted his teeth and swung a leg over the windowsill to go after her. No one got the better of the Wolf of Kendrick. No one.

Then he shrugged and drew back inside. *It's better that she's gone,* he decided grimly. Something about that girl was distracting, and he didn't like it. She'd made him lose his concentration on the quest ahead of him. He needed to think only about the forest and the search for the Necklace of Nyssa. And about the dream that was his guide to the prize.

He couldn't afford to let himself be distracted by some stubborn little imp with a sensuous pink mouth and eyes that glowed more brilliantly than any jewels he'd ever seen. Let her venture into the forest tonight if she chose. He would no doubt come upon her lifeless body in the morn.

And she'd have only herself to blame.

Blaine of Kendrick turned away from the window, and when the wine came he drank it himself — every last drop. But even as he threw himself down at last upon the narrow bed where only a short while ago the imp had lain, he couldn't stop thinking about her.

And wondering if he would ever see her again.

Think about the necklace, he told himself. *And the princess.*

Better yet, think about kissing the princess. And bedding her.

He'd never kissed a princess before and he was looking forward to it. *Think about that.*

But as the night crept toward morning and the cool autumn air drifted through the room, he found himself thinking about kissing the lips of a flame-haired girl with a beautiful freckled nose, a girl who had refused to give him so much as her name.

4

A pale, pearly dawn glimmered high above
the trees as Willow mounted Moonbeam and
once more set upon her way. She'd entered
the Perilous Forest last night in the darkest
hours after midnight, and even she, who
prided herself on her bravery and good sense,
had felt a prickly unease at the back of her
neck as her mare trotted beneath the sinister,
gnarled branches of the forest's great black
trees. Not even a beam of moonlight had illuminated her path, but Willow had picked her
way slowly and steadily, ignoring the hooting
owl that swooped among the branches,
seeming to follow her, and paying no heed to
the glowing red eyes of shadowy night creatures that peeped at her now and again and
then disappeared into thick brush.

After several hours she'd made a silent
camp and allowed herself to sleep for a time
until the first whisper of dawn glowed across
the sky. The notion that she was alone in a

forest reputed to be evil and teeming with outlaws did not keep her awake, for she knew she must rest in order to survive. There was no time to waste on fear. She had to sleep, eat, and ride — and somehow find the Troll's Lair where the necklace was hidden. She refused to let fear stop her or slow her down, for her father had no one else to rely on for his rescue, and she would not fail him.

And if any handsome, overbearing, pig-headed, princess-pursuing bully happened to cross her path, she would quickly leave him very far behind.

A smile curved her lips as the sun burst through clouds high above and the mare quickened her pace. Willow was very pleased with the way she'd outwitted Blaine of Kendrick last evening. The thought of his fury when he returned to the room in the inn and found her gone made her giggle.

But remembering the relentless determination that she'd glimpsed in his eyes more than once, she suddenly felt a chill and hoped he would *not* catch up to her at all. In fact, nothing would please her more than if she never saw or thought about the Wolf of Kendrick again.

The trouble was, she kept thinking of him, remembering the strong grip of his hands, the gleam of those coal-black eyes — and the way he'd looked at her with concern when he'd thought she'd fainted. That showed that there was *some* compassion in the man — though not much, she decided. He wanted to marry some poor princess simply to outdo the competition. He didn't believe in love and probably not in friendship, loyalty, honesty, or responsibility either. Or in any other virtue she could call to mind.

He was exactly the kind of man her father had always warned her about — and the complete opposite of Adrian.

She sobered, thinking of Adrian. The familiar pang in her heart made her sigh, but her attention quickly refocused on the present as she suddenly reached a fork in the road and she realized she had to choose between two paths.

Straight ahead, the trees grew together even more thickly. An ominous, heavy odor hung in the air, like rotting flowers. To her right branched a more open path where green shrubs sprouted, and a bluebird perched on the limb of a tree. The path jutted down toward a steep embankment, then disappeared.

Which one would lead to the Troll's Lair with the least amount of danger?

The odor of rotting flowers, which seemed to come from the first trail, made her wrinkle her nose. She chose the second.

"This way, Moonbeam — and may it be the right path," she murmured to the mare as she spurred the animal forward at a quick clip.

Something seemed familiar about this place. Suddenly Willow remembered. She had seen it before — in the dream.

The dream had showed her the rows of green shrubs and . . . yes, the embankment. The bluebird swooped ahead, and she remembered that, too.

Follow the bluebird. Her father's voice, as she'd heard it in the dream. It was often this way in the dreams he sent forth — the images and details came back to the dreamer later, as the path of the dream unfolded.

With a quickened pulse, she followed the bright wings of the bird.

But even as she spurred the mare forward in pursuit, she felt a rope descend quick as a snake around her shoulders and slip down to tighten around her arms. She cried out suddenly as the rope bit into her flesh and pinned her arms uselessly at her sides.

There came the sounds of horses crashing through the brush, and suddenly she was surrounded by three armed, unsavory-looking men on horseback.

"What's this? A boy traveling alone through the Perilous Forest?" The shortest of the three men, a barrel-chested scoundrel whose black beard was as unkempt as his greasy mane of shoulder-length hair, rode right up to her and laughed uproariously as he surveyed her helpless posture.

A second man, the lean, rust-haired one who held the other end of the rope that had ensnared her, spoke from the saddle of his muscular gray destrier. "You're either stupid or addlepated, lad. Don't you know that no one gets out of our forest alive?"

"And now you won't either," the third man jeered in a voice so deep and hoarse that she could barely decipher his words. Yet she understood them well enough, and they chilled her blood, for they were almost as unsettling as his thin, rodentlike face and cruel eyes.

"I . . . mean no harm, sir." Willow moistened her lips, biting back tears as the rope cut painfully into her flesh. "I am only . . . passing through. If you let me go —"

"Let you go? Hah. Now why would we do a thing like that?" The lean man who held the rope chortled, but suddenly Blackbeard squinted his dung-brown eyes and began to study her more acutely.

"Well, well, 'tis something strange about this boy," he muttered, his ruthless gaze traveling from Willow's pale face down to where the rope pulled taut across her chest. She suddenly realized that it revealed the shape of her breasts, outlined beneath her cloak. Her heart began to thud as Blackbeard grabbed her pony's bridle, grinning savagely.

"Take the rope off, Liam, and ye might just find we've caught us more than we bargained for."

"Meaning?" The Rodent also rode closer for a better look, but even as he did so, Blackbeard snatched the cap off Willow's head, and her hair tumbled down, bright and vibrant against the dull brown of her cloak.

"A girl, eh?" Liam dismounted, still holding the rope. He let out a whistling breath and strode forward. Without warning he yanked at the rope, and she was tugged helplessly from the saddle.

Breathing hard, Willow suddenly found herself in the center of the group as Liam slipped the rope from her shoulders.

"Let's take off this cloak and see how comely you are, my lady," Blackbeard ordered, but as he reached for her, Willow spoke in a crisp, sure tone.

"If you touch me, you will die."

For a moment he froze, his mouth gaping. Then he pushed his greasy dark hair from his eyes.

"Now what does that mean?"

Willow drew a breath. She forced herself to look from one cruel face to the next. She didn't know who these men were, but she knew what they were. Their ragged garb and well-fed horses and rough ways told her all she needed. Outlaws. Brutal men who lived like animals, killing and marauding in packs, knowing no law but their own.

"I am here on orders of Lisha the Enchantress," she said as calmly as she could. "If you harm me or waylay me in any way, she will have her vengeance upon you."

She held her breath as they all stared at her. Slowly the men exchanged uneasy glances.

Blackbeard was the first to give his head a shake. "Methinks you are lying, my lady. What proof have you?"

"You'll have all the proof you need when Lisha turns you into stone," she replied gravely and fixed him with a stern look. "You have already delayed me. If you value your lives, you'll —"

"I say we take her to Eadric and let him judge the truth." Rodent ran his sharp, beady eyes over her. "Eadric the Terrible has a rule: all who trespass in this forest must pay him a toll. Whoever we find within these borders must be brought before him so he can decide what that toll will be."

"But Lisha the Enchantress —"

"I'd rather face the wrath of an enchantress than Eadric when he's crossed!" The lean man seized her by the hair. "Come along with me."

Terror bubbled through Willow as he dragged her toward his steed. She tried to pull free of the outlaw's grip, and he suddenly shoved her toward his horse with such force that she fell into the dirt. As the others laughed, he bent to haul her up. At that instant Willow grabbed a handful of dirt and threw it into the man's face. He screamed as the gritty particles blinded him, and quicker than a blink, Willow sprang up and snatched his sword from its sheath.

"Stand back," she ordered, whirling to face them all. She hefted the sword smoothly and eyed her enemies.

As Blackbeard and Rodent drew their own swords and advanced slowly toward her, Willow held her ground. Liam staggered blindly toward the brush, cursing and trying to rub the dirt out of his eyes.

"That was a mistake, wench," Blackbeard

muttered. "Now you've asked for it."

"Woman or no, we'll slice you to ribbons and then bring you to Eadric," Rodent snarled.

As they both closed in on her simultaneously, Willow swung the sword. Desperately she parried a blow from Blackbeard and then darted aside to strike out at Rodent. Her sword point bloodied his arm but missed his chest; she was suddenly locked in a life-and-death battle with them both, struggling to hold them at bay and to strike wherever she could.

Though she'd been well trained, these outlaws were soldiers-turned-marauders, and they had weathered many battles — battles against men larger and stronger than she. She was agile and quick, but in a prolonged fight against the two of them she knew she could not last. She would have to wound or kill one quickly so that she could use all her energies against the other — and she could only pray that Liam would be unable to recover enough to jump into the fray.

Suddenly Blackbeard sprang forward with a nasty thrust that caught her shoulder, and she felt a hot fire slice through her flesh. Then came the warmth of trickling blood.

The world spun for a moment, but she gripped the sword tighter despite the burning in her shoulder and parried another bone-jarring blow.

"We've got you now!" Rodent crowed, but suddenly there was a whooshing sound and a great rush of hooves, and she glanced dizzily up to see what looked like a dark cloud descending. A scream tore from her throat as Blackbeard charged at her, his sword lunging . . . lunging . . .

His screech of pain echoed through the forest long after he fell dead. A black-eyed warrior on horseback cut him down with one stroke. The warrior leapt from his saddle and planted himself squarely between Willow and the other man, but not before Willow saw that he was Blaine of Kendrick, his face set and cold, his black eyes locked upon those of his opponent with deadly intent.

"Stand back, imp," he ordered coldly without glancing over his shoulder at her, yet even as he spoke the words, Willow tried to take a step forward. She would fight her own battle. She didn't need help.

But each moment the world was growing strangely more dark. The pain in her arm seared like hell's fire.

Through a gray haze she saw a sword blade slash the air in a dizzying glint of silver, saw the rapid thrust and parry as

Blaine of Kendrick fought her enemy. She heard a grunt, an oath, both of which came from the direction of the brush to her right, and then suddenly Liam was flying toward Blaine, a cudgel in his hands. Blaine, intent upon his battle with Rodent, had left his back unprotected.

Willow's lips parted — she cried a warning, but the words died in her throat as the earth rose up to meet her, and then there was only the darkness and the silence and the cold.

5

"Don't try to move."

Willow heard the deep male voice as if from a great distance.

"Let me up," she whispered, but she felt as if there was no strength in any of her bones. She was floating, floating on a sea of air, and her limbs were heavy.

"Do as you're told, imp. And drink this. It will help."

That voice. It sounded familiar. It sounded like . . .

Blaine of Kendrick.

Memory flooded back, and with a start she forced her eyes open, only to discover that she was lying in Blaine's arms, her head lolling against his chest. Her cloak — it was gone. And her tunic —

Torn. The fabric had been rent, leaving her shoulder bare but for the cloth bandage tied around it.

"What did you . . . How dare you . . ."

"I had to see the wound, didn't I, to find out if it was fatal. It wasn't, my imp. It's barely a scratch. You'll live — not that you deserve to," Blaine said grimly. "You may thank me if you wish. I've cleaned and bound it for you while you slept."

"And what else have you done?" Panic swept over her as she gazed up at him, but he only shook his head. An amused smile touched his lips.

"Nothing you would not have me do. I killed those outlaws for you. No need to thank me for that. And . . . no!" he added sharply as she began to turn her head. "Don't look over that way, or you'll faint again." His arms tightened around her. "It's not a pretty sight. But I thought you'd be pleased."

"I'm . . . delighted. And I would . . . not faint." Willow struggled to sit up, but Blaine's arms held her snug against him.

"Can't you ever do as you're told?" He frowned in exasperation. "I said *don't move*."

She felt him shift, reach for something, though he held her firmly all the while. "Here, drink from this flask. It will give you strength."

"I don't want to drink any of your vile . . . Ooohhh!" She gasped and sputtered as he put the flask to her lips, and potent spirits streamed down her throat. They burned going down, almost as much as the wound in her arm, but when he at last took the flask away, she felt better. Some of the pain seemed to have ebbed, and the dizziness, too. The faintness in her head had cleared.

A few moments passed as she gazed up at the high clouds drifting in the bright sky. Not altogether unpleasant moments, Willow thought as she lay cradled against this man whose arms were so strong, who held her so carefully.

But suddenly she remembered her mission — and the need for haste — and she roused herself from the lulling sense of comfort that had overtaken her.

"Let me up."

His grip never slackened. "In due time. You're in no shape to ride further into the forest just yet."

"That is for me to decide," Willow retorted as she began to push herself up and out of his arms. But the world tilted crazily, and she quickly closed her eyes, falling back against him. He grabbed her before she could slide to the ground.

"I warned you," he growled.

Frustrated, Willow forced her eyes open

once more and glared defiantly at him. "And I . . . warned you . . . not to follow me into this forest."

"It's a lucky thing for you I happened along when I did."

"I had everything . . . under control." The fact that she knew it wasn't true, and that he had saved her life, only made her more cross with him than ever, and her eyes blazed with irritation. "I don't see how you caught up to me so quickly. I scarcely slept and I made good time."

"Don't you understand yet?" Blaine stifled the urge to shake her. "Nothing is going to prevent me from finding and claiming the necklace. Not even you," he added darkly. "I don't care how pretty you are."

Pretty? He thought her pretty?

Her eyes widened suddenly. Blaine felt as though someone had punched him in the stomach. When he'd been forced to tear her tunic at the shoulder to tend to that scratch of a wound, he'd glimpsed her soft, pale flesh — and even the tempting white curve of her breasts. He'd allowed himself to do no more than glance, but he'd seen enough to know that beneath her poor garments was a richly curved and beautiful female form. That knowledge, and the sparkling allure of her wide-set eyes and riotous spill of hair, were having a strong effect on him. He'd already experienced a tightening in his groin. Now, beneath that brilliant violet gaze of hers, he felt his blood begin to heat.

In vain he tried to summon up an image of Princess Maighdin, who was said to be tall and fair, with hair the color of spun gold. But his senses were full of this petite, slender imp with her glorious red-gold curls and a mouth that was made for kissing.

"You stay away from that necklace — and get out of this forest — and you'll be fine," he told her, his tone hoarse.

"That is my same advice to you!" Once again Willow wrenched free of him. This time she succeeded in clambering to her feet. Perhaps not so gracefully as she would have liked, for she wobbled a bit unsteadily, but she managed to face him, one hand holding her torn tunic in place.

She met his hard stare as he, too, scrambled up. He loomed over her, tall, formidable, scowling. With his powerful legs planted wide apart and his eyes regarding her with a mixture of irritation and admiration, Willow thought him more handsome — and somehow more intriguing — than ever, and was alarmed by her own reaction. There were strange feelings churning inside her, feelings she'd never experienced before.

She forced herself to remember that she and Blaine of Kendrick were at cross-purposes.

And that her father needed her . . . and the necklace.

"Don't think me ungrateful to you for what you've done. I know I'm in your debt," she said in a rush, "but you don't understand. I must have the necklace, and no matter what it takes, I can't let you get to it first."

He nodded. "That is exactly how I feel about you."

Her desperation mounted at the determination she read in his face. "If you turn back and leave the necklace to me, I'll see that you get a bag of gold worthy of a king's ransom. If it is riches you're after —"

"You can't buy me away from this quest." Blaine took a step toward her and grasped her arms, his expression unreadable. "I told you why I want the necklace. Now it's your turn to tell me why you want it."

"I need it," she said, startled by his direct assault.

"Why?"

Willow hesitated. The feel of his hands upon her was distracting. Her skin seemed to tingle where they touched. Yet she knew enough to realize that a man like him — for whom life was a game, a challenge, a chance to best his competitors — would understand nothing about the reasons that drove her: love for her father, loyalty, devotion.

"You won't understand." She moistened her lips. "Or care."

"Try me." His tone roughened. "You say you're in my debt. Then you owe me at least an explanation. And something else."

"Something else?" Willow stared at him. "What might that be?"

His eyes glittered. "A kiss."

She stood there, frozen, one hand still holding her torn tunic in place, her breath squeezing tight in her throat. The forest, the horses, the dead men lying somewhere among the gnarled trees, seemed to fade. She could see nothing but the strong lines of his face, the magnetic gleam in those dark, hawklike eyes. For a moment she couldn't speak, then the words burst from her.

"I would rather kiss a pig."

He edged closer. "Kissing me would be much more enjoyable," he assured her.

"Enjoyable?"

"Don't you ever do anything just because it's enjoyable?"

"Of course." She searched her mind for the last time she'd done something enjoyable. It had been long before her father had been imprisoned. It had taken her a week just to find him. And it was difficult to think just now beneath that intense stare of Blaine's.

"Picking flowers," she came up with at last. "Swimming in the river on a summer's night. Besting one of Sir Edmund's knights at swordplay, climbing the highest tree in the wood that runs behind our cottage at Brinhaven." She warmed to her topic. "Baking tartlets and feeding them to all the children in the village . . ."

"Enough." He interrupted her. "What about kissing? Have you done much of that?"

Willow felt her face flame. "No."

"But I thought you said you were in love."

Her chin lifted. "I *was* in love," she said quietly. Adrian's face swam into her mind. "But . . . he wasn't in love with me."

Before Blaine could mock her, she rushed on. "He always considered me a child — and he never would have tried to steal a kiss. He was the finest man you could ever hope to meet and not the type who would —" She broke off, certain that her cheeks must be brighter than the summer roses in her father's garden.

"He wasn't the type of man who would kiss you? Something wrong with him? Or do you think there's something wrong with kissing?"

"Don't be ridiculous. I'm sure it is very nice — with the right person. It's just that Adrian never knew how I felt — that I loved him with all my heart. He was older than me," she added quickly, "and he was wise and kind and good. Everyone loved him. And now he's gone. He died nobly . . . in battle . . . and I . . ."

"You're never going to give your heart to another," he said mockingly.

Willow drew in her breath, pain constricting her chest. His face looked so harsh — so cold. She hated him. Tears stung her eyes, but she blinked them back.

"No," she whispered. "I don't suppose I will. Not that you would ever understand anything that was fine and noble and good, anything about love!"

Blaine saw the shimmer of tears beneath those thick, sweeping lashes of hers and wished he could take back his words. He hadn't meant to hurt her. She was such an innocent, a lovely thing full of hope and courage and purpose, even if she did tend to chatter. He'd never cared for chattering women, but in her case there was something captivating about the way she rattled on.

"Tell me your name," he heard himself saying, his voice harsher than he intended.

She stared at him, thunderstruck. "Why?"

"I like to know the names of the women I kiss."

She swallowed. "You are not going to kiss me. But . . . it's Willow. My name."

"Willow, if I were to let you glance over there and see the men I slew today — all for you — I think you'd concede that you do owe me a kiss. One kiss. Payment for a service rendered."

"Knights aren't supposed to demand payment from those they aid. They're supposed to help others out of chivalry, because of justice and duty and right —"

"I'm not like other knights. I thought you'd realized that by now. I make my own rules." His arm clamped around her waist then, and he tugged her close. His other hand tangled in the spiraling curls that tumbled past her shoulders.

"Just one kiss," he urged softly. His breath was warm upon her cheek.

It was madness, but she felt herself wavering. Heat flowed through her everywhere he touched. Those dark eyes seemed to draw her in . . .

The temptation to kiss him was almost overwhelming. But he was a stranger. Her enemy. Competing with her for the necklace.

He saved my life.

"Think about it." Blaine's arm tightened around her waist. His voice was low, persuasive. How could a man's voice make her blood race and tingle? Her heart ache?

Some strange magic . . .

"Think about how you tried to put that sleeping powder in my ale. And that trick you played on me in the inn, when I was trying to come to your aid. That wasn't nice. Nor wise," he added, frowning.

Despite herself, she smiled. "You must have been furious," she murmured.

"With good reason." His hand drifted from her hair and began to trace the delicate curve of her jaw. "I could scarce sleep a wink thinking of you. I planned to wring your neck when I caught up with you. But now . . ." He smiled, a deep, heart-stopping male smile that made Willow's knees wobble. It was a good thing his arm was supporting her, she realized faintly.

"I'd much rather kiss you, Willow."

The sound of her name on his lips was her undoing. Without even realizing it, she nodded, almost imperceptibly. His smile deepened, and he leaned in closer. She held her breath.

Blaine's lips found hers.

It was a deep kiss and a gentle one. Willow knew only that the world fell away and there was nothing but this man, this moment, this magic, as his warm mouth laid sure and masterful claim to hers. Blaine of Kendrick kissed her long and thoroughly and opened her to sweet, wild sensations spiced with fire. A shock of pleasure rocked her, and she trembled in his arms. She kissed him back with instinctive ardor, and when at long last he lifted his head, she stared dizzily into his eyes.

"One more," he said hoarsely.

Before she could whisper permission, he drew her to him and kissed her again. This time the kiss was harder, deeper still, and hungrier than the first. Heat roared through her, and she clung to him, unaware of the pain that had burned earlier in her shoulder, aware only of his muscled arms around her, his mouth hard against hers, his tongue delving purposefully between her parted lips.

Then came more heat, more fire, a musky world far from innocence and sunlight, and she was beyond thought. Her senses reeled, her heart pounded, and she couldn't breathe . . . couldn't think . . . couldn't stop . . .

It was Blaine who stopped, drawing away from her so abruptly that Willow gasped in dismay. Her lips felt bruised and swollen, and bereft without his.

"I think . . . you've paid your debt now." His breathing was heavy, ragged. He dropped his hands from her and turned away.

By the devil, what was wrong with him? He couldn't let her see how the kiss had shaken him. She was an innocent, just as he'd thought, yet the way she kissed him had jolted him harder than any blow in a jousting tournament ever had. How could this be?

He'd kissed a hundred women, and none had ever affected him like this one. None had ever tasted so sweet, or smelled so clean and fresh, like wild mountain flowers. None had ever clung to him so softly — or kissed him back with such passion. He was used to being in command of such encounters, but she had made him hunger and thirst for more than he could ask of her.

More than he *would* ask of her.

She was too young, too innocent, and too vulnerable. Even he had limits — and rules.

Don't kiss her again, he told himself. *Think about your future bride. Think about beating everyone else to Maighdin's marriage bed. Then you'll get all the kissing — and everything else — you want.*

"Night is coming." He took a long breath. "We're deep in the forest now, and Eadric and his men — and who knows what other evil beasts — will be on the prowl. We'd best find shelter."

He turned back to find her still standing as he'd left her, her skin flushed, her eyes bright, her luscious mouth trembling. She looked as delectable as a ripe peach begging to be tasted.

But he couldn't taste her again, Blaine sensed warily, not without feasting on all of her.

"Did you hear what I said?" he asked. Even to his own ears, his voice sounded harsh. "We must find shelter. Come, I'll fetch your mare. Can you ride?"

Can I ride? Willow thought dazedly. *Can I think? Can I even speak?* Heaven help her, she was behaving like a dullard and a fool, but kissing Blaine of Kendrick had robbed her of her senses.

She wondered with a flash of panic if they would ever return.

She stared at him and finally took in his impatient expression, the tension in his face.

He was finished with her. One kiss, no, *two*, and her debt was paid. His interest was gone. It had all been a game.

Shame flooded her, and as it did so, saving pride returned.

His words at last sank in.

"I will find my own shelter, thank you, when I choose to halt my day's travel. I have already wasted enough time —"

"If you keep riding, wounded, in this haunted forest, I won't be responsible," he cut her off. "Other outlaws will find you, and they can roast you over an open fire without my lifting a finger to help you. A troll will come and pluck out your eyes and your fingernails, and I won't so much as pause on my way to finding that necklace."

"I wouldn't expect you to."

She lifted her chin once again. Did she have any idea how fetching she looked when she notched it up like that and her hair swung back from those fine-boned cheeks?

Blaine clenched his jaw. "Good. Because I'm not like your precious Adrian, you know. I'm not noble, I'm not good, and I'm not bound by any chivalrous code other than my own: do what you must to survive, and damn everyone else."

"I am well aware of that." She scooped her cloak up from the ground and slipped into it, her cheeks bright with fury. Not even glancing at Blaine, she started marching toward Moonbeam, grazing in a stand of birch trees. But it was then that her gaze fell upon the carnage no more than thirty feet from where she stood.

Nausea rose in her, and she swayed.

Instantly Blaine was at her side. "By all that is holy, girl, I told you not to look!" One glance at her utterly white face unleashed a stream of oaths. "That settles it. You're in no shape to ride anywhere."

That said, he swung her up into his arms and carried her to his own horse. She was busy trying to keep down the bile in her throat and erase the bloody scene from her mind. She didn't notice when he hefted her into the saddle, or when he vaulted up behind her. Even when they trotted forward and he grabbed her mare's bridle, her mind did not register what was happening.

Only when they were galloping through the forest together, as the encroaching dusk began to cast long, inky shadows and the menacing growl of unseen wild creatures reached her ears, did she realize that she was seated before Blaine in his saddle, that Moonbeam was being drawn along with them, that the bitter cold was seeping through her tunic and cloak, and that Blaine's powerful arms enclosed her on either side, providing some warmth and shelter from the biting wind.

"Where are we going?" She twisted in the saddle to peer into his face, which looked hard and grim in the failing light.

"I'll know it when I see it," he replied,

barely sparing her a glance.

The going became rougher. The trees, which earlier on this path had been widely spaced, now seemed to grow even more tightly together, their roots snarled and thick, interlocking one with the other, making it difficult for the horses to travel without stumbling. A black, impenetrable darkness, unbroken by moon or stars, descended over the entire forest. With it came raging gusts of wind — furious wind — and a sudden blinding whirl of snow. Numbing cold ate into their bones.

It was only autumn, yet the frigid air and thick snow and howling wind made it seem like late December.

This was an evil night, full of some wicked magic, Willow realized, shivering in Blaine's arms, and she was suddenly glad that she was not alone, that another human being shared her need to find shelter from the dangerous cold and wind. Any kind of shelter, even a cave . . .

"I don't like the feel of this," Blaine muttered in her ear, as if reading her thoughts. "I'd swear these trees are moving closer together all the time — forming some sort of trap."

His words echoed Willow's thoughts, and fear rose in her.

Neither of them saw the jet-haired figure perched in a tree branch high above. Her silver cloak blended with the white of the snow as Lisha the Enchantress waved an arm, and a sprinkling of silver sailed through the forest and fell upon a clearing in their path.

Then the magic dust and the enchantress were gone, and only the fierce night remained.

It was Willow who shortly after saw the dark hutlike shape ahead of them. "Look. *There!* Blaine, is it — can it be a cottage?"

She pointed, and he saw it, too. Swiftly he turned the horses in that direction as even thicker whorls of snow surrounded them.

"Empty or not, we're taking it for the night!" he shouted, and then fixed all his attention upon guiding the horses toward the rough dwelling, a wooden hut packed with mud and twigs.

Before they reached the door, the snow was already carpeting the forest floor and weighing down the branches of the trees.

"There's a lean-to behind. I'll settle the horses after I've got you inside!"

She could barely hear his shout over the rising scream of the wind. Willow had never seen such a night as this, and she knew it was borne of a dark magic. *The Troll King's magic.*

She braced herself as Blaine helped her down, and together they staggered toward the door. He kicked it open and drew his sword as they stepped inside.

Utter darkness.

And silence.

When they lit the tallow candle that Willow took from her cloak, they discovered that the cottage was empty.

Blaine kicked the door shut. "I'll build a fire."

"No. Leave it to me." Willow put a hand on his arm as he started toward the grate. "Take care of the horses, or they will surely die."

He glanced down at the small, icy hand upon his arm and then into her taut, lovely face. Her cheeks were reddened from the cold, and her mouth was trembling. The snow was still melting on her eyelashes.

Something clenched hard inside of him, something that was at once painful and sweet.

"I won't be long, then."

He lifted a hand, touched her face, then was gone.

A small stack of twigs was piled beside the hearth. Willow set about tossing them into the grate and setting them ablaze, even as she thought how strange it was that she awaited the return of the Wolf of Kendrick with a sense of something she could only describe as eagerness.

"As usual, my darling, you have made a rather large mistake." Lisha the Enchantress popped so suddenly into the dungeon that Artemus had to stifle a scream.

"Where did you come from?" he demanded, his brows drawing together. "And more to the point, are you prepared to let me out of here now?"

He started toward her but was rudely halted when she lifted a hand and he crashed into an invisible stone wall.

"Drat it, Lisha. Stop showing off."

"I've come to gloat. You deserve it."

"I deserve to be set free. Enough of this nonsense."

She regarded him from beneath a mop of dramatic black curls shot through with a few striking strands of silver. Her pale green eyes glimmered, as unreadable as a cat's. Lisha was beautiful, sleek, and sensuous — and she was powerful. While Artemus's strongest powers lay in the Realm of Dreams, and he was able to do a few simple tricks, like lower-level transformations and moving objects about with his wand — when he could *find* his wand — Lisha was known to be a cousin to Merlin himself, and she possessed powers that were truly splendid. Artemus eyed her warily, unable to help noticing how lovely she looked. Beneath her shimmering silver cloak, a rich turquoise velvet gown clung most provocatively to every single one of her curves.

Oh, my. But even as he admired her, he didn't trust her, for she had an infamous temper and bewildering moods.

He didn't understand women, not even his own daughter. So how could he hope to understand this intoxicating enchantress who was as unpredictable as a firefly on a summer night?

"Don't you want to hear about your mistake?" she fairly purred, stretching out on the fur rug she'd cast into the dungeon, arranging herself sensuously upon it. "It concerns your daughter."

"Willow?" Artemus took a deep breath, his eyes wide with alarm. "Tell me. What has gone wrong?"

"You sent her a dream, didn't you? To help her find the necklace. But you also sent another dream."

"That's right. To Sir Dudley. What's wrong with that? He will aid and protect her."

"He *would* have aided and protected her,

if you'd carried out the spell correctly, you bumbler." Lisha stroked her hand back and forth across the fur. "You sent the dream to the wrong man, Artemus. The man accompanying your precious Willow through the Perilous Forest is none other than the Wolf of Kendrick."

Artemus's blood curdled. He could only stare at her, an expression of horror creeping across his face. "The . . . Wolf of Kendrick?" He felt as if he was going to faint. "Who . . . is he?"

"An adventurer." She smiled carelessly. "Young. Brilliantly handsome. Ruthless. He is a womanizer, a mercenary. He wants the necklace for himself."

Artemus covered his face with his hands. "What have I done?" he whispered.

He sank down upon the hard stone floor, visions of Willow in danger, not only from what lurked in the forest but from the man he himself had sent in after her, filling his tortured mind.

"I don't care about the necklace anymore." The words tore from him. "I'll gladly stay here forever, if only Willow can come to no harm. Lisha, let me out of here. I must go to her, help her, then I'll come back, I swear. I'll come back for the next hundred years —"

"I've already assisted her. There's no

need for you to go anywhere. Thanks to me, she and the Wolf have a cozy place to spend the night."

"Spend the night?" Artemus bellowed. A terrible thought struck him. "Why do they call him the Wolf?" he demanded.

Lisha shot him a cool smile. "You don't want to know, darling."

For a moment Artemus closed his eyes and shuddered. "Why are you doing this?" he asked at last in a weary tone. "All because I turned your lover into a toad? It wasn't my fault that some stupid hawk ate him." He ran a hand through his thin, graying hair. "I should have turned him into a cockroach!"

Lisha rose from the rug in one lithe sweep of her body. "You know full well that is not the real reason why you are in here," she said, and for the first time there was a throb of emotion in her velvety voice.

"It isn't?" Artemus stared at her. "But you said . . . I thought . . ."

"Men." Lisha flushed with anger. "I'm going now, before I am tempted to turn *you* into a cockroach," she muttered between gritted teeth.

"But . . . give me some clue . . . some hint . . ."

"The Melwas Ball. Remember?" She spit

out the words, then vanished in a puff of fire.

The invisible stone wall vanished with her, and Artemus stalked across the dungeon and back, then paused to stare down at the fur rug.

The Melwas Ball?

"Oh," he said suddenly, incredulity filling him. For the moment he even forgot about the fix that Willow was in — trapped for the night in the Perilous Forest with the Wolf of Kendrick. He was remembering himself and Lisha the Enchantress, four months ago, dancing together at the Melwas Ball.

And then there was what had happened in the dark seclusion of the garden *after* the ball. "Oh. Yes," he murmured, stroking his jaw with long, slender fingers. He grimaced. *"That."*

6

Snow pelted the roof of the tiny thatched cottage. Within its humble walls, Willow and Blaine sat on stools at a small table near the fire and dined on what food Blaine had stored in his pack: day-old bread, a hunk of cheese, and wine.

Willow was no longer shivering with cold, but it was not the fire alone that warmed her. The heat of Blaine's eyes each time they settled on her seemed to melt her very soul.

What magic is this? she wondered as she sipped from the flask of wine and then handed it back to him, watching him all the while from beneath her lashes. A quiet mood had descended upon them both.

"Don't you think it time you told me, Willow?" His deep, steady voice brought a fluttering into her heart.

She didn't pretend not to understand. "Told you . . . the reason behind my quest for the necklace?"

He nodded. "Or do you hesitate because your cause has less merit than mine?" Despite this challenge, there was an oddly gentle smile upon his lips. That smile, boyish and frank and almost sweet, took her completely by surprise. If she'd been standing, it would have knocked her right off her feet.

"On the contrary, it has far more merit." Willow was finding it difficult to speak evenly with her heart pounding like an anvil. She continued with effort. "You will agree when you hear."

Blaine studied her, searching those breathtaking blue eyes, which were deeper, more intense, and more expressive than any other eyes he'd ever seen. "More merit than the quest to wed a princess? Doubtful, my imp. But tell me, and we shall see."

Somehow the words spilled out of her, and to her surprise, he listened without comment as she told him about her father, Lisha the Enchantress, and Artemus's misbegotten sorcery. She told him of the dungeon in the decaying castle, of Lisha's decree that she would not release Artemus until he managed to secure for her the Necklace of Nyssa.

"And he allowed you to set out on this quest to save him? He sent you alone into the

Perilous Forest?" Blaine demanded, clearly furious. "What kind of a man would —"

"He couldn't stop me." There was blue fire in Willow's eyes. She pushed away the crust of bread left on the table before her. "He begged me to bring along a male protector, but I refused. I travel lightly and more quickly on my own. Besides," she added before Blaine could comment on her penchant for landing in trouble, "he did help me in another way. A way that's going to be invaluable once I reach the Troll's Lair. He sent me the dream."

Blaine choked on his last bite of cheese, grabbed the wine flask, and washed the errant crumb down with a long, noisy gulp. Then he went perfectly still. "What's this you say . . . about a dream?"

"My father. He's a Dream Sorcerer. He can dream the future — also the past and the present. He can send his dreams out to others to guide them, or to warn them, or to steer them on a better course. He sent me a dream about this forest, and about the bluebird I was following this very afternoon. He showed me the Troll's Lair and where I will find the necklace once I am inside —" She faltered at his thunderstruck expression. "Blaine, what is it?"

"*I* had the same dream, Willow." His powerful shoulders hunched as he leaned forward across the table. "That's why I'm here, in this forest. That's what gave me the idea for my quest to get the necklace for Princess Maighdin in the first place. On the night of the full moon, I had a vivid and very specific dream — about the Troll's Lair, about the Necklace of Nyssa. I think it was the same dream as yours."

Willow paled. The night of the full moon. That was when Artemus had sent the dream to her. She pushed herself off the stool and began to pace around the cottage, her cloak billowing about her, the firelight burnishing her hair until it rivaled the brilliance of the flames.

Suddenly she whirled toward Blaine. "You don't by any chance know a knight named Sir Dudley, do you?"

Blaine stretched out his long legs. "I know him well. Dull, solid type. Been a soldier all his life. Decent fighter," he added fairly, "but not too bright. Matter of fact, the other night I stole his precious cloak as a jest, and he never even —"

He halted in mid-speech, his eyes narrowing.

"You stole Sir Dudley's cloak?" Willow began to pace again, raking her hands through her hair. She spun back toward

Blaine abruptly. "Did you by chance fall *asleep* with it wrapped around you?"

He didn't even have to nod. She saw the glint in those hard black eyes, and she nearly shrieked in frustration. "Sometimes Artemus needs to fix his mind on some feature of the person to whom he's sending the dream — or on something the person wears, perhaps a ring, or a medallion — or a cloak," she explained, grimacing. "He must have sent you the dream by mistake! It was supposed to go to Sir Dudley. Artemus must have wanted to direct him into the forest and to the Troll's Lair, no doubt to protect me."

Blaine came off the stool and stalked toward the fire, his face set. "That isn't *my* fault," he muttered. "I got the dream — and the idea for what to do with that necklace — and I'm entitled to it, same as you. And don't think I'm going to let you have it, Willow. Sounds to me like your father is getting exactly what he deserves. Maybe he needs to spend twenty years in that dungeon and begin thinking about getting his spells right for a change."

Willow's eyes flashed. "I won't ever let that happen."

"You shouldn't be here — in danger — in the first place."

"He's my father. I can't abandon him. Or

let him down." She shook her head, sending her curls flying around her cheeks. "Isn't there anyone, anyone in this world, that you care about, Blaine?" she asked wonderingly.

The wind howled at the door, the firelight danced and set the tiny cottage aglow with flickering amber light, but all she could see was the face carved in stone of this lean, dark man who had kissed her today with such force and such fire. Could a cold heart hold such passion, she wondered, or stir such heat as had sparked between their two souls?

"I don't understand you," she said softly. Her eyes mirrored the bafflement inside her. "Don't you understand at *all* what it is to love?"

"No." The word came quickly, harsh and certain, torn from the depths of him. His eyes glittered, frightening her with their sudden iciness, for they were as cold as the night beyond the cottage walls. "*My* father was a duke, a hated one as I recall. When I was a boy, he was murdered by his enemies, one or a dozen, who knows — they were too numerous to count. Among them," he added, gripping her shoulders, his jaw taut, "were his natural sons, my half brothers. I was only the little bastard, of no consequence to anyone."

Willow's throat went dry, aching for him, for the boy he had once been. "Surely your mother . . ." she whispered.

"Dead within minutes of my birth. I had a twin, you see, a brother, but he left this world with her, never having drawn a living breath."

"Blaine . . ."

"Don't pity me, imp." Never had he sounded so indifferent. A hard smile touched his lips. "I decided long ago that it was my fate to travel this world alone. To make my own way, look after my own skin. And I survived. *Alone*. Not only that, I grew strong. I learned that I don't need — don't want — anyone. You should do the same, Willow," he said suddenly, giving her a shake. "You'd be much better off."

Her gaze was soft and searching upon his. "I don't wish to go through this life alone. Without family, without anyone to love." She reached up suddenly, touched his jaw, shadowed now with a day's growth of beard, as his heart, she suspected, was shadowed with loneliness. "Nor, I think, do you, Blaine of Kendrick," she murmured softly.

Blaine's hands dropped from her shoulder. He took a step back. "You're wrong."

"Am I?"

He frowned and turned away, suddenly uncomfortable beneath that warm, steady gaze. "Believe what you want." He stalked nearer the fire, warming his hands. "But you'll have to beat me to get the necklace, Willow," he said in an offhand tone. "And as you remember, no one ever beats me."

"We'll see." Quiet determination flowed through her voice. "But I believe this is one battle you will lose."

His eyes narrowed, and he spun back to study her again, filled with anger, frustration, and reluctant admiration toward this slender, intractable beauty with her dusting of freckles and her mouth softer than flower petals. What was it about her that fascinated him so?

Everything. Everything from the graceful way she carried herself, to the determination that blazed in her soul, to the devotion to her father that would set her on a path of danger in a bid to save him.

That the Wolf of Kendrick would find her so noble, so enchanting, was ironic, Blaine reflected tersely, considering that he himself had never known devotion from or toward anyone.

He'd always stood alone.

He advanced toward her, his gut clenching when instead of retreating before him, she held her ground.

"Then let the battle be joined, my imp." He spoke with resignation. "Tomorrow, at dawn." His voice lowered, roughened. "But for now the hour is late. For tonight and tonight only, I propose a truce."

Before she could respond, Blaine caught her in his arms and drew her close. "Do you consent?" His breath ruffled her hair. "A truce until the morn?"

Willow wavered. She ought to pull free, stalk away, warn him to keep his distance until dawn, when the quest could begin again — for each of them. But she yearned to stay right here where she was. How warm and safe and snug she felt in his arms, as if she belonged there for all time.

How could that be? He was a man who cared for no one, nothing, only his own interests. And he was her enemy.

Surely it was wrong to want to kiss your enemy . . .

"I agree to . . . a limited truce. Tonight only," she conceded, keeping her tone steady with an effort. Without being able to stop herself, she reached up and touched the soft thickness of his hair. Being close to him always seemed to have an unsettling effect on her, and just now, in the firelit cottage with the wind and snow pummeling the forest beyond these four walls, and with his eyes so alight and keen, looking at her as no man had ever looked at her before, that effect was even more pronounced. A powerful current surged between them. Thinking clearly was a challenge, and pulling away seemed out of the question.

"Tonight only," he agreed, and with wonder she realized that his voice was no steadier than hers. His strong warrior's hand cupped her chin, gently but firmly, sending tingling sensations all the way down to her toes. He tilted her head up so that she could not have looked away from his penetrating eyes even if she'd wanted to. "As long as we're negotiating, there is something else to decide. Another kiss."

"You said just one. And then you took two," she murmured breathlessly.

"Indeed. Because I found it quite enjoyable. Did you?"

"It was . . . somewhat enjoyable." Willow swallowed, feeling herself drawn against her will into a kind of mesmerizing spell that she was powerless to break. "Perhaps not . . . as enjoyable as . . . climbing a tree, but —"

"Ahhh. You wound me." A wicked smile lit his face. "I suggest we try it again and see if we can improve."

"Improve?" Truth be told, Willow

couldn't imagine anything more wonderful than the kisses she'd shared with him, but as he leaned slowly down toward her and she realized he was going to kiss her again, she felt panic. And a hot jolt of desire. Blaine ignited feelings in her that no one else — even Adrian — ever had, and she didn't know what to make of that. She wasn't sure she liked it and . . .

He's going to kiss me again, she realized and made one quick, futile effort to pull away, but he slid those iron arms around her and held her even more closely and kissed her before she could squeak a protest.

And kissed her . . . and kissed her . . .

Before, she had been cold, but now she was hot. The snow and ice and wind might not have been raging outside the tiny cottage at all; the small, rough chamber might have been carved of gold; the very night might have been blazing day, for all she knew of anything but the power of his kiss, the need that rushed through her, the pleasure that ran from the top of her hairline to the underside of her dainty little toes. Sweet, hot, dizzying pleasure.

Her arms flew around his neck, and she found she was kissing him back. Ardent, hungry kisses that burned from her soul to his.

Somehow, as the fire flickered and the blue-orange flames cast their shimmering light across Blaine's strong-boned face, she found herself being swept up into his arms and cradled against his chest. It was not the first time this had happened, but it was the most delightful, for this time his lips never left hers as he carried her across the room to the pallet against the wall.

He had spread his cloak upon it earlier when the fire began to blaze, and now he lowered Willow to it as gently as a fresh spring leaf.

"Is this still not as enjoyable as climbing a tree, Willow?" he asked as he leaned across her, lifting his mouth from hers only long enough to gaze down into her eyes.

"I . . . shall try to decide." She gasped and pulled him down to her, her mouth seeking his with a boldness she'd never known she possessed. Her very blood seemed to be on fire as he stroked her hair and her throat with tender caresses, and pressed gentle kisses upon her cheeks and eyelids.

Despite Blaine's strength and his powerful body, she wasn't at all frightened by his hungry touches. She was lost in a world of vivid sensations, of sweeping pleasure, as a hot, demanding need began to throb deep inside her feminine core.

"Blaine, this might prove . . . even more enjoyable than . . . jousting against King Felix's . . . men-at-arms," she whispered with a small laugh, and he laughed along with her.

"It will be far more enjoyable, imp. You will joust with me — in a battle unlike any you have ever waged before."

A delicious battle. Her fingers twisted through his hair even as her lips parted to admit his tongue, which challenged and swept against hers, drawing her into a dark, dusky game of sensuous war.

When his hand found her breast, she gasped with pleasure; when he stripped the woolen layers of her cloak and her tunic from her and kissed her bare shoulder just above the bandage he had put in place, she pulled him down to her and began to tug at his garments with a wild insistence.

A tremor shook her. He was splendid — bronzed, magnificent. She wanted him, all of him, this man with his searing kisses and gentle touch, this man who professed to care for no one but who had saved her life and found her shelter and carried her to this bed with such tenderness. She wanted him with a desperate hunger that came straight from her heart, with a sureness that came not from reason or logic but from a magical knowing place inside her soul.

245

"Blaine . . . Blaine," she said softly, cherishing the sound of his name upon her lips. She moaned when his tongue found her breast, teasing her sensitive, swelling nipple. As his hands stroked her hips and her belly, slowly, lingeringly, igniting torturous tingles everywhere he touched, she writhed with a fire that would not be denied.

The world spun away. The forest, the cottage, the snow, and wind. There was only the fire — their own raging fire as, naked and twisting together upon the pallet, they touched and kissed and discovered each other. There was no yesterday, no tomorrow, only tonight and this fever that gripped them.

Blaine made love to her, filling her with himself, with his strength and his power. She was so beautiful and seemed so fragile he was fearful of hurting her, but there was no hint of pain between them, only a desire that ran quick and hard and deep within them both.

Her hair smelled like flowers, Blaine thought in wonder as he thrust inside her with long, deep strokes that made her gasp with pleasure. Like sweet summer flowers. Her desperate writhing and those long, slim legs wrapped around him rocked him like thunder.

"Willow. Ah, Willow." He could barely speak, for he was hoarse with the wanting and the taking of her. Despite her delicacy, her passion was as fiery and all-consuming as his own.

Blaine groaned and pressed harder, drove deeper, raining kisses on her as he took them both to the edge of the world.

Locked with him, their bodies melding, clinging, fitting as though made for one another, Willow knew only that he obliterated everything else, air, color, light. There was only Blaine — his muscles taut and sheened with sweat, his eyes darkened with a desire that filled her with joy. He smelled of earth and spice and musk, tasted of wine and sizzling fire, filled her with wonder and an exquisite tension exploding at her very core.

Swept into a storm of their own making, they gave themselves up to roaring kisses and a passion that whirled beyond reason and doubt. Their lovemaking was as beautiful and pure and wild as the night that raged beyond the cottage, and as they clung together they rode the high, wild crest, shuddering in the joy and the pleasure. Release came with a dizzying fulfillment. Their bodies sweetly tangled, they shattered and became one, holding one another with every ounce of their strength, knowing for that fleeting eternity the splendor of radiant joy.

Then, spent and dazed, they curled in each other's arms — and at last slept.

It was hours later when the dream came to her.

At first it was all the same, exactly the same as before, except for one thing. This time as Willow saw the dim great hall of the Troll's Lair, and the looming staircase that dominated it, she noticed something she hadn't seen earlier. A doorway in the wall at the middle of the stairway — an invisible doorway that creaked open and in a shimmering burst of light revealed the chamber where the treasure was stored.

She awoke with a start.

Artemus!

He must have suddenly remembered the door from his long-ago journey into the Troll's Lair. He'd sent it to her to further guide her search for the necklace.

Her heart pounded as she realized something else. Blaine had not shared in this dream. Lying on the pallet in his arms, her head cushioned against his chest, she knew that the dream had been hers alone. Either her father had sent it only to her, or, if he had expanded the energy to direct it also to Sir Dudley, it would this time have reached the real Sir Dudley in his fine gold cloak.

Not Blaine.

So he didn't know about the hidden door. And she now had an advantage — a strong one — in the contest ahead.

Pondering this, she raised herself up and gazed into her sleeping rival's handsome face. The emotion that rose in her filled her with wonder. For years she'd thought she loved Adrian, and Adrian alone, that there was no other man in the world for her. Now she knew that what she'd felt for Adrian had been a pale illusion, as different from love as sea mist is from hard, driving waves.

Blaine of Kendrick was real and solid. He had saved her life, made her laugh, and taught her the power of a single kiss. He infuriated her and fascinated her. She felt a strange tenderness for this man who claimed to need no one.

What was happening to her? She must not fall under his spell. She must keep her mind and heart focused on the prize.

Yet, as he slept, she couldn't help herself. She reached out to gently touch that rough, stubbled jaw. At once his eyes opened.

They warmed as he saw her, and, grinning, he reached out to clench her velvet curls in his fist. "Ah, my beautiful imp."

His deep voice wasn't the least bit groggy. "Ready for another round of jousting?"

Before Willow could say a word, he pulled her down atop him, and it all began again.

7

When daylight came, Willow and Blaine rode out from the cottage into the brisk, frozen beauty of a clear, blue-skied day. Willow had abandoned her boy's disguise and her torn tunic and had donned the plain blue wool gown in her pack. She'd chosen to let her hair ripple freely down her back and had noticed Blaine's gaze lingering on her while they partook of a spartan breakfast before setting forth. Before they left the table, he'd surprised her by offering a proposition: that they travel together and extend their truce until they reached the Troll's Lair.

Willow had searched his face long and hard before nodding agreement. She was in no hurry to be at odds with him once again. Yet she knew with a heavy heart that it was only a matter of time. The closer they came to the Necklace of Nyssa, the more apart they must grow from each other, for they had separate goals and equal determination, and neither was willing to accept defeat.

For hours they rode, their horses' hooves crunching on the hardened snow. Memories of the dream returned to each of them as they passed marks and signs they had seen before. They compared what they remembered of the path that had been shown to them, and each wondered in silence what destiny this day would hold.

"Did you dream last night?" Willow asked at one point when they halted to rest and to eat.

"Only of you," Blaine replied, smiling, helping her down from the pony. His hands lingered at her waist. "And you?"

Willow did not answer, except to pull his head down and kiss him until they both forgot all about the question.

It was nearly dusk, and they were weary when the ground began to change. The horses' hooves sank in a boggy marsh, and they knew they were drawing close to the Troll's Lair. As the sun dropped and lavender shadows hugged the sky, they at last came to an opening in the wood and there, before a wall of jagged cliffs, towered a bloodred stone fortress that loomed like a dark, terrifying monster against the sky.

It was a good thing the Troll King was dead, Willow thought as Moonbeam reared and she struggled to get her under control. Bad enough that his evil spirit inhabited the place — she would not have liked to have to fight the Troll himself.

But she would have done it if she needed to. Now she had only to fight the dangers of the fortress — and Blaine.

"Moonbeam, hold steady," she urged as the mare tried to balk at the muddy path. All about was ooze and slime, with dead trees stranded in the midst of shifting gray bog. "Do as I say. Forward!"

To Willow's vexation, Blaine's destrier showed more mettle. Though she could see the whites of his eyes as he sensed something dismal and dangerous in this place, he did not balk or rear, but continued stolidly. Blaine pulled ahead of her.

"Wait," she called to him, spurring the mare forward, but Blaine was staring intently ahead and did not slow his pace or glance back at her.

She gritted her teeth and drove the mare on. *So, the truce is ended,* she thought bleakly. *He will give no more thought to me. He seeks only to enter the fortress first.*

Don't look back. Blaine gave himself a rigid order. The mantle of preparedness for battle settled over him like a shield. This brief interval with the sorcerer's daughter had been entertaining, he conceded, but it was time now to bring it to an end. He had set his sights on a prize hidden within those seemingly impregnable stone walls and he was going to see his mission through. Willow was resourceful and bright, he told himself as he narrowed his gaze on the forbidding fortress before him. She would find another way to free Artemus the dreamer.

As his black destrier moved stalwartly forward, Blaine could have sworn he felt the ground beneath him start to quake.

He left the destrier in what had once been the keep's yard, now a marshy open space choked with weeds, and spared one quick glance over his shoulder as he strode toward the door.

Willow rode doggedly on, despite her mare's skittishness. In the fading light, her lovely face was set and grim — and sad.

Something tore at his heart. He hardened it deliberately.

This is for the princess, he told himself. *For the prize. Don't let anything turn you aside now.*

Swiftly he entered the keep and stared at what had once been the Great Hall. Now it was naught but a towering ruin.

By the time Willow tethered Moonbeam

within the decaying courtyard and hurried through the great doors, her cloak whipping in the breeze, the sun was nearly set and a strange amethyst darkness shrouded the yard.

She entered the keep and found no sign of Blaine. But oddly, torches and candles glowed within the cavernous Great Hall, casting long, wavering beacons of light around the dank stone walls.

She turned slowly, her throat dry. There was something evil and horrible in this place. The spirit of the Troll King inhabited the very air of the fortress, every bit as much of a presence as the long-tailed rats that scurried through the corners.

She wanted to call out for Blaine, but bit back his name.

She was on her own now. As was he.

Remember the dream, she told herself as she moved cautiously toward the stairway. It looked the same as it had in the dream. As she set a foot upon the first step, she listened to the deep silence of the once beautiful castle. *Where was Blaine?*

It didn't matter. Only the Necklace of Nyssa mattered now.

Halfway up the stairs, she paused and studied the wall to her right, where the dream had shown her a door. Now, in the flickering torchlight that so eerily lit this place, she saw only the old red stone, rough and unbroken. There was no sign of a door.

She closed her eyes and recalled the dream once more. In her memory, she counted the number of steps before the door appeared.

Eleven.

She returned to the bottom and retraced her steps, this time counting.

Here. Willow placed a hand upon the wall. She felt a warmth beneath her palm. Studying the stone, she saw, waist high, a faint circle that began to glow. She pressed on it and the door swung open.

The long chamber inside was exactly like the one in her dream. She stepped into it, and the door closed behind her. But she was not in darkness, for here, too, candles flickered from sconces high above, throwing light wildly through the chamber. They illuminated the draperies of rich scarlet and gold, the marble floor, the huge gilt furnishings.

This had been the chamber of the Troll Queen. And there, on a raised dais at the far wall, sat the box inlaid with gold and silver, its lid adorned with rubies in the shape of a troll.

Willow approached cautiously and touched

the box with trembling fingers, scarcely daring to breathe. When she lifted the lid, she saw the necklace at once.

Ten shimmering crystal stones on a strand of glittering gold. Within the heart of each crystal glowed a perfect ruby.

The Necklace of Nyssa. She touched it, a shiver racing through her. When she lifted it, she was startled by its cool, airy lightness.

But even as she took it out of the box she felt a strange quivering beneath her feet. The entire fortress began to shake. Terror swept through her as the floor swayed beneath her and the very walls trembled. It lasted only a moment, and then all was still, but it was enough. Her heart pounding, Willow clenched the necklace tight within her fist and dashed toward the door.

She pressed the glowing circle, and the door swung in toward her. With a cry of thankfulness she rushed out — but charged straight into a wall of iron.

Blaine of Kendrick blocked the door.

For one heart-stopping moment their gazes met and held.

"Let me pass," Willow said breathlessly.

"Not so quickly." His face was grim, his voice hard. This was a different Blaine from the man who had made love to her in a firelit cottage all through the night. This was the

Wolf of Kendrick, a single-minded warrior, intent on his own personal victory at any cost.

His gaze narrowed upon the necklace clutched in her fingers. He reached for it, but Willow thrust her hands behind her back.

"I found it first! You cannot take it from me, Blaine."

"It is not the one to find it first, but the one to possess it last that marks the winner of this contest." His tone was low and heavy.

"Blaine, please . . ."

The desperation in her voice as well as the distress in her pale face struck him like a dagger straight through the heart. In his mind, the small boy who'd had to fight to live circled and screamed. *Take it. Take it.*

Blaine swallowed, torn by the image, by the too vivid memories of hunger, thirst, exhaustion, of never knowing whom to trust, of never being able to count on anyone but himself.

"Don't make me do this, Willow." He advanced toward her until she was backed into the chamber once more, all the way against the wall, her hands still behind her, still clutching the necklace.

Her face was lifted to his, proud, defiant, as lovely as a star. How he wanted to bury his fingers in that rich cloud of glorious hair . . .

"Willow —"

"You'll have to take it from me if you want it. Go ahead, Blaine, take it."

Take it, take it.

He swore and lunged out in anger, then froze as she flinched, her eyes bright with fear.

Fear. Of him.

Agonizing shame flooded him, and remorse. Remorse so heavy it was like a vise around his soul. Slowly he brought his hand up, and it came to rest gently upon the softness of her cheek.

"Do you think I would ever hurt you, Willow? For anything?"

She stared wonderingly into his eyes, unable to believe what she was hearing.

Blaine's chest was so heavy that the words came with difficulty. "Come, let us leave this accursed place."

"Do you promise — you will not take it from me by force, or trickery, or —"

She saw the flash of pain cross his face then, the grief in those unfathomable dark eyes. Willow sucked in her breath. She had hurt him, wounded him someplace deep inside.

"You have my word," he said in a harsh tone.

"Blaine, I didn't mean — I just wanted to be certain —"

"Don't apologize. You're right not to trust me. But let me say it plainly: the necklace is yours, my lady. I will even accompany you back to that dungeon to see that Lisha keeps her word and releases your father."

She shook her head, dazed. "But what about Princess Maighdin? Won't you need . . . to find another prize?"

"I can always find another prize." His mouth was grim. "I know of one even now, one worth infinitely more than this bauble. But for the first time in my life," he said slowly, "I don't know if I can attain it."

As another tremor rocked the marble floor beneath them, Blaine glanced sharply around, then caught Willow in his arms. "Now, will you come with me, before —"

A huge rumble vibrated throughout the fortress, a roar like thunder. Even as he held Willow close as if to shield her with his body, the floor began to sway even more violently, and this time it didn't stop.

"Blaine, it's giving way! The fortress — it's buckling!"

He was already pulling her toward the door. They staggered together as they reached the stairway and the floor rolled yet again. From high above, a chandelier full of candles crashed down, rumbling through the Great Hall below. The dank stone walls and ceiling began to crack.

"Run!" Blaine clamped his arm around her waist as together they raced down the swaying stairs.

Even as they reached the Great Hall, one wall collapsed with a crash. Bats began to swoop, rousted from the rafters by the commotion. Suddenly Willow smelled smoke, and a moment later they saw flames spiraling through the solar.

Fear tore at Willow as they ran for the doors. She clutched the necklace in one hand and Blaine's powerful fingers in the other as she nearly matched his giant strides with her own swiftly desperate ones.

They bolted out of the fortress as if pursued by a demon, which in a sense they were, as the Troll King exacted his vengeance by destroying the very lair that his spirit had haunted for centuries. The horses were rearing and neighing, but the destrier quieted when Blaine hoisted Willow into the saddle and then vaulted up behind her.

"Moonbeam!" Willow cried. An instant later Blaine had the mare untethered and was dragging the terrified creature by the reins as he spurred the destrier back through the bog.

261

Ensconced safely in front of Blaine in the saddle, his hard warrior's body pressed against her, Willow glanced around to see the towers of the fortress collapsing inward, and great arcs of black smoke and orange flames shooting toward the sky.

Then they were galloping through the bog, racing away from the doomed fortress, and Willow no longer looked back.

She leaned against Blaine, content to let him guide the destrier and the mare as she slipped the precious necklace deep into the pocket of her cloak. And she looked ahead, beyond the return journey through the Perilous Forest — wondering now what the future would hold.

8

"Look at her," Artemus whispered, as he poured Lisha a goblet of wine in the kitchen of his cozy cottage. From her seat upon the bench near the hearth fire, the enchantress glanced at the girl curled in a velvet-cushioned chair near the window of the darkened room. Only the firelight glowing from the hearth illuminated her pale face as she gazed out at the wintry darkness.

"That's all she does every night, and most days, too. Stares out the window. Watching for *him*," Artemus spat angrily. "I swore to her I wouldn't interfere, but by all that is holy, Lisha, I'm going to send that scoundrel a nightmare he'll never forget."

"You will do no such thing." Lisha accepted the goblet he handed her and took a sip, then smiled up at him.

"Sit down, darling. Pay attention to me. Willow's troubles will soon sort themselves out, you'll see."

He allowed her to pull him down onto the bench beside her and moodily took a sip of his own wine. "Is this your enchantress's intuition, or have you seen something in that looking glass of yours?"

"I've seen something," she purred, and smiled as his face lit up.

"Blaine of Kendrick? He's going to die some horrible death? Get eaten by a dragon, or torn to bits by a boar, or —"

"No, don't be silly. That would not make Willow happy."

"It would make *me* happy," he grumbled.

Lisha sighed. "If I'd known you would work yourself into such a tizzy over all this, I'd have never begun this chain of events in the first place." She placed their wine goblets on a small silver-edged side table and took both of Artemus's hands in hers.

"Do you forgive me?"

"I married you, didn't I?" He kissed the tip of her turned-up nose. Lisha smiled and snuggled closer.

Much had happened since the day that the sorcerer's daughter and the Wolf of Kendrick had stolen the Necklace of Nyssa from the Troll's Lair. Lisha, seeing that event in her looking glass, had realized that she was going to have to release Artemus from the dungeon one way or another, and she had immediately whisked herself down to confront him.

In the course of the discussion, much had been cleared up between the two of them. Artemus had told her most sincerely that he had *meant* to call upon her after the Melwas Ball, that he had *wanted* to call upon her, but he'd been afraid she had kissed him the way she had at the ball only because she had drunk too much of the powerful wine that they'd both enjoyed that evening. He'd thought she would laugh if he, a simple sorcerer with limited powers and only a small degree of fame and fortune, came to call upon so great a beauty and so powerful a woman as Lisha the Enchantress.

He confessed that he had not so much as taken a moonlit stroll or even an innocent summer picnic with any woman since the death of Willow's mother some ten years earlier, and he was, well, er, *shy*, he'd finally admitted — at least he was when he wasn't under the influence of strong spirits.

Lisha had seen the truth in his face, and she'd been ashamed of her hotheadedness. She'd always had a regrettable temper. When he hadn't called upon her in the weeks after their wonderful dance and that heavenly kiss in the garden, she'd thought he was as capricious and unreliable as all the other men in her life — and that hurt, because she'd thought, and hoped, that Artemus possessed a glimmer of something special.

So in an attempt to make him jealous, she'd taken a young lover and made no secret of it, but he'd gone and turned the poor boy into a toad, and then there had been that unfortunate business with the hawk.

Well, she'd overreacted. She'd admitted it to him in the dungeon that day as Willow and Blaine galloped headlong away from the Troll's Lair, making their way back through the Perilous Forest.

She'd apologized. And set him free.

Artemus had insisted that she blink them both to the White Hog Inn on the outskirts of the forest by the time Willow and Blaine arrived there, so that he could tell his daughter as quickly as possible that he was free.

Lisha had agreed. They'd reached the yard of the inn just as Willow and Blaine rode up. In all the confusion and greetings and exclamations of relief, amid Willow's happy tears that Artemus was safe and his joyous gratitude that she had surivived her dangerous quest and returned to him, amid Willow's laughing and offering Lisha the necklace, and Lisha refusing it because the necklace wasn't what she had really wanted after all — somehow, no one noticed Blaine of Kendrick slipping away, until he and his great black destrier were just *gone*.

Artemus had seen the hurt and desolation on Willow's face when the Wolf was nowhere to be found, and so had Lisha. They had exchanged guilty looks, knowing that their own mistakes had had a far-reaching effect on the girl who had risked her life over their foolishness.

That was weeks ago, and there'd been no word from the Wolf of Kendrick since. During that time, Artemus and Lisha had been quietly married and feted at the court of King Felix and had set up housekeeping at the sorcerer's cottage.

But though Willow had smiled over their happiness, danced at their wedding with several eager young knights and most attentive noblemen, they'd both seen the sadness that lay deep in her heart, a sadness that grew more apparent every day.

Then today a messenger had charged through the village, spreading word of the marriage of Princess Maighdin and a dashing young knight who had bested all others and won her hand.

Unfortunately no one seemed to have caught the name of the knight who had accomplished this feat.

The whole village was abuzz, but Willow spoke not a word.

She merely opened the chest where she kept the Necklace of Nyssa, gazed at it a moment, and then closed the chest very softly.

She'd curled up in the velvet-cushioned chair as soon as supper was over and the dishes washed, and she'd been staring out at the empty winter night ever since.

"I cannot bear to see her so unhappy." Artemus sank back against the cushioned bench and let Lisha stroke his cheek. "Even when young Adrian went away to battle and then was lost to us, she wasn't like this."

"I know, darling, but —"

"She will get over him, won't she, Lisha? You're a woman. Surely you know about such things."

"I never would have gotten over you," the Enchantress said softly. Then she gave him a smile. "Come, let us retire. All will look brighter in the morning."

"Of course it will. The sun will be up then. Truly, Lisha, what has that to say to anything . . ."

His voice trailed off as he allowed himself to be led to the chamber that he and Lisha shared.

Willow never even heard them call out

good night. All her attention was focused on the trees lining the path outside the cottage because she thought she saw some movement there.

Yes. Something . . . or someone . . . was out there.

She froze in her chair as she saw the horse and rider coming up the cottage lane. A sliver of moonlight illuminated a familiar figure, tall and muscular. As he rode closer she could at last make out his face — a strong, hawklike face, unsmiling, his dark gaze fixed intently on the cottage.

Her heart leapt into her throat, and for a moment she was certain she wouldn't be able to move from the chair. But suddenly she was flying toward the door, and she threw it open just as he raised his fist to knock.

For a moment neither of them spoke. They simply stared into each other's eyes. Willow could have sworn that somehow he had grown even more darkly, impossibly handsome since the last time she had seen him.

Since the day he had vanished without a single word to her.

"What brings you here at this hour, sir?" she asked with all the coolness she could muster. "It is a late hour to be calling."

He smiled, and her heart flipped over. "You know full well what brings me here, Willow." He pushed his way inside and drew her after him.

"Why are you sitting in the dark?" he demanded.

"Why do you feel you have the right to simply walk into my home and ask me . . . *oh!*"

It was a long kiss and a hungry one. "*That* is why," the Wolf of Kendrick said in a tender tone.

"Oh." Still warm and dizzy from the kiss, Willow tried to understand. "But . . . the princess . . ."

"Is wed. To Rolf of Cornhull."

For a moment she was overcome by dazzling relief, and then came the realization that brought her low. "I see. You have lost . . . because you didn't have the necklace." Her lower lip trembled. "I'm sorry. I would have given it to you. You may have it still, if you wish. I have no need for it."

"Nor do I. I have no desire to give it to Princess Maighdin or to anyone else. As a matter of fact, I removed myself from this particular competition — stood back and watched them all make jackasses out of themselves. If I hadn't been so preoccupied, I might have enjoyed the spectacle." He gazed at her intently. "But I found I wasn't nearly as interested in the contest — or in the prize — as I'd thought I was."

His arms tightened around her, making it difficult to think clearly. He smelled of leather and horses and spice. He looked more weary and yet more handsome than any man she'd ever seen — and infinitely more dear. For the life of her, she realized with a small shock, she couldn't remember a single feature of Adrian's face.

"You . . . weren't interested?" she asked dazedly. "*Why?*"

"I've had other things on my mind. Other things to attend to."

"Oh. I see."

But she didn't see. She didn't see why he was here, why he had kissed her in that way that made her head spin and her toes tingle, why he was looking at her as if he was memorizing her face to last him forever. Unless he was going away and he had come to say good-bye.

"You didn't even say good-bye."

He smiled and touched her hair, drawing his fingers gently through the length of her curls. "You mean back at the White Hog Inn? That's because it wasn't good-bye."

"You're not making sense."

"I didn't actually leave you, Willow. I just

. . . went to attend to some business. And now I am ready to embark on a new quest."

Her heart stopped. "What has that to do with me?" she asked quietly and shifted out of his arms. A thread of disappointment ran through her as he allowed her to move away. She lit some candles on the small table near the chair, fidgeted with a tasseled pillow on the low plum sofa, and turned back to him, her hands trembling a little as she smoothed her skirt.

"This is only the second time I've seen you in a gown." There was a glint of appreciation in Blaine's eyes as he surveyed her pale lemon gown with the green embroidered flowers upon the sleeves. "You are almost as lovely as when you wore nothing at all."

"Shhh!" She blushed and threw a quick glance toward the room where Artemus and Lisha had retired.

"I think it is time you ended this mystery and told me your business. Then you may continue along your way."

He advanced on her, smiling. Those black eyes suddenly held a gleam of amusement — and perhaps, she saw in surprise, a trace of nervousness. "I agree, my beautiful imp."

"I am not —"

"Will you be?"

"I beg your pardon?"

272

Blaine of Kendrick swallowed hard. "Will you be my beautiful imp? Mine. My woman, my bride, my wife." Suddenly, to Willow's astonishment, he dropped to one knee and took her hand in his, cradling it as if it were made of glass.

"I love you, Willow of Brinhaven. Will you consent to wed me and come to live with me? Before you answer, let me tell you," he rushed on urgently, "that I have been granted a fine parcel of land by King Felix for services rendered to him some time ago, in the War of Two Winters." He continued quickly, as if afraid she would refuse him before he could finish his plea. "I never had use for it before, but it happens to lie not more than half a day's ride from here, and there is a fine manor house, and you would have servants, as befits the wife of Sir Blaine of Kendrick, and —"

"I don't care about the land — or the manor house," Willow whispered. She tugged him up to her, her eyes shining with joy. "Sir Blaine of Kendrick, I love you, too. I would live with you in that tiny little cottage in the Perilous Forest if you asked me. I would live with you in a tree."

"That won't be necessary," he assured her, and kissed her again.

A long time later, when both of them

could speak once more, and think somewhat clearly, they sat side by side on the bench before the hearth fire and spoke of all that was in their hearts.

They made their plans for a future — together.

"I feel as if I'm dreaming," Willow murmured wonderingly, her head against Blaine's shoulder. "I thought I'd lost you forever, and now . . ."

"If you are dreaming, I share the same dream." He turned her so that she faced him, and he cupped her face between his hands.

"This is not your father's handiwork again, is it?" He grinned.

"No — he is none too pleased with you, I fear."

"I will win him over," he said with a confident laugh, sounding once again like the bold and brash soldier she had first seen in the taproom of the White Hog Inn. "I won you, didn't I, and your love, and that is the only prize worth having. The only contest worth winning," he whispered against her mouth, and this time when he slanted his lips to hers, it was the tenderest kiss of all.

"I haven't a doubt, Willow, that for the rest of our lives, you and I are going to share the same dreams."

"A home," she whispered, her heart in her eyes, "and children."

"Many children," he corrected, pulling her onto his lap.

"And much laughter — and much love," she added simply, lifting a hand to touch his face.

Blaine thought of his own loveless childhood, of the home he'd been tossed out of at an early age, of his lonely roaming and struggles and desperation. He gazed into the lovely face of the woman who was promising him all that he had ever wanted, all that he had never had.

"Much laughter, much love," he repeated, sounding almost dazed. "And I will do my best, sweet Willow, I swear on my life, to make all of your dreams come true."

And of course they did come true — beautifully true — every single one of them.

The Enchantment

Ruth Ryan Langan

For all who believe
And especially for Tom,
who always believed in me

1

"Afternoon, Annie." Melinda Mozey looked up from the waitress station of the Mozey Inn as Annie Tyler breezed in. "I've got that sandwich and coffee all ready for you."

"Thanks, Melinda." Annie reached into her purse and withdrew a couple of bills. While the older woman rang up the sale, she fumbled in her pocket for her pager and noted the number of the caller before looking up. "Something smells wonderful. What is it?"

"Bean soup. Howard's been simmering that ham bone all morning. Want to try some? It'll warm you up on this miserable day."

"Thanks, Melinda. No time." Annie gave her a quick smile, then picked up the carryout bag and started out the door, cell phone to her ear.

The older woman shook her head, then turned to her husband, who was wiping down the counter. "That girl just never slows down."

"Yep. Still running on New York time. But Doc Simmons said she's got her grandmother's debt nearly all paid down. She settled the hospital bill. Paid for all those round-the-clock aides. Promised Doc Simmons she'd have his final payment next month. The way she's working, she'll be free and clear in . . . oh, another year or so."

"If she lives that long." His wife glanced at the figure dashing across the street through a curtain of rain. "What a pretty little thing like Annie needs is a good man to show her how to have some fun in her life."

The object of their discussion turned up the collar of her trench coat as she raced along the main street of the little town of Tranquility, Maine. The calendar said April, but the rain and wind still had the bite of winter to them.

She pushed open the door of the small, freshly painted office and smiled at the young woman who was busy tearing off a fax.

"Hey, Annie." Shelly Kirkland, a young divorcée with two little girls, had eagerly offered to work part-time when Annie opened her real estate office in town. Because Shelly couldn't afford a baby-sitter, she was forced to bring her daughters with her after school. Annie had surprised them with a low wooden table and a variety of art supplies. Now the two girls, aged five and seven, played happily while their mother manned the telephone.

Annie fished two cookies from the carryout bag and raised an eyebrow at Shelly for permission. At her nod of approval, Annie offered them to the girls, who chirped their thanks before digging into the warm, gooey chocolate chips.

Shelly grinned. "Every time I see you with my daughters, I wonder why you don't have a couple of your own."

"Yeah. That's what I need in my life."

"But you're so good with them." Shelly put the fax on Annie's desk and efficiently changed the subject. "Here's the description of that little house just outside of town. The Drummonds are worried that they've set the price too high. Think you can estimate what it's worth?"

Annie nodded. "I'll drive out there tonight and take a look."

Hanging up her coat, she moved to her desk and nudged off her shoes, wiggling her toes.

"How'd the showings go?" Shelly watched as Annie tore the wrapping off a sandwich and opened the lid of her coffee while scanning her computer screen.

"Not so good." Annie sipped gratefully. It was her first break since dawn. She'd had to skip breakfast and lunch because of scheduled appointments. Now it looked as though she'd have to skip dinner, too. "I took the Featherbys through six different houses. Judging from Mrs. Featherby's reactions, which ranged from boredom to outright dislike, I'm pretty sure I won't see a sale."

"That's just like Margo Featherby. What a waste of four hours."

Annie shrugged. "It's all right. I've come to expect it in this business. But look on the bright side, Shelly. I've sold enough this month to justify the rent on this place and pay your salary."

"Yeah, but have you made enough to pay yourself?"

Annie gave a wry smile. "Not yet. But I'm getting there."

She scanned the fax, then turned to look out the window at the bleak rain that pelted the windows.

It had been a tough decision to make the move from New York to Maine. She'd loved the excitement of the city, and her job in one of the top commercial real estate firms had been challenging. She'd found herself dealing with representatives from some of the biggest names in the industry, all vying for multimillion-dollar buildings in the heart of Manhattan. But the move, no matter how wrenching, couldn't be helped. That was what family did when they were needed.

She sipped her coffee and idly reached for the phone on the second ring. "Tyler Real Estate."

"Anne Louise Tyler, please." The woman's voice on the other end of the line was clipped, with none of the distinctive New England inflection.

"This is Annie Tyler. How can I help you?"

"Ms. Tyler? I'm told you are related to Sara Brinkman Tyler."

"Sara was my mother." Distracted, Annie began rummaging through the pile of papers on her desk, searching for her pen.

"Splendid. Sara and I were girlhood friends in Bar Harbor. We attended the conservatory together many years ago. Perhaps you've heard of me? My name is Cordelia Sykes Carrington."

Annie sat up a little straighter. "Mrs. Carrington. Of course I know of you. My mother spoke of you often."

"She was a dear friend, but we lost track of one another when she moved away. I was sorry to hear of her passing all those years ago. She was far too young." There was a slight pause before she went on. "I've decided to sell my estate, White Pines. I was hoping you might drive up to evaluate what needs to be done before it can be shown to prospective clients."

"I'd . . . be happy to, Mrs. Carrington."

"Fine. I'll have a representative of my legal firm deliver a set of keys to your office before you close for the day."

"Keys? You won't be there?"

"No. I'm leaving today. I've been here for the past week with some of my staff, tagging antiques and mementos that I'd like shipped to my home in Palm Springs. I'd like you to pay particular attention to the grounds, Ms. Tyler. You'll need to hire a company to spruce things up."

"I'll . . . see to it."

"You'll need to hire a cleaning company, as well, to handle the grime that has accumulated and to dust the interior before you show the house."

"You . . . want me to show the house? You want me to handle the sale of White Pines?" Out of the corner of her eye Annie saw Shelly's head come up.

"That's why I'm phoning you, Ms. Tyler. Do you have a problem with that?"

"Of course not. But . . . I ought to warn you, Mrs. Carrington. Mine is a very small company."

"My law firm assured me that even small companies can reach the proper clients, via the Internet and magazines geared exclusively to the sale of multimillion-dollar estates. Isn't that so?"

"Yes, it's true. I just thought you ought to know that I don't have the amenities of some of the larger firms, with legal departments and high-powered sales representatives."

"I have my own legal firm, Ms. Tyler. My son's firm. And there's no need for any high-powered tactics to sell White Pines. It will sell itself. I don't want just anyone handling this, you understand. It's been a painful decision to dispose of something that's been in our family for so many years. But it can't be helped." There was another pause. "I hope you can see to this promptly."

"I can drive up after work and spend the weekend, Mrs. Carrington. And if you'd like, I'll phone you with my report on Monday."

"I'd like that. Thank you. I'll expect your call."

Even after she'd hung up the phone, Annie sat staring at it.

Shelly, who'd been watching and lis-

285

tening, hurried over to her desk. "Carrington? Of the Sykes-Carringtons?"

"That's the one."

"She's selling White Pines?"

"She is." Slowly the smile came, until it grew into an irrepressible grin. "And she wants me to handle the sale. Do you realize what this means? Do you know what my commission will be? I've just been given the opportunity of a lifetime."

Shelly touched a cautionary hand to Annie's arm. "I've never seen White Pines myself, but a neighbor, Penny Hartman, has told me about it." She lowered her voice so her daughters wouldn't overhear. "She said that it's haunted."

Annie's grin widened. "Um-hmm. Well, you tell Penny that this is the wrong season for ghosts and goblins, Shelly."

"I'm only telling you what I heard. Penny said just passing White Pines in her boat every summer gives her a creepy feeling."

"Shelly, for the money I'll make on this sale, I'm willing to put up with all kinds of creepy feelings." Annie pushed back her chair and stood. "I'd better get out to the Drummond place. I'm going to want to leave for White Pines before it gets too dark."

She paused. "I'll stop by later to pick up

the keys that are being delivered. Can you take up the slack for me while I'm gone?"

Shelly nodded. "The girls will be delighted to spend more time here. Ever since you told them the art supplies are all theirs, I never hear any complaints about the hours I have to put in." She looked up. "Will you be back Monday?"

"If I can't make it back, I'll phone you." Annie clicked the mouse on her computer and made a fresh file labeled "White Pines." Then she picked up her attaché case.

She couldn't wait to get started.

"Shelly." Annie held the cell phone to her ear and listened to the static caused by the rain pelting the windshield. "I stopped by the Drummond place. I'll work up the estimate when I get to White Pines and E-mail it to you." She paused. "Sure. I can hold on." She waited, then smiled. "Good. Tell Mr. Canfield I can meet him first thing Monday morning." She pulled her pager out of her pocket and noted the number of yet another caller. "Okay, Shelly. Got to go. Got a call to make."

While she punched in numbers, she lowered the window, allowing the sudden breeze to whip her dark hair into tangles. She was revved about the weekend. How many people had a chance to sleep in a mansion and stroll the grounds of one of the country's finest estates?

Minutes later, as she finished yet another business call, Annie caught her breath at her first glimpse of White Pines. She'd seen the pictures and read the legal descriptions, which a messenger from Mrs. Carrington's law firm had delivered along with the keys. She'd already begun to chart some of the outbuildings that might be incorporated into the sale brochure. A beach house and gazebo, as well as a fully equipped stable. All set on fifteen acres of prime beachfront property. Those were excellent selling points. But the photos were probably ten years old, taken when the estate had been a high-society darling.

Now it seemed more like a tired dowager, clinging to her faded glory.

The house stood on a sweep of land that was absolutely breathtaking. Jagged cliffs. Massive boulders. And that lovely expanse of water, as far as the eye could see.

Annie stopped the car and simply stared, allowing herself to drink in the beauty of the scene before her. Earth and sky and water seemed to blend into the most amazing watercolor of greens and blues. The house had been cleverly designed to suit its surroundings, as though it had always stood there like an impenetrable fortress, facing into the sea and wind. Three stories high, made of stone and wood, it managed to look both rugged and majestic. Tall, rounded windows softened the look. Still, there was a dark, brooding quality about it, as though it harbored plenty of secrets.

Annie engaged the gear and drove up the curving driveway. On closer inspection she could see that the trees that lined the way were misshapen, the gardens overgrown with weeds. Fountains and statuary were discolored, the victims of wind and weather. Several had fallen to the ground, where they lay half buried in tangled vines. Still, despite all the decay it was easy to see the possibilities.

Why had this place remained unused for years? Why had the Carrington family abandoned something so magnificent? The ominous warning from Shelly began to play through Annie's mind.

She shivered and brushed aside the little flicker of fear. It was the rain, trying to dampen her mood. This was no time to get caught up in fanciful ideas. She'd always been blessed with a wild imagination, which at times seemed more like a curse, since it was directly opposed to her basically sensible nature.

Nearly a mile later she came to stop at the front steps. Moss had begun to grow between the cracks in the cement. The steps and porch were littered with leaves and debris.

Annie tossed the strap of her purse over her shoulder and took her duffel out of the trunk, as well as a sack of groceries. At the top of the steps she set them down and fished the key out of her pocket. She unlocked the heavy door and shoved it open, stepping into the massive foyer. A flick of a switch brought dazzling light from a dust-covered Waterford chandelier overhead. She glanced down at a dusty floor of gold-veined Italian marble. To her left was an elegant Louis XIV table, and above it a mirror framed in a most unusual twisted rope design of pewter and gilt. Both bore tags, which she assumed had been put there by Mrs. Carrington's staff.

Leaving her things in the foyer, she made her way toward the sumptuous great room.

"Not bad for a summer place." She grinned, recalling Mrs. Carrington's description of White Pines as the family cottage.

She looked around at the furniture, some shrouded in white cotton sheeting to prevent dust, other pieces uncovered and tagged for removal. There was something sad about a house as beautiful as this lying silent and somber instead of ringing with the voices of a family.

She paused in front of a wall of windows that offered a spectacular view of terraces and gardens and a lawn that sloped toward the water. Here was more evidence of decay, with the bricks of the patio crumbling, and the lawn overrun with weeds.

An adventurous soul had taken a sailboat out on the turbulent bay, and it bounced across the whitecaps like a cork.

Shaking her head at the sailor's stupidity, Annie decided to explore the upstairs. Mrs. Carrington had said the guest room was on the second floor. After retrieving her duffel from the foyer, she climbed the curving marble stairs.

At the top of the stairs was a portrait of a handsome young man, a beautiful young woman, and two boys, one blond, one dark-haired. The brothers, miniatures of their father, were dressed in suits and ties.

Annie stood a moment, enjoying the play of light and shadow across the faces of the boys. They stood on either side of their pretty mother, who was seated in a chair. Behind them, looking proud and protective, was their father.

The older, dark-haired boy was staring

straight ahead with a look of concentration. A serious child, Annie thought.

The younger, fair-haired brother stared adoringly at his mother, as though trying to catch her eye. A born flirt, Annie decided with a grin. Plying his charms on the first woman in his life.

She tore herself away from the Carrington family to poke through the various bedrooms until she located the guest room. It was actually a suite of rooms. A lovely sitting room with peach silk moiré walls and a white marble fireplace flowed into a bedroom that overlooked the ocean. Annie removed the dust cover from the bed to reveal a fabulous peach satin duvet.

The walk-in closet was bigger than Annie's bedroom in her little rental in Tranquility. The bathroom was done in peach and white marble, with a sunken tub, a shower big enough for a soccer team, and a lovely dressing area that separated the closet from the bath. Though everything was dusty and more than a little faded, it was still elegant.

While Annie unpacked, she took the time to admire the scented drawers, the padded, scented hangers. Even after years of disuse, the hint of fine perfume lingered, like faded rose petals.

She wondered how many famous people had been in this suite. Rumor had it that White Pines had been the scene of fabulous society parties since the time of Prohibition.

After unpacking and stowing her duffel, she glanced at the window and caught a glimpse of lightning, followed by the distant rumble of thunder. She shivered and snatched up a sweater before hurrying down the stairs.

She was glad now that she'd brought along groceries. It wasn't a night she'd care to go out hunting for a restaurant, especially when she wasn't familiar with the area. The last town she'd driven through had been nearly twenty miles back.

She picked up the sack and headed toward the kitchen. Like the rest of the house, the room was oversized yet warm. It boasted a wall of cabinets in ash with beveled-glass fronts and marble countertops. The hardwood floor was softened with area rugs in deep burgundy and teal in a rich floral design.

Annie located a heavy skillet and coated it with oil. Then she broke several eggs into a bowl and began to whisk them with a little milk. While she chopped an onion and green pepper, she could see in her mind's eye the way this place must have looked when the family was in residence. Children swimming, boating, playing tennis. A maid serving lunch on the terrace. Or possibly cocktails served by a white-gloved butler.

She hoped she could show it to potential buyers while it was still furnished. Mrs. Carrington's designers had done a wonderful job of making it both homey and elegant. The antiques she'd seen so far were truly impressive. No wonder Mrs. Carrington wanted them shipped to her home in Palm Springs.

When the ingredients were ready, she turned her attention to the loaf of hard-crusted French bread she'd brought from the bakery in Tranquility.

She was rummaging through the drawer in search of a slicing knife when the door to the kitchen was yanked open. Annie's head came up sharply. She spun around, dropping the knife to the floor with a clatter.

At first she thought it had been caused by the wind. But then she caught sight of a man standing in the doorway. His white pants and navy windbreaker were soaked clean through. His dark hair was wind-tossed, his cheeks ruddy from the cold. On his face was a scowl of such anger that fear skittered along her spine.

"What are you" — Annie bent and retrieved the knife, holding it in front of her like a weapon as she straightened and faced him — "doing here?"

"Coming in from the cold." He glanced at the knife, then up at her face. "What are *you* doing here?"

"I work here." With false bravado she raised her chin. "And you'd better step back. I don't think Mrs. Carrington would be happy to find stains on her precious rugs."

He glanced down at the puddles of water forming around his deck shoes. Then he looked back at her with a mixture of surprise and disbelief.

"You must be joking." His voice, when he regained it, was low with repressed fury. "Who the hell are you?"

She lifted the knife in a threatening gesture. "I'll ask the questions, if you don't mind. Now I think you'd better leave before —"

In one smooth motion he grabbed her arm and twisted it until she was forced to release her hold on the knife. It dropped to the floor between them.

"How did you get in here?" His voice deepened, though whether from anger or exertion, she wasn't certain.

With a burst of strength, she pushed free of his grasp and backed away. "With a key. Given to me by Mrs. Carrington." She lifted her chin again. "I also set the silent alarm, which you activated when you opened that door." She could feel the heat stinging her cheeks at the bold lie. But she was desperate now. Her heart was racing like a runaway train. She was miles from civilization and at the mercy of this stranger who looked like the devil himself. "So if you know what's good for you, you'll be gone before you find yourself surrounded by armed guards."

At that he looked at her for a moment, then threw back his head and began to laugh.

Laugh?

"Didn't you hear what I said? Unless you leave . . ."

"Yeah." He was still grinning. "Armed guards. You forgot to mention the vicious attack dogs."

She knew at once that she'd been caught in her lie. She looked around wildly, wondering where she could run to escape him.

Reading her intentions, he snagged her wrist. "Hold on, now. There's no need to be afraid."

She pulled back, more terrified than ever.

"Who are you, and what do you want here?"

"My name is Ben. Benedict Carrington."

"Carrington?" Her jaw dropped. "But I . . ." She tried again. "Mrs. Carrington told me the house would be empty."

"Sorry. I didn't bother to let my mother know my plans. When she told me she'd decided to sell the house, I came up here on a whim." He bent and picked up the knife, then stepped closer, all the while studying her through narrowed eyes. "Why would she give you a key to White Pines?"

Though his tone wasn't nearly as haughty as Mrs. Carrington's, there was the same proprietary inflection. Though he was years older than the boy in the portrait, Annie realized he was the same person. The same dark, serious eyes. The same fierce concentration.

Her voice was breathy as she struggled to compose herself. "I run a real estate firm in Tranquility. Your mother hired me to handle the sale." She gave him a long, steady look. "If you drove here, where's your car?"

"In the garage." Up close, those eyes were fixed on her with an intensity that made her feel extremely uncomfortable. "Now it's my turn. Where did you meet my mother?"

"I didn't. She phoned yesterday and had a

key and a list of instructions sent to my office."

"That doesn't sound like Mother. She rarely hires anyone without knowing everything there is to know about them."

"She said she knew my mother. They attended the conservatory together when they were girls."

He nodded. "That sounds more like it. If my mother knew your mother, she wouldn't consider you a stranger. Here, you can have this back, as long as you promise not to plant it in my chest." He handed her the knife, all the while watching her in a way that deepened the color in her cheeks.

She accepted it from his hand and ignored a curl of heat along her spine as their fingers touched.

He glanced at the food. "Planning a party?"

"Just me. But there's enough for you if you're hungry." It was the least she could do to make amends for the way she'd behaved. Now that she'd had time to compose herself, she was feeling more than a little foolish at the way she'd reacted. She had allowed Shelly's suggestion to trigger her overactive imagination.

He nodded. "Thanks. I'll take you up on that. I'm starving. Crashing my sailboat onto a pile of rocks always gives me an appetite."

Through the window Annie caught sight of the overturned sailboat, its torn sails flapping in the wind.

Her eyes widened. "You're the fool . . ." She caught herself and amended, "You're the sailor who was out in this storm?"

He was amused as her cheeks turned red — and unwilling to allow that little slip of her tongue to pass without comment. "Yeah. I'm the fool." He was rewarded by a deepening of the flush on her cheeks. He found it oddly appealing.

He picked up a handful of chopped green peppers and popped them into his mouth. "I'd better change into something dry. I'll be down in a few minutes."

He turned and strode out of the room.

When he was gone, Annie took a long, deep breath. Then she tore off a handful of paper toweling and began mopping up the puddles on the floor. While she worked she called herself every kind of idiot.

Talk about first impressions.

She'd just confronted Ben Carrington with his own kitchen knife. Benedict Carrington, the son of the woman who had just handed her the deal of a lifetime. And she'd called him a fool. Right to his face.

Not the way to keep a client happy, she chided. She found herself wondering if she would still have Cordelia Sykes Carrington for a client after Benedict Carrington had a chance to speak with his mother.

2

"Tracy? Were you able to book me a flight to New York in the morning?" Ben stood by the window, a towel draped loosely around his hips. Water from the shower glinted in his dark hair. He held a cell phone to his ear. "Great. What time?"

His eyes narrowed as static blurred the voice of his secretary. "Sorry. Can you repeat that?"

Again he heard the static, and then nothing. He decided to resort to his laptop. Crossing to the desk, he dashed off an E-mail, then impatiently read half a dozen incoming messages before walking away.

Outside, the sky had grown dark as midnight, and rain pelted the windowpane.

He couldn't pretend to understand what had compelled him to return to White Pines. When his mother had phoned to tell him she was selling the family estate, he hadn't objected. In fact, he'd felt a sense of relief. He'd left here three years ago, vowing never to return. At the time he'd meant it. He had certainly never expected to see this place again. Despite the fact that his childhood summers here had been happy, those early memories had been completely blotted out by the pain that had come later.

So why was he here? He had no answer to that. One minute he'd been in San Francisco, planning a business weekend in New York. The next he'd been on a plane bound for Maine. Maybe it was the power of suggestion. Maybe the knowledge that this was his last chance to see his boyhood home had blurred his reasoning.

He'd wanted, needed, to be alone here. He'd never dreamed his mother would move so quickly once she'd decided to sell. It had never occurred to him that there might be a real estate agent here to look over the place.

He sighed. It was only for a night. He'd be gone in the morning. Now that he'd had a chance to see how neglected the place was his only thought was to escape. That was why he'd taken the *Odyssey* out on the bay. As a boy that had been his greatest pleasure. He loved the feel of the wind in his face, the flash of sun-dappled water racing past the bow. Today he'd been sorely tempted to keep right on sailing and never turn back to the sad reminder of his past. Had it not been for the storm, he might have done just that.

But here he was. Stuck for the rest of the night in a place that was bound to unleash all sorts of demons.

Maybe it was just as well that he wouldn't have to face them alone. There was that intriguing woman cooking an omelette in his kitchen and looking good enough to eat herself. It occurred to Ben that spending one evening in her company wouldn't be too much of a hardship. She could help keep his mind off other things, and in the morning he'd be on his way.

Good riddance, he thought. The lovely Annie Tyler could have this place all to herself.

He slipped into black pants and pulled a black silk sweater over his head. He picked up the watch from his night table and strapped it on while he stepped into loafers. For good measure, he tucked his cell phone and pager into his pockets before hurrying down the stairs.

He paused in the doorway, watching as Annie tended something on the stove.

He took the moment to study her. She had a model's body, tall and slim, the sort of leggy frame that managed to look elegant even in denims and a baggy sweater. She'd kicked off her sneakers, and her bare toes kept time to Ricky Martin's Latin beat. Her dark hair was pulled back in a ponytail that bounced as she reached for a spatula. Tucked between her shoulder and ear was a cell phone. She was quoting real estate prices while neatly turning the egg mixture.

He glanced around. She'd set two places at the glass table in front of the bay window. On the kitchen counter a pot of coffee was slowly perking, sending up its rich fragrance to perfume the room.

Annie carefully transferred the omelette from the skillet to a platter, then turned and saw Ben watching her. She almost bobbled the platter before getting a firmer grip.

"I'll talk to you later, Shelly." She tucked her cell phone in her pocket.

She would have to be more careful about letting him sneak up on her like this. It was the second time he'd caught her off guard.

She looked him over as she carried the platter to the table, and felt her pulse leap. He had the look of a sleek black panther, stalking his prey. She felt a thread of fear along her spine. Not the fear she'd experienced when she'd first seen him, soaked and scowling, in the doorway. This was a very different sort that had her heart doing strange little somersaults.

"Well." She forced a smile to her lips. "That was quick."

"I might say the same for you." He crossed the room and held up a cup. "Want some coffee?"

"Sure."

"Cream or sugar?"

"Black."

He filled two cups, then took the seat beside her. "This smells wonderful."

"It's pretty simple fare."

He studied the basket of French bread, the slices of tomato and onion in vinaigrette, and the perfectly turned omelette dripping with melted cheese. "Sometimes simple is best."

She glanced at him. "You don't strike me as a man with simple tastes."

"You know what they say. Don't judge a book . . ." He took a bite of omelette and paused while he savored it. "Now that's too sinful to be called simple."

"I'm glad you approve."

For a moment they both grew silent as lightning burst across the sky in a brilliant display of fireworks. It was followed moments later by thunder that rattled the windows.

Annie shivered as she broke off a piece of bread. "Why did you take your boat out in such a storm?"

He arched a brow, which made him look even more dangerous. "Maybe I just wanted to tempt the fates."

"People who do that usually have a death wish."

When he made no protest, she turned to study him more carefully. "Do you?"

"Not that I know of." He paused a beat before adding, "The truth is, there was no hint of a storm when I started out. Just some misty rain. I was probably an hour from shore when the first clouds rolled in. But it came up so quickly, I was lucky to make it back home. I was watching every cove in case I had to anchor somewhere and wait it out."

She picked up her coffee. Sipped. "You must be a pretty good sailor."

"Fair. I've been sailing this bay since I was a kid."

"Tell me about White Pines."

"Let's see. There are fifteen acres . . ."

She lifted a hand to stop him. "I know about the legal description. I'm interested in the personal history."

She saw something flicker in his eyes. Whatever he was thinking, it was far from happy.

She decided to tread very carefully. "Did your family spend the entire summer here?"

"We'd usually come up in late June. We were always gone by mid-August, so we could get ready for school." He smiled, and she thought how handsome he was when he allowed himself to relax. "The natives say there are only two seasons in Maine — July and winter."

Annie laughed. "My grandmother used to say that."

"Did she live in Maine?"

She nodded. "All her life. She remained in her family home until she died."

"So you grew up here?"

Annie shook her head. "My mother was the first in four generations to leave. She and my father moved to California shortly after they were married."

"And you became a California dreamer."

She gave a short laugh. "Hardly a dreamer. Those who know me would tell you I'm a hardheaded realist."

"A pity." He studied her over the rim of his cup. "They tell me there's a lot to be said for dreaming."

"I don't have time." She began fiddling with a spoon. "Never have."

"Really?" He leaned over and put a hand over hers to still her movements. "A woman in a hurry."

She pulled back as though burned. "I

guess you could say that."

His eyes narrowed. Had he just imagined that jolt? It was the most purely sexual tug he'd ever experienced. Judging from her reaction, he'd be willing to bet she felt it, too.

The evening had just become more interesting.

Seeing that he'd finished his omelette, she picked up the dishes and headed toward the sink.

He sat for a moment, watching as she loaded the dishwasher. Her hurried movements told him she was evading him. Intrigued, he snagged her coffee and his and walked up beside her, leaning a hip against the counter.

"So. Have you always had this affliction?"

She looked up, puzzled. "What affliction?"

"You show all the symptoms of being a classic workaholic. And I ought to know. I've been called one myself. Let's see. An unwillingness to linger over coffee. A need to keep your hands busy." He caught her hand and felt the way she jerked back. This time he'd anticipated her reaction and was ready for her. He absorbed another jolt and continued holding her hand while he ran a thumb over her wrist. He was pleased to note the flutter of her pulse. At least he wasn't the only one affected.

"I'll bet when you were a kid you always had to be first in your class." He looked up. "Am I right?"

She nodded, unwilling to trust her voice. He was too close. Too potently male. And though she didn't know why, the mere touch of him caused the blood to pound in her temples.

"And after school it was the same with work, I'd bet. Why real estate?"

She shrugged. "It's what I knew. What my father and mother did."

"Did you work with them?"

"No." She said it too quickly, and he realized he'd hit a nerve.

He shifted gears. "Did you start your career in California?"

"New York."

"That's about as far as you can get from California. What brought you to Maine?"

"Family. My grandmother. I came back to take care of her and stayed on after she . . ." She couldn't say the word. It was still too fresh. She suddenly felt the lump in the back of her throat.

"I'm sorry." He poured more coffee and handed her a cup.

There it was again. That quick flutter of nerves in the pit of her stomach as their fingers brushed. She looked up to see him watching her in a way that told her he'd felt it too.

There was another crash of thunder, seeming to rumble directly overhead. Suddenly the lights flickered, then died. The room was cast into complete darkness.

Ben's voice was right beside her. "Just stand still. I know the layout of this room better than you."

Annie needed no coaxing to remain where she was. She listened to the sound of drawers being opened and closed.

Finally he exclaimed, "Here's a flashlight."

She heard the click as he turned it on, but there was no beam of light.

He swore. "Batteries must be old. I'll have to find some candles."

She heard him rummaging through more drawers, then he gave a murmur of approval.

A moment later a small circle of light sliced through the darkness.

He made his way back to her and offered an arm. "Come on. I'll lead the way. There's a fireplace in the great room. I saw some logs stacked beside it. If I can coax a fire, we'll soon have heat and light."

She couldn't hold back the little shiver.

"Do you think the power could be out all night?"

"Who knows?" He lifted the candle and peered through the gloom until he located the doorway. Then he started forward, with Annie beside him. "But don't worry. There are fireplaces in almost every room of this old house. And plenty of candles. We'll have enough light to find our way around."

"That's good."

In the great room he led her toward a sofa and waited until she was comfortably settled, then turned toward the fireplace. Within minutes he managed to coax a thin flame into life with a long wooden match held to some kindling.

From her position on the sofa, Annie watched the way the muscles of his back and shoulders bunched and tightened as he worked, straining the fabric of his sweater.

There was no denying that he was dangerously attractive. Tall, trim, with that spill of dark hair over his forehead. And though his eyes were a bit too compelling, seeming to see things she'd rather not reveal, there was a softness around his mouth, especially on those rare occasions when he smiled. Then he was pure charm.

He wore his clothes with casual elegance and he moved with the air of one who was completely self-assured.

Before long, fire licked along the bark of the log, filling the room with warmth and light.

He turned. "Isn't that better?"

"Much." She watched as he drew the fire screen closed before crossing to sit beside her. "Did your family ever experience a power outage when you were young?"

"It happens a lot up here in the summer. My mother used to keep supplies for just such an emergency."

She glanced over with a smile. "I'm really glad this didn't happen to me while I was alone." She pressed her hands together. "I'd have been petrified."

"I doubt that. Like all clearheaded realists, you'd have simply rolled up your sleeves and figured out a way around this little inconvenience." He caught her hands in his and turned them palms up, studying them with a critical eye.

As he moved his index finger across her palm, tracing a line to her ring finger, he felt her flinch.

His eyes narrowed as he looked up at her. "Of course, you could be wrong about yourself."

"What's that supposed to mean?"

"The woman I just saw in your palm isn't

at all the woman you described."

"Really? Who is she?"

"She's not afraid of hard work. But she's also a tenderhearted romantic who's afraid to reveal that side of her nature, for fear of being hurt."

Annie pulled her hands away. "That's . . . silly. You don't believe that sort of thing, do you?"

"Palm reading?" A slow, dangerous smile tugged at his lips. "I'd say it's as accurate, or inaccurate, as any psychological profile."

"And are you a psychologist?"

"Even worse. A lawyer." His smile grew wider. "But in the courtroom I'd trust a palm over a psychologist's report anytime."

On a sudden impulse he lifted her hands to his lips and pressed a kiss to each palm then closed her fingers over the spot. He wasn't at all certain just which one of them was more surprised by the gesture. When he looked into her eyes he could see the heat, and knew she wasn't nearly as cool and composed as she was trying to appear.

So much for the clearheaded realist, Annie scolded herself. One touch of this man's mouth on her skin, and she felt it all the way to her toes. But that didn't mean she had to show him what she was feeling.

"I've put in a long day. I think I'll turn in."

She started to rise and was startled when he stood up beside her.

He was too close. Too intimidating. She took a step back, but he stopped her with a hand to her shoulder. She lifted startled eyes to his, but he merely smiled and handed her the candle.

"You wouldn't want to face the darkness without this."

"Thank you."

He could have carried it off if their hands hadn't touched. When they did, the fire was back, hotter than ever. His eyes narrowed as they stared down into hers. He had the most incredible desire to crush her in his arms and kiss her until they were both breathless.

She looked up to find those sweetly curving lips hovering just above hers. And as strange as it seemed, she could almost taste them.

It took all her willpower to turn away.

"Good night," she called over her shoulder.

"Maybe I should go with you. You could get lost in the dark."

"No." She said it quickly before she could change her mind. "I mean, you'd better stay here and bank the fire."

He nearly laughed aloud. She may have meant the fire blazing on the hearth, but there was another one, burning a path through his veins. Just looking at her, being this close to her, had him vibrating with the most amazing feeling of need.

He stood where he was, watching as she hurried out of the room and up the stairs. Then he dropped back down on the sofa and stared into the flames.

What was wrong with him? He was fantasizing about a woman he'd just met. In the very house where another woman had betrayed him and shattered his heart beyond repair.

He stretched out his long legs toward the heat of the fire and listened to the storm raging just beyond the walls. It was nothing compared to the storm raging inside him.

3

Too restless to go to bed, Ben held a match to another candle and walked to the pantry, returning with a bottle of Scotch and a tumbler of ice. He poured, then stared down into the amber liquid.

When was this ever going to end? He'd thought that if he stayed away from White Pines the pain would dull in time. But there was no escape from it. And he was a fool if he believed that selling White Pines would put an end to it. Long before he'd returned, he'd felt the sting of all those memories. They had a way of sneaking up on him at the oddest times. In a courtroom. While he was interviewing a client. Late at night, when the nightmare would jolt him out of a sound sleep.

He was smart enough to know that he needed to get on with his life. Heaven knows, he'd tried. But the memory was always there, just below the surface, threatening to drag him down. The minute he began to let himself feel, it would rise up to haunt him. There was no escaping it.

He could sense it now, circling the edges of his mind, ready to snap and snarl like a vicious dog. And all because he'd allowed himself to feel something for a stranger named Annie Tyler.

It was a good thing he was leaving in the morning. Otherwise he would want to find out a whole lot more about her than was good for either of them. There was no point in pursuing her. As long as he continued wallowing in this personal misery, nothing could ever come of it.

Still, he couldn't quite shake the image he'd seen in her palm. Not at all the woman she showed the world. He'd called her a romantic. In fact, he'd seen much more. A deep, simmering passion that spoke to a similar passion within his own heart.

He smiled. He'd made her nervous. That pleased him enormously, because she definitely had the same effect on him, with those big eyes like liquid honey and that quick, shy smile.

He tipped up the tumbler and took a long pull, feeling the heat snake through his veins. Then he set it down with a clatter.

Why was he tempting himself like this? Nothing could possibly come of it. Even if he wanted to know more about her, how was he supposed to accomplish that and still make his business meeting in New York tomorrow?

He briefly entertained the thought of taking the rest of the weekend for himself. But it wasn't possible. He'd already made commitments. The truth was, he thrived on the press of business, counted on it to keep his mind off less pleasant things. What would he do without his work? It had been tough enough taking even this one day away from his desk. He could picture it, the neat stacks of client letters, depositions, legal papers. A workload that would stagger most men. But his work had been his salvation these past three years.

Just thinking about it had him smiling and uncurling his fingers, which he'd fisted by his side. It was definitely easier to think about business than it was to think about Annie Tyler.

He glanced at his watch and was puzzled to see that it had stopped more than an hour ago. Seven forty-five. He shook his wrist, then held it to his ear. There was no sound. Hadn't his jeweler just replaced the battery less than a month ago? He frowned. Probably defective. Like everything else in this crazy world.

He filled the tumbler again and drank, and found himself hoping the rain would let up soon so he could get a few hours of sleep and be on his way by dawn.

Annie undressed quickly and slipped on an oversized football jersey before heading to the bathroom. After scrubbing her face, she pulled the band from her hair and brushed it loose, allowing it to tumble about her face and shoulders.

She hoped the power came on soon. Her computer screen had remained blank even when she'd tried to switch to the battery pack. She hated losing that comfortable link to the outside world, but at least she still had her cell phone.

She carried the candle into the bedroom and placed it on the night table before drawing back the covers. Once in bed, she leaned up on an elbow and blew out the flickering flame.

The darkness was eerie. Except for an occasional blinding flash of lightning, it was impossible to see her hand in front of her face.

She lay listening to the rain pelting the window and thought about Ben Carrington. Smooth as silk. But brooding over something. Deep waters, she figured. It was the last thing she needed in her already complicated life. Still, the simple touch of his fingers had caused more heat than a kiss from most other men.

It was simply the isolation of this place, she told herself. She was letting that wild imagination loose again. He wasn't some romantic, battle-scarred, world-weary hero. More than likely he was just a moody, self-absorbed, self-centered man who thought he deserved every good thing that had been handed him.

Still, he intrigued her.

A jagged slice of lightning pierced the darkness. Minutes later it was followed by a crash of thunder that had her leaping out of bed. The old house shuddered as though struck by a giant hand.

She raced across the room in the darkness, feeling for the door. When she found it she flung it open and was confronted with an eerie white light coming toward her. She let out a scream.

"Hey." Ben caught her roughly by the shoulder. "You okay?"

"The thunder. It sounded . . ." She paused and swallowed, mortified by her behavior yet unable to control herself.

He held the candle up to see that her eyes were wide with fear. "Yeah. I heard it, too.

Sounded like it might have hit something."

"It nearly tossed me out of bed."

"Okay." He kept his hand on her shoulder, ignoring the quick jolt to his system. She looked warm and rumpled and entirely too tempting. "Let's take a look."

He led her back to her room, and they peered out the window. All they could see was darkness.

"I don't see any trees burning or electrical wires sparking. I think we're fine." Ben held the flame of his candle to the one on her night table until it ignited and began to burn. When he caught sight of the bed, he had a quick impression of Annie lying in it, and was surprised by the surge of heat that went straight to his loins.

He needed to get out of this room. "Just to make sure, I think I'll climb up to the attic and take a look."

"If you don't mind, I'd like to go along." She no longer cared if he heard the tremor in her voice or saw the way her hand was shaking. She wasn't about to be left alone in a room that spooked her.

"Sure thing." He handed her a candle. "Stay close."

She followed him out of the room and along the hallway until they came to a door. When he opened it, the sudden draught of air made the candle flicker wildly.

They proceeded up the stairs, feeling the brush of cobwebs as they climbed. When they reached the top, they peered around. The floor was littered with trunks and boxes and stacks of yellowed papers and photographs.

Ben held his candle aloft and studied the ceiling. "There's no trace of fire. Not even a whiff of smoke. I think it's safe to assume that the house wasn't hit."

"That's a relief." As she turned away, she caught sight of an open trunk beside the stairs. A plumed hat lay atop a black satin cloak. "What's all this?"

"Relics." Ben smiled. "I remember playing up here on rainy days. Whenever I wore that hat I became the hero, using my trusty cardboard sword to fight for truth and justice."

She grinned at the image. She'd had similar experiences at her grandmother's house. "Were you ever a villain?"

His smile faded. "No. That was always my brother's role. He thought heroes were boring and villains had all the fun. If there was one thing Win knew how to do, it was have fun."

He turned away abruptly, his jaw clenched. "Coming?"

Annie followed him down the stairs, wondering at his sudden change in mood.

When they reached the second floor they continued on to the main level. The glow of the fireplace drew them toward the great room.

As they passed the grandfather clock, Ben paused. "Odd."

"What?" Annie halted and turned.

"This old clock hasn't been a minute off in more than seventy years."

Annie arched a brow. The clock had stopped at seven forty-five. "That had to be hours ago."

Ben nodded. "Right after that first clap of thunder. But why? This clock doesn't run on electricity."

Annie shrugged. "Maybe the batteries wore out."

"It doesn't require batteries. It winds itself with these weights. See?" He tugged on a chain, but nothing happened.

Puzzled, he held the candle closer, studying the mechanism. Just then there was a gust of wind against the windows, blowing out both candles. Had it not been for the flame of the fire, they would have been thrust into total darkness.

"Come on." Ben led the way toward the fire and lifted several candles to the flame.

He nodded at the Scotch on the table. "Would you like a drink?"

She shook her head. "No, thanks. What I'd love is some coffee. But I suppose with no power that's out of the question."

He gave it a moment's thought, then said, "I'll be right back."

Minutes later he returned with a small copper pot and two empty cups. "There was still some coffee in the coffeemaker on the counter. I figure we can heat it over the fire in this."

Soon the room was filled with the wonderful aroma. Ben filled their cups and handed one to her.

"Ummm." She sipped and lifted her cup in a toast. "That was brilliant. I feel better already."

"Yeah. Me, too." Especially now that he had a chance to take a good look at those long legs before she tucked them under her and settled herself on the sofa.

He set aside his coffee to add another log to the fire. Then he picked up his cup and joined her. "Not ready to go back to bed?"

She shook her head. "Too nervous, I guess. I don't think I've ever heard thunder that could shake a house to its foundation."

"Probably because we're so close to water. Though I don't recall a storm this fierce before." He drained his cup and shot her a sideways glance. "I like that thing you wear to bed. I don't believe I've ever seen the Packers look that good in their uniforms."

His unexpected display of humor made her laugh.

It was, he realized, a wonderful sound. Soft and light and clear as a bell. His own heart felt lighter just hearing it.

He tried not to think about the way her breasts strained against the clinging shirt. "Tell me about yourself, Annie Tyler."

"There's not much to tell. I grew up in Santa Barbara."

"A beautiful part of the country. Any brothers or sisters?"

She shook her head. "Just me. My parents died when I was fifteen."

"How?"

"A plane crash. They were looking over some property they'd intended to develop." She sipped her coffee for a moment, looking pensive. "Gram was all the family I had. She flew out to comfort me and ended up staying for the next three years, until I was ready to go off to college. Then she went home to Maine, and I went up to Smith. These past two years, after she had a stroke, it was my turn to offer her a little comfort."

She said it all simply, without bothering to go into detail, but Ben found himself fascinated by all the things she left out. She would have had a career. A place of her own. A life of her own. But she'd simply packed up and headed to Maine to be with her grandmother, without a thought to what she was giving up.

"Why are you staying on? Why not return to New York?"

She shrugged. "Loose ends to tie up." She thought of the debts still owed, the threads of her life that had come unraveled, and the loneliness she sometimes felt at the knowledge that she was the last survivor of a family. "Besides, I've decided I like Tranquility. The people. The pace. It's becoming home." She turned to him. "Where do you call home?"

"San Francisco mostly. I have a place there. Another in New York. But I don't think of either of them as home."

"Then why stay there?"

He shrugged. "My work. It keeps me hopping from coast to coast. Maybe it's best that way. No time to get restless."

"Restless for what?"

Roots, he thought. But aloud he merely said, "Did I say 'restless'? Maybe a better word is 'bored.' "

"Do you get bored easily?"

"I wouldn't know. There's never been time to find out." He stood up, uncomfortable talking about himself. "Hungry?"

"A little. But there's no way to cook anything."

"Want to bet?" He pointed to the fireplace. "We heated our coffee, didn't we? Besides, we ought to be able to find something that doesn't require cooking. What would you like?" He picked up a candle and led the way toward the kitchen.

"Something simple." Annie took up her own candle and followed.

He rummaged through the refrigerator. "My mother was up here last week with her housekeeper, Rose, and a couple of the staff to catalog all the furniture. If I know my mother, she would have left enough food behind to feed an army." He grinned. "As long as the army had gourmet tastes. Mother has a fondness for champagne and caviar."

Annie sighed. "I like the sound of your mother."

"You'd like her. She can be rather abrupt. She can't abide fools. But she has a marvelous sense of humor."

"And exquisite taste." Annie studied the silver coffee service artfully displayed behind the glass doors of a cabinet. Her grandmother's had been similar and had been in the family for generations. It had broken her heart to sell it. And the house. But the medical bills had left her with little choice and even less pride.

"Ah. Here we are." Ben held up an assortment of cheeses. "We don't have to cook these. What's your pleasure? We have Brie, Cheddar, Gouda."

"Brie."

"My choice, too." He returned the others to the refrigerator, then searched through the cupboards until he located a package of thin wafers.

Annie found a knife and plate and a little silver basket for the wafers.

Ben was laughing when he snatched up a round tin. "Good old Mother. I knew she'd have something to satisfy that sweet tooth. How about some petit fours for dessert?"

"Perfect." Annie handed him the knife, and he unsealed the tin. Then they carried their treasures to the great room where they arranged them on the coffee table.

Ben settled himself beside her on the sofa and watched as Annie spread Brie on a wafer before handing it to him.

He tasted, then gave a sigh of pleasure. "Perfect."

Annie nodded as she bit into hers. "I can

see that it doesn't take much to make you happy. Cheese, stale coffee, and a warm fire."

"There's something to be said for being warm, dry, and well fed." He chuckled as he leaned back, thoroughly enjoying himself. "Listen to that wind and rain outside. I'm just glad I'm not out on my sailboat."

"Or anchored in a cove somewhere. You'd be spending a pretty rough night."

"It wouldn't be the first time. I've spent plenty of nights riding out a storm."

She sipped her coffee. "Then you're not just a weekend sailor?"

He chuckled. "I suppose I am now. But when I was younger I thought seriously about joining a crew to vie for the America's Cup."

"Really?" She turned to look at him more closely. He had an athlete's body. Lean. Muscled. And the casual confidence of a man who took pride in everything he did. "How exciting. Why didn't you?"

"It would have meant at least a year's commitment in New Zealand. My father's health was already beginning to fail. It wouldn't have been fair to my family, or to my team. So I took a pass."

"Did you ever regret it?"

He shook his head. "No. My father died

six months later. I'll always be grateful for the time we had. Those last months were especially sweet. We learned a lot about each other, and about ourselves, that I'll always cherish. No trophy in the world could mean as much to me."

Annie nodded, moved by his words. "It was the same for me. My friends couldn't understand how I could give up my career in New York and move to a town like Tranquility to care for my grandmother. But the simple truth is, I didn't give up anything. I got much more than I gave."

Ben spread cheese on a wafer and offered it to her. As their fingers brushed, he smiled. "It's nice to find someone who understands. Not too many people do."

She sighed, struggling to ignore the rush of heat from his touch. "I suppose it has to be experienced before it's understood."

"Like love." Now where had that come from? He hadn't meant to say it out loud. He gave her a sideways glance. "Ever been in love?"

She stared down into her coffee, avoiding his eyes. "I thought I was."

But that was before. Before she'd boldly told Jason she was giving up her job in New York and starting over in Maine. Before she'd learned that love meant something very different to some than it did to others.

"Tranquility?" he'd said with a laugh. *"You want me to relocate with you to a town called Tranquility? And what am I supposed to do there?"*

"The same thing you do here. You're a song-writer, Jason. Why can't you write songs in Tranquility?"

"Because I need this city. I need the hustle, the drama, the pressure that only New York can offer. This city is my muse."

That had cut. Deeply. *"I thought you said I was your muse, Jason."*

"You are, baby. As long as you're here with me in New York. But if you leave, Annie, you leave without me."

And she had. Without a backward glance. But, oh, how it had hurt.

She dragged herself back from her thoughts and reached for a petit four. She bit into it, then sighed. "Oh, that's heavenly." She took another bite and finished the confection.

Ben watched her through narrowed eyes. She'd gone somewhere unpleasant in her mind. But to her credit, she'd pulled herself back without too much trouble. If only he could do the same. Whenever he allowed himself to venture into the darker parts of his mind, he usually ended up wallowing in misery for hours.

To keep from going there, he concentrated on the woman beside him. He enjoyed watching her eat. She seemed to derive a great deal of pleasure from such a simple thing. It suddenly occurred to him that he was having a marvelous time. It was something he hadn't experienced in quite a while.

A simple conversation with another human being. And not just anyone. A beautiful, fascinating woman. One he wanted to know better.

"Well." She glanced up. "We haven't seen a flash of lightning or heard a rumble of thunder in more than an hour. I think it's safe to go up to bed now."

"So soon?" He hated the idea. He didn't want her to leave. He was having far too good a time.

When she got to her feet, he stood up beside her and shot her a dangerous smile. "We could continue this upstairs. Your room or mine?"

She struggled to keep her tone even. "I sleep alone."

"That's what I was afraid of. But you might be sorry." He caught her by the shoulders and stared down into her eyes with a look that could have melted glaciers. "You never know when the storm could heat up again and you'll wish you had someone to turn to."

"Thanks for the offer. I'll let you know if I need you."

He drew her fractionally closer. "What if I need *you?*"

"Don't, Ben." She put a hand to his chest to stop him.

"I can't seem to help myself." His voice was low now, seductive, as were the hands that moved ever so slowly along the tops of her arms. "I don't know what's come over me. But I have to taste those lips." He whispered the words against her mouth as his lips covered hers.

She hadn't been prepared for the heat. Or for the jolt to her heart. The blood roared like thunder in her ears. Her pulse hammered against her temples, and she could have sworn the floor tilted beneath her feet.

It lasted no more than a few seconds, but it was long enough for her hands to curl into the front of his sweater, though she didn't know how they got there. The breath backed up in her throat, and her mind spun like a top.

"I think . . ." She finally managed to surface and push herself stiffly out of his arms. "I'd better get upstairs." Fast. Before she embarrassed herself by begging him for another breathless ride on that roller coaster.

"What's your hurry?"

"You." She put out a hand to his chest before he could draw her close again. "You're making moves I'm not ready for."

"Sorry. I didn't plan it. It just . . . happened." In fact, he was as startled as she. Where had all this come from?

"Well, see that it doesn't happen again."

She looked up. His eyes were in shadow, and there was that dangerous curve of his mouth. Oh, what a mouth! One that was simply made for kissing.

She picked up the candle and backed away. "Good night."

"Good night, Annie."

He watched as she climbed the stairs. Then he turned to stare into the fire.

He'd never before met a woman who had stirred him so with a simple kiss. And the mere thought of going upstairs and following up on that kiss agitated him more than he cared to admit.

So much for satisfying his curiosity. What he'd learned about Annie Tyler was that touching her was dangerous. And kissing her was deadly.

4

Annie managed to open one eye, but she quickly shut it again at the stab of light that assaulted her. How could it possibly be morning so soon? Hadn't she just closed her eyes a few minutes ago?

She remembered climbing the stairs to her room, could recall blowing out the candle and sinking back onto the pillows. She'd spent what seemed an agonizing hour or more thinking about Ben Carrington and her strange reaction to his kiss.

His sizzling kiss, she reminded herself. She had never in her life been kissed like that. Without touching her in any other way, he'd engaged her senses so completely that she had continued to vibrate with need until sleep claimed her.

And now she was awake. Though she wished she could roll over and steal another hour, she knew by the way her mind was racing that she would never be able to get back to sleep.

A glance at the darkened bedside clock confirmed that the power still hadn't been restored. She picked up her watch. It read seven forty-five. Then she realized that was the exact time when the grandfather clock downstairs had stopped. She shook her watch and tapped it repeatedly against her palm, but it remained silent. She moaned in frustration. At least the storm had blown over, she told herself.

She padded to the bathroom, where she endured a frigid, and very quick, sponge bath. A short time later, as she rummaged through the closet, she was distressed to discover that the ceiling had leaked and all her clothes were thoroughly soaked. She glanced down at her nightshirt and groaned aloud. There was no way she could parade around all day in this. Not with Ben Carrington watching.

Swallowing her pride, she made her way downstairs in search of him. She found him in the great room, just putting another log on the fire.

He looked up with a grin. " 'Morning." He gave her a long, slow look, and the heat instantly rose to her cheeks. "Were you hoping to challenge me to a game of touch football?"

"Maybe some other time. Right now it's too early for games."

"It's never too early for the games I have in mind."

"I'll bet." She cleared her throat. "I have a problem. A leak in the ceiling ruined all my clothes. Is there something I might borrow?"

"As a matter of fact, my clothes were drenched as well." He glanced down at the dark, pin-striped pants and old-fashioned cardigan sweater he was wearing. They looked completely out of character on the man who'd been so fashionably dressed the night before. "I found these in my grandfather's closet. Come on. Maybe there's something of my grandmother's that will fit you."

Instead of climbing the stairs, he led Annie to a suite of rooms at the far end of the house. "This is part of the original design from the twenties and thirties. When my parents remodeled, they had a master suite added upstairs and left this wing intact. You won't believe the clothes that are still here."

He led the way across a fabulous sitting room with a white granite fireplace and ornate Italian furniture that featured lions' heads on the backs of chairs and white marble columns that served as bases for tables. The bedroom was equally exotic, with an enormous bed draped with gauzy hangings tied at all four corners and a white satin spread outlined with a gold crest. The walk-in closet featured row after row of men's and women's clothing encased in zippered plastic covers. There were beaded gowns with matching bags and shoes. Elegant, slinky dresses with dropped waists and hemlines that would brush the floor. There was one entire row of tennis clothes, both men's and women's, all white, and all with matching sweaters.

Annie looked around, trying to take it all in. "What a treasure trove for a collector. Why did your family save all these things through the years?"

Ben shrugged his shoulders. "Who knows? I suppose in the beginning my parents simply couldn't bring themselves to part with such personal belongings. Later it became easier to simply ignore the presence of all these things than to deal with them."

He swept a hand toward the clothes. "Feel free to wear whatever suits you." He grinned at his own choice. "I have to admit I'm enjoying wearing something that my grandfather once wore, but I certainly wouldn't want to be seen in public in this."

They shared a laugh. Annie was still chuckling as she began sorting through the ladies' clothes until she paused in front of a plastic bag filled with wonderful draped trousers and crepe shirts. "Your grandmother wore slacks?"

Ben grinned. "Nana was a free spirit. She admired Katharine Hepburn and said if pants were good enough for a Hollywood star, they were good enough for her." He pointed to a dressing room just beyond the closet. "Go ahead. Try on whatever you want. I'm going downstairs to see to our breakfast."

When he was gone, Annie unzipped dozens of bags and examined clothes that would have been fashionable when her grandmother was a young woman.

The cares of the world seemed to slip away as she stood before a floor-to-ceiling looking glass. With each new outfit she tried on, her enjoyment grew. It was as though she had suddenly stepped back in time. There was no job waiting for her. No debts to be paid. No deadlines or pressure. Just the pleasure of slipping into another era. Another lifetime.

Annie walked down the hallway, loving the way the cuffs of the long, draped slacks brushed her ankles with each step. The sleeves of the old-fashioned crepe blouse fluttered as she moved. The open-toed sandals she'd chosen were butter-soft against her feet. She gave her grandmother's generation credit. They certainly knew about style and comfort.

She had no idea how long she'd been in the dressing room trying on clothes. Without a watch, it was impossible to gauge the passage of time. But she knew this much. She couldn't recall the last time she'd enjoyed herself so thoroughly, doing nothing more important than playing dress-up. In fact, she'd had the time of her life.

Even before she reached the kitchen, she could smell coffee brewing. But how was that possible with no electricity? She found the answer. The French doors were open. Ben was standing on the brick-paved patio, tending a charcoal grill. A coffeepot perked alongside a tray of scrambled eggs. A plate of toast stood on a warming shelf.

He looked as sophisticated and self-assured as a character straight out of *The Great Gatsby.*

"Well." He turned to give her a long, slow appraisal. "Katharine Hepburn had nothing on you. Great choice."

"Thank you." She twirled, giving him a chance to view the complete outfit. The pants and shoes were taupe, the blouse a creamy white that accentuated her flawless skin and dark, burnished hair. At the admiring look on his face, she felt the beginnings of a blush.

Using a pair of long-handled tongs, he turned sausages on the grill. "Breakfast is ready."

She watched with approval. "Very inventive."

"Necessity." He pointed to the patio table set for two. "There's juice. Unless you need caffeine."

"I'll take both." She picked up a glass of juice and sipped, then filled two cups with coffee.

"Did you sleep, Ben?"

He shrugged. "I think I dozed on the sofa. But I feel as refreshed as if I'd slept all night. In fact, I woke up thinking I haven't slept this well in years. How about you?"

"I feel fine." It was true, she realized. She felt as if she'd slept for eight hours. Maybe it was the fresh air. Or the change of scenery. Whatever it was, she wasn't about to complain. "Need a hand?"

"It's all ready. Just sit and enjoy." He carried a platter of sausage and eggs to the table and returned with a plate of toast and a little crock of jam.

"What are your plans for the day?" He

held the platter and waited until she'd filled her plate.

"I think I'd better walk around the estate and see what needs are most pressing. I've already decided to hire a landscaping firm to tend the lawns and gardens and prune the trees. I'll need a cleaning crew to begin work on the exterior. Paint the trim. Wash the windows. Then I'll have a second crew see to the interior. I'd like to get started showing the house before your mother has her furnishings removed."

"Good idea." He buttered some toast and dug into his eggs.

Annie tasted, then looked up. "This is good."

"Thanks. I used to enjoy cooking once in a while. Haven't had time to do much of it lately." He spread jam on a piece of toast. "A shame, too. It really relaxes me." He looked up. "Do you cook anything besides omelettes?"

"When I have to. I usually just pick up some carryout on my way home. But then, I often don't find time to eat until eight or nine at night, after I've finished showing clients through houses." She sipped her coffee. "What do you have planned for the day?"

He gave a sigh of regret. "I'd love to stay around, especially now that the weather has turned so gentle, but I have commitments. I'll be leaving for the airport as soon as I finish eating."

Annie ignored the momentary twinge of regret. After all, she hadn't expected him to stay. Considering the way she reacted whenever he got too close, it was just as well. "I guess if the power doesn't come back on by this afternoon, I'll be leaving too. There's no way I'm going to spend a night alone in the dark." She pushed aside her plate. She'd suddenly lost her appetite. "What time is your flight?"

"I don't know. My phone and computer are both down. But it seems to me my secretary was trying for a ten o'clock flight."

"You can borrow my phone. It's upstairs in my bag." Annie hurried away. Minutes later she returned and handed him her cell phone.

"Thanks." He punched in a series of numbers, then listened, and shot her a puzzled frown. "No dial tone."

"Are you sure?" She took it from him and tried several times before meeting his eyes. "This doesn't make any sense. How can both phones be dead?"

He shook his head. "I don't know." He sighed. "I guess I'd just better get to the airport early so I can catch whatever flight is available to New York."

As he started to gather up the dishes, she stopped him with a hand to his arm. She knew she wasn't imagining the jolt that shot through her fingertips. She took a step back and tried to adopt a casual tone. "You don't have time for this. Besides, you cooked. The least I can do is clean up."

He was watching her closely. Too closely. What was it about this woman that a simple touch had him burning? It was a good thing he was leaving. Being with her made him behave in the strangest way. Like a clumsy teenager on his first date. "You don't mind cleaning up alone?"

"Not at all."

"Thanks. I'd better load my stuff in the car."

She watched him walk away and found herself wishing things could have been different. Maybe if they'd met at a more convenient time they might have thoroughly enjoyed each other's company.

She carried the dishes to the sink and chided herself. Who was she kidding? With her lifestyle, there was no such thing as a convenient time. The chronic workaholic. Hadn't she admitted as much to Ben? And his life was no better. They simply weren't meant to be.

Still, just thinking about the kiss they'd shared brought another rush of heat. She couldn't think of any other man she'd ever known who'd had such a stunning effect on her.

"I guess this is everything." Ben paused in the doorway, holding an overnight bag and a briefcase. He was wearing a trench coat to hide his out-of-date wardrobe.

"Safe trip." Annie stayed where she was. It was definitely better to keep some distance between them. "It was nice meeting you, Ben."

"Nice meeting you, Annie." He was looking at her with that same intensity she'd seen on their first encounter. For a moment she was certain he was about to come charging across the room and haul her into his arms. The mere thought had her heart beating overtime and her breath backing up in her throat.

Instead he turned and strode away.

Annie watched him with a sinking heart. She had the almost overpowering desire to call him back. But common sense forced her to tackle the dirty dishes.

Work, she thought with a wry smile. It had always been what she did to keep her mind off other things.

She was just turning off the taps when she

heard a sound in the doorway and spun around.

"Ben." Her eyes widened, and though she wasn't aware of it, her lips curved into the most beguiling smile. "What are you doing back?"

"I never left. The car's dead." He shook his head. "Can't trust these rental cars anymore. I know it's a long way, Annie, but would you mind driving me to the airport?"

"No. Not at all." She dried her hands and hoped she didn't look as happy as she felt. She'd just been given another hour or more in his company. "I'll just go upstairs and get my purse."

Minutes later, as Ben was stowing his bags in her trunk, Annie turned the key in her ignition. The only response was silence.

He opened the passenger door and climbed inside, then caught the look on her face. "What's wrong?"

"My car's dead, too." She bit her lip in annoyance. "Ben, what's going on here?"

He shook his head, then slumped back against the seat. "I don't know." He looked over. "Try it again."

She did. With the same results.

He walked around to the hood of the car and lifted it, then began poking at wires and cables. "Try it again," he called.

Nothing.

Finally he slammed the hood shut and walked around to the driver's side. Through narrowed eyes he looked up at the clear, bright sun starting to climb over the trees. "Okay. For some unexplained reason, the storm knocked out all the power. As for the rest of this, I don't have any explanation. Maybe some sort of electrical surge. But we can't be the only ones affected. Sooner or later we'll see a crew from the power company getting everything up and running again."

Annie could feel the beginning of panic. "But what if they don't bother because we're so far from town? It must be fifteen miles, at least."

"More like twenty. Too far to try walking." He frowned. "And with the boat out of commission, there's no way we can sail to town."

Seeing the look in her eyes, he tried a smile. "Look. We're not in any trouble here. We won't starve to death. Or freeze. The worst thing that can happen is that we'll miss a few deadlines. My New York meeting is out of the question, and it looks like you won't be getting back home tonight. In the meantime, we may as well enjoy the day.

Whether we like it or not, we're not going anyplace."

Annie nodded. Though she was more than a little puzzled by these strange twists, she couldn't deny the tiny thrill of excitement at the realization that she and Ben Carrington weren't about to part just yet. They'd been given a reprieve.

Was that happiness she was feeling? Or a healthy dose of fear?

Annie stood at the kitchen counter, loading film into her camera. She looked up when Ben entered, carrying a toolbox he'd found in the garage.

"I figured I'd work on the sailboat. See if I can get it seaworthy." He glanced at the camera. "Should I smile?"

She shot him a teasing grin. "I wouldn't want to break it. I think I'll save it for really important things. Like the beach house. The gazebo. The stables."

"Too bad. Your loss." He tugged on a lock of her hair. Then he twisted it around his finger while he looked down into her eyes. "I thought I'd drop in a fishing line while I'm working. See if I can catch our dinner."

"Good thinking." She struggled to hide the feelings that curled along her spine at the mere touch of him. "Are you going to clean and cook them, too?"

He arched a brow. "And just what are you going to contribute to this feast?"

"My appetite. And if your dinner is as good as breakfast, I'll wash the dishes."

"Deal." He watched as she took a step backward. Though she gave very little away, he had the distinct impression that she wasn't nearly as cool and composed as she pretended to be. And that was good. Very good. Because just touching her made him itch for more, and he'd hate to think he was the only one suffering this way.

He followed her out the door. She made her way across the patio, and he hefted the toolbox and started in the opposite direction, toward the beach.

At the end of the dock he baited a hook and dropped a line into the water, then waded through the shallows until he reached the *Odyssey.*

There was a hole in the hull, and the sails were shredded. It occurred to Ben that he'd been very lucky indeed. If this had happened farther out in the bay, he'd have been forced to abandon ship and swim for his life.

Was it just luck? He sat back on his heels and turned to stare at the house. How many strange things could he accept as coincidence before he began to question just what was happening here?

He'd had no intention of coming up to White Pines. He'd had no intention of spending time in the company of a beautiful young woman. And he'd certainly had no intention of remaining for the entire weekend. Yet here he was. Not only doing a bunch of things he hadn't intended to, but enjoying them as well.

He was beginning to feel like a puppet. But just who was holding the strings?

5

Annie pulled out the description she'd been given of the various buildings on the estate. After reading through it, she decided to begin at the farthest end of the property and work her way back to the house.

She walked along a curving gravel drive overgrown with weeds, which had once been used as a trail for maintenance trucks and horse trailers. As she rounded a bend she caught sight of the stable in the distance.

She veered off the gravel drive and into the field, where early spring wildflowers grew in abundance. Tiny wild violets made a colorful carpet underfoot. Apple trees sprouted lacy leaves and the beginnings of buds. Chickadees flew back and forth, from ground to branch, eagerly lining their nests. Patches of brown grass were giving way to new green growth.

Annie fumbled in her pocket for the key to the stable. But when she inserted it, she was surprised to find the door already unlocked. She swung the door wide and looked around at the deserted stalls. Though they had been swept clean, the odor of hay and dung still lingered in the air, along with something else.

She sniffed the air as she began climbing the stairs to the apartment above, which, according to her description, had once housed the caretaker. Paint. The air was heavy with the unmistakable smell of paint and turpentine.

At the top of the stairs she paused with her hand on the knob. Before she could turn it, the door was yanked open. She stood staring in openmouthed surprise.

"Hi." The man was tall, blond, and boyishly handsome. "I've been expecting you."

"You've been . . . ?" She stopped, closed her mouth, then tried again. "Who are you? And what are you doing here?"

"Win Carrington. Actually it's Winston, but nobody ever calls me that. And Win suits me, since I much prefer winning to losing."

She looked at him more closely. "Of course. Ben's younger brother. I recognize you from the portrait."

He stuck out his hand. "And you're Annie Tyler."

"How did you know? Oh." She laughed. "You've been talking to your mother."

He continued holding her hand. "I was only nine in that portrait."

"And already an accomplished flirt." She heard herself laughing like a schoolgirl before she remembered to remove her hand.

"I'm so glad you noticed. I consider flirting to be a dying art. One that isn't appreciated nearly as much as it ought to be. Beautiful women are a weakness of mine. One of many, in fact. And you, Annie Tyler, are beautiful enough to take a man's breath away."

"Well." Her smile grew. "You didn't have to tell me you were a flirt. After that stale line, I'd have guessed as much."

"It's not a line. Well," he added with a grin, "maybe it is. But I meant every word of it." He placed his hands on either side of her face and lifted it to the light, turning it this way and that as he studied her. "Wonderful bone structure. Small, even features. Eyes a man could drown in. And lips that could tempt even a saint. Could I persuade you to pose for me?"

"Oh, I should have guessed. You're an artist." Now she understood the odor of paint and thinner.

"Of course. And I'd very much like to

paint you. Naked, of course. It's the only way a beautiful woman should be painted. The way nature intended."

It was impossible for Annie to take him seriously. Or to be insulted at his good-natured remarks. He was simply too charming. "You'll excuse me if I don't leap at your offer. It's just that I have this job, you see. It takes up a great deal of my time."

"Time should never be wasted on work when there are so many more pleasant ways to spend it."

"Really? And how do you spend your time?"

"If I had my choice, I'd spend it making love with beautiful women. As many as I could coax into my bed. And sometimes, when I was restoring my energy, I'd spend it simply enjoying great art."

Annie stared around in astonishment. "Oh, this is wonderful."

"I like it. It suits me, don't you think?"

"It seems to."

The apartment was one big open room with a living space on one side, dominated by a bed and dresser. The other side, facing a wall of windows that overlooked the orchard, had been turned into a studio, with canvases lining every inch of available space.

Unopened jars and pots of paint were everywhere, as well as tins of thinner. There were containers of brushes and several easels holding works in progress. A long wooden table was littered with sketches.

Annie moved closer to the table and examined a sketch of a sailboat on the bay. It was the same scene she'd witnessed the previous day, before she'd known that the sailor was Ben. With just a few strokes of charcoal, Win had managed to capture the feeling of speed as well as the ominous threat of storm clouds overhead.

She looked up from the sketch. "Why didn't Ben tell me you were here? He never said a word about it."

"He doesn't know yet. And I'm hoping you'll keep my secret."

"Why would you keep your presence here a secret?"

"It's just for a little while longer. I'm planning a surprise for him."

"Is it his birthday?"

"No. It's something even better. Maybe I'll call it his re-birthday." Win gave her his most charming smile. "What do you think of White Pines?"

"It's beautiful. The cliffs. The rocks. The bay. I can see in my mind the way it must have looked when it was the center of your family's life." She walked to the window, to stare at the scene spread out below. "It's sad, really. As I was walking here I could see so many possibilities. That orchard, for instance. What a shame that the fruit has been allowed to rot on the trees. The ground is littered with last year's crop." She glanced around. "And this stable. The stalls should be filled with horses again. And children to ride them." She spread her arms, allowing herself to get caught up in the moment. "Oh, Win, I hope I can find the perfect buyer who will love it and restore it to its former beauty."

She turned to see him watching her. His boyish features lit with a devilish smile. "With that kind of enthusiasm, I have no doubt you'll do just that, Annie."

He crossed to where a bottle of champagne sat chilling in a bucket of ice. "Let's drink to it. To your success with White Pines, and to its restoration as a thing of beauty."

"Sorry." She shook her head. "It's much too early for that. Ben and I just finished breakfast a little while ago."

"Of course. I lose track of day and night when I'm working. What do you think of my brother?"

"Think of him?" She watched as he filled

a fluted glass and drank.

"Solid? Steady? Dependable? Wouldn't you say all those things describe my older brother, Ben?"

She heard a faint note of derision in his tone. And though she didn't know why, she felt the need to defend Ben to his brother. "Yes. I'd say he's all those things. They're admirable qualities. Why does that bother you?"

"It doesn't bother me. It just makes me sad for him. Poor Ben has never learned how to have fun. Given a choice between dancing and working, he'll choose work every time. Do you know that he carries lists of things to be done and actually enjoys crossing items off, one after the other? Ben's idea of a good time is to plow through his paperwork with a vengeance, so that by quitting time his desk is clean. It never occurs to him that it'll just be filled with new work in the morning."

"What's wrong with that?" She felt the sting of embarrassment, since he'd just described her own lifestyle as well. "Why are you mocking him?"

He studied her over the rim of his glass. "Do I detect a bit of fire in those eyes, Annie Tyler?"

She flushed. "I just don't see why you

should make fun of your own brother, especially to someone like me, who hardly knows him."

He continued to stare at her, watching her color deepen. "Seems to me, for someone who hardly knows Ben, you're taking this as a personal insult." He stepped closer. The boyish smile grew. "Could there be some feelings between you and my brother?"

She stiffened. "I told you. I hardly know him. We just met yesterday."

"And you and Ben are hardly the type to believe in love at first sight."

"That's right."

His tone softened. "Don't be offended, Annie. I'm not mocking you. As for Ben, I make fun of him because he makes it so easy. I used to accuse him of being so stiff and perfect, he'd probably break in two if he ever tried to unbend. But I admire him. Really I do. In fact, I've always wished I had some of his discipline. Heaven knows, I've tried. Too many times to count. But each time I started to walk the straight and narrow path, I found all those temptations in my way. And the next thing I knew" — he shrugged — "I would be knee-deep in sin and debauchery again." Grinning, he held out the flute of champagne. "Sure you won't have a sip?"

"No, thank you." It was odd. Though she'd

been stung by his words, she found she couldn't stay angry with this man. He was simply too charming. Which, of course, was something he was much too aware of. It was an art he'd probably perfected from his earliest days. Because he was the younger son, his family no doubt not only tolerated it but encouraged it as well.

"It's a pity some of Ben's more admirable traits haven't rubbed off on you, Win. You really ought to go easy on the champagne this early in the day."

He merely grinned.

She turned away. "I'd better go."

"All right. Remember, Annie." His voice lowered conspiratorially, and he put a hand on her shoulder in an intimate gesture. "I expect you to keep my little secret."

She felt a coolness where he was touching her and found it odd, considering the heat she always felt at his brother's touch. "When will you let Ben know you're here?"

His smile was bright enough to light up the entire sky. "As soon as my surprise is ready."

Annie glanced around. "Are you painting something special for him?"

"You don't really think I'm going to tell you? All I'll say is this. He's going to consider my little surprise the greatest gift of his life." Win drained the glass, then began to mix some paint on his palette. "Now I'd better get back to work if I'm going to have . . . everything ready in time."

"Then I'll leave you. Will you come up to the house for dinner this evening?"

"Sorry. Can't. I have plans."

"I see." She walked to the door and turned, but he was already absorbed in his work. "It was nice meeting you, Win."

He looked up suddenly and shot her a brilliant smile. "The pleasure was all mine, Annie Tyler. A pity I couldn't have met you first. You're really quite something, you know. I think it would be wonderful to have someone defend me the way you leapt to Ben's defense."

"I wasn't defending . . . well, I was, but . . ." She realized her attempt to explain was falling on deaf ears. Win had already turned his attention to his work again.

She closed the door and descended the stairs, wondering why she had indeed been so quick to defend Ben to his brother. After all, she and Ben had known each other such a short time. Still, she couldn't deny that she'd begun to care about him. There was something good and decent about him. She paused. There was also something sad about him, as though he'd been deeply wounded. She could see it in his eyes when he let down his guard.

Once outside, she started across the orchard, turning once to look back. She thought she saw Win's hair glinting gold in the sunlight, but she couldn't be certain. It might have been merely the sunlight glinting off the windowpane.

What a strange twist, she thought. Two such different brothers, and both of them paying a last visit to their childhood home.

Despite Win's sarcasm, it was plain that he loved his brother. She only wished he would finish his surprise tonight, so that he and Ben could have some time together before they had to leave White Pines for good.

Of course, there was another reason why she found herself wishing Win would join them tonight. She wasn't at all certain that she ought to be alone with Ben Carrington. There was no telling how many self-imposed rules she might be tempted to break if he kissed her again the way he'd kissed her last night. Just thinking about it made her pause to touch a finger to her lips.

With a sigh she pulled out her camera and clicked off several shots of the stables and the orchard. It was time to get her mind back on the business that had brought her here in the first place.

She decided to investigate the rest of the outbuildings while the sun was still high in the sky.

Annie took several photos of the interior of the beach house, then stepped outside. The sun was already beginning to set behind glorious golden clouds. She'd had a wonderful time exploring the buildings on the grounds of White Pines. And though everything showed the effects of years of disuse, it also showed great promise.

Annie had no doubt that she would find interested buyers. That thought didn't bring the flash of excitement that usually accompanied the prospect of a sale. Instead, there was just the slightest twinge around her heart. It seemed a shame that this lovely place should be abandoned by a family that had loved it for generations.

As she locked the door and turned away, she saw Ben stepping off the dock carrying a string of fish.

"Perfect timing," he called as he caught up with her. "This will save me a second trip. Would you mind holding these while I go back for my tools?"

She held out her hand and took the string of fish. When he returned a few minutes later, he was grinning like a kid. Annie couldn't help thinking how much he resembled his brother, despite their differences in color and temperament. Now, like the first time she'd seen him, his dark hair was ruffled by the wind. His clothes were wet. But unlike that unpleasant first time, he now seemed relaxed and content.

"What made you so happy?" She matched her steps to his.

"I'd forgotten how much I enjoy puttering. There's just something so satisfying about being able to work with my hands. I was able to patch the hull of the *Odyssey*. It's pretty crude, but it'll keep her from sinking until I can contact someone at the marina to come and haul her in to dry dock."

"Oh, that's good news." Annie paused to glance back at the sailboat, bobbing in the shallows. "What about the sails?"

He shook his head. "Not too much I can do about them. She'll need to be outfitted with new sails and rigging over the wintertime. But at least she's seaworthy."

Annie looked down at the string of fish. "I'm glad you were able to catch our dinner."

"Want to help me clean them?"

She wrinkled her nose. "No, thanks. Not my idea of a good time."

"Come on." He closed a hand around her shoulder. "It'll be fun. I promise."

Laughing, he looked down into her eyes and absorbed a purely sexual jolt.

For a second Annie simply couldn't breathe. Her blood ran hot from the way he was looking at her.

His voice lowered. "I don't claim to know what's happening to me, Annie. I've never been one to act on impulse. But right now I want to kiss you more than anything in the world."

His gaze lowered to her mouth, and she felt the kiss as surely as if he'd already covered her mouth with his.

She ran her tongue over lips that had gone dry as dust. "I . . . don't think that would be wise, Ben."

"To hell with being wise. It occurs to me that all my life I've been too damned sensible."

He dragged her against him, covering her mouth with his.

Heat. It engulfed Annie in waves and buckled her knees. Though she knew she ought to resist, it just wasn't possible. One hand dropped limply at her side, still holding tightly to the string of fish. Her other hand curled into his sleeve and clung as his lips moved over hers.

Ben breathed her in, loving the intriguing scent that was uniquely hers. In fact, he loved everything about her. The taste of her. The texture of her skin. The way she seemed to fit so perfectly against him.

Where had this need come from? The need to kiss her until they were both breathless. One minute he'd been happily thinking about the work he'd accomplished. The next he'd found his mind wiped clean of all thoughts but one — Annie. The need to hold her. To kiss her until she was weak and clinging.

His hand tightened at her waist, drawing her closer as he drank her in. She tasted as cool and as fresh as spring rain. He kept his eyes open, watching the way her lids fluttered, casting shadows on her cheeks. Such high, perfect cheekbones, he thought. The kind models would kill for. As he deepened the kiss he saw the slight flush of desire. Felt the way her breath hitched, the way she shivered when his thumbs skimmed her breasts. It was absolutely intoxicating, and he thought he could go on like this for hours, pleasuring himself with only her.

With an effort he stopped himself just short of devouring her. "Has anyone ever told you you taste as good as you look?"

"No." She found even that single word an effort as she took a step back, lifting her head. "But then, I haven't had too many men sampling the wares."

"Fools. They don't know what they're missing." He ran a hand lightly up her arm. "Want to go for seconds?"

"Not likely." It shamed her to admit that, even while she was denying it, it was exactly what she wanted. This kiss had left her hungry for much more.

He merely grinned. She was as transparent as the glass-topped table on the patio. It was obvious that he made her as uncomfortable as she made him. That pleased him more than he cared to admit.

He pointed to the string of fish. "Are they tugging on the line? Or is that your hand trembling, Annie Tyler?"

"My hand, damn you." But she managed to smile as she said it. There was something in his eyes, something hot and fierce that put her on edge. She didn't think it wise to push too hard.

She took a step back and set the string of fish on the grill. "I think I'll leave you to the joy of fish-scaling. I'll just go inside and start writing up my impressions of what I've seen so far."

"Okay, coward. Run away. But we haven't finished this."

She fought to ignore the flutter in the pit of her stomach.

When he turned away, his voice cooled. As did the heat in his eyes. He was in control of his emotions again, at least for the moment. But that was only because he wasn't touching her. "Give me about an hour, and dinner will be ready."

"All right. Want me to set the table?"

"I wouldn't want to deprive you of all the fun of your paperwork," he deadpanned. "Leave the table to me."

When she stepped inside the kitchen she paused to let out the breath she'd been unconsciously holding. How were she and Ben going to get through another evening without giving in to all this passion that was heating up between them?

Maybe, if they were lucky, Win would complete his surprise in time to join them. There was safety in numbers, she reminded herself.

If Win didn't join them, she would just have to play it very cool and retire to her room as quickly as good manners would allow. It was, after all, their last night together.

So why did that thought bring her no pleasure? Because, she realized, she'd really wanted him to take that kiss further. To push them both to the edge. And maybe even take the tumble.

6

Annie kicked off her shoes and noted that they were damp, as were her stockings and the cuffs of her slacks. Her own clothes, which she'd left hanging in the closet, were still too wet to wear, so she was forced to return once more to the store of vintage clothing. This time she chose a long, slinky dress in shell pink with matching shoes. As she studied herself in the full-length looking glass, she was startled by her reflection. She looked like one of the pictures in her grandmother's album. She stepped closer, examining herself more carefully. It wasn't just the clothes. It was something else as well. Her eyes were the same, though she'd always thought them a bit too wide. The same turned-up nose dusted with freckles. The same generous mouth. The same teeth, one of them slightly crooked. But there was something new. Maybe it was her attitude. She felt completely relaxed, as though the cares of the real world had slipped away.

She shook her head and took a step back. Silly. The power may have been lost in the storm, but that didn't mean that her responsibilities had disappeared. She still knew how to work. She would do what she'd come here to do. Chart the possibilities, the selling points, and then return to her office in Tranquility and get to work for her client.

She made her way resolutely to the guest bedroom, determined to stay busy until dinner was ready. She settled herself at the lovely Queen Anne desk in the upstairs sitting room and began making notes on the property and buildings she'd examined. Next to this house, she estimated the beach house to be the most important building at White Pines. Just steps from the shore, it was a small guest cottage, with a simple, open design that incorporated a galley kitchen, great room, bedroom, and bath. The wall facing the water was all glass, filling the rooms with light. There were skylights in the ceiling, allowing for even more light. Though the interior showed its age, with faded paint and outdated carpeting, it could be upgraded at minimal cost. That would be an important selling point.

Then there was the stable. The apartment above it added even more value to the property. It could be billed as a caretaker's apartment, something an estate of this size would need.

She leaned back, thinking about the current tenant of the apartment. How long had Win Carrington been here? From the looks of his studio, he appeared to be a longtime resident. Yet his mother hadn't said a word about him. In fact, she'd led Annie to believe White Pines would be deserted.

Maybe he planned on leaving as soon as he presented Ben with his surprise.

Ben. What was she going to do about him? The more time she spent in his presence, the more intrigued she became. The angry, impatient stranger she'd first encountered seemed to be changing before her eyes. That veneer of sophistication was slipping away. As was the pain she'd seen on that first evening. Despite the fact that he'd missed his plane and had been cut off from all communication, he didn't seem to mind nearly as much as she'd have expected. But then, the inconveniences weren't bothering her, either. In fact, she'd almost forgotten about the fact that she and Ben had been cut off from the outside world for almost twenty-four hours.

Life had gone on without any noticeable interruption.

She blinked, wondering how long she'd been sitting here. She'd better head downstairs to see if Ben needed any help with their dinner. As she descended the stairs, she felt the whisper of fabric brushing her ankles. She slowed her movements, loving the way this old gown made her feel. Sexy. Sophisticated. Glamorous.

She paused when she saw Ben standing across the room, watching her.

He was wearing a pair of his grandfather's dark pants and a white tennis sweater, which gave him an air of sophistication as well. On his face was a look of intense concentration that she'd begun to recognize.

"Sorry. Am I late?"

"No. Wait." He held up a hand.

"What's wrong?" She froze in mid-stride.

"Nothing. I just wanted a minute longer to admire the view. You look" — he started toward her — "like a character out of one of those old black-and-white movies." He caught her hand and helped her down the final step. "Only better. Much better."

"Thanks." She felt herself grinning. "As a matter of fact, you do, too. We could do a Fred and Ginger impersonation. Want to dance?"

"Yeah. Sorry there's no music." He pulled her into his arms and swept her into a graceful circle. This time he was ready for the jolt. He absorbed it and enjoyed the way the heat begin to spread through his veins. "Can you whistle?"

"No. But I can hum. What would you like to hear?"

"Something with a beat."

Instead, she started humming an old waltz as he moved with her around the room. His lips were pressed to her temple in a most provocative way that had her heart beating overtime.

She looked up and found to her dismay that their lips were almost touching. "Not bad. I'd say you've been practicing."

He shook his head and kept his gaze steady on her mouth. "I haven't danced in years. I'd forgotten how pleasant it can be."

She took a step back. "Are you going to offer me a drink?"

"Yeah." Keeping hold of her hand, he led her to the patio, where the table was already set, complete with candles.

A bottle of wine sat chilling in a bucket of ice.

Annie stared in surprise. "You did all this?"

He shrugged, more than a little pleased at the look on her face. "I thought the evening called for candles and wine. It's probably the last time I'll have a chance to eat here at White Pines. I thought it was a fitting tribute to the old family homestead."

"More than fitting." She waited while he filled two goblets and handed one to her. She sipped. "Nice wine."

"Merlot. I told you, my mother has good taste." He stepped closer, inhaling her intoxicating fragrance. "And so do you, Annie. That dress looks like it was made for you."

"It's funny. I thought I'd feel foolish wearing something of your grandmother's. But I don't. In fact, it feels just perfect. This dress seems to suit this house. This occasion." She felt herself flushing under his scrutiny. "I guess that sounds silly."

"Not at all. I was thinking the same thing." He caught her hand and led her across the patio to a low stone wall. Beyond was the lawn that sloped to the water.

"While I was cooking, I found myself thinking back to all the good times I've enjoyed here through the years." Ben smiled with the memories. "Sailing on the bay. Fishing from the dock. Chasing fireflies after dark. And the parties. Every Fourth of July my grandparents used to invite all their family and friends to celebrate. My grandfather would hire a barge to anchor offshore and send up a fireworks display. We would all sit here on this wall, or spill out there on the lawn, and watch the night sky turn into the most amazing show."

Annie lifted her head. "Even without the fireworks, that's quite an amazing show."

The sky was glorious ribbons of pink and mauve, with a setting sun that gilded the edges of the clouds. A movie director couldn't have ordered a more perfect background. It was a scene that couldn't help but soothe away the cares of the day.

Without thinking, she touched a hand to Ben's arm. "It must have been wonderful growing up here."

He closed a hand over hers and smiled. "It was."

"How can your mother bear to part with something filled with so many happy memories?"

"Strange." He looked out at the peaceful bay. "A day ago, I'd have said the bad memories far outweigh the good. But now that I've had a chance to spend some time here again, all I can remember are the good times." He turned to smile at her. "Such good times."

They stood for long minutes, drinking in the beauty of the evening.

He turned away, still holding her hand.

"Come on. Our dinner will get cold."

She followed him to the table, where he held her chair. When she was seated, he placed a platter of appetizers in front of her.

Her eyes widened. "Shrimp?"

"They were in the freezer, along with a fabulous assortment of seafood. I just sautéed them in a little garlic and oil."

"Do they taste as wonderful as they smell?"

"There's only one way to find out." He took the seat beside her and spooned some onto her plate. He watched as she bit into one. "Well?"

"Fantastic." She tasted several, then looked up in surprise. "Is this one lobster?"

His smile was back. "I told you. My . . ."

"I know." She laughed and put a hand over his to stop his words. "Your mother's exquisite taste again. Remind me to thank her."

"I will." He wondered if she knew what her touch was doing to him. Just the merest press of her hand, and he was pleasantly warm again.

He topped off her wine, then his own. "Wait until you taste the fish. There's nothing better than fish fresh from the bay."

"You mean you cheated and already ate some?"

"The privilege of being the cook." He took a bite of shrimp and another of lobster. "I make a fantastic seafood gumbo. You'll have to taste it sometime."

"I'd love to. How'd you learn to cook, Ben?"

"Necessity. While I was in law school I shared my first apartment with three buddies. It was always littered with take-out cartons and fast-food wrappers. I think the only thing we made from scratch for three years was peanut-butter-and-jelly sandwiches."

She laughed. "Sounds a lot like the apartment I shared with my friends in college. But you forgot to mention the mounds of dirty laundry. And music blasting at deafening decibels at all hours of the day and night."

He joined in the laughter. "Yeah. That, too. I have to admit I don't miss any of it. Well, not much, anyway. I promised myself that when I had a place of my own, I'd fill it with good books, good music, and good food."

"Seems to me I promised myself that, too. But somewhere along the line I got too busy to follow through. So how did you learn to cook? By trial and error? Or did you invest in a library of cookbooks?"

"Trial and error mostly. Whenever I tasted something I really liked, I'd ask the cook for the recipe. Then I'd go home and try it out."

"I'm impressed."

"Don't be too quick to heap praise. Let's see if you still say that when you're finished." He pushed away from the table and crossed to the grill. Minutes later he set down a platter of sizzling fish surrounded by grilled vegetables on a bed of rice.

Annie tasted and sighed. "All right. I've decided you're in the wrong profession. Forget the law. You really ought to be doing this for a living."

He couldn't hide his pleasure at her words of praise. "I'll admit it's satisfying. But only when there's someone to enjoy it with me. It isn't much fun cooking for one."

"I know what you mean." Annie sipped her wine and savored her meal. "Most nights I'm so tired by the time I get back to my apartment that the last thing on my mind is cooking. I just take something out of the freezer and nuke it."

"How many hours a day do you put in at your business?"

She shrugged. "Who counts? I just squeeze in as many clients as possible. When I run out of hours I start over the next day."

"Sounds familiar." He topped off her wine again and thought about his own days and nights of never-ending work. How long had it been since he'd taken a vacation? Or even a day off work? How long since he'd spent this much time with a beautiful, fascinating woman?

She was beautiful, he thought as he watched her finish her meal. And fun to be with. He loved the sound of her voice. That low, breathless quality that never failed to move him. The way her laughter made his heart feel lighter.

"Oh, look." She touched a hand to his shoulder and pointed to the sky. "A falling star. Quick. Make a wish."

He turned in time to see her close her eyes.

When she opened them she saw him smiling. "What's so amusing?"

"I didn't think anyone still believed in that."

"You mean you don't?"

He shook his head. "But you do."

She shrugged, then gave an embarrassed laugh. "It's just an old habit from my childhood. I remember my father telling me to always wish on a shooting star. But one night after he and my mother had been lost . . ." She took a deep breath, amazed that even all these years later, she could still feel the shadow of pain. "I stayed awake all night, hoping I could see a falling star so I could wish on it."

"And did you?"

She nodded. "I remember wishing with all my might. And crying the next morning, when I told my grandmother that it was silly and stupid, because nothing was ever going to bring my parents back." She smiled now, remembering. "Gram said that sometimes, even when wishes can't come true, it's because there's something even better just around the corner."

"Not exactly what a teen wants to hear, is it?" He wondered if she had any idea how inviting she looked in the dark with candlelight weaving its magic around her.

"Maybe not. But it left quite an impression. From that day on, I've always believed that it isn't so important to have what I want. I can always live on the hope that something better is about to happen."

"Don't tell me you're one of those who believe that out of every lousy thing that happens in our lives, something good will come."

"Only if we let it. If we close our hearts to the possibilities, how can the good find its way in?"

She saw his eyes narrow as he thought over what she'd said.

A sudden gust of wind ruffled her hair and

threatened to extinguish the candles.

Ben touched a hand to hers. "I think we'd better get inside and start a fire."

He stood and began to gather up the dishes, surprised at how dark it had grown. Where had the time gone? Time. He'd lost all track of it since the power went out. Or maybe just being with this fascinating woman made him forget about the time.

"I'll carry these candles in so we can find our way." With a candle in each hand, Annie led the way while Ben stacked the dishes in the sink.

Then she returned to the patio for the carafe of coffee bubbling on the grill. As she poured two cups and set them on a tray, the fragrance perfumed the kitchen.

"I'll take that." Ben took the tray from her hands and led the way to the great room, where more candles gleamed on the mantel. After setting the tray on a table, Ben lifted one of the candles and held the flame to kindling in the fireplace. Soon the room was ablaze with warmth and light.

"There now. That's better." He turned and found Annie standing beside him, holding out a cup of coffee.

He accepted it and touched it lightly to the rim of hers. "Here's to our last night at White Pines."

She wondered at the sudden ache in her heart. After all, this place meant nothing to her. Nothing except a hefty bonus when it was sold. Still, she couldn't help thinking that the Carrington family would one day regret their decision. But by then it would be too late. Someone new would be living here, creating wonderful new memories.

"Will you be sorry to leave, Ben?"

He studied her a moment before nodding. "Yeah. I never thought I'd say that. But tonight, remembering the good times, I realized just how much of my childhood is wrapped up in this place."

"Maybe you should urge your mother to reconsider."

He shook his head. "White Pines has sat empty now for three years. It's time to sell it to someone who can enjoy all that it has to offer."

"But why not your family?"

He merely smiled as he stared at her. "You know what, Annie? You ask too many questions."

"But that's my job. If I'm going to represent your family in the sale of this place, I need to know everything I can about it. I need to know if there's some flaw in the design that caused your family to stop coming to White Pines."

He seemed not to hear as he stared into her eyes. Abruptly he took the cup from her hands and set it on the mantel beside his.

Her eyes went wide. "Ben, what are you doing?"

"I'm going to do what I've wanted to do ever since you floated down those stairs." He drew her close and covered her mouth with his in a kiss so hot, so hungry, it melted every bone in her body. She could feel them, one by one dissolving, disappearing. Just a kiss, and she felt boneless and fluid. And completely undone.

When he looked at her, her eyes were huge with shock. It pleased him more than anything. "I really wanted this instead of shrimp and lobster. Instead of wine." He ran nibbling kisses across her jaw and heard her sigh of pleasure. His teeth nipped lightly on her lobe. "All wine can do is go to my head. But you, Annie. You go straight to my heart."

He darted his tongue inside, sending piercing little arrows all the way to her core. She made a sound that might have been pleasure or protest.

"Now I'm through wanting." He ran his hands lightly down her sides, then closed them over her hips, and dragged her against him. "I've decided I have to have you, Annie. If I don't, I'm not sure my heart will survive."

She simply stood there, her eyes wide and unblinking. She couldn't seem to move. Or to speak.

"Need some coaxing, do you?" He framed her face with his hands and kissed her so softly, so gently, it seemed almost no kiss at all. As gentle as a snowflake, as sweet as a single raindrop. But it was the sweetness that was her undoing. With just the mere touch of his lips on hers, she felt her blood heat, her pulse rate begin to climb.

When he raised his head, she could see him watching her, his eyes narrowed on her with a look that was both pleading and puzzled. "It's your call, Annie. Tell me you want this, too."

It was on the tip of her tongue to bolt, but she was rooted to the spot. She couldn't have moved if she'd tried, and though she had at least a dozen good reasons why she ought to refuse his offer, at the moment she couldn't recall a single one.

Like someone in a dream she wrapped her arms around his neck and offered her lips for another drugging kiss. Her voice sounded husky in her own ears. "Oh, Ben. I thought you'd never ask."

7

For the space of a heartbeat the only sounds were their shallow breathing and the hiss and snap of the log on the fire. He stared into her eyes and saw the same smoldering need that was driving him slowly mad.

"I hope to hell I'm not dreaming." He covered her mouth with his and took the kiss deeper. Against her lips he muttered, "If I am, don't wake me."

Without warning he lifted her into his arms and headed toward the stairs. Halfway up, he couldn't wait any longer for another taste of her. As he lowered his mouth to hers, he felt a need that shook him to the core.

He couldn't recall another time when he'd known such a hunger. To taste. To touch. To possess.

He continued up the stairs and prayed for the strength to make it to the top before he gave in to the unbelievable passion that was nearly blinding him. With all the strength he could muster, he made it. Barely. Then he paused to kiss her again. A mistake, he realized at once. He should have waited until he'd reached his bedroom. Or hers.

"Annie." Pressing her back against a closed door, he struggled to keep the kiss gentle, as the others had been. But it was impossible. The need for her was humming through him, threatening to break free and rip apart the last shred of his control. "I'm not sure we can make it to a bed."

"Okay. I guess." She tried to laugh, but the sound came out on a choking sob.

His kisses were no longer gentle. Nor were the hands that moved over her, setting off sparks wherever they touched. Beneath the thin veneer of control was a violence that excited her even while it frightened her. This wasn't the urbane, civilized man who'd cooked dinner and served it by candlelight. This was the dangerous sailor she'd seen on the bay. A pirate, pitting his wiles against nature's storm.

And what a storm. It howled and raged between them, hurling them into a frenzy unlike anything they'd ever felt before.

His mouth demanded, devoured. His hands moved over her, possessing, arousing, until she was trembling with need.

"Wait." She put a hand on his chest. "I need to catch my breath."

"I don't want to wait, Annie." He lifted her hand to his lips and pressed a kiss to the palm, then to her wrist, then higher to the bend of her elbow. "I'm beyond waiting."

"I can't . . ." Her sigh was laced with frustration and pleasure. She turned blindly up the hallway, toward her bedroom. "I need . . ."

"All right." Sensing her fear, he dropped an arm around her shoulders and moved by her side. But after only a couple of steps he turned her into his arms and brushed his lips over her cheek, her jaw, her lips, loving the way her body reacted with a need that matched his own.

She drew back until she bumped against the closed door of her room. But he kept his hands on her, his lips on hers.

This was a mouth to savor. Full, generous lips. And a taste so sweet he had to keep returning to it, again and again. He couldn't get enough of the taste of her.

He cautioned himself to slow down. When he did he saw the way her eyes glazed as he nipped her lower lip, then dipped his tongue inside. Her eyes fluttered closed.

He could almost feel her skin soften and heat beneath his fingertips. Could feel the way she tensed, then released a breath, filling his mouth with the taste of her. Her heart was pounding almost as much as his.

He'd always felt a need for control, and now that it was slipping away from him, he realized he didn't care. The only thing that mattered was this woman, this moment, this all-consuming passion threatening to devour them both.

"The bed." With his mouth on hers, he reached behind her and twisted the knob.

As the door opened, the two of them nearly fell into the room. It was only Ben's arms around her that kept her upright. And then she was hauled against him, while his mouth fed on hers with a hunger that matched hers.

He sighed with frustration. He wanted her naked. He desperately needed to feel her flesh. As he lifted his hands to the buttons of her dress, he felt the way she trembled.

Trembled? It thrilled him as nothing else ever had. Though he wanted more than anything to strip away her clothes, he forced himself to put aside his needs and think about hers.

With a patience he'd never known he possessed, he skimmed his mouth over her face, whispering soft butterfly kisses across her forehead, her cheek, the tip of her nose.

She sighed. A long, drawn-out sound that

went straight to his heart.

Calmer now, he brought his hands to the buttons at her throat. This time he was able to move slowly and deliberately, without fear of tearing the delicate fabric. One by one, as the buttons opened and the bodice parted, he kept his eyes steady on hers. Finally, as he slid the dress from her shoulders, he lowered his gaze.

The sight of her nearly staggered him. "You're so beautiful, Annie. You take my breath away."

"And you, Ben." She tugged his sweater over his head and tossed it aside, needing to feel the warmth of his flesh. "You're beautiful, too."

He was — all hard, muscled flesh and skin burnished from the sun. She moved her hands over his hair-roughened chest, the flat planes of his stomach. She loved the way he quivered at her touch. Her hands splayed over his chest, and she could feel his heart thundering in rhythm with her own.

Somehow it steadied her to know that he was as caught up in the passion as she, to know that they were taking this crazy ride together. And it was crazy. Or at least it had seemed so just minutes ago. Now it seemed the most natural thing in the world to be standing here in the dark, the only light in the room coming from the spill of moon-light through the window. The play of light and shadow over his face gave him an added look of danger. And this man, who just a day ago had been a stranger to her, now excited her as no man ever had. He was about to take her to the most intimate of all places.

He lowered his head to run soft, nibbling kisses down her throat and across her shoulder. As he did, she felt her breath catch in her throat. But when his mouth dipped lower, to the swell of her breast, she couldn't hold back the little moan of pleasure. In-stinctively she arched against him, driving them both mad with need.

He tugged on the last button of her dress, allowing it to glide soundlessly over her hips to the floor, where it pooled at her feet. Then he lifted her to the bed and shed the rest of his clothes before lying beside her.

Moonlight turned the ends of her dark hair to flame and gilded her skin. For several seconds he studied her, loving the way she looked. Like a beautiful, beguiling angel.

"You should always wear nothing but moonlight, Annie."

She gave a husky laugh and reached out a hand to him. He surprised her by lifting it to his lips, where he kissed each finger. Then he leaned over her, allowing his mouth to roam over her torso, her ribs. With each touch of his mouth, she could feel the heat growing, and with it the need. Her breathing became more shallow as she felt herself slipping, slipping, deeper into that dark, demanding tunnel of desire.

"Ben, please." She reached for him, but he resisted.

"Not yet, Annie. Not yet. Let me pleasure you. Pleasure both of us." With lips and tongue and fingertips he roamed her body, fueling his own passion even as he drove her ever closer to the edge of madness.

He'd thought he wanted only relief from this blinding, aching need. But now he realized he wanted more. Much more. He wanted to touch, to taste, to savor. He wanted a feast, and here was a banquet of delight. The way she moved in his arms. The way she sighed with each new pleasure. It occurred to him that he wanted to touch not only her body but her heart and soul as well.

She thought she would die from the feel of those clever fingers moving over her. But when he found her, hot and wet, pleasure speared through her until it was close to pain. Sensation after sensation ripped through her, like arrows piercing her heart. She cried out until his mouth covered hers, swallowing the sound.

The air rose up between them, hot and thick, filling their lungs, making their breathing labored. Annie's body was on fire. Each touch brought fresh heat, threatening to sear her flesh, melt her bones.

Ben struggled to hold back, keeping relief just out of reach. Seeing her like this, without a shred of control, was the most erotic thing he'd ever experienced. He could feel his own control teetering on the very edge.

Somewhere in the deep, dark recesses of his mind was the fear that he had driven them both too far. The last thing he wanted was to take her like a savage. But even as the thought formed, it was gone. As was every other thought save one. He had to have her now, this minute, or die. For there was a beast inside him, clawing to be free.

"Annie." He breathed her name against her lips as he entered her.

He saw her eyes go wide, then flutter closed.

"Look at me, Annie."

Her eyes opened, and he could see them glazed with passion.

"I want to see you. I want you to see me."

As he began to move, she gave a moan and wrapped herself around him, moving with him, taking him higher, then higher still. Then they were sailing, skimming the waves until, caught in a whirlwind, they found themselves spinning out of control.

It was the most dizzying ride of their lives.

"Are you still alive?" He pressed his mouth to the hollow of her throat.

"Mmmm." She touched a hand to his cheek, then let it drop limply against the pillow.

They lay, still joined, their breathing shallow, bodies slick.

"Sorry. I didn't mean to be so rough."

"Me either."

He leaned up on one elbow to look down into her eyes. They were crinkled with unspoken laughter. Ribbons of gold played across her face, giving her the look of a gilded angel.

He trailed a finger across her cheek. "That was . . . amazing. You're amazing. But then, you probably already know that. I'm sure you've been told that by dozens of men."

"Hundreds."

Again he caught that quick smile and he was able to smile with her. He pressed his lips to her forehead and felt himself beginning to settle down. It was amazing how this simple act had quieted all the nerves. What he felt now was a sense of peace. Of contentment. It was something he hadn't felt in years. And it occurred to him that it was all because of this woman in his arms.

"Am I too heavy?"

"No." It was the truth. She found the press of his beautiful body on hers to be pleasurable. She liked the feel of his long legs on hers. His hair-roughened chest brushing hers. Those arms, so strong they could break her in two, holding her as gently as though she were made of spun glass.

When he rolled to one side, and gathered her against him, she almost moaned in protest. Instead, as he ran a hand along her spine, she found herself purring like a kitten.

He lifted a finger to trace the curve of her brow, the softness of her cheek. Now, feeling pleasantly sated, he could take the time to really look at her. "Do you know how beautiful you are, Annie?"

"Tell me." Her breath was warm against his throat. He found himself thinking that if she kept her mouth just there, he might go quietly mad.

"When I first saw you standing in the kitchen, I was sure I'd bumped my head harder than I'd thought and that you were just a figment of my imagination."

"When did you decide I was real?" She skimmed a hand along his side, and he found the scrape of her nails against his flesh the most exquisite torture.

"When you threatened me with the knife. The minute I touched you, and felt that heat, I knew you were real."

She sat up, her hair falling over one eye in a most seductive way. "You felt it, too?"

He merely stared at her. "So. It was the same for both of us."

"I thought . . ." She shook her head. "I thought at first that I was imagining it. But when it happened every time we touched, I knew it couldn't be all in my mind."

"As long as we're in the mood for confessions, I'll tell you one more thing." He reached up to play with a strand of her hair, twisting it round and round his finger. "I wasn't at all sorry when neither of our cars would start. I'd already begun to think it might be a fine idea to stick around for another day."

She felt the curl of pleasure along her spine and wondered if he knew what his touch was doing to her. "And here I thought you were angry because you had to miss your business meeting."

"I should have been. Any other time I

would have been." He tugged gently on her hair, drawing her face closer to his. "But the thought of spending another day in the company of the intriguing Annie Tyler certainly cushioned the blow."

He cupped a hand to the back of her head and guided her mouth to his. Against her lips he muttered, "Why don't we go for seconds?"

"So soon?"

"You mean you're already bored with me?"

She laughed. "I mean, I didn't think you'd be up to such a feat."

"You bring out the best in me. Or maybe it's the beast." He drew her down on top of him and ran a hand along the length of her. "What do you think?"

"Why, Mr. Carrington, what a surprise."

"Yeah. I'm just full of them." He tangled his hands in her hair and pulled her close for another kiss.

This time, he promised himself, he would move slowly and give her the care she deserved. But as their kisses heated and their heartbeats started racing, all his good intentions disappeared. They were hurled once more into the eye of the storm. All they could do was cling desperately to one another, until they reached the next calm shore.

"Sorry our coffee got so cold. I hope this will make it up to you." Ben was barefoot and naked to the waist, wearing only his grandfather's old pin-striped slacks, which he'd hastily pulled on. He handed Annie a flute of champagne, then climbed into bed beside her.

"Mmm." She sipped, then looked up at him with a smile. "This more than makes up for it. Besides" — her laughter came again, quick and light — "it seems we got a little sidetracked before we could drink our coffee."

She was wearing his tennis sweater for warmth. The deep V at the neck revealed the cleft between her breasts.

Across the room a cozy fire burned on the hearth.

On the bed between them lay a tray of assorted snacks. She spread a thin wafer with cheese and held it to his mouth.

He plumped the pillows behind him and leaned back, sighing with contentment. "Do you know, Annie, I can't remember when I've had a better time."

"I was just thinking the same thing." She shook her head, sending dark waves tumbling. "Wouldn't you think the loss of power, combined with the malfunction of all our gadgets, ought to have us wild with anxiety? Instead, here we are, feeling as relaxed and refreshed as though we'd been on a month's vacation."

He nodded. "I really ought to be feeling at least a little guilty about my missed appointments. But I don't." He drew her close for a slow, lazy kiss, enjoying the taste of champagne on her lips.

She spread more cheese and offered him another bite, then made a second one for herself. He topped off her flute with more champagne before filling his own.

As she sipped she wondered if it was the alcohol that made her lightheaded or the man beside her.

He had his hands on her again. It seemed he couldn't help himself. He loved touching her. Her hair. Her skin.

He leaned close to press a kiss to the slope of her shoulder, where the oversized sweater had slipped to reveal a tempting expanse of flesh. "I've been meaning to tell you. You look much better in this than I do. And I'd be willing to bet my grandfather never looked this good in it."

"I'll bet your grandmother would disagree."

He chuckled. "You're right. There were times when the two of them looked at each other that I could almost hear the sizzle. She'd smile, he'd wink, and the rest of us just seemed to fall away, leaving them alone in their own little cocoon of love."

"That's so sweet."

"Yeah." He took the flute from her hand and set it on the night table beside his.

"Wait. I'm not finished."

"Neither am I." He turned to her, and she saw that the dark, hungry look of a pirate was back in his eyes.

"I meant the champagne."

"I know what you meant." In one smooth motion he tugged the sweater over her head and dragged her into his arms.

Then there was no need for words as he took her on another fast, dizzying journey into that place where only lovers can go.

8

Annie felt herself drifting on a cloud of contentment. There was something heavy pressing her into the mattress, and it took her a moment to realize it was Ben's leg, tossed possessively over hers. His arm was around her, pinning her to the length of him.

It felt good, so right, lying here beside him, feeling the warmth of his body seeping into her pores.

They had stayed the night in this big bed, alternately loving, then dozing, then waking to love again. Looking back on it, she marveled that they had indulged themselves like two greedy children, wanting more, and then more. At times their lovemaking had been as comfortable as if they'd been old lovers. At other times they'd been caught in a torrent of emotions, tossed and buffeted like driftwood in a hurricane. Taking each other with a savageness that left them both dazed and breathless.

It occurred to Annie that the night had seemed to spin on forever. Without a clock, they were completely unaware of the passage of time. Even now, with the sky outside the window still in darkness, she wasn't certain whether it was midnight or almost dawn. But her stomach told her it had been hours since she'd eaten.

She tossed aside the blanket and started to sit up. A hand closed around her wrist.

"Does this mean you're tired of me already?"

She turned to find Ben watching her with that dark intensity that always seemed to touch her heart in a special way.

"I've decided to throw you over in favor of food."

"Oh, yeah? Maybe I can tempt you with this." He dragged her close and brushed a kiss over her lips.

At once she felt the heat and was amazed that even now, sated from a whole night of lovemaking, he had the ability to arouse her so easily.

"Mmmm." She nibbled his mouth. "Very nice. But I can't live on love alone."

"You really know how to hurt a guy. How about this?" He took the kiss deeper and ran his hands along her spine, lighting fires with each touch until she sighed from the pure pleasure of it.

"Well. Maybe I could stand a few more minutes of this."

"I'm happy to oblige." He dragged her down until she was pinned beneath him. Then he pressed his mouth to her throat and heard the little hum of delight. "How about an hour?"

"Okay. As long as you promise not to stop doing what you're doing."

"I promise." He chuckled, then moved his mouth lower, until he heard her gasp of surprise. "You see. I'm a man of my word."

But she was already beyond hearing. Under his ministrations, she'd slipped into that dark cavern of pleasure, and he was only too happy to follow.

"I can't remember ever feeling like this." Ben lay on his side, cradling Annie against him.

Her hair lay in dark curls against the pillow. He played with the ends, loving the way her eyes stayed steady on his. He would gladly drown in their depths.

The bed linens were tangled around them. They were both pleasantly sated, though they knew it was only a matter of time before passion would rise up again to thrust them back into the whirlwind.

He touched a hand to her mouth. "I've never believed in love at first sight. But I don't know what else to call this."

Annie felt her heart bounce once and fall nearly to her toes, before leaping to her throat. She'd been thinking the same thing, but had been terrified to speak the words aloud.

She touched a hand to his cheek. "This has been the most amazing night of my life."

"Mine, too. And what I feel for you isn't just lust." He gave her one of those heart-stopping smiles. "Though I must admit the lust part isn't bad either."

She chuckled until he brushed his lips over hers. At once she felt the jolt to her already charged system.

Would it always be like this? she wondered. Would he always have the power to make her heart jump through hoops with a single kiss?

"But there's more here, Annie." With a finger he traced the outline of her lips. "There's the fact that I love everything about you. The way you talk. The way you laugh. The way you've chosen to live your life. I especially love the way you handled this awkward situation, with no power, no conveniences, and no way to leave."

She brushed a lock of hair from his forehead. "If you hadn't been here with me, I'd have run the twenty miles to the nearest town. I'm basically a coward."

"Not you, Annie. Aren't you the woman who gave up her life in New York for the unknown here in Maine, just because your grandmother needed you?"

"But that's not the same as this. I stayed because you're here with me, Ben. I would never have stayed here alone through all of this."

"But that's just it." He linked his fingers with hers, loving the way their two hands looked. Hers small and soft. His large and slightly calloused from his work on the sailboat. It had felt so good to work with his hands again after years in a confining office. "We're here together. And we've found something special. I know it's sudden, Annie, but I don't want this to end. I'd like us to find a way to stay together."

She sighed. "You make it sound like some sort of fairy tale. We meet, we fall in love, and we live happily ever after."

"Why not? We're two adults. We know what we want. Why can't we make it happen?"

Why not? she wondered. At any other time she could probably come up with a dozen different reasons why this wouldn't work. But at the moment, with his hands linked with hers, his hard, firm body pressed against hers, and her head spinning from his touch, she couldn't come up with a single one.

He lowered his head to whisper against her temple, "Do you feel the same way about me, Annie?"

She nodded, too overcome at the moment to speak.

He tucked a finger under her chin and lifted her face so that he could look into her eyes. "What's this? Tears? Over me?"

"I . . . feel so silly. But I never thought . . ." She sniffed. "I never thought I'd feel this way about anyone. Ever again."

"Neither did I. Oh, Annie. You've made me believe in the impossible." He drew her close and pressed his lips to her temple. "This is too wonderful for words."

Then he showed her, in the only way he could, just how much he cared. With slow, deep kisses and soft, whispered sighs, they took each other to a higher, sweeter place than they'd ever been.

"What's this?" Annie stepped out onto the patio to see Ben closing the lid on a wicker basket.

"Our lunch." He looked up, then gave a smile of approval. "You'd better watch out. I might decide to make you lunch. In that outfit you look good enough to eat."

"You like it?"

He watched as she slowly twirled. The dress of ivory voile had short, fluttery sleeves and a softly fitted waistline, then fell in a long, straight column to her ankles. To fill in the deep V of the neckline, she'd pinned a cameo brooch to a velvet ribbon tied at her throat. Her dark hair was swept up and held with mother-of-pearl combs. The effect was stunning.

"I'm beginning to really love wearing your grandmother's clothes. I think I'll actually be sorry when my own are dry and I have to go back to wearing jeans and sweaters."

He traced a finger down her arm, watching the way her eyes heated at his touch. "I think I'll be sorry, too. I like looking at you in these old-fashioned things."

She gave an exaggerated flutter of her lashes. "Maybe it's because I'm just an old-fashioned girl at heart."

"You're making a joke. But in truth you are."

"And how would you know?"

He brushed his lips over hers, and though he thought he was prepared for the jolt, it still managed to catch him by surprise. "I just know. Every time I touch you, every time we kiss, I know you, Annie Tyler. As though I've known you for a lifetime."

Strange, she thought as he picked up the wicker basket and caught her hand, but it was true for her as well. She felt as though she'd been waiting for this man, and this moment, all her life. And that everything that had happened before had been in preparation for this very special time.

"Where are we going?"

"On a picnic."

"Where?"

"There's a little sandy cove. It's ringed with rocks and very secluded. But it has a great view of the bay."

"Sounds like fun." She linked her arm through his and they started out.

They crossed the overgrown lawns of White Pines and slipped into the cool darkness of a pine forest.

Annie breathed in the fragrance of evergreens as they made their way between huge boulders and around fallen logs. Then, just as suddenly as they'd entered the forest, they emerged into a sun-dappled cove overlooking the bay.

"Oh, Ben. This is wonderful." Annie stared around, enjoying the spectacular view of water ahead of them, the towering forest at their backs.

She slipped off her shoes and followed him across the sun-warmed sand to a shady spot between two egg-shaped boulders.

"When I was a kid, I thought of this as my secret place." Ben opened the basket and lifted out a blanket, which he shook and lowered to the sand. "I thought of these two rocks as giant dinosaur eggs. I used to climb them and balance on the very top, staring out to sea. All alone here, I was master of my universe."

"I can see why you loved it." Annie walked to the water's edge and felt the brush of waves against her bare toes. "I don't think I've ever seen a prettier place."

"Then I'm glad I brought you." He walked up beside her and caught her hand, lifting it to his lips. "A pretty woman deserves a pretty place."

"Such lovely words rolling off that silver tongue of yours, Mr. Carrington." She was laughing when she looked up into his eyes. But the smoldering look she saw there faded her smile.

"I've never said such things before, Annie. I never felt the need. Until now." He drew her into his arms and kissed her. "Until you," he whispered against her mouth.

She could have sworn that the sand shifted and her world tilted as he took the kiss deeper.

When he lifted his head he caught her hand. "Come on. I promised to feed you."

Annie knelt on the blanket and watched as he opened a bottle of champagne. "I've never been on a picnic before."

"Really?" He looked up. "Never?"

She shook her head. "My parents were always working. After they were gone, my grandmother and I never seemed to have time for anything except getting through the next few years." She looked over as he popped the cork. "Have you been on many picnics?"

"Too many to count. My parents used to take us across the bay in their boat. They always brought along a picnic lunch. We'd walk the shore, searching for driftwood and fancy stones." He stared into the distance a moment, lost in thought. Then he shook his head. "Funny. I'd forgotten how many wonderful memories we've shared here. For too long now I've thought only of the reasons why I didn't want to be here."

She waited, hoping he would explain. What tragedy had driven this loving family away from White Pines? Why had they allowed it to fall into such disrepair?

Instead, he held his silence as he filled two flutes and handed one to her.

She smiled. "Shall we drink to happy memories?"

He nodded. His eyes were steady on hers. "To happy memories. And to happily-ever-after."

They sipped in silence, watching each other over the rims of their glasses. Then he turned away and began unwrapping an assortment of foods. Croissants, which had been sealed in foil and warmed on the grill. Several types of cheese — Cheddar, Gouda, Swiss — cut into cubes. Shrimp and lobster still steaming from the barbecue.

Annie burst into laughter. "Who's supposed to eat all this?"

He looked up. "Aren't you the one who told me you couldn't live on love alone?"

She shook her head. "I may have been in need of a little food, but this is a lot more than a little. This is a feast."

"You'd better enjoy it, then, because I'm not sure how long I can wait to try the love diet again."

She laughed until she saw the fire in his eyes. She turned serious and touched a hand to her chest.

His tone was rough with passion. "What's wrong?"

"Nothing." She managed a smile. "It's just my heart. It keeps on turning somersaults whenever you look at me like that."

"Good. I'm glad to hear I'm not the only one suffering like this." He offered her a bite of cheese.

When she swallowed it, he reached over and took the glass of champagne from her hands, setting it beside his. "Okay. That's enough food for now. If you don't mind, I'd like to get back to that other thing we do so well."

"Ben." She allowed herself to be drawn into the circle of his arms and shivered slightly as he reached to undo the buttons of her dress.

"What?"

She sighed as his mouth followed his fingers and began to weave that wonderful magic once again. "Nothing. I just wanted to tell you that I approve of this diet."

They came together with laughter, which quickly changed to sighs as they lost themselves in the wonder of their newly discovered love.

The sun was at their backs as they made their way back to the house. Annie glanced at their linked fingers and thought how easily she and Ben had slipped into this slower, lazier rhythm.

As they approached the patio, they both began to slow the pace, almost as if they dreaded what they might find.

"Think the power's back on?" She saw Ben frown before he shrugged.

"We'll soon see." He opened the French doors, then reached for a light switch.

When nothing happened, they burst into laughter and realized they'd both been holding their breath.

"Looks like we're stuck with candles and wood fires for another night." Relieved, Ben set the basket on the kitchen counter, then turned to Annie. "I think I'll head out back to the woodpile for a fresh supply."

"Good idea. I'll get more candles and bring them to the kitchen."

She walked to the great room and started toward the fireplace where candles were massed on the mantel.

Seeing a blur of movement outside the window, she hurried over. Win, she thought, smiling. With all that had happened, she'd completely forgotten about him. He must have finished his surprise for his brother and was now planning a visit.

As she walked closer, she could see that it wasn't Win. This was a stranger, a white-haired man peering in the window. She hurried to the door and stepped out onto the wide front porch.

"Hello." She watched as the man stepped away from the window and turned to study her.

"I saw the car." He pointed. "Figured I'd better investigate."

"My name is Annie Tyler. I drove up from Tranquility, where I have a small real estate office. I've been hired by Mrs. Carrington to handle the sale of White Pines."

"She's selling it, is she?" He walked closer, wiping his hand on his pant leg before extending it. "Name's Oscar Gabriel. Used to be the gardener here. My wife and I live just up the highway a few miles. Not surprised they're not coming back."

"You aren't? Why is that?"

He gave her a long look, then shrugged. "Most folks around here know about what happened at White Pines. We figured once the family left, they wouldn't want to come back to such unsavory memories."

"Why, Mr. Gabriel? What happened here?"

He cleared his throat. "Don't abide gossip myself, but I guess it's old news by now. Win, the younger of the two Carrington sons, was an artist. Wild sort. Not at all like his older brother, Ben. Fine young man, that Ben. Anyway, Win always had an eye for the ladies, and Ben's wife, Laura, was a real beauty. It started out innocently enough, I heard. She posed for a portrait as a surprise for her husband. One thing led to another. Then one night she and Win left a note saying they were running away together."

"Win . . . stole his brother's wife?"

"That was his intention." The old man frowned. "Funny the way things happen. It was a rainy night. One of those bad storms we get now and again here on the coast. Their car went off the highway just around the bend there, past the stables." He shook his head, remembering. "It was the talk of the countryside."

"Were they . . . hurt?"

"Hurt?" He peered at her, then tucked his hands in his pockets and rocked back on his heels.

For several seconds he stared hard at the ground. It was obvious that it still pained him to talk about the incident.

"There wasn't much left of either of them by the time they were pried from the wreck. Win and Laura were both killed instantly."

9

All the color drained from Annie's face.

Alarmed, the old man touched a hand to her arm. "Here now, miss. You don't look so good. You'd better sit down a minute."

"No. I can't. I have to . . ." Dazed, she turned away and pulled open the front door. Then she seemed to catch herself. "Will you come inside, Mr. Gabriel?"

"Sorry. Can't." He shook his head. "Got to be getting home. My wife will have supper ready."

"Supper." She rested her forehead against the door, struggling to focus. She couldn't seem to make her mind function. Then it came to her. "What is she using for power?"

"Electricity. Same as always." He was watching her warily.

"Didn't you lose your power in that storm?"

"What storm, miss?"

"The storm Friday night."

He took a step closer. "You sure you're all right?"

"Yes. I just . . ." She turned away, but his voice stopped her.

"Today is Friday, miss."

"Today?" She turned back. "But it was two days ago that I drove up here. On a Friday evening."

He was shaking his head again, looking at her as though she'd just lost her mind. "I was here yesterday, miss. I always drop by on Thursdays, just to look over the place and see that nothing's been vandalized. I guess I've always been hoping that the Carringtons might decide to come back and turn this old place into a home again." He sighed. "Anyway, today's Friday." He glanced at his watch. "It's just a little past seven forty-five."

She blanched, then began running toward the kitchen.

The old man watched a moment longer. Then, shaking his head in alarm, he turned away.

"Ben." Seeing him striding along the hallway with an armload of logs, Annie halted.

"Hey." Noticing her pallor, he dropped the logs and caught her arm. "What's wrong? You look like you've seen a ghost."

She shivered. "Mr. Gabriel was here."

"Old Oscar? He was our gardener for years. Why didn't he stay? I'd have enjoyed seeing him again."

"Ben." She was beginning to tremble in reaction to what she'd just heard. She clutched her arms around herself, wishing there was some way to soften the blow. "Mr. Gabriel told me about your wife and your brother."

She saw the look that came into his eyes. As though he'd been struck.

"I'm sorry. I suppose I should have told you, Annie. But it's not something I care to repeat. It's the reason why we've never returned to White Pines. No matter how many good memories we had here, in the end that's the only one we have left."

"Ben, you don't understand." Though she was trembling, she reached out a hand to him. "Your brother, Win, isn't dead. I saw him yesterday. At the stables. In his studio apartment."

Ben's eyes narrowed on her. For several minutes he couldn't seem to find his voice. The silence hung between them.

Finally he closed a hand over hers. His tone was as patient as though he were addressing a child. "Look, I know this weekend has been something of a strain."

"You don't understand." She drew away. "I saw him. I talked with him. He was handsome and charming and . . . he flirted with me."

"Annie . . ." He reached out to her.

"No." She took several steps backward, then suddenly turned toward the door. "I'm not crazy or overwrought. Win is here. He's living and working in the stable. I'll prove it."

She began running.

"Annie! Wait!"

She heard Ben's voice but she refused to stop or even look over her shoulder to see if he was following.

She was desperate to get to the stables. Ben would see for himself that this had all been some horrible mistake.

Annie pushed open the door to the stables and stepped inside. She looked around at the empty stalls as she made her way across the floor to the stairs, which she took two at a time in her haste.

At the top of the stairs she paused and turned the knob. The door was stuck, and it took several attempts before she managed to nudge it open with her hip. As she did she heard the sound of Ben's footsteps behind her.

"Win!" she shouted as she stepped into the studio.

In the silence that greeted her, she stared around in absolute astonishment.

"Annie." She felt Ben's hand on her arm, but she pulled away and stepped further into the room.

Except for cobwebs that hung everywhere and dust that had settled thickly over the floor, the room was bare. Instead of the strong odor of paint and thinner that had earlier permeated the air, it was now musty and stale.

"His bed was there." She pointed to a corner where a spider was busy adding to his already giant web. "And over here was a worktable, littered with sketches. There were canvases and easels lining the walls. Those windows were clean." She noted that they were now streaked with an accumulation of dust and grime.

Her voice took on a note of urgency. "He was here. I didn't imagine it. We talked. He flirted and said he wanted to paint me. He even offered me a glass of champagne. When I asked him why he hadn't told you he was here, he said he was planning a surprise for you. He called it a . . . ." She struggled through layers of confusion to recall. "He called it a re-birthday gift." She turned. "He was really here, Ben. I didn't imagine it."

Ben seemed not to hear her. He was staring at a spot in the far corner. A single unframed canvas stood on an easel, turned to the wall.

Without a word he walked over and turned the canvas around. Annie went to stand beside him.

It was a painting of Ben and Annie, dressed as they were now, Ben in his grandfather's borrowed pants and sweater, Annie in the old-fashioned gown. They were standing together on the sandy beach, looking at each other as they had earlier that day. In their eyes was an unmistakable look of love.

Annie felt the sting of tears and couldn't stop them from spilling down her cheeks.

Seeing it, Ben drew her close and wiped them with his thumbs. "There's no need to cry, Annie."

"But there is. I don't understand any of this, Ben. But I know I'm not crazy. And I didn't dream Win. I didn't."

"I know." He shivered and looked around, then he picked up the painting and tucked it under his arm.

He took her hand in his. It was so cold.

In a voice gruff with emotion, he said,

"Come on, Annie. Let's get back to the house."

They didn't speak. Not a single word passed between them as they crossed the overgrown orchard and made their way across the patio into the kitchen. As they stepped inside, Ben put the painting on the counter, and the two of them studied it in silence.

It was then that they noticed that the lights were on. The refrigerator was humming. The clock on the wall was ticking.

Annie glanced at it. "Just a little past seven forty-five." She turned to Ben. "Isn't that the time the storm struck?"

He nodded.

"Mr. Gabriel told me that today is Friday."

At his arched brow she nodded. "I thought he was mistaken. But now, after all this, I'm just not sure of anything."

"There's one way to find out." Ben picked up the phone and listened for a dial tone. Hearing it, he punched in a series of numbers. The voice on the other end of the line spoke in a monotone.

When he hung up, he grew thoughtful.

"Well?" Annie waited.

He turned to her. "It's just as he said. It's Friday, April twenty-third, seven forty-five. The weather predicted for the weekend is clear and sunny and unseasonably warm."

Annie had to reach out a hand to the countertop to steady herself. This wasn't possible. It couldn't be. She put her hands to her temples, to blot out the nerves that were beginning to take over.

She was suddenly more afraid than she'd ever been in her life. This wasn't happening. None of it.

With a cry she ran out of the room and raced up the stairs. A short time later she descended the stairs, dressed in her jeans and sweater, which were as dry and untouched by the rain as they'd been when she first hung them in the closet.

In one hand was her purse, in the other the overnight bag. She knew that if she looked in the refrigerator she would find the groceries she'd unpacked earlier. And all of them would be untouched.

Ben was standing where she'd left him, staring at the portrait. His color, she noted, was as pale as hers. The look on his face was a mix of anger and puzzlement.

"Good-bye, Ben."

He looked up and struggled to focus. "Where are you going, Annie?"

"Home. Back to Tranquility. I'll . . . phone your mother on Monday with my recommendations."

He nodded, still too distracted to reply.

She walked to the door and opened it, then turned. He never even seemed to notice her. His attention was riveted on the portrait. His hands, she noted, were clenched at his sides.

She closed the door and made her way to her car. Inside, she turned the key, and the engine hummed. As she drove along the curving ribbon of drive, her eyes filled, and she had to blink furiously before she could continue on to the highway. She wasn't crying over Ben Carrington, she told herself. She was just crying because . . . because she'd almost begun to believe in fairy tales, and happily-ever-after. But a ghost? She shook her head. That was asking too much. Unless, of course, she was losing her mind.

What she needed, desperately, was to spend the rest of the weekend back in Tranquility. Back in the land of reality. Doing what she did best. Working.

"Hey, Annie." Shelly looked up when the office door opened. "I thought you were going to spend the weekend at White Pines."

"Morning, Shelly." Annie set her laptop on the desk, carefully avoiding her friend's eyes, and began removing papers from her attaché case. "I . . . didn't stay. Just drove up and took a look at the place, then drove back."

"Too spooky, huh?" Shelly poured coffee and set it on Annie's desk, then gave her a good, long look. "You really need to take some time off. I bet you stayed up the whole night working."

Annie shrugged and was grateful when Shelly was forced to turn away to answer the phone. Minutes later, with her computer calling up her accumulation of E-mail, she tore off a fax and paused to check the number on her pager.

"Annie." Shelly put a hand over the phone's speaker. "Melvin Jakes from the camera shop is on the phone. He said that roll of film you left with him is completely blank. He wonders if you want to bring in your camera so he can have a look at it."

No surprise, Annie thought, considering what she'd been dealing with. "Tell him I'll stop by tomorrow."

When her mail carrier delivered a stack of letters, Annie thanked him and began sorting through them. She never even bothered to look up when the door opened a second time.

It was Ben's voice that made her slowly lift her head.

"You were easy enough to find. Every-body in Tranquility knows Annie Tyler."

"Ben." Out of the corner of her eye she saw Shelly's jaw drop. And no wonder. He looked every inch the successful lawyer. Perfectly tailored dark suit. Designer tie. Italian loafers. "I figured you'd be in New York by now."

"Yeah. That's what I thought, too. In fact, I started out for the airport. Then I realized what a mistake that would be."

"A mistake?"

He was looking at her the way he'd looked in the cove by the bay. The way he'd looked in the portrait.

Except that the picnic by the cove had never really happened. And the portrait was as unreal as the man who'd flirted with her in the stable.

She had to keep reminding herself of that fact.

He pressed his two hands on her desktop so that his eyes were level with hers. "We were given a very special gift this weekend, Annie, and we very nearly tossed it away."

"You mean mass hysteria is something to be thankful for?"

"Is that what you think? Annie, we weren't suffering from mass hysteria. Win was really there."

He saw her glance at her friend, then away.

For Annie's sake he lowered his voice. "The storm, the time we spent away from the rest of the world, even the portrait, were real. We experienced those things together."

She pushed away from her desk and got to her feet. "I don't want to talk about this, Ben."

"Well, you're going to, whether you like it or not."

She was already shaking her head, about to turn away, when he rounded the desk, blocking her way. "I don't know how he did it, but Win managed to come back. And what he gave us was a very special gift."

"You call fear, terror, a gift?"

"You weren't afraid while it was happening. In fact, you never showed an iota of fear. Not during the storm, or the power outage, or any of the other inconveniences. It wasn't until you realized what had really happened that you bolted. I don't blame you for being afraid then. I was afraid, too. But now that I've had time to think about it, I can appreciate just how special Win's gift was."

Annie was watching him carefully. "I don't understand."

"Don't you see what he gave me? What he gave us both?"

She shook her head, determined to deny everything.

"Time, Annie. He gave us the gift of time. We were two workaholics running on a treadmill, without ever getting off. And now, thanks to that little . . . storm, we've had all the time in the world to meet, to fall in love, to think about a future together."

"Then you . . . think this really happened?"

He stared down at her, afraid to touch her. If he did, there was no telling what he might do. All he had thought about on the long drive here was the touch of her, the taste of her lips, the way she felt in his arms. He was aching to hold her again.

"I don't think anyone will ever believe what happened to us. But you and I will always know. And for that I have my brother to thank."

His smile came slowly. But when it did, Annie felt her own fears begin to evaporate. "Win told you it was my re-birthday surprise. A good choice of words. Because, thanks to his generous gift, I have been reborn."

She studied him carefully, noting that the little lines of stress around his eyes were gone, and the smile on his lips was as bright as the sun. "Does this mean you've forgiven Win?"

He nodded. "I never thought such a thing would be possible. The pain was too deep, the betrayal too vicious. But now I realize that sometimes a family's bonds are too strong to be severed, even by such a cruel act. However he managed it, Win found a way to come back and make things right. I'll always be grateful. Because of him, I've found you, Annie. And I don't want to lose you." He did touch her then. Just the press of his hands along the top of her arms. But it was enough to bring the familiar rush of heat to both of them.

"Annie, I love you more than I could have ever believed it was possible to love anyone." He took a deep breath, needing to impress on her the enormity of his feelings. "I've already asked my mother to reconsider the sale of White Pines. I'd like to buy it myself. That is, if you'd be willing to go up there with me on weekends and breathe life into the old place again. I think with a lot of love and hard work we could restore it to its former beauty."

"But my work. My responsibilities. I . . . have so many debts from my grandmother's illness."

He smiled that wicked, dangerous smile she'd come to know. "Annie, I'm a wealthy man. Your debts are the least of my worries.

I still don't know how I'll fulfill my obligations to a staff of employees on two coasts. I'll just have to figure out a solution. But I will. I have to. Because you're more important than anything else in my life." His tone lowered for emphasis. "There are probably a hundred good reasons why we shouldn't rush into this, but only one very good reason why we should. Life is so short. And we've just found the most incredible love. Why shouldn't we just reach out and hold on to it?"

Annie twisted her hands together. "Oh, Ben. This is crazy. Impossible. Impulsive. It's so unlike us."

"I know. But we can change. We can bend." He held his breath.

"Win said you were so rigid that if you ever tried to bend you'd break."

"He did?"

She nodded. A slow smile curved her mouth. "But he was wrong. And you're right. I love you. Nothing else matters."

He grabbed her and held her a little bit away from him. "Is that a yes?"

"Yes. Oh, yes. I love you, Ben Carrington. And right now, I want it all. Love. Marriage. The fairy tale. The happily-ever-after."

At her words, Ben felt his heart begin to beat again. With a shout he lifted Annie in his arms and swung her around, then kissed her until they were both breathless.

In that instant they heard a sound. Like a man's soft chuckle. Shelly would later say it had been the wind, but Annie and Ben knew otherwise. They looked at each other and began to laugh. Then they came together in another long, slow kiss to seal their bargain. As they did, they were convinced that a certain wild soul was watching with approval as the brother he'd admired, then betrayed, finally found the forgiveness and the peace he'd sought for so long, with the woman of his dreams.

This was, they realized, the finest gift of all. Love. Enough to last a lifetime. And beyond.

The Bridge of Sighs

Marianne Willman

To my favorite spinners of enchanted dreams,
Nora,
Jill, and Ruth, to Karen Katz, and to Dan.
May all your most beautiful dreams come true.

Prologue

Venice, Italy

Shadows filled the great room with its orna-mental plastered and painted medallions. The girl glanced about nervously, then hurried inside. The hem of her gold velvet gown, the soft leather of her green embroidered slippers, whispered over the rose-and-white-marble tiles of the floor. Water dripped nearby.

The tall shutters at the far end of the salon were closed, but bars of fading light told her that twilight was approaching rapidly. A sense of ur-gency compelled her. She was late.

Dear God, please not too late!

She hesitated by the stairs leading down to the first floor, which opened to the canal. Her escape would be quicker by water, but she didn't dare risk being seen. The girl sighed and turned reluc-tantly away. Passing through a small vestibule, she pulled aside the heavy curtain that covered the door leading to a neglected courtyard.

Lifting her velvet skirts to keep them from being soiled, she moved silently around the starlit gardens. A bit of Pointe de Venice lace caught on the rough bricks of the ancient stone well, and she yanked it free.

She took the wine-colored cape from its hiding place in the alcove behind a statue, then tied the strings of her mask securely. She had vowed on her life to meet him. He would already be there, waiting.

The door in the far wall that led to the calle *was locked, but she had the key tucked in her pocket. She peeked through the intricate wrought-iron design set in the thick wood, then slipped into the narrow alleyway. The hinges sighed, and the door clicked shut behind her. There was no going back now. The outer door had no handle and could be opened only from inside the garden.*

The blank walls of the buildings rose up four and five stories on either hand. As darkness deepened, their mellow tints of peach and pink and rose faded to dull terra-cotta and lavender. Soon they would be leached of color and merge into the night shadows.

She listened to make sure no one had followed. By daylight she felt safe here, as if she were in a secret passageway leading to adventure. Tonight, with only the deepening incandescent twilight to light her way, she was terrified. This path to freedom could so easily become a trap!

There were no footsteps. No sound but that of her own ragged breathing. After a moment she went on.

The calle *narrowed, then branched off into a maze of other alleyways. There was no way she could get lost. She had only to look for the tall, pointed roof of the* Campanile San Marco *rising above the tiles of the neighboring houses to guide her.*

Suddenly the plaintive call of a gondolier drifted on the breeze, and another picked it up in the distance, like an echo. The sound was so lonely, so wrenching, she felt as if her heart might break.

She touched the necklace at her throat for courage. It was the only thing she had taken with her when she fled the house. He *had given it to her. Her fingertips slid over the smooth beads that held the heart-shaped ruby pendant, as if she were telling the beads of her rosary. Starlight caused the matching ring on her finger to glow with intriguing lights. She'd never dared to wear it before.*

Thoughts of her lover, of their future together, made her brave. He would be waiting for her at the bridge. But the closer she got to the bridge, the more her heart pounded beneath her lace-trimmed bodice.

She hid in the shadows. Domenico was not there. She was suddenly afraid.

Deeply afraid . . .

*"I had had my dreams of Venice.
But nothing that I had dreamed was as impossible
as what I found."*

— ARTHUR SYMONS, Cities

1

Claire jerked suddenly awake, completely disoriented. The frightened girl in the long velvet gown and embroidered slippers faded and reality took over. The comfortable leather chair, the elegant cabin interior, the muted roar of the private motor launch as it sliced through the fog and rain.

Sandbagged by jet lag, damn it! And that dream. Again.

She always awakened before the girl reached the bridge. Before dream changed to nightmare.

Clair shook her head to clear it, then looked out the window beside her. Opalescent mists rose from the surface of the lagoon to meet the fine silver rain, almost totally obscuring the view. Somewhere out there was Venice, the most romantic and intriguing city in the world.

Now and then the mist shifted, creating a strange, dreamlike effect. Bits of Venice hovered in the air like apparitions: the spire of a church, a square bell tower, or the Gothic facade of a palazzo took shape, only to dissolve once more into the pearly, scattered light.

Claire felt as if she were floating softly back in time, into a world filled with decadent charm and unearthly beauty.

It was snug and warm inside the richly appointed cabin. Count Ludovici had insisted on sending his launch to pick her up. Leaning back against the luxurious leather chair, Claire smiled. This trip to Venice to appraise several of the count's paintings was the high point of her career.

Sterling Galleries in San Francisco, where she worked as a specialist in Renaissance art, had scored a major coup when Count Ludovici had commissioned them to offer several drawings from his family's extensive collection at private auction. Now he was planning on doing the same with some fabulous paintings.

But the real bombshell had come in a cryptic phone call she'd received from Ludovici himself, hinting that he had an unknown Titian. Why he would want to sell it was a mystery, but if it was true, Sterling Galleries and Claire would be on their way! Not that it was definite that Sterling Galleries would get the private auction. Claire had to convince the count that they were up to the job. That they'd deal with the Italian authorities, that they'd find the right buyers — discreet patrons of the arts who would only be too glad to pay fabulous fees for incomparable works and avoid the notoriety that attended a public auction. Then most of them would be donated by the philanthropists and art patrons who bought them to a local museum. A win-win situation. Everyone came out ahead.

She wasn't sure she could pull it off. Panic fluttered inside her breast. *I'm not a saleswoman or a dealmaker. I'm researcher, a bookworm. A behind-the-scenes kind of person, damn it!*

Tish Sterling, the ultra-fashionable gallery owner, had thought otherwise and was eager to clinch the deal.

"You'll do fine," Tish had assured Claire, her smile as bright as her expensively cut, copper-penny hair. "And you have a connection with Venice. That's a link between you and the count, right there."

Claire had splayed her hands and examined her nail polish. Venetian Pearl. Maybe it was an omen. "I just don't want to ruin this opportunity for you, Tish. I've never done anything like this before."

"Why are you always afraid of trying something new?"

It was an old question, and Claire still didn't have an answer.

Tish opened the window, lit a cigarette, inhaled, and blown a smoggy cloud out over the parking lot. With her bright green-gold eyes and spiky hair, she looked like a friendly dragon, with two streamers of gray smoke curling lazily from her nostrils.

"I'm a good businesswoman, Claire, and believe me, I wouldn't pack you off to Italy if I didn't think you could pull it off. Be yourself, but treat the count with kid gloves. Fitzgerald was right, you know: The rich *are* different. Especially the old, noble families."

She waved her manicured hand with its wide cuff of silver and gold at the marvelous burled-chestnut paneling of her office, the view of the Golden Gate Bridge beyond. "We're Johnny-come-latelies. The Ludovicis can trace their roots back a thousand years, to when Venice was nothing but a few huts stuck up on pilings in the mud flats of the lagoon. They don't think in terms of years but of generations."

Tish took a second drag on her cigarette, then stubbed it out carefully in the only ashtray allowed at Sterling Galleries. She let herself use it once a day. "Count Andrea Ludovici's ancestors were ruling Venice even then. Mine were raiding English cattle over the border from Scotland, wearing nothing but blue paint beneath their plaids. If they even bothered to wear their plaids."

She ran a hand through her hair, making it stand straight up, and still managed to look chic. "You go to Venice, Claire, and convince the count to sign the contract with us."

And here I am, Claire thought in amazement, as the launch changed course in the glowing mist. The engine slowed. The panic hardened to a dull lead fist, right in the pit of her stomach. The moment of truth was growing closer every minute.

Over a thousand years. She tried again to grasp the enormity of that span of time. To know exactly who your ancestors were for the past millennium! It seemed impossible.

Certainly it was for her. She knew her father's great-grandfather had sailed to America from Scotland when he was a boy of sixteen and started the family ranch in Idaho. On her mother's side, Claire's bloodlines were Irish and Italian.

That was about it, as far as her own family history went. Her mother had died too young to tell her more, and her father and grandfather were more interested in the future than the past. Perhaps that was why she loved the past so much. It was real and constant.

Once again she felt the launch swing right in a long arc. With her small map spread across her lap, she tried to guess how close the launch was to her destination. If only the mist would burn off and the skies clear! Off to one side, she knew, was the Isola de Guideca, the curving island of crumbling palazzi and neglected squares, with the elegant Hotel Cipriani set like a jewel at its tip. On the other side were the multitude of small islands, connected by humped bridges, that formed Venice proper.

She caught her reflection in the polished brass fitments. The interior lights winked off her emerald-cut topaz earrings and turned her wildly curling blond hair to masses of beaten gold. On their first date, her ex-husband had told her that she looked like a woman from a Renaissance painting. Val's deep voice floated through her memory: *"Botticelli's Venus, rising from the sea. Only with clothes on. Unfortunately."*

Claire remembered laughing up into his blue eyes — and that had been that. She ran her fingers through her hair. One thing about Val, she thought wryly. He certainly knew the way to an art major's heart. He just didn't know how to keep it.

His loss, she told herself, but an ache remained just the same.

The launch's engines reversed suddenly, slowing their forward motion. "Behold, *signorina*," the pilot said over the intercom. "Venezia!"

She swiveled her chair for a better look out the side window. The weather was changing. The soft rain that had been falling since the launch had picked her up at the airport suddenly ceased.

It was pure magic. The gray waters lightened, turned silver, and suddenly the sun burst through the clouds. Mists vanished as though at a conjurer's command. The scene, a monochromatic ink drawing a short time earlier, was now a glorious watercolor, the lagoon the same shifting, blending aqua and deep turquoise as Claire's eyes.

Claire was stunned. Distinct rays of gold radiated across the sky, like the background of a Renaissance Madonna and Child. All it lacked was a few angels descending to earth in fluttering robes with garlands of flowers in their hair.

A shock of pleasure rippled through her. There it was: La Serenissima, the most beautiful and mysterious city in the world.

The place where she'd been born almost twenty-six years ago.

It looked like a mirage, a dream of Byzantine domes, fantastic towers, and ice-cream-colored palazzi, shimmering in the liquid light dancing off the waters.

No wonder so many artists and writers have made their home here, she mused.

Claire sometimes dreamed of Venice — or thought she did. One of her plans was to visit the *penzione* where her parents had their apartment. Her father had been working in Venice when she'd been born. She wondered if she would recognize anything that she hadn't seen in a thousand pictures and photos and calendars. If there was a little piece of Venice somewhere that was truly hers.

The motor launch swept on toward the *molo,* the traditional landing place for visitors to Venice before the causeway and train station had been built from the mainland. Black gondolas filled with sightseers, a few launches, and the sleek *vaporetti,* Venice's aptly named water taxis, plied the entrance to the Grand Canal.

The air shimmered with the silvery incandescence the city was noted for, making everything seem just a little bit unreal. Slanting sun caught the forest of mooring poles rising from the water, the huge statue-topped columns that guarded the *molo*, the pale pink and white Gothic facade of the Doge's Palace, and the Byzantine domes of the Basilica San Marco beyond.

Claire blinked. It was like catching a glimpse of another world.

"I'm here," she murmured. Full circle. "At last."

Holding her breath, she waited in vain for the feeling she'd expected, the one that would tell her that she was home. Back in the place where she had begun life. Disappointment filled her.

Venice was beautiful, exotic, beguiling. And it was as alien to her as the moon.

The water had turned a lovely milky green as they entered the Grand Canal. Before she knew it, they were pulling up to the mooring poles at the landing of the Europa e Regina Hotel where she had booked a suite. She stood with her face to the sun as the pilot unloaded her bags.

"Your first visit to Venezia, *signorina?*" the launch pilot asked in a mix of Italian and English.

"I was born here," Claire told him. "My father was one of the engineering consultants brought in to help prevent the flooding."

"Ah!" the man shook his head. "The *aqua alta*."

Venice had suffered severe damage back in the sixties and seventies, and the world had responded in an effort to preserve her priceless treasures from the surging tides.

His dark eyes smiled down into hers. "Then you have Venice in your blood, *signorina*. You must go to see Nona Frascati . . . she has a shop in the Mercerie. Past the fashionable designers, you understand, and into the older quarter, where she sells old jewelry and reliquaries. If she likes you she might tell you your fortune. Tell her Pietro sent you."

"I will. *Grazie*."

She gave him a generous tip and went into the hotel. After registering in the elegant lobby and handing over her passport, she was taken up to her rooms. It was a fabulous suite with brocade-covered furniture, tall mirrors of Venetian glass, and a marvelous chandelier.

Tish must be out of her mind! Either that, or she's pretty damned sure I can convince the count to let us handle the auctioning of his entire collection.

Claire wished she felt as confident. She was secure in her knowledge and expertise. It was her persuasive powers that worried her. When she was vetting a painting or examining a piece of furniture, she was sure of herself. It was her people skills, as Tish called them, that were lacking.

Being raised alone on an isolated ranch, with only dogs, books, and a silent grandfather for companions, she'd somehow never learned the knack of talking to people. *And if I need any evidence to prove that to me, there's a divorce decree sitting in my desk back in San Francisco.*

Six months, she thought with a pang that might be anger, and not a single word from Val. He'd vanished from her life as if their marriage had been nothing but a remote dream, the kind that started out wonderfully and morphed into a nightmare.

Like the ones she'd been having almost nightly for the past eight weeks.

"The honor bar, *signorina*." The bellman unlocked an elegant gilt cabinet to show the rows of bottles behind the carved doors. Claire was glad he hadn't noticed how abstracted she'd become.

He showed her briefly where everything was, then left her. Once she was alone, her first thought was to flop on the bed in the other room and sleep for hours. Instead, her eyes were drawn to the terrace beyond the open double doors, and the splendid view.

Across the canal, the frosted white marble church of Santa Maria della Salute dominated the horizon. It was breathtaking. Although supported by more than a million wooden pilings sunk deep into the clay beneath the water, it seemed to sail upon its own reflection in the Grand Canal, like an enormous floating pearl.

The scene was familiar to her, not just from movies and travel books. The Salute was featured in several of the paintings in Count Ludovici's collection. She'd seen several fine reproductions of them. Oh, but the reality of it was so much more lovely!

As she took it all in, a black gondola filled with happy tourists was overtaken by a vaporetto filled with even more. It left a foaming wake and a waft of engine fumes on the canal. Otherwise, she thought, surely nothing had changed in decades.

Or centuries.

All thoughts of a nap vanished. Claire wanted to step out through the ivory curtains stirring in the breeze, relax in the chaise longue on the small terrace, and drink in the view as if it were a glass of sparkling wine.

She took two steps past the doors and stopped short. The chaise was already occupied. She could just see gleaming dark hair above the back cushion and the tips of a man's butter-soft Italian shoes.

"Oh! I'm so sorry," she stammered. "There must be a mistake . . . er, ah . . . *mi dispiache!*"

The figure on the chaise rose with sleek-muscled grace. "Good God, Claire!" said a deep, masculine voice layered with laughter. "Your accent is as bad as your cooking!"

She stiffened. The man who stood there wasn't wearing shoes with his khakis after all, just a pair of handmade cowboy boots. The boots, like the voice, were every bit as familiar to her as the man wearing them.

"What the *hell* are you doing in my hotel suite, Val?"

Eyes bluer than the Venice sky smiled down at her. "Is that any way to greet your husband?"

"*Ex*-husband. The divorce was final in May."

He shrugged lightly. "They don't deliver U.S. mail in the jungle."

"You don't need a mailbox to be divorced, Val. I'm sure your attorney has all the proper papers."

He strolled over to her, his tanned face suddenly somber. He tipped her chin up with a strong, nicely shaped hand. "Is it, Claire? Is it really over?"

Her breath caught in her throat. His cologne was as familiar to her as the scent of her own skin, the warmth of his hand as enticing as she remembered. He looked older, though, and even more handsome. There were new sun creases at the corners of his eyes, and the lines of his face were leaner. And he was still the only man who'd ever made her knees turn to jelly and her brain to cotton wool.

Damn him and his pheromones!

"Don't try that cowboy charm on me. It doesn't work," she lied. Jerking her head away, she stepped sideways to avoid him. That was a mistake. The balcony was small and there was no place to go.

She slanted a look from beneath her gold-tipped lashes. "One of us is going to go over the railing, Val. It won't be me."

He didn't answer but took her hands and drew her away from the railing. Claire felt the magnetism between them, as strong and as dangerous as it ever was.

Damn him! She couldn't think when he was so near. Memories slammed into her like the waves of the Adriatic Sea, beating against the sands of the Lido. If she wasn't careful she'd be swept away again — and left floating alone, out in the middle of nowhere, while he jaunted off to the latest hot spot for *Time* or *Newsweek*.

"Let me go, Val," she said quietly.

His mouth turned up in an odd little smile. "Never. You're mine, Claire. And I'm yours. We belong together."

"I see. And that's why I spent our honeymoon alone, painting our apartment and playing Solitaire on my laptop, while you were in the Middle East." She tried to sound cool and was surprised to hear her own voice so harsh.

So bitter.

"I also spent Christmas by myself," she added, "while you went off to Egypt or Africa or some remote Balkan village."

His mouth hardened. "You knew what you were getting into when we married," he said, a spark of heat in his voice. "It was part of the deal. I told you I had to take the assignments that no one else wanted while I got established and that it would lead to more reasonable ones in time. You agreed."

Claire felt a surge of guilt, but shrugged. "I didn't know you'd be gone for weeks on end. I suppose I was very young and stupid."

She left the balcony with its watery Renaissance views and went back into the high-ceilinged room. Reflected light made the pale yellow walls luminous, dappled them in shifting, liquid patterns.

Val came after her and grasped her arm, whirling her about. "Yes," he said harshly. "You were."

Her angry gasp didn't stop him. His fingers closed over her flesh. "Or at least you pretended to be. Now I wonder if I was the stupid one. I thought you understood. I thought we had a bargain of sorts."

"That was the problem," she snapped. "I thought we had a marriage!"

"We did, damn it." His eyes blazed with anger. "We could have made it work, too. But from the moment the wedding ring was on your finger, you tried to change me. To take everything that makes me who I am and turn it inside out."

"Was it wrong to expect to see something besides a potted plant looking back at me across the dinner table? To expect to warm my cold feet on a winter night with something a little more personal than an electric heating pad?"

His mouth was hard as flint. "If you wanted a desk jockey, you should have married a clerk instead of a photojournalist. If you wanted a house pet, you should have gotten a canary. I can be lured to hand, Claire — but I can't be caged."

She held out her left hand, where a pale circle showed where the diamond band

452

been removed, and was furious to see it shaking.

"It's gone now, Val. You're free. And so am I! So get out of my hotel room right now. Don't come back. I don't want to see you again. I thought I'd already made that clear!"

His jaw squared, but he reined in his own temper. "Oh, you have. But I'm afraid that will prove a little difficult. I've taken a sabbatical from the magazine. Tish Sterling hired me to do some freelance work for Sterling Galleries."

"I don't believe you!"

His eyes darkened. "I've never lied to you, Claire. I won't start now. I'm doing the auction catalog, and a photo spread on the Ludovici Collection."

As he turned away, her eyes stung with tears. It always ended this way, both of them hurt and angry, neither of them giving an inch.

Val strode to the door, then turned back with a hard smile. "If you need anything, sweetheart, just rap on the wall. My suite is right on the other side."

He went out, shutting the door.

2

Claire locked the door, went into the adjoining room, and threw herself across the wide bed. Lying on the luxurious spread, she watched the water lights dance on the walls. It was so lovely. So soothing.

God knew, she needed comfort!

She couldn't believe how much it had upset her to see Val again. At first she tried to convince herself it was because their parting had been so bitter, their meeting today so completely unexpected. She'd been so *damned* sure that she could will herself not to love Val. That she'd bolted away the memories and emotions — both good and bad — in the locked steel box of the past.

Yet it had taken only one look from those devastating blue eyes, one touch of his tanned hand against her skin, and she was a bundle of raw nerve endings, jangling with loss and anger. With yearning and emptiness, and a deep, aching need.

She brushed the hair from the nape of her neck with one hand and kneaded the tension knots. "You can't chain an eagle," her grandfather had warned her when she and Val had gotten engaged. "You'll break his wings."

She remembered that moment, the soft twilight sifting down around the narrow porch, the Idaho hills stretching away by starlight. "And if you build a nest with one, you'd better know how to fly."

It was the longest conversation she had ever had with her grandfather. He'd been a man of the land, not one of words.

Claire punched the pillow into an even more uncomfortable shape. She hadn't known how to fly and hadn't wanted to learn. Her dream had been of relaxed, firelit evenings, intimate dinners with friends, discussing art and life over wine and pasta. Hard to accomplish with your husband 10,000 miles away. She'd tried to be patient, to face the loneliness. She really had.

They'd managed to stumble on long after they should have called it quits. The marriage might have drifted along for years, their problems unresolved, one of those long-distance marriages that ended up as nothing more than two names on a marriage license and an album of neglected photos.

But then came that desperate time when she needed him. She hadn't even known what country he was in, much less how to reach him. The memory was still painful. To be fair, she hadn't told him that she was pregnant. She'd been only six weeks along. But oh, how she'd wanted that baby!

Claire watched the ripples of light weave glowing patterns around the room. She felt too jet-lagged and too edgy to relax. The iced-marble dome of the Salute was captured in the mirror over a console table, backed by an incredible turquoise sky. The beauty of it calmed her, and her rapid breathing slowed. Within minutes she slipped into an uneasy sleep.

. . . *The hinges sighed, and the door in the garden wall clicked to behind her. There was no going back now. The door had no handle and could only be opened from inside the garden.*

Her green eyes looked warily through the eyeholes in the silver mask, and her heart was like an iron hammer beating against the fragile glass of her ribs. Tucking a stray blond curl beneath the hood of her cloak, she gathered her courage. He would be waiting for her at the bridge.

Her father had locked away her jewelry casque, with its precious heirlooms of pearls and emeralds and rubies that had formed part of her dowry. But her lover's pendant lay against her skin, cool as water from the court-yard fountain on a summer's day; she imagined the ruby pendant and ring warming her blood, like flames.

Except for the clothes upon her back, they were the only items she had taken with her when she fled the house.

She glided along the calle. Through the slits of her silver Carnivale mask she made out the sides of the blank, three-storied buildings. To her right was the Palazzo D'Oro, where her fiancé lived. Like the homes of other wealthy merchants, the street level was given over to business, but the rest was opulent, filled with treasures from the four corners of the earth.

She had wept bitterly when her father announced her engagement to Giovanni Gambello. He was vain, arrogant. The ugly rumors of his reputation as a libertine had reached Bianca, even as sheltered as she was within the walls of her father's house. Venice was a city given to scandal and vice: to make a name for oneself among the most notorious was something indeed!

Worst of all, from her innocent young perspective, was that she did not love him, nor he her. He wanted only to possess her. And to cement the banking and import business between himself and her father.

Bianca shivered. But now, thank the Virgin and all the saints, she would never be his wife.

Soon, very soon, she would be safe in her lover's arms!

Suddenly the plaintive cry of a gondolier drifted on the breeze, and another picked it up in the distance, like an echo. The sound was so lonely, so wrenching, she felt as if her heart might break.

She paused when she reached the bridge, almost overcome by fright. What if she was discovered? What if her lover wasn't there?

What if she waited through the dark hours until morning lit the sky, and still he never came?

It would be a fitting punishment for her, she thought in misery. After all, she had failed him twice. Then someone moved out of the shadows on the far side of the canal, the Rio di San Moise. *She gave a shaky laugh. Her fears were groundless. There he was, waiting for her in his dark cloak on the other side, his hand outstretched. Taking a deep breath, she hastened toward the arcing bridge. Only a few more steps to freedom and the beginning of her new life.*

Then why was she so afraid — ?

Claire awakened to the drumming of her heart. The thick evening shadows of narrow *calle* faded to a splendid room flooded with sunlight, the gondoliers' cry to the plaintive call of seabirds from beyond the open window. She sat up abruptly, disoriented, as jumbled impressions of past and present sorted themselves out.

Then she remembered where she was, and why. Venice. Count Ludovici.

Val, damn him.

And the dream.

The dream always began in the same way: the frightened girl, crossing the marble floor and hurrying out the door to the courtyard. This time it seemed different somehow. But the more she tried to grasp it, the faster it slipped away.

Still, even now, she could almost feel the brush of the velvet cloak against her cheek, the weight of the heavy key in her hand, the smooth, cool kiss of the beads and pendant against her throat.

She never saw them in the dream, but she knew exactly what they looked like. The necklace was formed of long Venetian beads as clear as water, but with shimmers of real gold leaf trapped inside the glass. They were interspersed with tiny beads of granulated gold. The pendant that hung from it was a delicate ruby, set in a thin gold rim.

Claire tried to shake off the dream. It had been recurring more frequently and each time there was something more, something new. Each time the sensation of fear deepened. And she always awakened with the feeling that something terrible, something tragic and inevitable, was about to happen.

She swung her legs off the bed and sat up, afraid to fall asleep again.

The dreams had begun after she'd unpacked the crate of delicately tinted drawings that Count Ludovici had sent through an intermediary for a private auction: Titian, Bellini, Tintoretto, Giorgione, Caravaggio. Claire would never forget the thrill of holding them in her hands, of feeling a sense of the artists who had drawn them, across the centuries.

Her favorite had been the *Carnivale* scene: revelers celebrating the holiday in fanciful costume, their faces disguised with paint or elaborate papier-mâché masks. It was the best of the lot, attributed to Titian, and had been expected to be the high point of the private auction. Oddly, it hadn't met the reserve price and had been withdrawn.

Among the colorful throng was the figure of a young girl. She stood in the shadows of the foreground beneath an airy balcony, blond curls peeping out beneath the hood of a wine-colored cloak, her oval face covered by a silver mask. She wore a necklace of Murano beads, with a small ruby pendant in the shape of a heart.

From the moment she'd first spotted the

girl in the drawing, Claire had had the uncanny feeling that she knew her. Or that the face, forever hidden behind that painted silver mask, resembled her own.

She rose, shaking off a little shiver. Her first meeting with the count wasn't until dinner at the Ca' Ludovici this evening. There was an entire afternoon to kill. "I'll walk off some of this energy," she told herself. "Do a little shopping."

She dressed casually in a two-piece blue silk outfit, grabbed an ivory jacket and her purse from the sofa, and left. She wanted to put some distance between herself and the dream.

Her stomach rumbled as she went out through the gardens, but she didn't want to run into Val in one of the hotel's gilded restaurants. Claire decided she'd walk to the piazza and have a gelato, the heavenly Italian version of ice cream, and then stroll along the Mercerie, the main shopping thoroughfare, where many of the most exclusive shops were located.

It would be a sin against her femininity, she assured herself, not to buy some exquisite and comfortable shoes — a combination that seemed to be unique to the Italians. Something sexy and strappy.

Taking the Calle Barrozzi past the church

of San Moise, she worked her way back around to the waterfront. The café in the Hotel Monaco tempted her, as did the famous Harry's Bar, but she didn't give in to either. She wanted to feel the pulse of Venice and knew she should begin her explorations at its beating heart: the Piazza San Marco.

A few minutes more and she crossed the lovely bridge over Rio del Giardinetti, the canal that surrounded the gardens Napoleon had built on the waterfront after Venice had surrendered her thousand years of independence to him. Claire stood on the *molo*, with the former Mint building on her left and the fanciful pink and white arches of the ducal palace to her right. She headed toward the open space between the tall pillars topped with statues that she'd seen from the launch. One held Saint Teodoro with his crocodile — there's a story there, she decided — and the other with the winged Lion of Saint Mark, the city's emblem.

It was amazing to see tourists in shorts and baseball caps, with cameras and shopping bags, mingling with fashionable Italian women, suited bureaucrats, and colorful souvenir vendors in front of the graceful, ancient buildings.

It was unsettling, Claire thought. As if

time had collided with itself and been violently twisted about in the process.

A shadow fell across her, and she froze when a hand gripped her shoulder. It was Val, his dazzling eyes hidden behind sunglasses. "Don't go between the pillars," he told her. "It's bad luck to walk there."

"Dozens of people are doing it right now," she said curtly, "and I don't see lightning bolts blazing down from the sky."

"Executions used to take place between the pillars. Hangings and beheadings," he said cheerfully. He knew how superstitious she was. "Just thought you'd want to know."

She ignored him, threading through the throng of tourists snapping photos and locals on their way to meet friends for drinks at Florian's or Quadri's. He was still there, just a few feet behind her. She knew the sound of his footsteps as well as she knew her own.

She threw a quick glance over her shoulder. "Go away! You're spoiling Venice for me."

His eyebrows raised. "I didn't think you'd take it so personally."

"There are few things more personal than a divorce," she told him and walked a little faster.

Val kept pace with his easy cowboy stride. "You can't avoid me forever," he said casually. "We're both dining tonight with Count Ludovici."

Claire stopped dead in her tracks. "I didn't know you were included in the invitation."

"I wasn't. But I paid a courtesy call on the old gentleman earlier and made arrangements to photograph the collection. One thing led to another, and when I mentioned knowing you, he thoughtfully asked me to join the two of you for dinner."

She ground her teeth. She'd come to Venice hoping to put Val behind her. It wasn't going to be easy, but she had might as well be gracious about it. "I'll see you at eight, then."

Val shoved his hands in his pockets. "We could share a gondola."

"They're overpriced."

"Not if you know how to haggle with the gondoliers." He smiled down at her. "And think how romantic it would be, lying back on the cushions as we glide silently past the glowing palazzi by moonlight."

She shot him a glance of disgust. "And maybe I could push you over the side while we glide silently under a bridge, on some particularly dank and smelly canal."

His smile wasn't dented a bit. "Ah, now, that's the spirit, Claire. A little passionate wrestling while the gondolier serenades us home."

"Look!" She stopped and faced him, her arms braced on her hips. "This isn't going to work. It's bad enough that we'll be thrown together on this assignment. I won't have you following me around the rest of the time, trying to lure me back for a nostalgic romp between the sheets. I'm immune to your charm now. It's like catching the measles: a one-time event — then never again."

He just grinned at her, as if her lie was as transparent as glass. Claire felt her temper rising. "Go practice throwing out lures to some beautiful *signorina* and stop following me around."

Val rocked back on the heels of his boots and considered. "Do you really think that's a good idea?"

"I'm sure of it."

He turned his head. The arches of the piazza were reflected in the dark lenses of his sunglasses. "Hmmmm. What about that dark-haired beauty with the wide hat sitting outside Florian's?"

She cut a glance over at the tables outside the famed café. They were mostly filled, but she spotted the woman almost immediately. She was exquisitely dressed in the European style: elegant, polished, and absolutely stunning. Probably one of the five most beautiful women in all creation.

Claire smiled. "Knock yourself out."

Val bowed mockingly. "Your wish is my command."

He crossed the long piazza with his easy stride and went up to the table. While Claire watched in amazement, the woman looked up and smiled. Val leaned down and greeted the woman. She offered him her hand — and her cheek to kiss. A moment later they were sitting close together, talking like long-time friends.

As they probably were, Claire realized. He'd set her up, damn it!

What a fool she'd made of herself, accusing him of following her, when all along he'd been on his way to Florian's for a drink with the beautiful *signorina!* As she fumed, he looked up and smiled at her across the piazza.

"Arrogant bastard!" she mouthed.

Val lifted his drink to her and smiled his dazzling smile.

Claire swore, turned on her heel, and marched off.

3

Claire headed to the nearest gelato shop. After paying at the counter, she salved her wounded pride with a cone of three flavors, the way the Italians enjoyed it. She chose apricot, ice-white lemon, and what she thought was pale pink strawberry.

As she left the shop, she was still steaming. Why couldn't a pigeon have made a direct hit on Val as he leaned over the beautiful *signorina?* But things like that never happened to Val. He was too lucky. She stepped back into the sunshine and had to laugh. Val always knew how to yank her chain, but this time she'd been the one to set herself up. He'd just let her forge a few of the links.

And she'd be damned if she'd let him get away with it. The thought of pushing him into the Grand Canal grew ever more enticing.

He knew her too well. That was apparent.

He could always see through her, and yet Claire always felt as if she didn't have a handle on what made Val tick. The magnetism between them was always potent, the affection tender, the sex passionate. She felt her body temperature rising just thinking of it.

He could be a delightful companion: charming, easygoing, and laid-back. In fact, his quirky humor was always part of his appeal to her. Or he could be intense, impassioned by his work. So much so that he could focus on it to the exclusion of everything else.

Including me.

He could change from one to the other in the twinkling of an eye. Just like the eagle her grandfather had compared him to. *Ah, Val!* Her sigh turned into a chuckle. *I'll get even, you sonofabitch.*

Moving through the crowded piazza, Claire took a lick of the pink gelato. It was the most amazing flavor, delicate yet complex. At first she couldn't place it. Then it came to her as a complete surprise.

Roses, she thought. *Roses in the sun.* She sighed with pleasure. "Only the Italians," she murmured, "could make an ice cream that tastes like summer."

The piazza was suddenly more crowded

than ever, and she realized it was time for the feeding of the pigeons. As long as the birds stayed in Venice, so legend said, the city would remain in all her glory. A few fluttered down all around her, to the delight of the children and visitors. The local people, well-versed in the habits of pigeons, prudently ducked under the piazza's arcades.

Suddenly, from the corner of her eye, Claire saw a great swirl of movement, the flash of light from a hundred multicolored wings. For a moment she was a child again, gazing up at the pigeons swirling up past the domes of San Marco, the pale tiles of the Doge's Palace, their wings shifting color in the late-afternoon light. Could smell coffee and hot rolls on the outdoor table where she sat with her nurse, feel her fingers sticky from a striped piece of candy as she tried to wipe them, unseen, on her frilly blue dress.

Could see a woman's face smiling down at her, filled with love.

"I remember," she exclaimed beneath her breath.

She'd been only four when her mother had died in a fall down the steps of their ancient apartment building, and her father packed her up and went back to the States. He'd always told her that she was too young to have any memory of her early years in

Venice, but Claire had always known that he was wrong. She *could* remember if only she could find the key to her bank of memories. Pictures of the beautiful city might account for some of her dreams, but none of them captured the shimmering, transparent light of Venice in the way she'd always seen it in her mind's eye.

The way it really was.

"I do remember!"

Her eyes were filled with tears, her heart with emotions long buried, and her mouth with the taste of heavenly gelato. After all these years she was back in Venice, far from the Idaho ranch where she'd spent her grammar school years, farther still from the hazy San Francisco Bay Area where she'd gone to college. Half a world away from everything that was most familiar to her.

She was home.

She wished she could share this moment with someone. Couples strolled by, families of tourists, locals meeting friends for drinks. She seemed to be the only one alone in the crowds. She looked across the piazza to the table where Val and the Italian beauty had been talking, but the table was empty, and there was no sign of them. Had they slipped away to some lovely room overlooking the canal to make love?

Jealousy sliced through her to the bone.

It amazed and outraged her. *She'd* been the one to file for divorce. The one to say the marriage was a mistake, that it was over, and that she would pick up the pieces and go on as if he'd never existed.

Claire stood stunned while the crowd jostled around her. "It's not love," she told herself fiercely. "It's not even lust."

Although, thinking of the way heat had curled through her body when Val touched her back at the hotel, she had to admit it was close.

No, it was just a simple dog-in-the-manger attitude. She didn't want him. Not really. She just didn't want anyone else to have him either.

Laughing at her foolishness, Claire turned around and headed for the arched gateway to the Mercerie. Val was an adult, unmarried, and free to follow his own desires. And so was she.

The two bronze Moors above the gate swung their bronze hammers against the great bell to mark the hour. She pushed Val and the dark beauty out of her mind and lost herself in exploring Venice.

An hour later she had a Fendi bag, a pair of sling-back leather shoes, and another hour to kill before returning to the hotel to dress for dinner. Not enough time to drop in at one of the fascinating museums or galleries but certainly enough to visit one of the intriguing shops on the streets that branched off to either side. What was the name of that place the launch pilot had told her about?

She couldn't remember, so she just wandered contentedly. She stopped when she came to a tiny place displaying *Carnivale* masks in the window. Others hung on the walls inside. Claire examined them through the glass. Some were plain silk strips made to cover the eyes, while others hid the entire face. There was the eerie mask of the "plague doctor" with its long snoutlike nose funnel, and there were silver moons and gilded suns and spiky stars. Lovely female faces painted in rainbow colors or stark white, blank as stone.

There was something fascinating yet sinister about them. With the anonymity of one of the cleverly painted papier-mâché creations, it was possible to merge with the crowd and become anybody — or nobody.

She wondered if the girl in the drawing had done that. Or the girl in her dream. Claire was sure they were the same. Something about that drawing had triggered the dreams that started out so enchantingly and ended with her waking in terror. It was the only logical explanation.

Was she a young lady of a noble family, savoring an adventure? Or a servant who'd taken her mistress's cloak and mask so she might slip away and meet a lover? Did she ever walk along these same streets in her dainty embroidered slippers?

I wonder what her name was, and where she was going when the artist captured her likeness. Claire looked around. *Hell, I wonder where I'm going!*

She'd taken a wrong turn while her thoughts were rambling. She found herself halfway along a steep *calle*, and there wasn't another soul in sight.

Her heart stopped, then skipped a beat, when she saw the ancient door set into the blank wall. A familiar decorative iron grill was set high in the thick wood, and there was no handle on the outside. Just like the door in her dreams.

Wisps of panic curled through her. Something from the dream. Something she couldn't quite recall . . .

Claire forced herself to go to the door. Her fingers touched the time-roughened wood, and the panic grew. She wanted to run away, but she held her ground. The bottom of the wrought iron was at the level of her chin. She peered inside, although the dead leaves of a vining plant obscured the view.

There was nothing to distinguish the place. Nothing to see but sections of the terra-cotta-colored walls that formed the building, a pot of purple basil, the edge of a dark blue shutter, and a child's leather sandal. It might be any private courtyard in the city.

There was a sudden blur of movement, and Claire jumped instinctively. The low yowl of an irritated cat sounded nearby. A moment later a sleek yellow feline hurtled from the wall to the courtyard pavement, like a heat-seeking missile. Claire backed away from the door.

Rather than turn back, she continued on her way.

She was still thinking of the girl who haunted her when she came out into a small square. It was utterly charming. Real estate was so precious in Venice that it startled her to find a patch of green. Whoever had lived in the grand palazzi surrounding it must have had power and influence. Now most of them were made into apartments, their first floors turned into enticing shops.

She was about to enter the jeweler's when she saw the reflection behind her: FRASCATTI, a sign said in faded gilt letters on black. The place the boatman had mentioned to her. Crossing over the bridge to the opposite side, she examined the offerings arranged on burgundy velvet in the small shop window.

They were a mixed lot, with an engraving of the Rialto Bridge on an easel beside a porcelain doll, half a dozen antique Murano glass wine goblets the color of ripe plums, an ornate set of monogrammed silver hairbrushes, slightly tarnished, a cracked cherub's face of ebonized wood.

And a necklace.

An echo of her dream came shivering back. She stared at the antique bauble. It was made of clear Venetian glass, shimmering with gold and strung between granulated golden beads. There was some sort of pendant hanging from its center. Could it be the heart-shaped ruby?

No. Impossible. But her heart was ticking like a bomb inside her chest. Shading the glass, she tried to see it better. The light was wrong, bouncing off the window.

Was it really the same necklace as the one in the drawing? Claire couldn't be sure. And yet . . .

For just a moment she could feel it: the coolness of the dream-necklace against her skin, the light weight of the pendant at her throat.

Her heart fluttering as if it had wings, Claire reached out and tried the handle. The door opened softly.

4

The shop was in shadows. She heard the soft tinkle of a bell as the door closed. When her eyes adjusted, she could make out a Venetian mirror, a pair of filigree lamps, and collars of old lace in glass cases. She jumped when something brushed the back of her neck. It was just a stuffed monkey, its black glass eyes staring back at her.

"That's it," she murmured. "I'm out of here."

Before she could turn around, a curtain at the back of the shop parted and a plump, dark-eyed woman came out. She wore a marvelously tailored suit of black silk worsted and an armful of thin gold bracelets that jingled softly as she moved.

"*Bon giorno, signorina.*"

Claire answered in her fractured Italian, and the woman's face changed. "Ah, good afternoon, *signorina.* I mistook you for . . . for someone else. You are American?"

"Yes. I just arrived in Venice."

"We are honored. Is there something I can show you?"

Claire hesitated, feeling foolish. The necklace couldn't be the same.

But it was. The moment she saw it laid out on the square of black velvet, she knew it. But the pendant was missing. She saw the bit of gold in the center from which it had hung.

"There used to be a pendant."

The shop owner was startled. "Yes, *signorina*. I have it here."

Reaching inside the glass case, she removed a small box. When she straightened up and removed the lid, however, it was just a heart-shaped piece of granulated gold.

"The ruby is missing," Claire said, disappointed.

"It may have been another stone," the woman told her, smiling. "Or perhaps even a piece of Murano glass."

"No." Claire was certain. "It was a ruby. *Quando?*"

As soon as the word was out of her mouth, she realized she'd said the wrong thing. That meant "when," not "how much?" "Er . . . *Quant-è, per favore?*"

The woman named a sum surprisingly low to Claire. A quick transaction, and the necklace was hers. She touched a fingertip to the pendant.

It was cool, and yet a line of heat shot up Claire's arm and burst into small golden sparks. The sensation was so sharp, so startling, that she pulled her finger back and looked at it, almost expecting to see blood.

A vision floated between her and the necklace, took on shape and depth and texture:

> *. . . light stuccoed walls. The parapet of a graceful bridge. A glimpse of a cloaked figure in a gilded Carnivale mask. Then a moving mosaic: pale paving stones, the hem of a gold velvet gown, the tip of a dainty embroidered slipper. The luminous sheen of scattered starlight, reflecting off the black-green waters of the canal.*
> *Numbing cold. Fear. Oh, God, the fear . . .*

The vision was gone in an instant, leaving her feeling dizzy and ill.

The world had gone black, except for small, ragged spots of light. It was like looking through a black cloth full of moth holes. Then Claire realized that she was on the floor, with the shop woman leaning over her in concern.

Her patchy vision began to clear, and her hearing came back. The world was still out of kilter. She caught the tinkle of bells, over-laid by an exchange of words in rapid Italian — and she understood every word.

"She was just standing there, looking at the necklace. Then her face went white as this marble cherub, and she crumpled and fell."

"I'll fetch a cold cloth and some water."

"Perhaps the doctor, *nona?*"

A slight pause. An elderly face swam into view above her, and a pair of dark, dark eyes looked into Claire's. She felt as if she looked through them and out the other side, into endless tomorrows. Or yesterdays.

"She will be all right. She is sensitive, this one, and has had a glimpse of the past. It can be unsettling."

Both women looked up as a shadow fell across Claire, and the draft from an opened door swept past them like a wraith. She blinked. The women were still speaking in musical Italian, but suddenly she couldn't understand a word. Then Val was kneeling at her side. Beneath his tan, his face was as white as hers felt.

"Claire? Can you hear me? What hap-pened?"

"I . . . I don't know."

"A fainting spell, *signor,*" the elderly woman said. She shook her head. "It is not good to go all day without feeding the stomach. The *bella signorina* needs a bite to eat. Something more than gelato. *La minestra* for *primo*. *Risi i funghi* to follow. And," she said firmly, "a glass of good *vino rosso*."

He helped Claire sit up slowly. At first she was glad for the warmth and comfort of his arm, but the moment she felt restored, it seemed too intimate. A reminder of what they'd had — and lost.

"I'm okay. Help me up, please."

His eyes darkened, and his jaw squared, but Val pulled her easily to her feet, then removed his arm from around her shoulders. "You look like something the tide washed in."

She slanted a wry look at him from the corner of her eye. "I'm disappointed. Your skill at delivering graceful compliments seems to have deserted you."

"That's better." He grinned, but his eyes were still cool. "The *signora*'s advice is sound, Claire. Let's get you out into the fresh air. There's a neighborhood restaurant around the corner in the square. I can vouch for the food."

She knew he was right and didn't argue. "The necklace . . ."

"Of course, *signorina*." The younger woman wrapped the box in gold tissue paper and put it into a little bag with a corded handle.

As Claire and Val were about to leave, the elderly woman touched Claire's wrist lightly. "It is good that you have come to Venice. It will be even better when you leave."

"Well," Claire said later when she and Val were settled at a small table overlooking the calm Rio San Zulian. A gondola glided past, empty except for the lone gondolier. "I've never been told to 'get out of Dodge' before. That wasn't very friendly of her."

He laughed at her joke, but his voice was serious. "I don't think she was warning you off. I think she was telling your fortune." Val dipped a spoon into his thick vegetable soup. "Everyone in San Marco has heard of Signora Frascatti. They call her *nona* — grandmother. She's said to be able to see the future and cast love spells. Some say she can give the evil eye."

She examined his face. The reflection off the canal cast his face in light and shadow. "Do you believe such things are possible, Val?"

"I don't know if they are — but I hope so." The lines of his face grew stern, and his eyes were haunted. "Life can be pretty grim at times without a little magic."

Without thinking, she stretched her hand across the table and covered his. She wanted to reach up and touch his face, smooth away the sudden frown, see the shadows vanish from his eyes.

"Was it very bad?"

His jaw clenched. "I was standing on a ridge with an eager young British journalist and our guide when the mortar round hit. The next moment I was alone."

He set his spoon down. "That's enough of the soup for me. Let's order dessert. I'd recommend anything on the menu."

She snatched her hand away. He was always like this, damn it. Shutting her out. She'd spent their entire marriage pounding on the locked door of his silence, never knowing exactly what was on the other side.

The realization struck her then that she was being shallow and selfish. Stupid, too. Val wasn't as lucky as she had always thought. In fact, given what he'd just told her, he was lucky to be alive.

It had never occurred to her that he was in danger on his assignments. The air of golden invincibility that surrounded him had blinded her to it. Val had seen and survived terrible things. He was just good at hiding it. Damned good.

Their waiter came over. Claire let him

take her half-finished dish of rice with mushrooms and frowned at the chalked menu on the board outside the café.

The dark young woman across from them had a footed glass bowl of tiramisu, Val's favorite dessert. She dipped her spoon into the frothy concoction of coffee-soaked ladyfingers, mascarpone, and whipped cream with gusto.

Claire wavered. Tiramisu was one of her downfalls. She could almost taste the creamy confection on her own tongue right now. In a moment she'd be drooling. But she was afraid if she ate too much now she wouldn't have room for dinner with Count Ludovici.

The couple at one of the other tables were sharing a bowl of melon and berries. "That fruit looks good." She smiled at the hovering waiter. *"Il fritto misto, per favore."*

The waiter seemed bemused. Val choked on his wine and shook his head vigorously. *"La frutta mista."*

The waiter hid his smile, nodded, and went inside. Claire folded her arms and sighed. "I take it I ordered the wrong thing?"

He grinned. "Not if you wanted mixed fried fish for dessert."

"Ick." She wanted to bang her head on the table.

"You're getting a mixed fruit plate instead."

"Thank God!" She made a face. "I was born here. I spent my first years in Venice and I've always been good at languages. Why is the simplest Italian so difficult for me?"

Val sipped his *vino rosso* and shrugged. "Maybe you have a mental block about it: for some reason connected with the past, you don't really want to learn it."

"What the hell does that mean?"

He leaned forward. "I think you could learn anything you set your mind to. But you've always been as stubborn as a two-headed mule. And when there's something you don't want to discuss, you clam up. Shut yourself away."

Her temper fired. "Like you just did when I asked about your work. You always shut me out, Val. As if I were too stupid to understand."

"It's not that," he said sharply. "There are just some things that I want to forget. Maybe it's not possible, but it's the only way I can be at peace with what I've seen."

"I'm not a child. You don't have to treat me like one."

There was hurt in her voice, but truth, too. He looked at her steadily, as if seeing her anew. "I'm sorry, Claire. That was part of the problem between us, wasn't it?"

"You cut me out of your life."

"I wanted to protect you from it."

She lifted her glass and watched the light turn the wine to liquid garnet. "I'm a big girl, Val. And you know what they say: Life Happens."

He shot her a wry look. "I think I've heard that phrase in the past expressed just a little less politely from time to time."

The laughter they shared was light and easy. Like old times. He wanted to reach over and pull her into his arms, tangle his fingers in those riotous golden curls. Kiss that rosy, stubborn little mouth until they were both dizzy with it.

His voice was husky. "Do you miss me, Claire?"

It was the wrong thing to say. "Not any more than I missed you when you were off with your cameras and gear to the ends of the earth."

The silence between them was cold and clear and thick as ice. Val tossed back the remnants of his wine and signaled for another. Nothing had changed.

No, he thought. That isn't exactly true.

The Claire he had been married to would never have come to Venice on her own. She had shunted back and forth from Coeur d'Alene in Idaho to San Francisco as if there was an invisible rut in the sky. Once or twice she'd gone briefly to L.A. and even Chicago. But his suggestion of a honeymoon in Australia hadn't been met with much enthusiasm. They'd spent it in San Francisco instead.

In the end, she had been too afraid to leave her comfortable nest, and he'd been too angry to stay.

She was such a curious mixture: hungry for knowledge but afraid of adventure. Happiest exploring some long-dead artist's past instead of her own future. Confident on the outside, a bundle of jangled nerve endings inside. Strong and stubborn, yet afraid to trust. That had been the real rock their marriage had foundered on.

Whatever hurt her so was buried deep. He had never been able to get to the heart of it. And, God Almighty, after all they'd been through, she still took his breath away.

Need fisted in his gut. He wanted her as fiercely as ever.

"Don't look at me like that," she said softly.

He raised his brows and tried to look innocent. "Like what?"

"Like I'm a bowl of tiramisu, and you're

going to scoop me up."

"Does it bother you?"

"Of course."

He braced his hands behind his neck and smiled. "Good."

A flush of heat rose from the pit of her stomach and spread upward. She could feel the hot rush of blood stain her throat and warm her cheeks. Damn him! He still knew which buttons to push.

Raised voices drew her attention. A young couple stood on the bridge beside the canal, quarreling. Hands waved and eyes flashed as the spat grew louder. Claire felt her stomach drop.

Val was right. She'd been blocking something out. It came rushing back now: a window overlooking a church, flowered curtains dancing in the breeze. The sound of her parents' voices in Italian. They always switched to Italian when they argued, and they'd done so the day her mother died. Then footsteps, her mother racing around the corner to the landing, where someone had left a basket of laundry. Then a soft cry, something falling. After that, only a terrible, echoing silence. That's why someone — a neighbor? — had taken Claire to the Piazza San Marco to see the pigeons. And while the woman hadn't been looking, Claire had wandered off to see the birds at close hand.

She'd been lost for hours, looking for home and her mother. When they found her, she didn't have a mother anymore. Or a home. In less than three days, she was on a plane to Idaho.

The quarreling had now escalated to heated outbursts, accompanied by emphatic gestures and much waving of arms.

"What is it?" This time it was Val's hand that covered hers. He felt it tremble in his grasp.

"I . . . I don't know. I can't stand to hear a man and woman arguing like that. It upsets me."

He took her hand between his and smiled. "They're Italian. From the south of Italy, by their conversation. They're not arguing, sweetheart. They're making love."

"That's the stupidest thing I ever . . ."

She broke off. He was right. While the woman shouted and pounded the air with her fist, the man pulled her into his arms. He almost swept her off her feet and was kissing her passionately. She was responding with equal fervor. In fact, any more fervor and they'd both be cooling off in the canal together.

The same electricity arced between Claire and Val. She knew he was as aware of it as she. "And don't," Claire said lightly as she pulled her hand away, "call me sweetheart."

The waiter returned with Val's change. "Honeymoons? Newlywedded?" he ventured, practicing his English.

"No," said Claire.

"Yes," Val replied simultaneously.

The waiter nodded, smiled, and walked away. He scratched his head, thinking he must have used the wrong phrase.

"You shouldn't have lied to him," Claire said, rising.

The slow, simmering look Val gave her made her tingle from head to toe. His arm slipped around her waist so naturally. "You could make an honest man of me."

"The honeymoon is supposed to come after the marriage," she told him. "Not after the divorce."

But she let him take her hand and twine his long fingers through hers. As they walked back toward the Europa e Regina Hotel together, they fell into a natural rhythm, with Val shortening his long strides and Claire lengthening hers.

The piazza was less crowded, and they lingered outside Saint Mark's Basilica, examining the golden mosaics on the facade, the way they caught the liquid light of Venice and sent it darting, dazzling, back.

It was the long way around, but neither Claire nor Val cared. Something of the time-lessness of Venice seeped into them, bringing an inner quiet that was both sooth-ing and intimate. They were both silent as they walked from the *piazetta* to the water-front. Lagoon and sky were the same hazy shade of aqua, and the buildings gleamed softly in every shade of rose and white.

She wished they could have gone on for hours in such quiet companionship, but they reached the hotel all too soon. As she unlocked her door, Val stood looking down at her with a peculiar expression on his face.

"What are you thinking about?" she asked.

The corners of his firm mouth tilted up. "Tiramisu."

5

He wound one of her curls around his finger, the way he used to do. Dark lights shone in the depths of his eyes, and she was sure there was an answering spark in hers. She thought for a moment he might kiss her. Hoped it, too.

But Val only touched her cheek. "Until tonight."

He opened the door, and it swung in on silent hinges. She went inside and closed it softly, then leaned against it for a minute. When she walked away from it eventually, she felt light and unsteady, as if she were walking on water.

Until tonight.

Claire was ready early, and they took a gondola after all.

With the lantern lit and starry skies above, she thought this scene was straight out of a history book. Or a fairy tale.

Val had negotiated with the gondolier in advance, and they left the brighter areas of the Grand Canal to glide along the smaller *canale* that served as the streets of Venice. They went along places where the water sparkled darkly, making false moonbeams on the faces of the tall buildings on either side, and past gaily lit squares full of music and laughter, only to glide back into darkness again.

Then, to her surprise, they were back in the Grand Canal, not all that far from where they'd started. "We could have walked," she said, laughing.

"Not on your first night in Venice." Val smiled. "You've seen her now as she deserves to be seen."

She thought their arrival at the Ca' Ludovici would be an anticlimax. She was wrong. "I thought *Ca'* was short for *casa*. House."

"It is. I don't know how it came to be. An inside joke." Val laughed. "Like the Vanderbilts and their seaside 'cottages.' "

Count Ludovici's home was a huge palazzo of the pale pink brick that made up so much of Venice, fronted with elegant Gothic traceries and arched windows on every level.

Their host was waiting for them on the

water landing, smoking a cigarette. He extinguished it as the gondola moored and went to greet them. "A fine night," he said in a richly cultured voice. "Welcome, *Signorina* Johnston, *Signor* Blackford."

They went up a flight of marble stairs from the water level to the *piano nobile*, the main floor that held the public rooms of the palazzo. Claire felt as if she'd walked into a museum by mistake.

The first parlor was covered in heavily gilded wood in the Venetian style, with frescoed ceiling and mirrors everywhere. The main reception room was enormous and filled with paintings by the great masters of the Renaissance. It was overwhelming to be in a room with them and realize they were the personal possession of one man. They had been in his family for centuries. After all, some of the count's ancestors had commissioned them from the artists themselves.

The mellow light shone on the count's thick white hair as he guided them through to the balcony. "A cocktail? Or wine?"

What Claire really wanted to do was examine the pictures. That, of course, would be impolite. Ludovici poured them glasses of pale wine, so clear and golden it was like captured sunbeams. "From the Ludovici vineyards," he said when Val inquired.

He and the count talked as easily as if they were old acquaintances. While Claire mentally squirmed, the two men drew her into their conversation. She was aware of Val smoothing the way for her, giving her openings to drop a comment from time to time. How does he do it? she thought. It was as foreign to her nature as trying to fly.

"There is a little time before dinner," Ludovici said, almost regretfully. "Perhaps you would like to see my private collection?"

Claire was agog. The moment was here at last. He led them to a library that looked out across the San Marco basin, with a view of the old Custom House and the Salute. The domes of the church caught the starlight and held it.

In the end she preferred the view to the paintings. She liked Chagall, but not Picasso. Frankenthaler left her cold. The count gave a little laugh. "I am teasing you, a little. I know it is the Old Masters whom you love."

He opened a door and led them through to another chamber. It was wonderfully proportioned, all rose marble floors and white silk walls. The paintings glowed on them like jewels. Her breath caught in her throat. There were paintings she'd never heard of in all her research. A volume of beauty that the world had never read.

As they went around the room, the count would indicate by a nod or an airy gesture which of the paintings he wished to put up for auction. Val leaned down.

"When Tish sees these uncrated in her office, she'll be so excited she'll have to replace the rug."

Claire dug an elbow in his ribs to shush him. As they were coming around toward the door, she noticed a small alcove. A black curtain hung at the back of it. There was a small table before it where a lamp of brass and red glass burned, like the lights she'd seen in churches and cathedrals. A shiver danced up her arms. It looked like a memorial.

"The painting that hung here," she asked, "is it out for repair?"

"You do not know the story?" Count Ludovici seemed surprised.

Reaching up, he pulled a hidden gold cord. The black curtains parted to reveal a stunning portrait of a young woman.

Claire's cry of shock drowned out Val's startled gasp. Count Ludovici gazed up at the portrait. "So, you both see the resemblance!"

"We'd have to be blind not to," Val said

softly. "It's incredible."

The painting showed a young girl in the first blush of maidenhood. She was lovely, with a short, straight nose, small chin, full, rosy lips, and eyes as green as glass. Her cascade of curling blond hair was held back by a delicate headpiece of gold wire and pearls set with topaz. Her velvet gown was a wonderful shade of gold, so lustrously painted it seemed as real as the ivory sheen of her skin.

And that pale, oval face! Claire had seen it before thousands of times. The resemblance to her own reflection in the mirror was uncanny.

"How . . . how did you know?" she stammered. "We've never met."

The nobleman bowed. "I am a gentleman of the Old World, *signorina,* but I live in the new one as well. The computer is a part of my daily business. I was on the Internet when I saw your photograph and biography on the Sterling Galleries' Web site. We Venetians are a superstitious lot. I took it, of course, to be an omen."

Claire swallowed around the lump in her throat. It was a curious thing to come upon what looked like a portrait of yourself that was hundreds of years old. She tried to discount the emotional punch of it. To let her professional instincts take over. The portrait was in excellent shape, not affected by damp or clouded by age.

"She will be the highlight of the auction, Count Ludovici. Although why you wish to part with her —" She broke off. "Forgive me. That was rude. It is your business as to why you wish to do so and mine to evaluate the painting." The Ludovicis had been worthy custodians.

The light from the red electric lamp cast an interesting glow on the girl in the portrait. She looked so young, so infinitely tender. So . . . *in love!* Claire thought with surprise. Although she shouldn't be: this young woman was surely the same as the girl in the drawing that had not sold at the private auction.

And the same one who fled her house to meet her lover in Claire's disturbing dreams. She even wore the necklace of gold-flecked Murano glass around her slender throat. All it lacked was the pendant with the glinting heart-shaped ruby.

She must have added that later, Claire thought. The gift of her secret lover.

"You must not apologize," Ludovici said. "Come, sit here, and we will talk. I shall tell you the tragic tale of Bianca and her father. It is the shame of my house. She was beautiful, as you can see, shy and pampered. Too timid in the beginning to run off with her lover when her father arranged a marriage with another man. Too defiant in the end to bow to her father's will."

Claire felt sick to her stomach. She was afraid to hear what was coming. Val's hand was there, taking her own in his.

"It was shortly after this portrait was taken," the count continued. "Bianca learned that she was pregnant by Domenico Coleone, the son of a rising merchant house. She sent him a note when he returned from Florence, but he claimed never to have received it. She threw herself into the canal, some say. Her body was found floating beneath a bridge."

"A terrible story," Claire said, shivering.

"The penalties for loss of the wedding contract were heavy, but the other consequences of the tragedy were worse. The Count Ludovici of that time was a powerful man. He was rumored to be a member of the secret Council of Ten. If things had gone differently, he might have been elected Doge. Certainly he had dreams of it, as his diaries reveal. Instead he was ruined, exiled from Venice to terra firma. He died in Padua, a broken man. It took one hundred years before the Ludovicis became a power again."

"I don't understand." Val leaned forward. "Why was the father ruined for the daughter's mistake?"

"Ah." Count Ludovici sighed and sat back. "There was another story, you see: that her father murdered her in a rage and had her body thrown into the canal."

"And that's why the portrait has been hidden away so long." Claire gazed up at the lovely young face of Bianca.

The count nodded. "But now the time has come to show her to a wider audience. Perhaps then her ghost will cease to walk."

Val looked over his shoulder. "Do you mean that literally?"

"Oh, yes. She is seen from time to time, by lonely lovers. She gazes from the balcony or through the window of her bedchamber. The servants report her footsteps from time to time, as well as the scent of roses. Myself, I have never seen her." He paused. "Except once. In a dream."

6

They took another gondola back. On the way, when Val's arm went around her shoulder as they passed beneath a bridge, Claire didn't protest. Bianca's story had moved her profoundly.

Val was thinking of it, too. He quoted the lines from Thomas Hood's poem, "The Bridge of Sighs," about another girl who'd leapt from a bridge in Venice:

*"Take her up tenderly, hand her with care,
Fashioned so slenderly, young and so fair."*

Claire leaned her head on his shoulder. Lanterns lit the sides of a wide square, and muted laughter floated from open windows. Fairy lights glimmered from the water. The gondolier discreetly kept his eyes averted as Val's hand crept near her breast. They were taking the long way back again.

"It seems wrong," she said, "that something bad could ever happen in a place as beautiful as this."

He didn't answer, merely took her chin in his hand and tilted her face up for his kiss. His mouth was incredibly tender and arousing. His hands were, too. They caressed her body as if it were an act of worship, stroking slowly as he pulled her close. Wine and Venice had gone to their heads.

By the time they reached the hotel, in his haste, it was all Val could do to pay the gondolier.

Claire's body burned for him, ached for his touch. If she had only this one perfect night to remember him by, it would surely last her the rest of her life.

When they got to their hotel floor, neither spoke. They went to his door by one accord, and he opened it. The next minute she was swept up in his arms.

He carried her to the bed through the milky dimness and put her down, then stripped off his clothes in a few efficient moves.

He took more time with hers.

One by one, he undid the buttons of her evening suit, pressing his hot mouth against her flesh at every step. He slid the straps of her lacy bra down her arms, then unhooked the front clasp.

"So beautiful," he murmured, baring her

breasts to his gaze. The ripples of light that suffused Venice danced across her skin like willow-wisps. He groaned. He'd meant to take it slow and easy, but she was eager for him. She trembled when his mouth touched her and took the velvet tip inside.

One tug and she was wild for him. Her fingers raked over his shoulders and down his chest. "Don't be gentle, Val."

He was, though. The first time. He peeled away her skirt, her shimmery hose, bit by bit. He tasted her skin until she was in an agony of pleasure. And only then, when he felt her body arch against his naked chest, did he obey her. They were as impassioned as the first time they'd made love, pagan and unrestrained. A dance of give and take, building to a crescendo like a Flamenco and ending in mutual triumph and exhaustion. When she was calm and quiet, he began again, bringing her trembling to the brink beneath his skillful hand.

She shook and shuddered, crying out his name. Then he slipped inside her, sheathing himself in her warmth. He took it slow this time. Deliberately.

The long and sensuous way home.

Their joining was too intense for either to hold back. They peaked together, crying out in unison. When it was done, and they'd settled gently back to earth, they slept, exhausted, in each other's arms.

The next week went by too quickly for Claire. By day she was at the Ca' Ludovici, doing a preliminary inventory and description of the paintings the count wished to auction. But the evenings, and oh! the nights — they belonged to Claire and Val alone.

She'd been in Venice eight days now, working dawn to dusk among the masterpieces at the Ca' Ludovici, while Val shot dozens of rolls of film. Separate in their work, and yet together. In the evenings they dined with the count or strolled arm in arm, exploring Venice. Gondola rides, quiet candlelight dinners in some charming *trattoria* they chanced upon, kisses in the dusky shadows, with the sound of water lapping against the canal sides.

And every night was spent, content and satiated, in each other's arms.

He never spoke of the future, nor did she. Until now.

She lay on the soft embroidered sheets in his room, with morning light playing over her naked body. He'd done wonderful things to her, and she to him, until they were both exhausted and happy. They lay curled up together while ripples of light danced on the ceiling like webs of enchantment, with her breast cupped in his hand. He grazed the silken nipple with his thumb and kissed it erect.

"I could get used to this again, Claire. I could spend the rest of my life making love to you."

She was afraid to let him continue. "Don't. Don't say anything you don't mean or make promises you can't keep."

He rolled over atop her and pinned her down with his weight. His hands tangled in her hair as he covered her face with kisses. "I love you, Claire. I've never stopped. Not for a minute. Let's wipe out the past and try again." He lifted his head and gazed down into her eyes. "We can start over. Will you marry me again, Claire?"

Those were the words she'd wanted him to say, yet feared to hear. "I wish we could. I love you, Val, I do! But what if we *can't* make it? What's to stop us from making the same mistakes all over again?" She touched her fingertips to his mouth. "I think it would break my heart forever."

Whatever he was about to say was forestalled when the bedside phone rang. He snatched it up out of habit and rolled over on one elbow, frowning. The sound from the earpiece carried clearly to her: It was like a cartoon character on speed. She recognized the voice of Parker Farley, the editor in chief of *One World Magazine.*

"Hell, no," Val said into the mouthpiece. "I'm in Venice, in bed, with a beautiful woman beside me. Why in God's name would I want to leave for the Arctic Circle tonight? Besides, it's cold there, and I didn't pack my long wooly underwear."

Claire rolled onto her side, with her back to Val. Despite his joking, she could feel the excitement he radiated. She could hear Farley's voice, tinny and far away: "I'll buy you all the goddamn red flannel long johns you need for the trip. You know you can find a willing woman anywhere, Kincaid. But it's damned hard to find a good story. Listen, this isn't a warm and fuzzy feature on polar bears. The State Department and the Department of Defense are involved. This might be really big!"

While they discussed the breaking story, Claire slid out from under the sheet, grabbed her clothes, and marched through the connecting door. It was true that Val could find a willing woman anywhere. He'd certainly found her.

She wanted to smack herself.

That glib charm and winning smile had

suckered her again. She'd bought it all. But when it came down to the wire, when the choice was between herself and the almighty story, she knew who would win, hands down.

When he hung up, she was wrapped in his bathrobe, perched on the end of the bed. "You're going," she said dully.

He came to sit beside her, naked and handsome as a classical god. "Will you marry me, Claire? Remember, I asked my question first."

She rose and walked away. "It's getting late. The count will be waiting for us."

"We'll finish this later," Val said between his teeth.

As she was dressing, Claire heard him making phone calls.

They walked to the count's palazzo this time, and the moment they were alone in the gallery, their quarrel started anew. His voice was light, but his eyes were intense, even in the dimness. She couldn't meet them. "I won't give you my heart again so you can put it away on a shelf somewhere until you need it, as if it was a stack of contact sheets or an old camera."

Her shoulders were trembling with the effort to keep from weeping, but he was too angry to see it. "Goddamn it! I tried, Claire. Left *One World Magazine*. Took the newspaper job so I could be with you. And you still weren't happy with the long hours, the late calls on a breaking story." His eyes were dark and hard as diamonds. "In the end it wasn't enough. Not for you. Not for me."

She was shaking. "And so you went back to your old life."

He shrugged. "You went back to yours."

"While you were off saving the world, I was stuck back in the corner of the museum, writing fluff about artists who have been dead for centuries!"

Val's face darkened with anger. "You were never stupid, Claire," he said. "Don't try and act the part. Your work is as valuable as mine. It's just different. You can investigate the past at your leisure. I don't have that option. The present is happening *now*."

He was right. That only made her angrier. "Ah," she said hotly, "but your work is so much more important!"

"That was unworthy of you." His eyes flashed blue as lightning. "I never said that. Never thought that!" His voice was rich with passion. "There are stories that only cameras can tell. Stories that have to be told so the world will know and intervene. I can't turn my back on them. But the horror I report with my lens needs an antidote, and it's there in the beauty that you write about. Don't you see? There's a desperate need for both!"

There was anguish in his voice.

And truth.

It slammed into her as if she'd been hurled against a wall. A wall of stubbornness and false pride. Shame filled her. It clogged her mouth.

"I was pregnant when you went to the Amazon," she blurted. "I didn't tell you because when you left I wasn't sure. I lost the baby at six weeks. Afterward, there was no sense in telling you."

"No, of course not," he said bitterly. "I was only the father. Damn it, Claire, you didn't even trust me enough to tell me." His face darkened. "Or were you punishing me by holding it back?"

Claire just stood there, shaking her head, unable to speak a single word.

Whatever would have happened next, she would never know. While she struggled with her emotions, Count Ludovici returned to the salon. He stopped halfway across the room when he saw their faces. Not even his Old World manners were enough to overcome the awkwardness.

"Forgive me. I have intruded on a private

moment." He started to withdraw.

Val stopped him. "Not at all." He looked away from Claire. "We've said all there is to say between us."

Which seemed to be correct. She couldn't think of a word to utter.

Val held out his hand to the older man. "Thank you for your hospitality and cooperation, Count Ludovici. I'll send the proofs to you as soon as possible. Meanwhile, I'd best be on my way. I have a plane to catch."

"I wish you a safe journey, then."

With a cordial smile for his host and a nod to Claire, he walked out of her life.

7

Claire looked in the beveled Venetian mirror above the console table. The silvered glass reflected the ghost of the immature girl she had been, but it was fading fast.

Val had never lied to her. She'd lied to herself.

She'd been shunted from pillar to post during her early years, unwanted and unloved, except by her taciturn grandfather. And later by Val.

She'd been so hungry for love that she had starved it with her neediness. Now it was too late. He was gone for good.

The image in the mirror blurred as she viewed it through tears. She had put all the blame on Val. Yes, he'd been selfish at times. She hadn't had a lot of inner resources to fall back on then. Hadn't known how to be alone without being lonely. And so, instead of trying to find a common ground, she'd set about trying to change things.

No, her inner voice told her with the cool reasoning of adulthood. *You only tried to change* him. *To clip his wings and keep him by your side.*

Sighing, Claire rolled onto her back and watched the rippling lights dance across the ceiling in endless, fascinating patterns. It was true. She'd been immature and selfish, sure that if he loved her enough he would let her remold him into her perfect romantic vision of what a husband should be. Maybe that was the cause of their final rift, what had driven him away in the end.

She sat up and looked at the clock. It was after midnight. Val was in the air, winging away from Venice.

Away from her.

She fell back against the pillows and wept.

Shadows filled the great room with its ornamental plastered ceiling and painted medallions of nymphs and goddesses. It was Carnivale, and her father was away, attending a ball. She had been locked up in her room since yesterday, when they'd fought.

"I will not marry him!" she'd cried defiantly. "He is cruel, and I do not love him. I would rather be walled up in a nunnery!"

"That," he had told her, "can easily be ar-

ranged. *If you do not do as I tell you, you foolish, headstrong girl!*"

But Bianca knew she wasn't headstrong. She'd been timid and weak, afraid to leave the security of the only life she'd known. As the shy and pampered daughter of a wealthy family, she'd had a life of luxury and ease. Every step had been planned out for her, and there had been no need to accept responsibility for her future. To plan.

Until now.

Her father had chosen her a husband, without telling her until the contract was signed. The marriage would merge the two great banking families and consolidate their fortunes. The very thought of it made her blood run cold.

Especially now, when she was so deeply in love with another man.

Thank God that Guilietta, her old nurse, had taken pity on her. Guilietta had delivered the note to her lover and then returned to dress Bianca and help her escape. The old woman had trembled at her daring. "May the Holy Virgin have pity upon me when the count learns what I have done! And upon you, Donna Bianca!"

But Bianca had formed a plan to protect Guilietta. "No harm will come to you, I swear it."

She handed her servant a tiny flask of clear

blown glass. "Place this vial on the table beside my bed. Then lie down upon your pallet in the corner, with your cup beside you, as if it had fallen from your hand. When my father returns, you will pretend to be difficult to rouse. He will think that I drugged you in order to make my escape."

And now Bianca was on her way. The hem of her gold velvet gown, the soft leather of her green embroidered slippers, whispered over the rose-and-white-marble tiles of the floor. Water dripped nearby.

The tall shutters at the far end of the salon were closed, but bars of fading light told her that twilight was approaching rapidly. A sense of urgency compelled her. She was late.

Dear God, please not too late!

She hesitated by the stairs leading down to the first floor, which opened to the canal. It was tempting. She could slip a coin from the heavy purse at her waist to the boatman and be on her way. By the time he returned, even if her absence was discovered by her father, she would be gone beyond his reach — and safe in her lover's arms.

Unless he didn't come to meet her at the bridge. Unless her fears and timidity had given him a disgust of her, destroyed his love.

Unthinkable! He must come. He must still love her! He must!

Why didn't I flee with him three months ago, when he begged me to sail away with him? I was a silly fool!

The sounds of bells startled her. The great brazen voices of the many churches and towers in the city were marking the hour. The girl turned reluctantly away from the entrance to the water steps. Her escape would be quicker by gondola, but she didn't dare risk being seen.

Passing through a small vestibule, she pulled aside the heavy curtain covering the door that led out into a little-used courtyard. Once this had served as the main land entrance to the house, but when the smaller, original casa was enlarged to a palazzo, *it had become inconvenient.*

The paving stones beneath her feet were ancient, some composed of two-toned mosaics that went back to Roman times. Small bits of crumbled leaves were strewn over them. Lifting her velvet skirts to keep them from being soiled, she moved silently through the starlit courtyard. A bit of lace caught on the old bricks that formed the coping of the stone well, and she yanked it free.

She took the wine-colored cape from its hiding place in the alcove behind a statue, then tied the strings of her mask securely. She had promised to meet him. Domenico would already be there, waiting.

The door in the wall that led to the calle *was locked, but she had the key in her pocket. She peeked through the intricate wrought-iron design set in the thick wood. There was no one in the narrow alleyway. Inserting the heavy key in the lock, she twisted it. The bolt slid back with a low shriek.*

Something pinged away softly into the darkness. Bianca froze, sure that it had been as loud as Judgment Day, but no voice cried out to stop her.

That didn't mean she wasn't being watched. Or followed. Her father might have set another of the servants to the task.

Bianca propped the gate open, then stood with the key in her trembling hand. If she was intercepted and brought back, she would have to try her luck again. To prepare for that she must hide the key. Somewhere that no one else would suspect. She glanced quickly around the courtyard, and an idea struck her. Once she had hit upon the place, it was the work of only a moment to hide the key.

Bianca slipped through the open gate. She sighed as the door clicked shut behind her with solemn finality. There was no going back now: the door leading to the calle *had no handle, and could be opened only from inside the garden.*

She hurried through the maze of alleyways, panic fluttering in her heart. A wrong turning, followed by another, lost even more time. Would he wait for her, or would he fear her courage had failed her yet again?

New waves of doubt assailed Bianca. Her father had conspired with the Gambello family to ruin her lover. They would have no way to support themselves in a foreign land until he was hired on as a mercenary or ship's pilot. At least she had the ruby ring and necklace he'd given her when his career rode high with the Venetian Navy. If need be, they could go to a moneylender with them once they fled Venice.

If, that is, he still wished to flee with her. Oh, she was such a coward! So afraid to do anything unless she had a strong hand to guide her. But now she had finally acted on her own. The moment she'd heard that Domenico was back, she'd sent Guilietta with her note to him.

Reaching up, she touched the necklace at her throat for courage. Her fingertips slid over the smooth glass and gold to the pendant, as if she were telling the beads of her rosary. The ruby was gone!

Bianca came out in a quiet square, sick with trepidation. Somewhere a lute played softly, floating on the still night air. There was the bridge, a pale curve over the small side canal. It was not used as a water road. The bridge merely linked two parts of an ancient building, built centuries earlier, on separate islands.

She'd expected Domenico to be waiting in the shadows by the statue of Venus. No one was there, and her spirits sank.

Then she saw him, coming swiftly along the narrow pavement on the far side of the canal. His cloak was black, melting into the jetty shadows. He wore the golden mask of the sun, as he had promised. With a cry of relief, she called out his name.

He turned his head as she ran lightly toward the bridge. The gilt rays of his mask glittered coldly in the dim light. She wished that she could see his eyes, to know if they were still filled with love for her. Or if he had come merely out of pity.

Then he held out his hand to her. She gathered her skirts to keep from tripping. Her thin slippers whispered over the stones of the bridge. She was breathless with exertion. With excitement. His hand clasped hers, warm and strong. He pulled her away from the bridge, into the protective shadows of the arcade.

"Oh, my love! I was so afraid," she murmured.

He drew her fiercely into his arms. His voice was so low she could scarcely make out the words. "Why did you doubt me?"

"I feared that my cowardice had caused you to hate me. I thought that you had changed your mind. That you would not come to meet me when my old nurse brought my message to you." Her fingers clutched at his cloak. "It is all so terrible! They tried to force me to marry Giovanni Gambello. I would rather die than have him touch me, after you!"

His body grew rigid beneath his thick, muffling cloak. Bianca didn't notice. "I prayed each day that you would return for me. When I saw you on the molo during the ceremony yesterday, my heart nearly burst for love of you. And the child . . . the child changes everything."

His voice was muffled by the slit in the gilt sunburst mask. "What child?"

"Our child," she said raggedly. Bianca looked up as his arm tightened about her shoulders. "I dared not write it on paper! I am three months gone. It will be born in September. A lusty son or beautiful daughter! Oh, I should have gone away with you when first you asked me. Then these horrible weeks of worrying, of wondering if you still loved me, would have never been!"

The moon rose over the high buildings, touching them with silver. In the change of light all her comfort vanished. His eyes were not black as night. The irises were dark gold, like tarnished brass.

Bianca stiffened. "You are not Domenico!"

Her hand shot out and ripped off the mask. The face beneath it was suffused with rage, so distorted with jealousy and thwarted desire that she scarcely recognized her fiancé. "Giovanni!"

He took her shoulders and shook her cruelly. "Little fool. Your nursemaid is in my employ. Your note never reached your lover."

His laughter echoed hollowly. Bianca shivered and tried to pull away, but he held her fast. "So, you have played me false! I knew you fancied yourself in love with another, but I thought you pure and unsullied, a shy and gentle virgin. Instead you have been Domenico Coleone's whore!"

"No! Do not say so! My love for him is good and true."

He pushed her up against the stonework at the end of the bridge. "To think that I intended to wed you. What a fool I have been. Did you laugh at my ignorance, you and Domenico, as you lay together?"

Bianca tried to pull away. "I never promised to wed you. I told you that I would never be your wife."

"So you did," he said, his fingers biting deep into her arms. "But you shall wear my ring upon your finger as you say your vows. Ah, Bianca! I would have treated you like a queen. Instead you shall be my whore!"

"Never. I would rather die than marry you!"

"Before I am done with you, you will wish you had," he said violently. "And when my friends have finished with you as well, I will send you to a nunnery. Not the kind where pious women pray, but where they are kept for men's pleasure."

"You disgust me." Her arm swung out. Her nails raked his cheek, and he yowled in pain. A sharp prong of the ring she wore had caught the corner of his eye. Blood dripped from the torn lid, like black tears in the moonlight.

It happened then. He cuffed her hard, just as she tried to twist away. The momentum threw her to the side. One minute she was standing beside the canal. The next she was in it.

The water was cold. So very cold.

The shock of it made her gulp in a mouthful of salty, fetid liquid. Her garments billowed out around her like the petals of a fallen flower. Then the current tugged at her, and the weight of her velvet gown and heavy cloak dragged her down. She struggled and splashed.

Her hair came loose from her coiffure, and the wet strands floated about her shoulders like seaweed. She reached out an imploring hand.

"Giovanni! Help me!"

The cold numbed her limbs, and her garments were like lead. She was helpless against their pull. The waters of the canal closed over her like a ceiling of rippled glass.

His body jerked forward, as if he would throw off his cloak and save her. Instead he looked *down at her in the icy starlight, his face as cold as stone.*

Then he straightened slowly, turned, and walked away.

Claire jolted up in her dark bedroom, her blood pounding with despair, with terror. A scream echoed in her ears.

She realized it was her own.

8

Claire raked her wild curls out of her eyes. The window to the balcony in her room was open, cool night air billowing out the curtains, like the wet folds of Bianca's velvet gown.

She was shaking violently. She had lost Val. And Bianca had lost everything, including her brief, star-crossed life. The helpless horror of her final moments clung to Claire like a shroud. If she didn't break free of it . . .

The pounding wasn't just the pummeling of her heart against her ribs. It was Val, beating on the connecting door between their rooms.

"Claire? Claire, let me in goddamn it, before I break the door down."

The wood shattered as he hurled himself against it. Throwing back the rumpled sheets, she stumbled across the floor to unbolt it. A moment later he was in her room, and she was in his arms, gasping for breath.

"The dream . . ." she said through chattering teeth.

"Jesus, you're cold as death!"

He pulled the covers up over her, then shut the windows. When he returned, her face was so pale, her eyes so wide with shock, it frightened him. He'd known what it was to be afraid for his own life. He'd never realized, till now, how much more terrible it was to fear for the life of someone he loved.

Val dried her tears and climbed in beside her, wrapping his arms around her for warmth. Through her thin silk gown, he could feel the pounding of her heart against his bare chest.

"Hush, darling. It's all right. I'm here."

He was. She leaned her face against his shoulder, inhaling his scent. The dream was gone, but he was strong and warm. And real.

And he was here.

She nestled into his embrace. She was weeping wildly, pouring out all the tears she'd sealed up inside her heart. "I thought you'd gone. I thought I'd lost you forever."

His arms tightened. "I couldn't leave you."

"Everyone I've ever loved has left me . . ."

He heard it in her voice then, the thing she

couldn't get past: the fears of a lost child, abandoned with no explanation. It broke his heart with love.

"Even if you didn't want me, I still couldn't leave you. Not when you were in such pain. Not ever, if you need me." He took her face and held it between his hands. "Don't you understand that?"

She clung to him, weeping and shaking, and the whole story tumbled out. Not Bianca's but hers. A young girl, raised in the middle of loud and angry voices. Whether they were fueled by love or anger or disgust, she couldn't tell.

"After my mother died, I was sent to Idaho to live with my grandfather. That's almost my earliest memory. Standing in the middle of a wide green landscape, with my suitcase beside me, and not so much as another house in sight. Seeing this stranger I was to live with for the very first time."

Val's hand smoothed her hair as she went deep into the past, to the root of her pain:

Warm sunlight, cool wind. Land stretching out in the distance to the humped green hills, the purple peaks beyond. A spotted cow with yellowed horns that looked far bigger than the sports car she'd just exited. A low, weathered house with a single rocker on the front porch and not a pot of flowers in sight. She longed for the tall, colorful houses dripping with flowers, and their cool reflections in the green canal.

A man came out onto the porch. He wore faded coveralls and a blue plaid shirt. His hair was threaded with gray, his blue eyes tired, his body worn down by work and poor health.

"So that's the girl."

"Yes. Here she is."

"She's the spitting image of Helen."

"Yes."

"And that was it." Her eyes were bleak with memories. "I remember my grandfather beckoning to me, hearing a dog bark, and then the sound of the car as my father drove away. I remember turning and running, screaming for him to come back. Screaming for my mother . . ."

She buried her face against his shoulder. "I didn't see my father again for six years. And that was only to shunt me off to boarding school. The first of several. I loathed everything about it with every fiber of my being."

Val wanted to comfort her and didn't know how. How do you repair the damage done to a shy, sensitive girl? It was no wonder that she was afraid to trust love, when it was something that had vanished from her life in the twinkling of an eye. He'd seen that same look in her eyes on the faces of refugees he'd photographed. Val blamed himself for not recognizing it in Claire, for trying to keep her set apart from his work, so that the violent world he photographed would never collide with hers.

He'd been a fool.

For once he had the sense to keep quiet, to not try and rationalize what belonged on a deep emotional level. Christ, he wanted to kill someone.

Instead he kissed her tears and held her tenderly. They lay together a long time, with no movement in the room except for their breathing and the starry patterns of the shifting water lights that covered the walls and ceiling. Claire felt the anger pouring through him as if it were her own. His rage and indignation, his reflection of her pain, were revealed in the tension of his body and the sorrow in his eyes.

He wiped her tears with his fingertips, held her cradled against him as if she were something fragile and infinitely precious. Strength flowed from him to her. The pounding of her heart gradually slowed.

Dawn came at last, sliding bars of gold and rose through the space between the curtains, and the atmosphere grew luminous around them. There was no way in Venice to escape the water, the way it bounced the light from every surface until the air glowed and pulsed with it. But the very element that threatened to destroy the city was what made it so unique, so beautiful.

There was no way to escape the past that had formed *her*, Claire realized. She could only take what she had and transform it. What it became was up to her.

Her chest burned, but her eyes were dry. All the tears of a lonely childhood evaporated in the heat of her adult anger. She would never know why her father had left her. Perhaps he'd blamed himself for her mother's death and couldn't live with the guilt. Or the loss. Now she felt pity for him and for her grandfather, that silent old man on his isolated Idaho ranch, with nothing but memories left of his only child. Perhaps they had been as alone and aching as she had been.

Claire wondered if her grandfather had been an eagle, like Val, before his wings and heart were broken.

Forgiveness came with sudden understanding. With that forgiveness, something inside her heart opened up. It was as if a band of scar tissue had broken, releasing her from its restrictions. For the first time that she could remember, Claire knew she was free to love. To trust.

Val felt the change in her. He touched her cheek, kissed her softly, and saw the alteration in her face. She glowed from within. "I love you, Claire."

"I love you, Val." She trailed her fingers over his wide shoulders and down his chest. "Make love to me now. Then pack your woolly long johns for the trip to the Arctic Circle."

He nuzzled her throat. "The first part is a given," he whispered as he cupped her breast in his palm. "The second is on indefinite hold."

She offered her mouth to him, soft and eager. He tangled his hands in her hair, fisted the curls, and angled her face to meet his. The kiss was as full and heady as sparkling wine. She felt the heat of it like effervescent bubbles in her veins. She was drunk with joy. With need.

Val's hand splayed across her back, pulling her closer, so close that she couldn't tell where he ended and she began. He kissed her mouth, her eyes, her temples. "I've been such a fool," she whispered.

"Not you," he murmured. "Not you."

He held her face between his bronzed hands and looked down at her solemnly. "I'll do anything to keep you, Claire. I'll take a job at the Washington bureau. Hell, at the car wash if I have to."

She laughed and pulled him down for a kiss. She couldn't clip his eagle's wings, break his proud heart. "No, you won't. You can't. But we can work it out. We'll negotiate. We'll fight. And somehow, some way, we'll find a solution. Because I'll do anything to keep you."

Her face was filled with love and faith. "And it will be okay when you go away, Val, because now I know that you'll come back."

A shudder of mutual passion ran through their bodies. His love was tender, but his lovemaking was fierce. His hot mouth and skilled hands had her groaning with greedy pleasures. Claire arched against him and lifted her hips boldly to meet him. She yielded up the last of her held-back emotions, and all physical restraint as well. Wrapped in his strong arms, and the warmth of his love, she found the courage to fly free. Two golden eagles, with sunlight on their wings.

9

Claire stuffed a rolled-up silk camisole into the corner of her suitcase, slipped some lacy panties into the side pocket, and closed the lid with difficulty. "Whew! I was afraid I'd have to leave something behind."

Val watched with amusement. "I didn't think you'd get the last two pair of new shoes in there."

"It was either the shoes or the underwear."

His face brightened. "I'd vote for the underwear."

"You don't get a vote."

She twirled the combination locks. Beyond the open windows the Grand Canal was a pale apple green, and the domes of the Salute gleamed in the early-morning sun. "I can't believe it's almost time to leave."

He ambled over and kissed the nape of her neck, where the golden curls sprang out against her milky skin. Her hair, still damp from the shower, smelled like roses.

"Hmmmm. We do have a couple of hours to kill before the launch picks us up."

"Greedy! It's only been, oh, about forty-five minutes?"

He turned her around and caught her hands in his. "That long?"

His pulled her into his arms, and his mouth came down warm on hers. She fell into the kiss, let it sweep her away as his hands tugged her blouse out of the band of her apricot slacks and smoothed the silky skin of her back. The heat of his body warmed her; the strength of it made her knees grow deliciously weak.

It was tempting, but this time she didn't give in. "We'll be in Paris in a few hours. Besides, there's something I have to do before we leave."

Val brushed the hair back from her temple and kissed it. "Do you want me to go with you?"

"No." Her smile took the sting out of the word. "This is something I have to do on my own."

"Something to do with the dreams." It wasn't a question. His blue eyes were grave and tender.

Claire touched a finger to his cheek. "Everything to do with them."

"Do you believe in dreams, Count Ludovici? In fate?"

Claire stood on the canal-front level of the palazzo with her host. Beneath her feet the rose-and-white-marble squares stretched across the floor to where the tall shutters were open to the Grand Canal. Water dripped nearby.

For once the view was empty of *vaporetti*. A lone gondola swept by, a black swan against the opaque green water. Except for their modern clothing, Claire thought, they could have fit anywhere in time, in the Ca' Ludovici's six-hundred-year history.

Count Ludovici smiled. "But of course. One cannot live in a fantasy like Venice unless one believes."

Claire reached inside her purse and drew out a small velvet case banded with brass. "Then this belongs to you."

He took it, frowning, and snapped the lid open. Bianca's necklace lay against the satin interior. "Madonna!" He recovered himself. "Surely this is the necklace that Bianca wears in her portrait!"

His fingers touched the beads, caressed the twist of gold that had once held a heart-shaped ruby in the center of the pendant. "Where did you get this, *signorina?*"

"From Bianca. She wanted you to have it."

"I do not understand."

"May we go into the tiny courtyard that opens to the *calle?* The one with the old stone well? I'll explain it there."

He looked startled, then shrugged. "But of course."

Claire led the way as if she'd walked it a hundred times. And she had, at least in dreams.

She hesitated at the top of the stairs leading down to the water level, resisting the urge to look over her shoulder. She wasn't Bianca. It didn't matter if anyone saw her.

She realized she might be making a complete fool of herself. Or that things might have changed since Bianca's desperate flight.

Count Ludovici was right behind her. Passing through a small vestibule, she pulled aside the heavy curtain that covered the door, leading out into the little-used courtyard. The hinges groaned from disuse.

It was exactly like her dream.

A shudder passed through her like, like a cloud sweeping over the sea. This, too, was exactly like her dream. Pots of flowers flanked the door, and tendrils of new vines clung to the ancient walls. And there was the locked door that led into the alleyway.

"Bianca was not a suicide, and she was not murdered by her father." She took a deep breath. "That fateful night, she left through that gate to meet her lover. She'd sent him a note via her nurse that she would defy her father and run off with Domenico Coleone. The note was delivered into the hands of Giovanni Gambello instead."

"How do you know this?" The count eyed her steadily.

"You might say that Bianca told me." Claire lifted her chin. "In dreams."

Count Ludovici was puzzled. "You say that she did not throw herself into the canal."

"Beyond that door is a narrow *calle*. If you follow it long enough, it leads to a tiny open square with a statute of Venus on one corner. An ancient bridge spans the small canal, so narrow that two people cannot pass one another."

The frown lines on his forehead deepened. "You intrigue me. The square is difficult to find, even with a map. The bridge is so old not even a gondola can go beneath it. It was originally meant only to link two parts of a palazzo. Few people know of it except those who live nearby."

"Bianca knew. She made it as far as the

bridge, where she expected to find Domenico Coleone, but her note to him had never been delivered. It was her fiancé, Giovanni Gambello, who was waiting to confront her in his *carnivale* disguise. He didn't know until then that she was carrying her lover's child."

Ludovici digested this. "You seem very sure, *signorina*."

A slight shadow passed across Claire's face. "As sure as if I had been there. He threatened her, and she tried to run away. In the struggle she fell into the canal." Her green eyes grew clouded, like the waters that lapped at the palazzo's steps. "Giovanni Gambello walked away and left her to die."

Bells rang out on the warm, still air, the voices of the churches and *camponiles* mingling in a chorus of regret. Ludovici's eyes were dark with it.

"I believe that *you* believe this is the truth. But in my heart of hearts, I wish for proof."

This was the sticky part. "Do you have the key?"

"No." The count shook his head. "I do not recall there ever being one. There is another door that leads out of the garden court. It is that garden door which is used."

She went to the old well and eyed the brick coping atop the ancient stone. "This is where Bianca snagged the lace trim of her gown."

Claire went unerringly to the spot and knelt down. Her fingers scrabbled at the brick, and it came loose in her hand. Bits of crumbled leaf and ancient mortar fell away. She reached in, and her fingers touched cool metal.

Relief whooshed through her. "Here's your proof," she said simply.

She pulled out the tarnished key. It was green with age, but the intricate design was still apparent. She held it out on her palm to him. Tiny pieces of patinated metal flaked away against her skin.

"But . . . how did you know it was there?"

"Bianca hid it, in case she was caught and needed it to escape again. She showed me — in a dream."

She'd had the last one that morning, as she lay content in Val's arms. There had been no fear, no terror in it this time. Just a smiling girl with Botticelli curls in a gown of gold velvet. Bianca's task was complete. She had cleared her family's name.

The count closed his eyes. When he opened them, they were bright. "Thank you, *signorina*, from the bottom of my heart." He took her hand and kissed it. "I would like you to handle the auction," he said lightly, as if it were of no importance. "And I would like you to have this."

He pressed the velvet case into her hand. Claire was startled. "I can't accept. This is an heirloom. It belongs to you."

"No," he said with an odd little smile. "It was Bianca's and now it belongs to you. I will have the ruby put back in the setting." The count smiled at her surprise. "Yes, Bianca's ruby. It was found on the stairs the night she vanished. It is in the vault with the family heirlooms."

The bright air shimmered around them, and Claire blinked. For just the fraction of a second there had been someone else in the garden with them. No, more of a *presence*.

"You feel it, too," Ludovici said softly. She nodded and took the jewel case, her heart pounding.

"In Venice," he went on, "the past is very much alive. A dozen years, a hundred . . ." He made an airy gesture of dismissal. "For centuries the shadow of her tragic story has haunted this house. Thanks to you, *signorina*, she has regained her place of honor here. Her father, Andrea Ludovici, as well. Take the necklace and wear it in remembrance. You can never know what a gift you have bestowed upon me."

"Nor you upon me." Claire's smile was

warm. If not for Bianca and the count, Val would be halfway around the world by now. And she would be alone.

"You will call me when you make the arrangements," the count said, leading her back inside the palazzo. "And when you return you will be my guest here. You and your husband."

It was her turn to be startled. "How did you know?"

The count laughed. "Perhaps Bianca told me. I, too, have dreamed of her *signorina*. She came to me last night while I slept. She is with her own true love. And you with yours."

10

A short time later Claire's Italian heels clicked over the rose and white tiles that paved the *piano nobile* and down the marble stairs to the water level.

She was going to meet her own true love, not timidly and with a fearful heart as Bianca had. Claire went down the water steps of the Ca' Ludovici boldly, filled with hope and love.

Val was waiting for her there with a private launch. Claire paused on the landing. Her bags were beside his on the deck. Just the way they should be.

Clouds were gathering in the distance. It would rain soon, but the lagoon beyond the canal was a translucent aqua, blending almost imperceptibly into the sky. Claire's own horizons had expanded in the past few weeks. She would no longer try to cage her eagle. Blue sky was half covered with pearly gray clouds, but the sun shone brightly down on him. It burnished his tanned skin, struck fire from the depths of his blue eyes. She could not change him, nor he change her.

They could only change themselves.

And they would succeed, because their love was deep and strong. Because they understood now how precious love was and how much they had to lose. And because she finally believed in his love, and that if she gave him his freedom, he would wing safely home to her.

He looked up and saw her, and his face shone. Then he raised his arms and lifted her down to him. He drew her against his chest for a long, deep kiss that poured through her like sunshine, warmed her to the core.

Val felt the difference in the way her body curved to his now, the faith that this was how it would and should be. The scent of her skin and hair were like perfume as he gathered her to him. It was, he thought, the most perfect moment of his life.

"I love you, Claire," he murmured. "I want you and I need you. Forever."

She raised herself up on tiptoe and threw her arms around his neck. "I love you, Val. I always have. I always will. Forever."

The pilot cleared his throat. "*Signor, si-*

gnora. It is time to leave."

Claire looked up at Ca' Ludovici, its faded pink and white facade luminous in the shifting light. The count was smiling down at them — and for just a moment she thought she saw another face beside his: a lovely young girl in a velvet dress, with a cloud of curling, golden Botticelli hair.

Then the image faded and was gone.

Claire's heart soared. *Thank you, Bianca! For your faith and trust in letting me uncover the truth for you. And for teaching me the courage to love.*

It started to rain lightly, a faint sheen of pewter in the air, as the launch headed out of the Grand Canal. The island of San Giorgio Maggiore was wrapped in mist. They'd be back to see it soon. Venice had become their city.

Claire went into the cabin, Val's strong arm wound around her waist. Contentment filled her. Bianca was at peace and with the man she loved. And so was she.

As the launch cut through the waves of the lagoon, they curled up together on the leather couch at the back of the cabin. The drone of the engine was soothing, soft as a heartbeat. Claire felt herself drifting away. Then Val's lips were on her hair, her eyelids, nibbling the lobe of her right ear.

"Save it for Paris," she told him with a soft little laugh.

He kissed the tip of her nose and pulled her head against his shoulder. They both glanced out the window for a last glimpse of Venice.

The playful wind off the Adriatic tossed the sheer veils of rain aside. For a magical moment the beautiful palazzi, the tile-roofed towers and domed churches, seemed to float on a molten pewter lake.

Venice vanished in the soft silver mist like a mirage. Like an enchanted island in a fairy tale.

Like a fabulous dream.